MEET

KNIGHT GLEASON—An Olympic athlete with a perfect sexual physique, transformed into the biggest star of the silver screen.

Sexual destination:
the White House

ARNIE BRUNO—An internationally adored crooner and insatiable seducer who's never satisfied himself twice in the same bed.

Sexual destination:
airborne

ROGER GIFFORD—The ballet dancer whose delicately choreographed performances have given rise to nasty rumors about his masculinity . . . rumors he is determined to prove false.

Sexual destination:
Grand Central Station

EDUARDO BRANT—The art world's most sought-after celebrity, attracting beautiful women to himself like a magnet.

Sexual destination:
a women's prison

Other Avon Books by
Gerald A. Browne

HOT SIBERIAN
THE AROUSERS

Coming Soon

IT'S ALL ZOO

GERALD A. BROWNE

The Ravishers

AVON BOOKS NEW YORK

This is a work of fiction, and all characters are products of the author's imagination. Any resemblance to persons living or dead is purely coincidental.

AVON BOOKS
A division of
The Hearst Corporation
105 Madison Avenue
New York, New York 10016

Front cover photograph by Anthony Loew, Inc.
Published by arrangement with the author
Library of Congress Catalog Card Number: 89-91354
ISBN: 0-380-70418-8

First Avon Books Printing: January 1990

Printed in the U.S.A.

RA 10 9 8 7 6 5 4 3 2 1

to:

Whip, Peggy, Roberta, Mark, Kathy, Hap, Cindy, Helen, David, Neal, Al, Deanna, Mike, Dino, Ann, Charles, Sandy, Bob, Ali, Dorian, Sophia, Adnan, Soraya, Marlo, Len, Peter, Sam, Gudrun, Kurt, Jacqueline, Shirley, Warren, Julie, Hugh, Maud, Roy, Hunt, Howard, Britta, Alberta, Judith, James, Pam, Tully, Lisa, Maggie, Vera, Frank, Natalie, Wilhelmena, Bruce, Steve, Nancy, Audrey, Omar, Lauren, Alexis, Truman, Joey, Richard, Liz, Harold, Grace, Graham, Virginia, Karen, Milton, Gardner, Pia, Rona, Gus, Bert, Penny, Chris, Buddy, Fred, Ninika, Mamdouh, Anita, Claire, Greg, Tammy, Faye, George, Ben, Rock, Angela, Gene, Johnny, Geoffrey, Kirk, Norman, Tony, Burt, Jack, Arthur, Gwen, Met, Alan, Sal, Jean Pierre, Terrence, Deborah, Raquel, Barbara, Kenneth, Stella, Skip, Cary, Sue, Phillip, Jane, Ursula, Gina, Paul, Victor, Mary, Nick, Michael, Bill, Bernie, and especially Jer.

1

A half hundred floors up.

Above the level of the ordinary world.

The only light in the room a faint pink, a calculated, helping color.

The only sound from the concealed hi-fi. His voice, him electronically, highest highs, lowest lows.

The king-size sheets now not just laundry-smelling. Now a more complicated pleasant mixture from skins, colognes, and the love-made wet of her.

She was now eyeshut in the nice aftersoft below reality. But he hadn't come, so he was wide open, looking the ceiling and hearing himself. One of his knees was just touching some of her.

He had pretended coming this time. He often did—acted the appropriate rhythms and sounds—and he was sure she didn't know he hadn't really finished. Not that he didn't enjoy coming, but he felt if he let flow every time he'd be drained. It was better, he thought, to hold back and preserve his want for variety. When he didn't come he didn't need time for refill. Instead of dry, emptied dry, he felt ready for the next.

He related his holding back to a religion he'd once read about and needed to remember: some Far East worshippers who used sexual incompletion as a source of energy to help them feel constantly high on life. They would, as he partially understood it, go to the very perimeter of release and stop. That is, the men would. He assumed the women got their kicks as usual.

Besides, he believed holding back was unselfish and contributed to his image, that was the best of the better lovers.

Now his solid eighteen-karat butane Dunhill lighted a cigarette for him, and he used its flame to let his Piaget watch tell him it was nearly eight-thirty.

He was going to be late for the game.

He got up and, having not come, his legs were full and strong, actually felt better than they had at the recording session that afternoon. He'd been especially good that afternoon, with plenty of voice to use, and emotionally he'd been so right that they'd done two numbers more than scheduled. It had been an easy session with nothing bothering, and the results were excellent, typically him—the identifiable phrasing with the message of experience in it for lovers lost or gaining.

For lovers, typically Arnie Bruno.

He hadn't planned on pulling the studio receptionist. That had been a flash idea on the way out, because he felt good from having been so good. She'd sent obvious signals, so he'd pulled her and brought her to his place. On the way he'd read her eyes and fifteen minutes after arrival he was doing her.

He'd been good then too. As advertised.

Now he looked down at her there. She was on her side with her thighs and bottom making a line to appreciate. He'd noticed a physical mistake about her: her stomach wasn't tight enough. Not potted out but not ideally tight either; just enough too much to spoil her hips some. Probably from sitting all day. In her favor, however, was the rest of her and her try. She'd tried to be special, hoping to qualify for a return or perhaps making the forever team.

Arnie thought now about the men there had to be who spent on her, this girl, Lois something. Spent time, money, words, wanting to see her all over, wanting to get her around it, playing it slow, believing that was the way in. And most of them getting zero, while it had taken Arnie Bruno less than an hour from the pull to making her moan nonstop. He thought that with an inside smile as he went to the next room, careful with the door not to bring her up out of it, because he didn't want to have to talk with her now.

There in the next room was Winner, reading. Winner said hello with his head.

Arnie told him, "I need something to eat."

"I put a frozen chicken pie in the oven for me. You want it? You said no dinner tonight, remember?"

"My stomach thinks my throat's cut."

Winner went. Arnie sat on the couch, and the leather was cool on his bare-ass cheeks. He looked the turned-off television ten feet away, as if he were creating one of his special shows on it. Winner came back with a tray under chicken pie and a Kentucky whiskey on the rocks.

"How about her?" asked Winner for Lois. "She hungry?"

Arnie didn't answer, punctured the chicken pie, swallowed cold Kentucky.

"She out?" asked Winner.

"Yeah, all done," said Arnie, vague.

"Wild-looking bird."

"Just a bird."

"Got better milky-ways than the one yesterday."

"You noticed?"

"I got eyes," defended Winner.

"Sure, bigger than your joint," abused Arnie.

Winner laughed because it was better to laugh. Winner was Arnie's man. For ten years always around him, the shadow with muscles ready to move between Arnie and violence—for two hundred a week and all the birds Arnie let fly his way. Winner had once been a pro heavyweight fighter and a loser.

Arnie chewed chicken pie and complained, "Slop. You know, you're ruining my health."

Winner was willing. "I can fix you a steak. Only take a minute."

"I'm late already," said Arnie, getting up to be stopped by Lois in the doorway. She had her shoes on and Arnie's shirt with the tails of it wrinkled where it had been tucked in. Nothing else.

"I woke up," she announced, smiling a try.

Arnie noticed she'd brushed her hair. Winner was stealing from where the shirt split in front to show some of her lower hair. She caught him and crossed a leg over to conceal.

There was no way for Arnie to leave the room without touching her. He didn't want to, but he held her a short hold and slid past to go into the bedroom and through to his dressing room. She followed, wondering about now.

He showered and she watched without talk. He dried and

began his second electric shave of the day. She took a towel and wiped the wet he'd missed from his back. He thanked her with a sound through his hands that were putting on after lotion.

"No," she said, "thank *you.*"

"For what?" he asked, knowing. He wished she'd go, get dressed and go.

"Was it good for you? It was for me," she said, while he shoved a door aside and chose things to wear.

"You mean by comparison?" he asked. That went into her because it was exactly the reason she'd asked. Arnie was used to them trying to be best. He saw her hurt. He didn't want her to cry because he'd have to give some cruel or kind if she cried and he was out of give. For something, he said, "You think I ball a lot, don't you?"

"I've heard." She tried to nonchalant it.

"It's a bunch of shit. If I balled as much as they say, I'd be dead."

A true lie.

She looked for proof. She saw him underweight, small-boned, not apparently a sexual athlete. She came out of it with reassurance that he couldn't possibly do many the way he'd done her. She reasoned that famous people always had such things said about them. Especially Arnie. He was a legend. Her mental additions came to the total feeling that she was special. She smiled for him.

By then he was dressed. She'd been so preoccupied with her rating that now, for the first time, she realized he intended to go out somewhere. She asked him.

He didn't answer. All he told her was, "If you're hungry Winner will fix you a steak."

She started dressing, put on her skirt, and while she was topless he stole some from her good breasts to remember. She had different nipples for a brunette, unusual pink like two pale points of lipstick. She didn't put on her bra. She didn't need it anyway. She stuffed it into her purse and got into her blouse, buttoning with hurry that told Arnie she expected to go with him. It made him angry some.

He covered it. "Why don't you stay and watch television with Winner," he suggested, letting her know.

She got it. She went for her best weapon, a sort of half bump with a hip, only a shifting of weight but it was like grinding pepper with her groin, when, along with it, she said, "Maybe I will."

Arnie didn't think she had anything left. He was almost sure she couldn't have. Most likely she was sensitive sore downstairs from him. But she spun and went out and was sitting deliberately close to Winner when Arnie went past that room down the hall to the foyer. Arnie remembered some D.H. Lawrence words about a woman being a hole constantly wanting to be filled. So before he went he called Winner and told him, "I don't want her here when I get back."

"What time will you be in?"

"I've been in." Arnie clipped words to remind.

But in the elevator was another world, and Arnie, descending, didn't care if Winner fucked her ass off.

2

Average 5 a week each.

That's 260 each a year.

2600 each over the past ten years.

For the four men who were at Eduardo's for the pool game, figure an altogether total of 10,400. And that was only for the preceding ten years, not counting the many who had come before.

Come they did. That impressive number of birds, pulled and pleased. More than 20,000 attention-getting nipples belonging to forgotten first names. As forgotten as meals.

On a straight basis that was more than 3,000,000 in and out strokes at 300 per. Not that it was all old-fashioned pumping.

Of course, the four men didn't keep such accurate mental ledgers. Only the extreme were remembered. Only the fervent freaks and those performers who had some exceptionally large or small or grotesque body part.

For these men, time erased time. One over one over and over, as repetitive as religion.

Actually they were a sort of cult, though never formally organized. And if they had been, they wouldn't have structured their temple with stiff columns of heaven-headed cocks, wouldn't have placed the most magnificent blood-expanded erection on their altar.

No. The opposite.

More divine for them was the vagina. Not holiness. Portable paradise, pulpited by nerve ends of revival and with nearly identical slippery and sweet enchanting passages around the organ during services.

Trinity: above, within, and behind.
Really love thy neighbors.
Reassure erection.
Come unto me.
It is better to give and relieve.
Blessed are the makes.
Do others as they do you.
Ball, baby, ball.
Cue ball.

Eduardo sent the special white sphere to collide hard against the triangle formed by its bright brothers, scattering. The orange five dropped into a pocket. They were playing eight ball. Eduardo and Knight versus Rog and Arnie. Eduardo aimed an easy shot and dropped another low ball, but he left himself bad position and missed his next try. He came over near Arnie, who was impatient to shoot because the week before he'd lost two thousand, mostly to Eduardo, and he was anxious to recoup. The amount lost didn't bother him. It was the down aspect of it.

"You look good," Eduardo told Arnie.

Arnie thought Eduardo looked tired but didn't say. One of Eduardo's attractions was his gaunt face that announced and promised excesses. Eduardo's eyes were always slow and seemed to be constantly stating they'd be more comfortable if the rest of him were horizontal, in the pleasure position.

"How's the painting coming?" Arnie asked him.

Eduardo shrugged negative.

"Maybe what you need's a better brand of bird."

"So send some."

"What size?" asked Arnie, watching Knight make a clean bank shot that told him Knight was really on tonight. Knight ran several more balls and had only one more to sink before going for the money eight. It was a long rail shot, not easy, but he put it in without any slop and left himself a close straight try at the eight. He chalked and smiled, kept smiling as he confidently stroked the black ball in. He took four hundreds from a corner pocket and divided with Eduardo.

That was the first game. After the next two, after more alcohol was in them, none of them was so serious about it, not even Arnie. When they missed they laughed and talked about birds. When they didn't miss they laughed and talked about birds. It didn't matter who was talking. The voices were different but the subject was the same.

"You still balling that skinny model?"

"Nipples like gumdrops."

"Mouth full of cognac. She went wild."

"Crotch flambé, baby."

"Put an Alka Seltzer in a rubber. You get fizzed off."

"What's a rubber?"

Laughs. Together laughs. League of laughs.

"She had these two Dobermans. Biggest lap dogs in town."

"Animal acts are tough to follow."

"Especially boxers."

"I pulled her at the Whitney."

"We fell in love for three hours."

"What's love?"

"Eight in the corner. That corner."

Their ears received only fragments, cut only the hearts from the various verbal contributions. The duplications of their experiences enabled them to do that.

"She did everybody on the set, including the propman."

"Probably had an unusual prop."

"Infantile vagina. Couldn't even get my little finger in."

"She asks would I like to snatch a kiss or vice versa?"

"No better vice than versa."

"I pulled the same one twice. First time she was brunette. She felt familiar."

"Every time she changed the color of her hair she got a merkin to match."

"Anything I hate it's the taste of glue."

"Thought that's how you learned."

"How?"

"Licking envelopes."

"She came over to the table and said she got off at two. The bird I was with had eyes for her. They were beautiful together."

"There was all the gear, the boots, the whips and everything all laid out and ready on the bed."

"Remember her? The one we called Spanky?"

"No."

"She used to say, 'I'll come early if you flagel*late*.' "

"First thing she does is smash this whole bottle of perfume against the bedroom wall."

"Plug it in, she says, handing me her vibrator."

"She didn't look like a hooker."

"She's hot for double features."

"Synchronize your joints."

"I take her to her place and tell the cabdriver to wait. And when I came down the next morning he's still there. With eighty-five bucks on the meter."

"She gives great head."

"Lipstick on her nips and even all around her fern."

"Weird bird."

"Full freak."

"Don't scratch. Play it in the corner you'll scratch. Play safe. Leave the cue ball up there and don't hit it too hard."

"I'm out eight hundred."

"I told her she was the only bird I know who gives me a soft on."

"She's so dumb she goes into an Italian restaurant and orders fellatio."

"One fellatio coming up!"

"With a side order of cunnilinguini!"

"Want to go to the fights next week?"

"I've got a bird who told me she can almost come off watching fights."

"No birds. Let's just go."

"Who breaks?"

"You broke last time."

"It's your break. You follow Arnie."

"That'll be the day."

"All the while I was doing her I thought she was grabbing a pillow, but I find out it was a teddy bear she was talking dirty to in baby talk."

"This phone freak used to call me."

"What did he say."

"Not a guy. A bird. She'd call me once a week, sometimes more. To get talked off."

"Maybe she was using a French phone."

"Ever find out who she was?"

"No, but I felt sorry for her. Poor bird."

"Why?"

"Because usually she had to call collect."

"She goes into the bathroom for over a half hour and when she comes out she's washed off all the good smells. It was like balling a bar of soap."

"In Rome one afternoon, honest to Christ, he tried to pull this nun. Didn't you? C'mon, admit it."

"She had eyes."

"She wanted to convert you."

"He wanted to convert her."

"Eight in the side."

"Make a beautiful subject. Hot nun with all her robes dropped around her feet."

"So paint it."

"Arnie will pull a nun for you."

"Get some bird who looks like a nun."

"Wouldn't be the same. Have to be a real one. Imagine her standing there bare-ass, with maybe just her rosary beads dangling."

"They shave their heads, you know."

"Do they shave everything?"

"Shit, how do I know?"

"You shot out of turn, you bastard. You follow me."

"I have a few times. They said I was better."

"She looked tight. You know the look. Anyway, when I went to put it in, it sort of dropped in."

"Would have felt better if I'd just taken it out in a warm room."

"I told her she ought to get laced up, about ten stitches."

"She was a buzzer."

"I had one like that last week. Kept coming so fast it got to be one long buzz for her."

Serious silence. Thoughts about the unfair distribution of possible passion.

"She wanted the television on while I was doing her. Had her head propped up and her eyes fixed on the set. All the way. Guess what was on?"

"Arnie."

"You mother, how'd you know?"

"She was having Arnie while you did the job."

"I've got it, baby," boasted Arnie, making a very fine cut shot to end that game.

"For kicks they cruise along Sunset or Wilshire in Andrea's white Cad. About three or four in the morning. What they look for is some nothing guy, some loser like a gas station attendant. They stop and ask if he wants a ride, and when he sees who they are it really shakes him. Two of the most famous stars in the world. Not one, but two, and he's probably been jerking off for years with them in mind. Anyway, they get him in the front seat between them and right away they start talking it up. Next thing he knows they're groping his joint, and of course it ends up with them both doing him. Think of it. The poor bastard living a dream. Wanting to never take it out, coming until all he can get off is dry shots. Then what they do is dump him out anywhere and laugh about it. Imagine the poor son of a bitch trying to tell somebody what happened to him. Nobody will believe him."

"I'll bet if he's married he even tells his wife."

"And it turns her on so he has to do her too."

"Andrea told me one guy they did like that came breaking through the crowd at a premiere of one of her pictures. She was getting out of her limo and all the lights were on her when this guy comes from nowhere. She sort of recognizes him. Anyway, he remembers her and thinks he's entitled to a grab. All the dumb mother gets is a lot of cops."

"What time is it?"

"After five."

"Make this the last game."

"For a thou."

"I'm in. Who's not in?"

"Everybody's in."

"It's Arnie's break."

Arnie smashed the racked balls but nothing dropped. If he won this one he'd be up six hundred. Otherwise down four. Eduardo examined the placements of the balls and decided to go for the highs. He ran three and then missed the kind of shot that was usually easy for him. Rog made three lows. Knight scratched.

Arnie pulled everything in him into concentration. He tried to make himself believe it was five in the afternoon and he wasn't feeling thick, that he was sharp and the only thing to do was put it in the hole.

Put it in the hole. Three ball.

Put it in the hole. The one ball.

Put it in the nice hot hole. The four ball.

Put it in the fucking hole. The two.

Hello, eight. Big eight. It went swimming before his eyes. The quiet was loud. A tough shot. Arnie chalked and looked the mouth of the pocket. All he had to do was put it in.

Put it in. Please put it in.

"In the corner," Arnie announced his intention and tried to get all of himself going for that direction.

One more time, baby.

It wasn't a clean hit. The black ball slopped around the mouth, unwilling, but finally fell.

"Like it had hair around it," said Rog.

"Lucky shit," said Eduardo.

The change of the game being over woke them all some. Eduardo offered breakfast and they were hungry so Knight went to fix it with Rog for help. Arnie and Eduardo sank in the down of a sofa. Through the town house windows they could see dawn happening.

"What have you got today?" asked Eduardo.

"Nothing."

"I've got one I pulled at a party the other night."

"You up to it?"

"I'll get up."

"You can always get down."

No laughs. All out of laughs.

"It feels good," said Arnie.

"What?" asked Rog, returning.

"Having nothing. No one to do."

"That's exactly what I was just thinking," said Rog, true.

"That's a bunch of shit," said Eduardo. "By this afternoon you'll be out pulling."

"Not today," Arnie promised himself.

"Me either," said Rog.

Knight came with Danish and coffee and some burned scrambled eggs that they ate without manners. They talked the same common subject. Knight said he had a matinee and a late one but thought he'd cancel both. Eduardo thought aloud that maybe the reason he wasn't painting was too many birds.

"Maybe what we should do is take an oath," suggested Rog.

"Fuckers Anonymous?"

"Not me."

"Better I stop breathing."

Eduardo let some words come up through his thoughts. "The trouble is too many too easy."

"So how'd you like to be the poor creep who has to really work for it? Maybe scores only once a month?"

They all counted their prolific blessings.

"I've got no problems," lied Arnie.

"I say the last was the best and the next will be better," claimed Knight.

"I'm with you," said Rog.

While Knight got up and restuffed his shirt in, he said, "I know a guy who goes into a retreat for a whole month every once in a while when he gets fed up with birds. A real monastery where's there's no talking and no birds. Absolutely no birds for a whole month."

"Yeah, and first night out he fucks himself into a coma."

"You ought to go into a retreat," Rog told Arnie.

"Me?" arched Arnie.

"We ought to all do it."

"Us?"

A long moment of silence. Eduardo finally said what they were all thinking. "Things aren't what they used to be."

"Not like the good old days."

"Like four or five years ago."

"When at least we had to ask twice for it."

"It's not our fault. It's today, the way things are now," said Rog thoughtfully.

"Permissive."

"Excessive."

"For instance, Arnie, when you pull a bird, right away what does she expect?"

"Nine inches," quipped Knight.

"And is she ever disappointed," grinned Eduardo.

Arnie defended by feinting a move to his fly for proof. He told Eduardo, "A bird hits your studio and she's practically on her back before you can get a drink in her hand. Right?"

Eduardo had to admit the paradoxical truth. "Like I said, too many too easy."

"Easy come, easy go."

"But there's nothing else to do."

"Birds," said Eduardo, hardly using his lips.

Knight yawned.

It was contagious. They all yawned.

"One time I was in Long Beach," said Knight inside a remembering look. It was as though he were talking to himself. The others were hearing without listening. Knight continued, "I was staying at this hotel and one night I came in about three sort of stoned. There was this bird running the elevator and while she was taking me up we got something going, so she stopped between floors and we balled. Right there. Never forget it. One of the best I ever had."

The others considered it just another bird story, nothing special.

He went on. "It just came to me why. Why it was better. It wasn't because the bird was so great. She didn't have a magic box or anything." He paused for a moment and then told them. "It was the elevator."

That registered. They all looked their attention at Knight.

"Where we made it is what made it good," he said. "The place."

"I did a bird in a bakery shop once," Rog recalled. "She was working there, so she locked up and we made it behind the counter. I still get a hard on whenever I smell that good bakery smell."

"Ever have a bird give you head while you were driving?"

"That's nothing. Happens a lot."

"Same thing, to a degree."

"In a hospital in Switzerland, when I broke my leg skiing, there was this night nurse. Had me in traction."

"How about the Metropolitan Museum, bent over a mummy case?"

"Did you?"

"No, but how about it?"

"A Christian Science reading room."

"Quiet, everyone!"

Now they were alert, playing with the idea. Eduardo went for more coffee and they continued suggesting places. Just for kicks.

"Maybe where's just as important as who."

"More maybe."

"Where instead of who."

"Who's the same. Where's different."

"Yeah."

They got higher and higher on the thought of it. They were inspired to invent such locations as the YWCA swimming pool and the electric chair at Sing Sing. Eduardo began writing places down on separate slips of paper. Not the impossible ones like home plate at Shea Stadium between doubleheaders, but only those that would require imagination and ingenuity.

It grew into an actual thing to do.

Eduardo folded the slips of paper and put them into a Galli vase. For their fingers to pick by chance. But first they decided on some rules.

1. It had to be done where specified.

2. They had seven days to do it.

3. Any bird previously pulled was ineligible. Had to be a new one.

4. No pros, no paying for it.

5. It couldn't be a quickie. The bird involved had to be very well done.

That last stipulation was a matter of faith in their sexual competence. Eduardo gave the vase a few good shakes. He held it out for them to pick from it. Knight stopped him. "We ought to have a bet," he said, "some kind of stake."

"How about twenty thou each in the kitty? Losers forfeit, winners take all."

"No, not money."

"Make it something important."

"Like what?"

They all thought.

"I've got it," said Eduardo. "We'll bet the retreat."

"Huh?"

"Losers have to go into a retreat for two months. Two whole months without even seeing a bird."

"Forget it," said Arnie. "I'm out."

Knight told him, "You're the one who was bitching about too many too easy."

"So were you."

"Well, I'm in," said Knight.

"I'm in," said Rog.

"I'm in," said Eduardo.

"You mean if I don't score in one of these places I've got to go into a monastery for two months?" Arnie asked incredulously. "A real monastery?"

"What do you want, a convent?"

"I was just feeling sorry for you guys, that's all," said Arnie. "I don't think you could take sixty days solitary."

"Worry about yourself. You in?"

"I'm in."

It was, of course, a perverse, farcical idea. But it was seriously important to them. It was better than going on and in, on and in. It was a new dimension. They needed it. Now they were recharged with spirit. Satiated empty, they now felt replenished, their sexual ennui transcended.

Eduardo held the vase out. They each picked a place from it. Confident, sure of success. Because they had everything going for them. They were the most wanted, the most envied, four of the most notorious swingers of our time.

Four of the beautiful.

Especially in this age, the beautiful are more sexually corrupt. At least, more sexually corrupted. Beauty and erotic vice are most compatible. They thrive together and one becomes the habit of the other. It is ironic that the beautiful must be such victims. As all others, the moment they are born they are alone and they also must anticipate a singular death, but the time of life between, for them, is more sacrificial. It may appear less lonely because it is spread with attention. But the beautiful are sentenced, by the very virtue of being more divinely formed, to early dissipation. Their shapes seem to fit more precisely into the pattern of futile physical attempts to compensate for human separateness. Also, the beautiful must pay the penalty of hypocrisy. They are demanded as performers in the fantasies of those plain and ugly, those who most critically condemn them with magnified scrutiny.

The beautiful are unfortunate, really.

They are the ravished.

They are the ravishers.

In their inescapable libidinous cells they are martyrs for us all.

3

Knight Gleason.

Everyone, except those in the other world of Marion, Ohio, who were the live mother and remote cousins and all the others who'd been in his early time, assumed Knight Gleason was a good name created by the big studio. But it was on his birth certificate.

Knight was the superhero. Physically shaped into one by sperm and ovum and United States nourishment, with perhaps some partial determination by unfair God, who so many claim has the final say regarding anatomical law.

Six feet six with a swimmer's waist and a face that tempted touch to prove it was not an ideal mask, Knight was superhero number one. Publicly emulsified into one through the fiction of thirty-seven movies in which he was never allowed to lose against overwhelming bad odds.

Unlike the fable, Knight wasn't discovered by those ever-culling experts, who shine like a high-set gem on the lower West Coast of nearly everyone's mental map of America. Rather, one day when he was full-grown and ready for public kissing, Knight went to the big studio gates and was let in all the way. It didn't matter if he could act or not. He could talk and he could move, looking beautiful. And, although it was never an actual written part of his fame, Knight's appearance said he must surely possess the longest largest between his legs.

The world's women secretly wished it true and used it for private attachment, trancing. Men, according to the measure of their envy, had to admire and wanted to believe it. Men of the farms unconsciously accepted and compared Knight's abstract endowment to certain animals. Many city men, with direct comparison at stake, compensated and reassured with the accusation that Knight had to be a homosexual, noncompeting.

Of course, there is the constant denial that sexual size is an advantageous attribute. Women especially say it's not how large it is that matters. But perhaps that is mere guile to protect their own desirable image of tight. And perhaps they need to say that to excuse their choices, compromising. Only they know.

Anyway, in the case of Knight Gleason, the creator was most generous with cells, did not disappoint an inch. Knight had it just as long and large as he looked like he had it.

For some encounters it was too much, but these were exceptional instances. Most times Knight's ample size merely confirmed the true elasticity of female tissue. Besides, some hurt is beneficial.

With so much advantage physically, it was assumed by all that Knight was intellectually limited. Not so. He was able to control the volume of his mental reception as needed. On the studio set between scenes he'd lock the circuit between his eyes and brain into one-way absorption of Schiller, for example. Not until the cameras and others were ready, absolutely awaiting him, did he leave the deep to skim in the shoals.

En route anywhere, being driven, being flown, he read. It was not uncommon to see him walking with a book up like a face guard, and both jacket pockets always contained extra literary ammunition. Books. In any room where he spent any time, no matter how transient, they were consumed and dropped, left dead, the life read out of them. Especially the bedroom of his New York apartment. The island of the oversize bed was surrounded by stacks, and more than a few birds stubbed toes on various volumes on their way to that promised land. It also disconcerted them that he read before and immediately after. However, his performance in between was always adequate.

But where did they go—all the words and all the ideas formed by combinations of words that Knight devoured? In but never out. Ever adding to the huge hoard, kept. The big beautiful man presented ideal flesh to the world but withheld his substance more complex.

He hardly ever gave more than a surface opinion to anyone, contributed no more than necessary to any conversation, and when the going got deep he deserted. Perhaps somewhere in his time he'd passed the normal point of knowledge and now his mind was mesmerized by the endless meaning of it all. Or more probably, he felt he must live up to the shallow that was expected for his image.

Knight was the first to leave Eduardo's that morning. The others stayed on to discuss their mutual prospects. It was between eight and nine, and the usual hurrying to work was on the streets. Knight walked some and was recognized too much, so he tried for a taxi. He got one from a girl who'd reached her destination and who, when she saw him replacing her in the yellow carrier, wished she could get back in. She saw that he needed a shave and looked as if he hadn't slept, and that excited her more. Anyway, it was something to tell the other girls at ordinary desks on this ordinary morning, that possibly, if she'd been brave enough, might have been thrilling. Opportunity runs through time and time again never.

In the taxi Knight took out the slip of paper he'd drawn from the vase. Printed in Eduardo's artistic letters was Knight's destination, simple geography that now made all else secondary:

The bedroom
of the President of the United States
in the White House,
Washington, D.C.

Knight had never been in Washington. He knew that city's landmarks and even some of its history, but he'd never had to go there and never been interested enough to make the trip voluntarily. Until now. Now he wanted to know exactly how the White House was constructed, every room of it. And for that purpose he was taken as ordered to the huge hard gray of the New York Public Library.

There he found what he sought. Among the hundreds of volumes on the White House, he found several illustrated. He sat in the silence and digested. One in particular he studied longer, a huge book with foldout sections that were detailed plans of the mansion. They were technical, meant for reference by architects, and Knight had to translate. He concentrated, trying to memorize, but although he retained a good general impression of the place, that wasn't enough. He decided he needed to take that book home, so he carried it to the check-out desk and waited his turn to face a dry woman with glasses that magnified her eyes.

"Do you have a library card?" she asked, sour.

He told her no.

"Fill out an application over there," she directed, not recognizing Knight. Perhaps she was as anti-movie as she was anti-people, Knight thought when he turned from her. She made Knight wonder why those who most dislike others seem to work at the most people-meeting jobs.

He went to the nearby counter where there were forms. He filled one and returned to a line that finally subtracted so he was again confronting the magnified eyes. She stamped an inky impression in a corner space of the form, hard, as if to hurt it. Then she printed his name and address on a card that had the word "Temporary" in red diagonally across it. "Sign," she ordered, and he scrawled his known name, impatient.

She told him with her transcribed voice, "You may use this card for the period of time noted upon it. Your regular card will be mailed to you."

"I want to take this book out," he told her.

She looked the book. "You may not remove this book from the library."

He asked her why.

"Reference books are not to be removed from the library," she said, dismissing, her glass-bugged eyes going past him to the next in line.

"Then perhaps I might borrow some paper," said Knight.

"You must supply your own."

He wanted to make some tracings of the plans, so he went back into the reading room and placed the book on the table and left the library to find paper. He walked east on 42nd to a large drugstore. In there, not far from combination hot water bottles-douche bags-enema syringes and a skyscraper of sanitary napkins, he found school supplies and a notebook that was adequate. At the counter for paying he was immediately recognized by the girl in drug white with "Miss Kumming" in red plastic over her left breast. She gave all her attention to his famous face, disregarding the dollar he was handing.

He was used to it. He took three packs of gum from a convenient rack, thereby reducing his change to pennies and not waiting for them. Then back up 42nd with eyes on him.

"Guess who I saw on the street today?"

"Knight Gleason."

"What did he look like?"

"He had on an old sports coat with baggy pockets and no tie."

"Maybe it was someone who looked like him."

"No, it was him."

"I saw John Lindsay on Park Avenue the other day."

"He looks better in movies."

"Lindsay's not in movies. He was on television but not movies."

"I mean Knight Gleason."

"They all look better on the screen. It's the makeup they use."

The secret wish drama was *Knight Gleason came right up to me and asked me who I was and while people gaped and wondered who I was he took me into a taxi and someplace that was his and gave it to me for a long long extra-long time. Me.*

Back in the reading room of the library, Knight saw that the books he'd left on the table weren't there. He went to the shelves where he'd first found them and saw their places vacant. He wondered and was answered by a cart being pushed down the long aisle between the walls of books. He went to it and saw his special book among many, so he reached for it. He was stopped by the pusher, an old man who was a small skeleton hung with white skin and liver spots.

"Books are not to be removed from this cart," the bony voice decreed.

"But I was using this one," pointed Knight. "I wasn't through with it." He started to reach again just because there it was.

"You'll have to wait till the book is returned to the shelf."

"That's absurd."

The skeleton gritted a sharp grunt and ignored.

Knight walked back to wait where the book would be replaced. He took out a pack of gum and unwrapped three sticks for his mouth, one after one. The needle green flavor helped dissolve the all-night brown thick in his movie-star mouth.

The skeleton was purposely slow, knowing he was awaited. Knight thought about time, comparing his own potential to that of the skeleton, and believed that people with less are those who waste most. Finally the cart of books was pushed against Knight's thighs and the skeleton had to put that special book in its place. Knight immediately removed it and went into the reading room.

The paper he'd bought was too thick for tracing, so he had to copy the plans freehand, not able to make very straight lines. He drew with all his mind for two hours and was nearly done when a piece of yellow paper was inserted under his eyes by fingers with pink painted nails. His immediate reaction was to autograph it, and he'd already put his first name on the yellow before he realized he was writing over a note that asked: "What are you doing?"

That made him look up and across to a girl with blonde hair middle-parted and down like slow golden water splashing on her shoulders. She was pretty with an American nose. Her eyes asked the same as her note.

"I'm doing some research," he told her, normal loud, his voice slicing the silence of the place.

The girl put a finger to her lips and hushed him. She scribbled another note that she passed across: "I've been watching you since ten o'clock."

He read and looked his watch. It was twenty after eleven. He wrote, "Why?" under her words and sent the yellow back to her.

She wrote: "It's cheaper (and better) than going to a film."

He noticed she had the kind of skin he usually liked. Her throat told him the quality her other skin would be. And he stole some from her front, going by his rule that was—if they looked large dressed they were usually too dependent and dropped when unsupported. Hers, he saw, were small enough to be nice on their own. So he wrote to her: "Are you an actress?" Flattering some.

She answered in writing, quickly: "All women are."

"Are you a woman?" he wrote.

"Physically yes, legally yes, emotionally maybe," she scrawled.

Knight was amused at the note passing, remembering the way-back other time of some school. But he cleared, reminding himself of what he was there for. He didn't have time for her. He wrote her off with: "I've got work to do," and concentrated again on the White House plans.

A fresh sheet of yellow came from her with two words large printed and without exclamation point, signifying some submission: "I'll wait."

By then he'd copied all but the White House attic area and decided it wasn't important. He folded in the foldout of the book and closed it along with his notepad. He stood. He didn't look but he felt she was also standing, and when he went the way out he felt she was behind him, all the way to outside where the air was different. He walked down the wide granite steps to the first landing and saw that Fifth Avenue was traffic, mostly yellow with taxis. He turned, and there she was, within reach. She was tall, maybe five-nine.

"Where do you want to go?" he asked, looking down at her shoes that he saw weren't cheap leather.

"Wherever," she replied, punctuating with a shrug and smile.

He put a hand under the angle of her elbow to steer gently down the rest of the hard city steps and find a taxi. During the ride he said anything she wanted him to say, while he told himself he couldn't afford the distraction that was her. He had only seven days. But her legs, he saw, were very good, and it was already started, so they went to his place, in and up to where there was a view of the river that she looked out at and then helped herself to all the other rooms that defined him. She touched some things and came back to where he was, to sit on the couch, loose. "They're real, aren't they?" she asked.

"What?"

"All the books."

"Yes."

"Want some coffee?"

"Do you?"

"No. But I'll make you some. You hungry?"

He was.

"I found the kitchen," she said and got up to go to it.

When she was out of the room, Knight asked a mirror that told him his looks, so he went to wash and shave quickly and feel better in a fresh shirt. She found him turned to any page of a Sartre in his bedroom.

"Come eat," she said.

Bacon, lettuce, and tomato on toast.

"My name's Selena," she told him.

"Selena," he said because it sounded good to say. Of course, he didn't have to introduce himself. She also told him her last name but it went unregistered.

"Why were you in the library?" he asked.

"Getting ideas."

"For what?"

"I'm a designer."

"Really?"

"No. But I want to be."

"Designer of what?"

"Fashions. Women's clothes."

"Do you draw?"

She nodded. "Badly," she said.

"Then why not an actress or something?"

"Actress is out."

"Who says so?"

"Somebody."

"Who?"

She didn't answer.

"You mean your father?"

She laughed short.

"Your husband?"

She didn't answer again. He didn't care anyway. All that mattered was she was there, and Knight wasn't even sure he wanted that.

They were on the couch. "I avoid your movies," she told him.

"So do I."

"Don't you ever go see yourself?"

"Never," he lied.

She thought and said, "I would if I were you."

The phone rang. He let it ring until it stopped.

"Aren't you curious about who it was? I could never let it ring like that without answering."

"My service will get it," he said.

She looked the room. It was a signal. She asked, "Who keeps house for you?"

"Why do you ask?"

"It's messy. You ought to have someone."

"I have a housekeeper."

"She's not very good," she criticized lightly.

"Take off your shoes," he said, not asking.

She slipped them off and dropped them. She got him eyes to eyes. "Anything else?"

"Everything."

Her look went female angry. "Just because I come up here with you you think I'm easy, don't you? Well, let me tell you something, Mr. Movie Star." She paused.

He looked what.

She faded the fight in her expression and replaced it with truth. She smiled a smile she considered wicked enough and told him, "You're right."

She stood within reach, facing him, and undid her skirt off. She had on bikini panties, clean white, and he could see her lower hair through them, little bristles sticking through the fabric and some curling out around the elastic of them.

Knight was tired but his want was on the way up. She was pretty and she was clean and she walked some for him while she peeled her silk jersey blouse up and off to show him her bare back and tell him no bra. She didn't turn around for a moment, waited for enough tease and then turned a slow turn and brought her drumhead stomach and good hips and breasts to him, stopping when she was within range of his hands, sure they would reach.

But they didn't. He didn't let them. Only his eyes moved, appreciating. He felt like playing it a different way. No touch.

His advantage lowered her. She knelt and pressed her breasts against his trousered knees. He liked the falling gold of her hair. She avoided his eyes, but he saw hers, wetter with anticipation, intent on her hands, her eyes watching her hands as if they were separate little amusing animals that undid his top trouser button and unzipped him open and went inside to find and take his center out into the air of the room. She claimed it with both hands.

"God," she said with more breath than sound. "You're so big.

"God," she said again, more worshipping.

* * *

After an afternap she touched him one final touch to believe it, but there were no kisses. She got dressed because she sensed he wanted her to go.

"Will I see you again? Ever?" she asked as she made her hair smooth.

"I don't know."

"It doesn't matter." She smiled to validate her words. "It was unexpected, so I shouldn't expect it, should I?"

He said no because he believed her. No need to promise lies. He wished there were more like her.

"I'm satisfied," she said and kissed him a good-bye kiss with only her lips, and then he was alone to call his answering service.

There had been several calls from birds wanting to be called back, but he forgot them as soon as he was told. His agent had called three times the night before and twice that morning. And there was a long distance from California that he was supposed to respond to as soon as possible. Knight dialed his agent, Glenn.

Regular hellos followed by a portion of careful hell from Glenn. "You ought to let your service know where you are. I told you Tuesday I'd be getting some word this week."

"Sure," said Knight, passive.

"They want you in Rome the day after tomorrow. Andrea's already there. They just want to go over the thing with you."

"Day after tomorrow?"

"Just to get everything clear. They won't start shooting for a couple of weeks, but they want to go over the script."

They, thought Knight.

"They," continued Glenn, "expect you to be there. I made the commitment. I had to."

"They," said Knight, "just want me to decorate their lousy fucking parties and you know it."

"You like Rome."

"I can't go."

"Shit, don't say that, I promised."

"You should have asked me first."

"I couldn't get you. I didn't know where the hell you were."

"That's your ass."

"You've got to go."

"I don't have to do anything. Tell them to shove their picture."

"You're already signed."

Knight heard Glenn's impatience in the wordless space between them. Then Glenn said, "All right. I'll get you out of it, but you'll be there before shooting date, won't you?"

Knight agreed and asked, "Who do you know in Washington?"

"A few people. Why?"

"I may go down there for a few days."

"What the hell for? Some bird?"

Knight didn't answer.

"You want me to make some arrangements for you down there?" Glenn offered.

"I'd appreciate it."

"I'll call you back. But shit, I don't know why anyone would want Washington over Rome. I'll call you back."

"Not right away. I'm going to sleep."

After Glenn, Knight looked at his scribble that said operator 813 Los Angeles and decided not to call, because if it was a bird it didn't matter and if it was business he didn't have room for it. He picked up a small green leather book that looked even smaller in his hands. He opened to any page. He sank into sleep in the middle of a line of Wordsworth.

When he arrived in Washington, Knight was met by photographic flashes and questions.

"What brings you here?"

(If you only knew.)

"Will you be seeing the President?"

(Christ, I hope not.)

"Are you planning on running for public office?"

(How about pubic office?)

"Is it true about you and Senator Killworth's daughter?"

(I don't think I've ever done her. What's her first name?)

He pushed out of flash range and past all the questions without giving any exterior answers.

That question about his running for public office wasn't really absurd. In former times movie stars were invited officially to the capital only when it was appropriately amusing to include a famous profile or cleavage. And then it was always done with anxious uncertainty, for who could predict when one of these beautiful ones might lapse into the antics of their rumored perversities?

Perhaps the runners of government were right to be concerned. Who knows how many foreign diplomats or wives of same were guilelessly groped between courses under the executive tablecloth? There were never any complaints.

Anyway, now is a different time. Now the government is becoming star-studded. And it is not considered consciously ridiculous to watch an actor act an act on television that is a serious speech criticizing foreign policy and the very same night see him make a ninety-nine-yard football run to win the game and the cheers and the rosy kewpie-doll girl in the end of the late late old movie.

There are child stars trying for Congress and hoofers fast-stepping in the Senate. So it was entirely possible that Knight was in Washington to get his role in the big big show.

"Take Mr. Gleason to his suite."

Two highest-up corner rooms where the over-age bellboy got a five-dollar famous-person tip for carrying the key and one Gucci bag and flipping the light switch and opening a window a crack.

"Thank you, Mr. Gleason." The bellboy smiled a lot of cheap dental work and left, thinking he'd ask for an autograph next time.

Glenn had arranged the reporters and the car and the hotel and given Knight two names with unlisted phone numbers. One was a Senator and the other Knight thought was surely a heavy hostess. So after Knight got settled in, had hung what had to be hung in the closet and made the large bathroom look less lonely with his toothbrush and various other personal things, he took out the slip of paper with the names on it and thought about which to call first. While he was deciding, the phone rang.

"Mr. Gleason, this is Lottie Winston." Pause. Obviously the name was supposed to mean something. Knight almost said, "Yes, Miss Winston," but she didn't really have a Miss voice, so he didn't say anything and finally she went on.

"I know it's presumptuous, my calling like this, but I wanted to be the first to welcome you to Washington," she said.

Knight thought perhaps she was the hotel's social director until she continued, "As soon as word gets around, you're going to be bombarded with invitations and I wanted to get my chance at you first."

"How did you know I was here?"

She giggled an older giggle. "Darling, I know everything that happens in Washington, sometimes even before it happens."

Knight was looking the slip of paper with the names on it. Lottie Winston wasn't there. Knight asked her, reading from the slip, "Do you know Babs Bannon?"

That made her breath catch. "Now, don't tell me Babs beat me to you. I don't see how she could have. You've only been in your hotel for five or ten minutes."

Knight resented her knowing that. He felt like telling her to go sit on her heel but controlled when it came to him that if she was so knowing perhaps he could use her. He told her, "I haven't talked with Babs yet," purposely using the first name familiar.

Lottie made a sound that communicated her delight. She asked, "How long will you be in Washington?"

"A week at the most."

"A whole week. Marvelous. That's plenty of time to do things."

"For example?"

"Well, if you'll pardon the short notice, tonight I'm having a small important dinner party and I'd love to include you."

Knight had an immediate yes in mind but hesitated for effect.

She filled the space with the important names of others who would be there.

"What time and where?" asked Knight, answering.

She victoriously told him the hour and the place and added, "Black tie, of course," before she clicked off.

Her voice left Knight with the image she had to be. A hundred-seventy-five-pound stump, hopelessly harnessed by a made-to-enormous-measure girdle. He dissolved the repulsion of her by going out and down to get the feel of the city.

It felt good. It was lunchtime and birds were in abundance on the streets. He absorbed the nourishment of their recognizing eyes and he knew he could pull all he could ever want here.

One delicious expensive brunette in a surely Ungaro suit

bumped him on her way from an understated jewelry store to a black chauffeured limousine. Face up to his face for only a moment. He saw her briefly stunned by the familiar stranger that was him and he knew by the measure of her recovery that she was impressed, pullable. He remembered that. She was choice.

Of course, Lottie Winston's address was in Georgetown. But as it turned out, she wasn't the heavyweight Knight had imagined. Lottie had an excellent figure for her years and a good genuine tan. She was definitely a time fighter, slowly losing, but not without a battle, using frequent two-week stays at health farms and every cream that had an ounce of hope in it. Knight guessed she was or would soon be sitting on sixty, although her body was adequately alert to deny it and she wasn't foolish enough to try camouflaging with makeup, letting her sun-soaked face say youth in that special, healthful way.

"I'm so glad you could come," she said, greeting Knight with both her well-lotioned hands.

Knight said something polite, while he stole from the plunge of Lottie's dress front and thought her pair were too good, that they must have been worked on, surgically somehow.

She joined herself to his famous arm and took him in to get everyone's attention. There was no need to tell his name.

Handshakes.

Nods.

Manners.

A recommended fresh mint vodka concoction for his fingers and throat.

Expected words.

"Not more than a week ago I saw that movie in which you played the soldier."

"I enjoyed it. You were superb."

"I especially remember that one about you in the underground. I forget the name of it."

"I've seen every movie you've ever made."

"I've always been a Knight Gleason fan. Always."

"In the one about the diamond mine when you had to dive from that swinging bridge, did you do that or was it some trick?"

"Who thinks up those things anyway?"

"You look the same as you do on the screen."

"I didn't think you were so tall."

Movies. In Knight's first ones the enemy had varied from arrogant Nazis to muscle-bound Apaches to all the most menacing black natives the studio could hire from Watts. But lately the foe had been constantly communist, either bulky, bushy-browed spies or slant-eyed military fanatics, attacking.

It was expected that Lottie's other guests should try to make an immediate connection through their reactions to Knight's public image. They felt, each in his or her own way, that they already knew him. Besides, it was taken for granted that that was what he wanted to talk about. They didn't know he didn't give a damn and was suffering through it until he'd been among them long enough for them to get off the subject and back to talking about one another. They didn't know he'd have preferred a regular hello and such normal getting-acquainted questions as "How's the weather up in New York?" He ran the gamut of their idolatry, proof to him that his being there made them as uncomfortable as he was. He drank his first false-frosted glass empty and nibbled on the minty leaves of his empty second. And all the way to when he was seated between Alecia Killworth and Lottie, facing a bleeding slice of prime rib, he thought the time was wasted. Two days now subtracted from his allotted seven.

Then it was Kenneth Hill who asked, "Are you in Washington on business?"

"Yes."

"Will you be making a film here?"

"Eventually."

"You're here to soak up some of the atmosphere?" asked Hill. He was the Secretary of the Treasury.

"Yes. To get the feel of it. I always do it before a film," lied Knight, while his mind quickly pulled vague fragments into a vague idea.

Hill went on as Knight hoped. "What will the film be about, the one you'll make here in Washington?"

Knight didn't answer immediately because he was inventing. His hesitation was made dramatically advantageous by Lottie who said, "It's confidential, isn't it?" Her eyes twinkled for her ears that thrived on disclosures.

Knight nodded.

That spurred Lottie. "At least you can give us a hint."

"Something to do with espionage?" asked Secretary Hill.

"In a way," Knight evaded, baiting.

Lottie leaned and touched his forearm. "You're tickling our curiosities," she smiled.

Senator Killworth almost ruined everything. "He told you it was confidential," said the hardly lipped mouth under the nose that breathed loud in the falling fat face.

Knight hurdled with, "It's a very involved plot."

"Anything to do with my country?" asked the French Ambassador, hoping.

"No."

"The CIA?" probed Lottie.

"That's close," Knight lured.

"You big teaser, you. Tell us," Lottie begged, girlish.

Knight acted helpless, unable to resist. He allowed some silence to hang for a backdrop and then asked, "Who guards the President?"

Everyone knew and said, wanting more from Knight.

"At the White House, for example," said Knight.

"He's well protected," said Secretary Hill, sure.

"Have you ever been to the White House?" asked Senator Killworth.

"Tomorrow," said Knight.

"Official invitation?" asked Lottie.

Knight smiled exactly the right kind of smile. "No, I told you I'm here on my own just to get the feel of the place."

Secretary Hill didn't even wait to swallow the sugared baby carrot he was chewing. As Knight had expected, it was important for the important to prove it. "Maybe I can make things a little easier for you," offered Hill.

Knight went sincere. "That's kind of you. Right now all I have to go on is a tourist map." That got some laughs, Knight Gleason a tourist.

"Well, we'll have to do better than that for you," said Hill.

"I'll do my part," said Lottie, eyes batting, "if you promise."

"Promise?"

"That you won't let Babs Bannon get to you," said Lottie.

"I'm in your hands," Knight told her.

* * *

After dinner Secretary Hill hadn't forgotten. Close, brandy friendly, he looked up diagonally to Knight, rotated a Havana-via-Montreal cigar to feel it in the slick cave of his mouth, and said, "I'll make some arrangements for you tomorrow."

"Sure it won't be too much trouble?"

"Not at all. Just a matter of a few phone calls. But let me be sure I'm right about what you want." He cleared his throat with a short popping cough. "From what I gather you want to get a look at how the Secret Service operates."

Knight saw himself on a long tour of fingerprint files and karate classes, so he risked asking for a direct route. "One phase in particular," he told Hill.

"What's that?"

"Perhaps it's not within your power," inserted Knight to prime.

"I run the goddam department," Hill informed with some smoke.

"The White House?"

"Hell, yes."

"I'm sorry. I told you I don't know who's who around here." Knight waited for Hill to offer, but the Secretary seemed preoccupied with the sensations he was getting from his cigar, so Knight had to come right out with it. "If I could see how things are done there in the White House, it would be very helpful."

"We'll show you the whole show," Hill guaranteed and chuckled a rakey little chuckle with his chest. "And maybe sometime when I'm out in Hollywood you can show me inside there," he said with visions of starlets deviating through his brain.

Lottie slid between Knight and Hill. "Whatever you're talking about, I'm changing the subject," she said and waved the air to breathe less of Secretary Hill's smoke. The Secretary retaliated by puffing another defiant cloud and then backed away.

Lottie led Knight from that room to another for alone. There were shelves with books to the ceiling, rich leathers. While Knight read some golden titles, he felt Lottie's eyes on him. He took down any book and broke it open. Lottie moved to be beside him, against just enough so Knight's arm had to feel her breasts and he knew he'd been right about them. They were injected firm. He had an urge to put his hands on them.

At the same time she was wanting his hands to do it, to take and like the scientific shape of them that she'd paid to have. Only she had seriously touched them since they were created, and she wanted it.

Knight had never done anything with a woman as old as Lottie. He was temporarily intrigued with the idea, wondering if he could activate her.

In all her life, all the ins and outs and downs, Lottie had never had anyone with as much physical pull as Knight, and in reaction to him she felt a flash of victory over time, inside, just above her retired opening—a vague tinge that tried to surge but swiftly faded.

Knight sidestepped from contact.

"I'm going to be candid," said Lottie.

Knight turned his eyes and caught her throat skin that made him hope she wasn't going to come right out and ask for it. He was relieved when she told him, "You've got Alecia all upset. She wants to go home."

"What's the matter with her?"

"She's bothered. You know. By you."

Knight acted. "Really?"

"She says it's a headache, but we know that's not where her head is, don't we?"

Knight laughed some inside and a little out. All through dinner he'd been aware of Alecia Killworth's disturbance. But he hadn't considered it extraordinary.

Lottie shook her head and ate him with her eyes. "You can't be," she said.

Knight looked what with his eyes.

"As good as you look," she explained.

"Suppose I am?"

"Then, darling, it's not fair."

"To Alecia?"

"Or me."

Knight used time to replace the book he'd taken down.

"It's late," he said.

"Please stay," begged Lottie for herself and then gave. "Go out in the garden and I'll send Alecia out to you."

Knight didn't want to, but Lottie didn't give him a chance to refuse. She hurried away, and Knight went out through the wide double doors to a terrace and down steps to an uneven walk of old bricks where it was dark. Bugs were making brave night noises. All along were the heavy heads of prize roses and everything conscientiously manicured, leading to a large important tree. It was darker beneath it. White chairs could be seen because they were white, and there was a glider that Knight sat on to face the rear of the house. The cushions were not too damp and he was content just to be there, away from all.

He thought some about Alecia. She was older than her age. She was attractive but one of those who refused to help herself to extra prettiness. She would, he thought, make a fine editorial subject for one of those women's magazines that delight in taking basically pretty people and remaking them lovelier. During dinner Knight had noticed her mouth especially, pale dry and tight-looking without lipstick or even a touch of gloss. And her unexaggerated eyes. Alecia the plain. She was coming now. He saw the bobbing beam of a flashlight that brought her down the steps and toward him. She shined and hurt his eyes with it.

"There you are," she said, keeping the light on him.

Knight had the fast foolish fear that it was a death ray. She finally turned it off and kept standing there, as if waiting for instructions. "Sit down," he told her.

"It's wet," she complained, but sat. She waited for him to speak, hoping he'd say anything to take the edge off being there. After some silence she said her excuse, "Lottie told me you wanted to talk to me."

"It's peaceful here," he said.

"Lottie keeps a nice garden. Some people seem to be able to grow anything, but not me. The only thing I ever have any luck with is tulips. Do you like tulips?"

"Tulips are interesting." He remembered miles of them in Holland with a girl from Amsterdam who sang to his center in her native tongue.

"Where were you born?" she asked.

"Marion, Ohio."

"Really?" Evidently she liked Marion, Ohio.

"Ever been there?"

He expected yes but she said no. "Where were your mother and father born?"

"Same place, Marion."

That pleased her more. "What extraction are you?"

Knight first thought of his dentist. He told her, "English mostly, I think."

"Don't you know?"

He didn't answer.

"Chances are your family goes way back," she said, "to early American days. Probably they were pioneers."

"Probably."

"You ought to find out. Have it traced. It's important."

"Why? What difference does it make?"

"A lot. Especially these days. It makes a person feel good to know he has roots that go deep into our country. My family fought at the Bridge."

Knight saw a gang fight on the East River under the Brooklyn Bridge with swearing and groin kicking, but he really knew the particular bridge she was talking about. "At Concord?"

"We had many, many ancestors in the Revolution. You did too, I'll bet."

He decided to play. He told her, "Valley Forge."

That made her jump. "Honest?"

"Crossed the Potomac with George," he lied for good measure.

"Then you belong, don't you? I felt you did."

"Of course."

"I knew it. I knew it," she exclaimed, excited.

Knight didn't know what he was supposed to belong to.

She said, "I'm very active in the D.A.R. We have a huge chapter here."

Knight thought, I'm active, too, with a big chapter, baby.

"Now I know," she said.

"What?"

"There had to be something about you. Something more than just a mere man." She left a space but Knight didn't fill it, so she had to go on. "I mean, it was this—this mutual thing I felt."

"Where did you feel it most?" asked Knight, playing.

She evaded. "At the dinner table."

"Deep?"

"Very deep."

"And warm."

"Oh, yes, warm."

"Inside?"

"Yes."

"In your lower stomach?"

"Yes, there."

"Lower?"

"Oh, yes."

He almost sent one of his hands to her crotch for a surprise but stopped it with the strange fear that if he touched her there her eyes might Fourth of July sparkle red-white-and-blue and she'd start whistling "The Star-Spangled Banner." He put his arm around her and pulled her to kiss. Her mouth was closed. His wasn't and his tongue soon persuaded hers to come out. He felt the breath from her nose on his cheek and heard a little pleasure sound excite itself out of her. He made it a long various kiss so her body tensed and gave in, tensed and gave in, climbing. When he removed his mouth, he separated completely, letting her shake it off. She got up to do it, walked all the way around the big tree and back to her place on the glider.

"Are you a Democrat or Republican?" she asked.

"Neither," he answered, true.

She almost shrieked, that made her so happy. She asked, "You're not middle, are you?"

"No."

"And you couldn't be far left?"

"No."

Actually Knight had never voted. He'd tried to vote for Kennedy but wasn't registered so they wouldn't let him. He'd had to be satisfied with voting for him in his mind, but that was the only time he'd been at all interested and in the end that had turned out badly.

She said, "Then there's only one direction left."

"Left?" he played.

"No. I mean there's only one other thing you could be." She paused and asked, "Are you?"

"Are you?" he asked back.

"Of course."

"Why?"

She thought it was a little test he was testing her. She couldn't fail. She said, "Someone has to stop the Jews."

He wasn't surprised. To draw her out he contributed, "And the niggers."

"The niggers are just tools for the Jews. The Jews are using the niggers. All those race riots and everything are just cover-ups for the real problem. The Jews are behind it."

"They're very clever," inserted Knight.

"The Jewish Conspiracy," she said as if it were a title.

Knight saw a little man with a distinctive mustache yelling from a Berlin balcony while the crowd roared worshipping approval.

Alecia went on, "The fluoride plot, for example. In the toothpaste and the water. It's cerebral poison, you know. Slow accumulative cerebral poison. The Jews are doing it. Poisoning our minds so they can take over."

He couldn't let that one go by. "But how about the Jews who drink that water and use the toothpaste?"

She had the answer ready. "They'll sacrifice the few to get the many," she said.

"The thing to do is go thirsty with dirty teeth," said Knight.

"They say it's for our health, but it's really a cover-up. The Jews have all kinds of cover-ups. But thank God, they haven't got everyone fooled. Right?"

"Not us," Knight overplayed.

"Poor Daddy," she whispered for him, "he has to be so careful. He has to pretend in order to keep himself in a position where he can watch it all and fight it. He really serves our country. One of our true patriots. Do you know he sometimes has to vote yes on things he actually feels no about. It hurts him so. Poor Daddy."

"I feel sorry for him," said Knight with sarcasm she was too involved to notice.

She said, "We've all got to protect America. Did you read the latest A.F.A. bulletin?"

"A.F.A.?"

"Americans For America."

"Oh, of course. No. I didn't get the last issue. Was it good?"

"It was all about LSD and what it's doing to the minds of youth. That and marijuana. It's putting them into a euphoric state so they can't resist the conspiracy. LSD was created by the Jews, you know."

Knight almost told her so was the Salk vaccine but decided she'd have a one-way explanation for that too.

She said, "I got so riled up when I think about it, the underhanded gangster tactics they use. Even the small things like the way they're buying up all the great art treasures of the world."

No comment.

"Flying saucers," she said. "There's more to them than anyone's letting out. Only the Jews know."

A little silence while she thought. Then she said, "Egypt—Egypt didn't have a chance. We should have backed Egypt all the way. But of course the UN is under Jewish control, so the Jews get their way any time they want."

She waited for him to say something about them. She believed his silence was agreeable. She said, "You know how they've twisted the Bible around, don't you? So it says everything the way they want it said. They call them translations but what they are is revisions. They've infected the churches too. And the schools. Many schools don't even salute the flag anymore."

"What a shame."

"They're getting more and more aggressive every day. You know what I think we ought to do?"

"What?"

"Fight. Like Daddy says. Fight before it's too late."

"Wipe them out?"

"All of them. We've got the bomb. We could do it."

"How do you know they haven't got the bomb? You said they control everything."

"No. We've got the bomb."

"That's reassuring," said Knight with thought.

Alecia fell lightly against him, snuggling. "Mmmm, I feel nice with you. Not because you're famous and good-looking. Honest, really. It's because we have so much in common. It's wonderful to have someone to talk to and be understood."

Some of Knight felt sorry for her. But most of him hated her hate. He was tempted to throw her back that instant and spread her and jam it into her rough. That she might like it stopped him. Besides, there was the silhouette of Lottie coming from the house, calling to warn them of her approach.

"Hello out there."

Alecia had eyes shut and Lottie's voice was a needle that made her jump and straighten.

"Alecia darling," said Lottie, "your father's ready to leave. He wants to know if you're going with him. Or shall I tell him that Mr. Gleason will see you home?"

Alecia didn't answer, hoping. Knight told her, "I'll call you."

"Promise?" whispered Alecia with pout. She was turned toward Knight so Lottie wouldn't hear.

For his answer and good night, he placed one of his hands on one of her breasts and squeezed an exact measure of hurt.

When he got back to his hotel rooms, Knight found three messages. They were all from Babs Bannon. He added up the progress of his first evening in Washington and decided he didn't need another hostess.

Five days to go.

The next morning at eleven Knight was in a long official black limousine. On his left was Gray Suit. On his right was Brown Suit. Gray and Brown both appeared to be relaxed men, except for their hands. Knight noticed their hands were constantly active, digging pockets, tapping fingers, fisting, opening. They were the kind of men that would dissolve into the crowd of any crowd, but when they were standing alone or as a pair, anyone would say they were police of some sort. Whenever Knight looked at them they tried to smile.

"You're going to make a movie about us, eh?" asked Brown Suit, without looking.

"So it seems," answered Knight.

Gray Suit asked, "You going to use real people in it?"

"It has to be authentic," said Knight.

Brown Suit sat higher. "I've been in the service for twenty years."

Gray Suit tried to sit higher than Brown Suit. "This is my fourth Chief assignment."

"What's that mean?" asked Knight.

"Protecting the Chief. It's the most important duty in the service," Gray Suit told him.

Brown Suit slouched.

"How about you?" Knight asked him.

Brown Suit pretended his attention out the window. Gray Suit answered for him. "He's been on foreign detail."

"Overseas?"

"No, guarding foreign visitors, like the Princess and Tony and Kosygin."

"That's a hell of a responsibility," said Knight for Brown Suit's benefit, inflating.

"I could really tell you some incidents," said Brown Suit.

Gray Suit wanted to know, "When you going to start making this movie?"

"I don't know exactly. Soon."

"Christ. Hope I'm not on leave when you do," said Gray Suit. He already saw himself in a shooting chase, heroic. And Brown Suit was enjoying a similar fantasy, including close-ups in color.

For their sakes, Knight made an indirect equal promise. "You're both good types," he told them.

Gray Suit couldn't take that sitting still. His hands had to unbutton his suit jacket, and that let Knight see the little blue-black butt of a revolver underneath, tucked in a leather holster. The realistic danger of it made Knight's belly grab and then radiate pleasantly, flowing excitement that went to his groin. It was a taste of the stimulation he was there for.

The limousine slowed and turned in at the White House. Official nods were thrown to the guards at the gate, so they didn't stop until they were all the way in. Out of the car, Knight faced his destination for the first time and found the building was larger, higher, stronger-looking than he'd thought it. Somehow, all his pre-impressions of it had been influenced by the suggestions of its name. The White House. That intimated purity and warmth and welcome, but this structure with its huge columns and unreachable windows was as overpowering as a cold asylum.

Brown Suit and Gray Suit led Knight into the lower foyer. And then for the first hour they opened doors and guided him through rooms with names derived from their colors and shapes. On the way they related places and things to various Presidents. Knight was partially interested but more anxious to see where the personal living was done, and they finally took him up to it, to the higher floors and to a certain empty corridor in that special wing of the house.

There were several doors on each side of the passage, as well as chairs and tables and a single large mirror. They stopped at the mirror. Brown Suit told him, "The Chief doesn't like men standing around out here in the hall, so we worked something out.'' He reached to a light bracket on the wall just left of the mirror and swung it up to reveal an adequate opening. He invited, ''Look here.''

Knight looked into a small lighted space. In there two men similar to Brown Suit and Gray Suit were sitting, just sitting with legs and arms crossed, looking ahead.

Gray Suit pressed the edge of a nearby table to make a part of the wall slide aside silently—a narrow opening. They went in. The men on duty were introduced and given handshakes. Brown Suit turned Knight around to show him. ''One-way mirror,'' he informed.

Knight saw the hallway through it—a total view.

''We also have an electric beam,'' said Gray Suit, pointing to a black box attached to the inside wall about eighteen inches up. ''It's coupled right across the hall so nobody can pass without hitting the circuit. Of course, it's not on all the time, only at night when everyone's settled down. Just an extra idea we had. Nobody can break that beam and get away with it.''

''I suppose it fries them right on the spot,'' said Knight.

''No, but that's not a bad idea,'' said Gray Suit, serious.

Knight quickly appraised the secret space to see there was a two-way radio and a pair of automatic guns on the shelf, ready for anything. Brown Suit saw him notice the weapons, so Knight smiled and inquired, ''Loaded?''

''Not even on safety,'' answered Brown Suit through closed teeth, overacting.

They went out and the wall slid back into place. ''What do you think of that?'' asked Gray Suit.

''Interesting,'' said Knight, thoroughly examining the mirror and its placement and noticing exactly where the electric beam crossed the hall.

They went farther down the corridor. ''This is where the First Family lives,'' said Gray Suit.

''Can we look in?'' asked Knight.

''No. They're in there.''

''Do they eat and everything up here?'' asked Knight.

''Most of the time.''

Knight had hoped for a complete inside look, but now they were at the end of the hallway. Any of the closed doors could be the place, and, evidently, neither Brown Suit nor Gray Suit was going to say. ''What's in there?'' asked Knight, pointing a door.

"Sitting room."

"And in there?"

"Bedroom."

That was the wanted word. Knight was counting doors to remember that special one, when Brown Suit told him that was where the Chief's daughter slept.

Knight had to ask. He acted the question, nonchalant. "Where does the Chief sleep?"

Gray Suit pointed to the last door on the right, deepest in the hallway.

"Want to see the kitchen?" asked Brown Suit.

Gray Suit answered for them. "Let's go down and have some coffee," he said.

And that's what they did.

In one of the few bathtubs that was big enough for him, Knight slid his asscheeks forward on the slippery porcelain bottom so his upper half was submerged in the high hot water that was cloudy white from hotel soap. After a few moments of relax, he arched and his center surfaced. The legendary sea serpent of Scotland, thought Knight for private fun. He lathered it until it was covered with slick suds and the hair there was frothy curls, giving the area more cleaning attention than needed. He broke the arch and drowned it, watching the water cloud more white from it. He manipulated the chrome drain handle with toes and let all the water run out. Then he closed the drain again and started a perfect mixture of fresh hot and cold to fill up and rinse him. He allowed a dribble of hot to continue and stayed in the tub longer than usual, while he took a mental audit of his progress. He started with the President's bedroom. At least now he knew where it was, knew its door. To it he added the cooperation of Secretary Hill along with Brown Suit and Gray Suit. And then there was Lottie. And Alecia. Altogether, they amounted to something that was taking him closer to the fulfillment of his obligation. Although they were still all circulating in vague positions, he felt sooner or later they would congeal into a clear helpful unit. It would have to be soon, he thought. He had four days.

He thought about Arnie and Eduardo and Rog and how they were making out. He wondered if any of them had already scored, and the possibility determined him. He thought what a loss it would be if he were the only one who failed. Of course, he could lie, but he knew that would only be cheating himself. No. He had to do it, remember every detail of it and take it back to New York with him.

He got out and dried with two towels and wrapped another fresh one around him to go out to the bed. It was half past seven. Message slips were on the bedside table near one of the phones. He looked through them. That person, Babs Bannon, had called four times. Persistent. Lottie once and Alecia twice. Glenn had phoned from Hollywood, probably having trouble with the Italian producer that was actually trouble with the Italian producer's overheated wife. He decided not to call anyone.

He closed his eyes and concentrated on the tiny nothings that swam on his lids. He was thinking about Italy, about the pleasures of not going there at all, when the phone rang. It was Lottie.

"Were you a good boy today?"

"No one to be bad with."

"Did you meet the Chief?"

"Not quite."

"See all you wanted to see?"

"Almost."

"When I called the second time and you weren't in, I thought Babs Bannon had stolen you away from me."

"Not a chance."

"What are you doing right now?"

"Just lying here."

"Alone?" asked Lottie.

"Just me and a towel."

A little silence while she got the picture. "I can imagine," she said.

"Tell me about it."

"You tell me."

"Well, right now I'm wiggling my toes." He just felt like talking.

"What else?"

"I'm not much of a wiggler."

"I used to be."

"That's for sure."

"Am I that obvious?"

"It shows," he told her.

"I was thinking this afternoon how sad it is that our times didn't match."

He didn't know what to say about that. True, he thought.

"I wasted a lot," she said, "a lot of time."

"If you could get it back now, what would you do with it?"

"Well," she breathed, big, "I wouldn't be here."

"Where would you be?"

"There."

Knight saw a twenty- or thirty-year-younger Lottie and knew she must have been great. The quality was still there. Heat that probably wouldn't stop until she was dead cold. Again he was fascinated by the idea of doing something with her. If not all the way, at least something, defying the life law that she represented, the futile simmering out.

He was thinking that, and she mistakenly translated his silence into verification of her inability. "Alecia called me today," she told him. "We talked about you. She's badly bitten."

"I never laid a tooth on her."

"She didn't sleep last night because of you."

"How did you sleep?"

"As usual, four or five hours, badly."

"For no reason?"

"You can stop right now. I'm not going to be fodder for your voracious ego."

"Why not?"

"You're a bastard, a cocksure bastard."

"Odd you should choose that word."

She knew which one he meant. "What I called about was to tell you that I've come up with an official White House invitation for you."

That made him sit up. "For when?" he asked, controlling.

"Friday night."

"Just me and the Chief?"

"Sure. Just you and the Chief and two hundred others. It's a costume ball in honor of the Brazilian president or whatever he is. You'll get your invitation by special messenger tomorrow."

"Costume ball. What shall I come as?"

"Come as you are," she suggested.

"I usually do."

"Just put a raisin in your navel and say you're a cookie."

"You'd eat me up."

"I'd eat you down," she said bravely and then gave him to Alecia again. "Alecia's expecting you to take her to the ball. I think you ought to."

"All right."

"Call and tell her."

"I will."

"Now. Anyway, tonight sometime."

"I don't have her number."

She gave it to him and asked, "You have my number, don't you?"

"Yes, shall I use it?"

"Only in case of emergency."

"Like if there's a fire?"

"If there's anything I can do for you, call. Okay?"

"Thanks."

"Forget it."

"You forget it."

"Don't worry, that's easy. I only wish it weren't."

Good nights.

He looked down at his center. It was half hard. And just from talk. That Lottie, he thought, had something.

He didn't call Alecia right then because he wasn't in the mood for her. It was still early and he'd have to make an excuse for not wanting to see her. Later on, late would be excuse enough. He dressed and went down to the lobby, hoping to choose some paperbacks to read. But the place for them was closed, so he had to go outside. He walked three long blocks to a bad magazine store where there were three rotating racks full, most covered with violence being inflicted on front bulging blondes. Unmerciful heavens, he thought as they spun before his eyes. He managed to find two different and not bad—a Kafka and an F. Scott Fitzgerald; both he'd read before but long enough ago.

On the way back to the hotel he saw an empty narrow hamburger place and went in. The guy working the grill was a Greek only three months in this country who spoke English not very well, and Knight liked it because it allowed him to talk about anything without the movie-star handicap. After a while a couple came in to recognize and spoil it.

Back in his rooms he found a message slip. Babs Bannon. He was glad she'd missed again. He undressed and went into the sitting room of the suite to turn on the television and watch nude from an indestructible hotel chair. It was a thin boy and girl movie with the girl in it cleverly saving her virginity for the essential wedding night. Actually, she was an actress with whom Knight had once shared acrobatic upright passion in a swimming pool. He clicked the television off and reduced her to a pinpoint of leftover electronic light. He thought perhaps now it was late enough to safely call Alecia.

She answered before the second ring.

"I thought maybe you'd forgotten me," she whimpered.

"I said I'd call."

"I suppose when someone's as famous as you they never get lonely," she said. Alecia's left breast still ached from his rough good-bye squeeze. It wasn't hurt really. There were no bruise marks. But it felt different from her right one. "There's a masquerade party at the White House Friday night," she told him.

"I know. I talked to Lottie."

"I've already got my costume. I thought it would be nice if we went as a pair. You know, in matching costumes."

"Skirts are drafty," he played.

"You know what I mean. I'll take you to the costume place where I got mine."

"It'll have to be tomorrow, won't it?"

"Yes. How about the afternoon?"

"The morning would be better for me."

"Maybe we could have lunch."

"I've got a business lunch."

"I want to see you," she said. "I've been thinking about us all day. I thought maybe I'd see you tonight."

He knew all he had to do was say and she'd be there in ten minutes. "I'm already in bed," he said.

"Sounds comfy."

"I'm sleepy," he told her.

"You do have to get your beauty sleep, don't you?" There was a trace of anger in her.

"Yes."

"I want to see you."

"Tomorrow."

"I need to see you."

"Tomorrow."

She gave up. "I spoke to Daddy about you today. He said he'd like to have a long serious talk with you while you're here."

"What about?"

"He thinks maybe you can help the cause. I told him you'd probably want to."

"How can I help?"

"I don't know exactly. But Daddy said you were in a Jew-controlled business. The Jews dominate motion pictures, you know. He said they use movies to get their dirt into the minds of everyone."

"Your daddy is very smart," said Knight, thinking about how many Jews must have voted for Daddy.

"I'll tell him you said that," she promised, as if Knight would be rewarded for it.

After some silence she exhausted a sigh. "Are you sure you're sleepy?"

"I can hardly keep my eyes open."

"But it's only half past nine."

"Must be the latitudinal change," he said. "Or maybe I've caught some special kind of Washington sickness."

"I doubt that. Anyway I hope you have more zip tomorrow."

More unzip, thought Knight as he said good-bye.

After that he ordered some ripe and some green olives and celery and two pieces of lemon chiffon pie from room service. He finished all the pie and celery first and then, while consuming Kafka, he had the olives, alternating green and black. They weren't pitted and he tossed their little hard cores at the mouth of the waste basket across the room. He averaged 60% hits.

Some rooms of the White House are open daily to the public. There are girl guides wearing special uniforms and doubtless smiles to show people where and where they can't go.

Knight went in with everyone. Hoping to prevent recognition, he had on large horn-rimmed glasses and an anonymous suit and his hair was combed a ridiculous way, middle-parted. He followed the crowd, staying well back until they were on the second floor, where, when they turned left, he turned right. For no attention he didn't hurry, merely walked away in the opposite direction at a normal, rather official pace. He opened a prohibitive door and went down a prohibitive passage and through several prohibitive rooms, aiming for the part of the mansion he knew contained the bedroom of the Chief. Several times voices and footsteps made him hide. In one room he had to squat behind the brocade back of an overstuffed chair for a long while and wait until some servants dusted around and vacuumed the rug. Another time only the recess of a doorway prevented his being discovered when four important-looking men walked past with papers in their hands and Vietnam on their minds.

Finally he reached that stairway he remembered and went up to an interim landing and up more to reach that special private corridor. He saw the vigilant mirror and, farther down, the final door. From that angle and distance he was sure the men of the Secret Service behind the mirror couldn't see him.

So far so good. His watch told him four-thirty. Now what he needed was a hiding place. He retreated to the landing where he saw two doors. One that he tried was locked, but he opened the second and saw it contained mops and other cleaning supplies. He looked to see if anyone was seeing and then went in to close the closet absolutely dark. He sat on a large carton of the softest toilet paper in America.

It was strictly reconnaissance. He wanted to find out if it could be done.

The first hour in the closet was easy fast, but after that the dark seemed tighter and each minute slower, persecuting.

Solitary confinement.

In the hole with him!

For control he played with remembering a part he'd acted movies ago. The Red enemy had him captured to punish the secrets out of him, and there had been the tricky, true-looking blows to his face, making the bogus blood trickle from his mouth. Time out for the spraying of glycerin that was the artificial perspiration caused by the artificial pain.

Torture me all you want.

They had him stripped to the allowable waist for appreciation, his shoulders and perfect pectorals and the little forest of his chest hairs glistening from torture.

I won't talk.

The optical spin to unconscious black.

I won't dance.

Remembering he'd always wanted to do a musical with a slick reflecting infinite floor for his patent leather shoes among silver slippers on hundreds of feet on the best legs ever cast.

I can't dance.

Remembering a bronze by Degas, a little ballerina with a very frayed tutu. Thinking that a lot of them, those he'd done, had too-frayed tutus. Too bad.

He felt in need of sound. He wanted to hum but couldn't.

He scratched his ear for the sound of it.

Remembering grass instead of a sheet in a younger time with someone forgotten. His knees grass-stained, and his elbows. Greensleeves. Again he felt like humming and remembered in that same other time nowhere alone enough for doing it and trying for her father's car in her father's garage and her father's electric alarm catching them for her father.

"If you were a man I'd kick the shit out of you," said her father, looking up at Knight, who was already then a six-foot fit piston working in life.

Now footsteps outside, going down the stairs, down and out of hearing. Two hours and ten minutes spent. More than double that more to wait. More footsteps, closer more.

His imagination saw them opening and finding him, jumping back frightened, calling out for help to come and drag him out and take him somewhere for questions. Recognizing him.

Headline: MOVIE STAR CAPTURED IN WHITE HOUSE CLOSET triple exclamation points.

But those footsteps went and as their sounds diminished so did his anxiety, all of it, and he felt completely relaxed, nearly blasé about being there. He uncramped, leaned back, shut his eyes, and allowed his mind to take him skimming over the soft disciplined surfaces that were lines of favorite memorized poetry.

Until quarter after eight.

He opened the door a crack and saw no one. He went swiftly out and up the stairs and into one of the doorway recesses on the same wallside as the mirror. After a short appraising pause, he moved along that wall past doors and chairs until he saw the little metallic inset that was the electric beam near the edge of the mirror near him. The mirror itself was heavily framed and placed above the baseboard. The depth of the frame was about eight inches. The baseboards about six. Together they gave him about fourteen to work with.

He went down on the floor on his back. He pushed with his hands and heels and slowly inched beneath the electric beam without disturbing it. The wood floor was waxed slick and he was going with the grain, the wool of his suit helping slide. He kept his shoulder pressed tight as possible against the baseboard underneath the mirror. He didn't know if they could see him or not. He thought perhaps the width of his body would show them the outer edge of him. If they couldn't see him, he knew he was only a fraction out of view, so he couldn't lift up to get any push. It all had to be done with his hands at his sides pushing the entire weight of him inch by inch until the upper third of him was past the seeing point.

Then he lifted his head to look the length of himself, and his feet alarmed him. They were too big, too tall, the tips of his shoes dangerously up to the mirror's lower edge. He was almost certain they could be seen from in there, but he had to move them. Every moment he expected to hear the whooshing of the wall panel for them to rush out and point guns down at him. He moved by small measures, controlling the urge to jerk his legs and feet quickly to safety. It took nearly a half hour for all of him to be more than past the mirror.

It was relief for him to be upright again. He felt taller than he was. He went down the hall without noise to the last door. The door. He listened against it and heard no one. He took the brass knob of it, and, evidence of his anxiety, it seemed to dissolve with his touch.

He turned it to click and opened. No peek. He opened all the way wide and went in and his eyes immediately found the bed in there in the soft electric light.

Hello, bed, he said inside, feeling himself brightening. He went to it and pressed on its silk spread with his fingers, testing. He sat on its edge and then lay back to bring his legs up and squirm to the middle of it. It was a big bed. He put his hands behind his neck for a while and looked up to the ceiling where he knew the Chief probably looked a lot. He looked the rest of the room and caught on a pair of cowboy boots paired next to a chair with a cushion that was indented by someone's sitting. Probably the Chief's, he thought. He looked left and there was a clean telephone panel with many plastic push-buttons neatly initialed. Also three phones. Red, white, and blue. He believed the white was direct to the Kremlin and wondered why not the red. Pure white. He was unseriously tempted to make a Moscow call and reassure them over there that we over here don't want more than our share, and how about an even split, and how would the man over there like to trade four tons of chocolate chip ice cream for a hundred pounds of large gray Beluga? Fifty pounds? Well, comrade, you go out and strip the sturgeon while I see how much choc chip there is in my freezer compartment. Knight guessed all the initialed plastic push-buttons on the panel were direct connections to various advisers. They made him think about Louis XV and his taborets, the little king-given seats that permitted few to sit in the royal presence while others stood, envied and developed varicose veins beneath their male and female silk stockings.

Dialogue: "If you're real good, baby, I'll give you something to park you ass on."

Not so different from: "I want you to keep in touch, sweetheart. Keep in touch. You're getting a direct line."

I choose you.

"Guess what, darling?"

"Guess what?"

"He's putting a line in for me, direct."

"But what if he calls?"

"We'll just have to chance it."

"Did you hear what happened to Senator Somebody? His new cook got on the direct line and ordered three pounds of chopped chicken livers."

"And?"

"They were delivered in less than an hour."

"I wonder."

"Wonder what?"

"If they've got any blintzes."

Knight was laughing a third of the way up his throat. He'd gotten there. He'd done it and now he knew he could do it again and next time he'd bring someone for kicks. The whole damned thing was falling into place. For triumphant expression he began bouncing. He bounced little bounces and felt like shouting so he bounced bigger instead. The bed made its noises under him.

A different sound made Knight stop. It was water running. In the bathroom. Water off and on again. Someone.

A man's voice asked, “Is that you, honey?”

Knight almost answered no as he got up.

“Honey?” the voice asked for answer.

Knight went for the door, got its knob, got it open, and turned to see if he was caught.

The Chief had a towel on and half a jaw of shaving suds. His neck stiffened and his eyes squinted to focus on Knight, who hoped the Chief had the right kind of eye trouble. Knight went into his act, made his head make his shoulders make his arms make his hands loose. He smiled his best Western smile.

“Howdy,” said Knight with a brief hand up.

The Chief unsquinted and snapped his head a small accepting snap as he said, “Howdy.”

Then it was up to Knight in the doorway, stay in or get out. He decided out was less incriminating, so he kept smiling at the Chief who was almost smiling when Knight left.

Out in the hallway he waited. He thought the Chief might open or look or call his SS men. Knight waited for either for a while and then put his ear against the door panel and heard what he thought he heard.

The Chief was singing a lonesome cowboy song. Pretty good in the middle range but definitely sour on the high and lows.

Everything was all right.

Knight retreated as he'd come. With more confidence and less difficulty.

The invitation's engraved information said costumes but no masks. Evidently they wanted always to know exactly who was who.

There were lots of pairs. A fat Indian brave was with a fat Indian squaw who had a sack on her back for a papoose that was a wetsy doll everyone thought cute because it had been given a beaded headband to hold a canary feather. A pretend maharajah was with a chiffon princess who had a blue dot between her eyes, bells on her toes, and finger cymbals on each hand that she dinged for hello at everyone. There were several baggy clowns with baggy clowns, as expected. There was a silver spaceman suffocating inside his plastic sphere helmet and colliding with his spacegirl's plastic sphere helmet.

Knight and Alecia matched the way she wanted. She was early American, naturally, in true blue with a dozen petticoats making her float, and her waist and ribs so cinched that her front pushed way up. She asked Knight several times if it was too daring. Knight was a Revolutionary officer complete with white stockings showing between silk knickers and square buckled shoes. He also had a three-cornered hat he had to carry. Alecia had on a high white wig that was knocked off balance early. She'd wanted Knight to be authentic as possible, but he'd refused to wear a white curled hairpiece.

Secretary Hill was there as a jowly ancient Roman.

Senator Killworth was a comic Nazi general with a wooden luger.

The French Ambassador wanted to come as Marie Antoinette but settled for being a floor-length sheik.

Lottie was South Sea for her tan in a man-made grass skirt thick enough, and a more modest than native bright top along with an ankle bracelet of flowers. She also had a blossom over her ear, although she couldn't remember if it signified taken or virgin or what.

They gathered in the Oval Room to flatter and laugh according to costume and influence. This was only the social overture. Nothing really began until music from somewhere shut mouths and stopped movement.

Hail to the Chief.

Some serious-suited men entered first, like a spearhead. Then the First Lady in fringed white buckskin on the arm of the most important Brazilian who was a stumpy unconvincing matador. Next was the Chief with the visitor's wife. She was so short that even her high mantilla didn't get her up to the Chief's armpit. She looked uncertain, as if ready to leap aside, afraid if the big man fell it would be on her. The Chief was a white cowboy, absolutely clean, not a speck of barbecue sauce on him. His cheeks were pulled just enough to create what was supposed to be a long-term smile. He nodded all ways at anyone. As he passed close by Knight, he blinked, trying to remember where and when.

The march music was stopped halfway through and the

other music began, a demanded smooth number for the First Lady to get pushed around some by the important Brazilian's belly and the Chief to be a rhythmic tower bent threatfully over the Brazilian's stunted wife. After a few bumping steps the Chief signaled permission for everyone to dance.

Alecia pressed her lifted bosom against Knight and felt melting. Knight had to regulate his steps to half length to avoid her dress and petticoat hems. He suffered through that first dance and used thirst as excuse from the next.

"I've already had my one limit," said Alecia.

"Tonight is special," Knight told her, persuading.

"I'm already a little tipsy. I'm not a drinker," she said, but took the glass of champagne from him.

He clinked her glass with his. "Here's to it."

No sips. She drank it all, seeing him through the etched White House seal. He could have stopped her but didn't, and then he complained. "You didn't let me finish my toast."

"You said here's to it and I thought we were drinking to it, whatever *it* is."

"But I wasn't finished."

"So finish." She raised her glass.

"Not with an empty. Never with an empty. It's very bad luck," he said and grabbed a full for her from a passing tray. "To it and us." He clinked again, sure she would drink to that.

She did. Her mouth gulped while her mind was on him.

Three, thought Knight and calculated that ought to just about do it.

Lottie came to them, swishing her grass and twirling a loop of fresh baby orchids. "Aloha, young lovers," she greeted with a cheek kiss for Alecia and a left breast jab for Knight's arm. Knight noticed Lottie's tan seemed deeper than when he'd last seen her. Her shown skin was extra rich with sun and barely oiled to shine some. She caught Knight stealing from her front and her eyes gave him permission.

"I'd love to dance," announced Lottie, claiming Knight's shoulder, while handing her nearly full glass to Alecia, who wanted to assert her assumed monopoly of her movie star but wasn't quick or brave enough.

Lottie pressed herself against Knight who pressed, and all through the dance they didn't talk much, allowing the physical its social opportunity. After the first few steps that got them out of Alecia's range and into the mix of the crowd, they didn't dance patterns at all, just short easy moves with a variety in all directions, permitted rubbing. For two pieces. Then Lottie returned Knight's hand to Alecia's hand, again surrendering to youth. She said, "He's a divine dancer."

While waiting, Alecia had nervously finished Lottie's drink. Knight noticed. He transferred the empty from Alecia to Lottie and gave Alecia his arm around. "Your turn," he told Alecia and danced her.

In his hold she was much more willing now than before, more pliable. Knight tried to press for some lower contact, but there was the layered thick of her dress and petticoats, so he shifted his attention to her upper half, going against her with tight little counter sways, making her breasts roll pleasantly under pressure. Also, his fingers played a message on her bare backskin, alternate cruel and tender tips.

Alecia snuggled her head in the curve of his neck and let her eyes close. By the end of that music there was perspiration above her lips and she felt she needed to swallow to pop her ears. In the talking space between songs she voluntarily remained against him, waiting in eyeshut for the motion to resume. Halfway through the next number, Knight tested. He stopped all his moving to measure her contribution and found that she was helping herself.

"How do you feel?" he asked.

"Nice," she answered, moaning the word downscale.

"Like the other night at Lottie's?"

"More."

"You want more?"

"More."

He steered her through the other dancers, including a near collision with the great white Chief, who was still pulling cheeks for his mouth to be smiling. Knight steered all the way to the entrance and out, unnoticed.

He said her name.

She said his name.

He said, "You and I are going to make some American history."

"History," she said.

"You want to?"

"Want to," she slurred. The champagne and Knight had reached her up and down.

He walked her to the grand staircase and hesitated there to make sure. She immediately looked to him, and over her head he saw no one looking. Up the stairs then at normal speed with her floating beside him. Up and around and out of sight into a room and room to room with as much hurry as caution would allow. He knew exactly how to get there from two times' actual experience and numerous mental practice runs.

The special corridor. They stopped at the start of it.

"Where we going?" asked Alecia, rolling her head at him.

"To make history, darling," he told her. He thought she might need some regenerating, so he took her to him and ran a kiss from her ear down her neck and back up again to nibble her lobe and give more attention to her ear's little cave.

"That tickles." She squirmed and giggled.

"Be quiet," he whispered into her. "You have to be quiet or we won't do anything."

"I want to," she pouted.

"I know," he said. "But you've got to do exactly what I tell you. Promise?"

"Promise."

"Good girl."

"Bad girl," she giggled.

He gave her neck more kiss with some appropriate suction for good measure. He heard her nose breathing louder from it. He guided her by hand to the corridor wall and the mirror.

It was his plan to get past by sliding under as he'd done before, only this time he'd do it belly down with her ahead of him, to be pushed if necessary. But he suddenly realized it couldn't be done. Her costume made it impossible. All those freaking petticoats would hump up too much. He thought about making her take them off and leave them there, but a hallway strewn with petticoats was surely enough cause for alarm.

He revised his plan. He carefully raised the secret wall light bracket and looked into the guarding space. In there he saw Brown Suit and Gray Suit. Knight considered that fortunate. He watched. The two men were both in their duty positions, sitting close together facing out. Brown Suit was reading aloud from a small book. Gray Suit was listening intently. From the moment he looked in, Knight felt there was something unusual about them. Although they seemed to be just sitting there, something wasn't normal, and finally when Brown Suit brought a finger up to turn the page, Knight realized what it was. Brown Suit and Gray Suit were holding hands.

That's sweet, thought Knight. He let the light bracket down into position and turned to find Alecia using the wall for lean. Knight instructed her to stay where she was and she nodded with a champagne grin. Knight pressed the secret edge of the nearby table. The secret panel slid open and in went Knight to make Brown Suit and Gray Suit spring to attention.

"Hi, fellas," acted Knight. "How's it going up here in good old secrecy?"

Brown Suit and Gray Suit offered strong handshakes and unusual smiles.

"I was just downstairs with the Chief," Knight told them for authority, "and Secretary Hill," he added for extra power.

Brown Suit tried to sit on and hide the little book he'd been reading aloud, but not before Knight saw it was *Sonnets of Love*. Knight's sudden appearance had the two men off balance, more self-conscious than alert, an advantage that Knight exploited.

"I'm leaving Washington tomorrow," said Knight, "and I wanted to see you two before I go. It's about the movie."

The movie made them light up.

"To get right to the point," continued Knight, "I've looked at everybody around here and I've decided that you, both of you, might be perfect for it. But you've got to understand these aren't just little parts I'm talking about. Actually, what you'd be playing is my right- and left-hand men all through the picture. Think you could handle it?"

An eager yes from them.

Knight told them, "Usually we do a screen test, but no need to bother you with all that."

"What about Hill?" asked Brown Suit.

"He's too old for the part," answered Knight.

"I mean, will he give us permission?"

"Don't worry, I've talked to Hill," assured Knight. "He's all for it."

Brown Suit saw himself being recognized by everyone on some future street. Gray Suit thought about signing autographs.

Knight went on building. "You know, everyone thinks

movie people make a lot of money. Five figures, six figures, even more than the Chief. And let me tell you, confidentially, it's true.''

That made Brown Suit go driving in the biggest kind of car with his initials on the door while Gray Suit went underwater in a private pool behind his future typical mansion.

Knight narrowed his eyes, examining them. ''Yes,'' he said thoughtfully. ''I'm almost absolutely sure about you. There's only one thing I'm not certain about.''

''What?'' they asked, duet.

''Well, whether you know it or not, the camera is a merciless instrument. It sees everything. For instance, an actor I once knew looked great from every angle except one and the camera caught it. It ruined his career.''

Brown Suit and Gray Suit were ready to show profiles.

Knight told them. ''The trouble was he didn't look at all good from the back. Obviously you can't always be facing the camera, so you've got to have a good back view. Right?''

''Right!'' they agreed, automatic.

''Turn around,'' instructed Knight. ''Let me take a look at you.''

They did an about-face for him. Knight made some appraising sounds to keep them turned while he stepped back quietly to reach the power switch that controlled the electric eye beam. He snapped it off.

''Most important is how you look in close-ups,'' Knight told them, going closer to inspect. ''Good ears,'' he complimented. ''Backs of necks look okay. Nice head shapes.''

Brown Suit and Gray Suit smiled happy at the rear wall.

''I know we can use you,'' said Knight, true.

They started to turn. Knight stopped them. ''No, stay just like that. Now I've got to check for long shots. I know you're great for close-ups, but how do you look from a distance?''

The two men corrected their positions, stood tall as they could, turned from him.

''Stay as you are,'' instructed Knight, backing away. ''Hell, I wouldn't be surprised if the producer offered you a contract. Don't move. I want to really study you from way out here.''

Knight was out and there was Alecia still leaning. He took her by the arm and, as if he owned the place, walked her past the guardian mirror, right down the middle of the forbidden corridor, all the way to the Chief's bedroom door. And in.

The bed was like a fresh open envelope with its clean sheets turned down ready for sleeping. Oversize pillows were plumped and propped, and placed there against them, not to be missed, was a thick manila folder tied and titled, "The President's Night Reading."

The moment she saw the bed, Alecia fell upon it, her multiple petticoats billowing up. Knight carefully slid the Chief's reading matter from under her and tossed it to the lap of a nearby chair. He clicked off two of the three burning lights and then removed his shoes and hers. He put his length down next to her. His arm under her head brought her face to a kiss. Her lips were open loose, inactive, but her tongue was playful. Knight tried for her front with a hand but she was so bound in it was impossible. He felt around back and found her zipper. She didn't arch to help, remained deadweight. He could have rolled her over to unzip but he didn't, and after a brief attempt at it he took his effort elsewhere.

Keeping her mouth occupied he pulled up her dress to pull up her petticoats that were crinoline and starched. He tried to invade them but they fought back, springing resistance. One up, two up, bunching, three up. He wondered if he'd ever reach flesh. Too much bunch. He gave up trying from that position, broke the kiss, and sat up, kneeled up, looked down at her eyes that were half-lidded. She lifted an arm as if it were horribly heavy and wiggled fingers for a silly wave at him along with a grin over the humpy rise of her costume. Then she let her arm drop abruptly to again be as lifeless as the rest of her.

Knight's feel found her ankle skin to go nonstop up against the down growth of her hairs, all the way up, the petticoats accumulating around his arms. She didn't object or assist. Her legs were straight, thighs together, and he had to push them left and right for space. She was wearing tight underpants that were warm moist where his fingers touched her through them for a while and then forced under the side elastic to reach exactly.

Although he knew by the measure of her wet that she was ready, he gave more perfect friction, expecting response. But she remained completely inert and silent. It made him angry some. He gathered the crotch of her underpants and pulled roughly until he heard the threads of them break. He tugged them down and off to let him climb over and be between her.

He was also ready. His want was expanded by the frail tissues of chance, the emotional reward of thieving ballooned his stomach and sharpened his mind and pumped his blood hard. He was in the bed of the President of the United States. Doing it. The intellectual part of him retained a narrow connection with his awareness that told him it was ridiculous, stupid to do, ridiculous. But that only nourished the doing, italicized the perversity of it.

His appetite was also increased by her. She was the perfect partner for this time because he disliked her so much. He loathed the acquired ignorance of her, hated her hate and the body that contained it. She was a robot, a soft robot, programmed to campaign for the cause of loneliness, and he was stirred by the idea of ramming, stabbing, puncturing into her to make her passion bleed and swamp all her despicable mechanisms. Unreachable otherwise, at least it was temporary destruction of her.

He took his center out and moved into better position between her. He lowered to be over her. Her petticoats flounced around, fighting his chest and stomach with their stiff float, and down below some were folded into a barrier against the aim of his center. She could have helped, could have reached to clear the way, spread to receive, but she did nothing, just lay there while he eliminated the obstruction and found her.

With a beginning measure, he made sure he was in the way in. She stayed still. He hesitated to muster his pleasure and malice.

Then he let her have it, plunged her. All at once. It hurt a scream out of her. Her arms and legs flailed and the rest of her exploded furious. She heaved but he held all of him in her to make her throat repeat the screams like a female beast, impaled. He felt fear constrict her center around him trying to close but already invaded.

It was not the first time for Alecia. She'd gone horizontal for some before. But never had she helped, never, because she believed she did her share by allowing. Each of those times before had been grateful probings, shallow and short, unlike this long enemy that jammed its attack. In automatic defense she tightened to shrink her entrance to safe infantile dimensions and printed the excusing red letters of the word "rape" on the black of her squeezed eyes.

Knight extracted some length from the tight slip of her and

felt her clamping the vacancy. But she was disturbed slick and could not prevent the forward force of another deep fast filling.

She suffered the sensual shock. Fear and pleasure volted contrapuntally through her and to her extremes. She pulled her center down and under to have his out of her, but failed because she had to go up to meet him. There was another scream in her; however, the point of it was softened too wide for her throat, so it came from her a mixture of helpless baby whispers and full-grown moans, while her mind ricocheted.

This isn't beautiful at all.
This is beautiful.
This doesn't hurt at all.
This hurts.
This is fucking.
I don't like it.
I do.
I want it.
Out.
This isn't beautiful at all.
I hate it.
Please.
Take it out of me.
I want it out.
But in.
Too far in.
I'm being hurt.
This is fucking.
Don't.
I'm just a little.
I'm just a little.
You bastard you.
I don't like it.
I do.
This is fucking.

She flung her hands from his back as if they were stones, far as possible several times. And, by her, some of the plastic push-buttons on the direct lines phone panel were shoved in and phones were hit from their cradles, including the most important white one. At once there was a chorus of filtered fidelity.

"Yes, Mr. President."

Knight had to remove and get up. He replaced the white phone first, quickly, thinking this was no time for a nuclear crisis. Then he restored all the others to their proper disconnect position.

It was when he was climbing between Alecia again that he discovered she'd fainted. He didn't know it immediately because she was no different than she'd been before—lifeless. He thought she'd return to reaction as soon as he was in her again. But she didn't. She was limp as dead.

He got up again to go into the bathroom where he found a small towel that he soaked with cold water. He made sure it was cold cold and hurried to plop it sopping on her face. He waited for her to respond but it seemed to have no effect and he had to remove it, afraid she might suffocate. As a secondary measure he slapped her cheeks a few times, not gently. Her eyelids fluttered some and then locked again.

All that was wrong with Alecia was too much. Too much champagne but mostly too much feeling. Her mind, on behalf of her body, had taken the unconscious escape.

According to the rules Knight remembered, his obligation included his partner's orgasm. And there she was, as insensible as if she'd taken anesthesia. Another problem for him was time. Each forward second was less safe, taking him nearer to being discovered. He thought some four-letter words at Alecia, blaming. Futility sunk him. He was deciding to give up when he was called a name.

"You crazy son of a bitch."

His nerves went full current for a moment but stabilized when he saw it was Lottie in the shadows of a corner. She moved to him and asked, "What are you doing here, of all places? Why here?"

"How long have you been with us?"

"I followed you."

"You've been watching?"

"I saw it all." She nodded, eyes to eyes with him, meaning everything.

He wasn't embarrassed. "Alecia's out of it."

They leaned over Alecia, appraising her unconsciousness. Her mouth was open dumb and she was breathing loud, cleavage up, cleavage down.

"We've got to get her out of here," said Lottie. "I'll help you."

"I need your help."

"Someone could come any second. Even *him.*"

Knight closed the separating space. He kissed Lottie his best kiss. Her anxiety broke it shorter than she wanted. "We've got to hurry," she said to his lips.

Her words were ignored. He kissed again, brought all of her tangent to him, tight, with his hard center sandwiched.

"We'll go to my place," Lottie told him, "or yours. Anyplace. But let's get out of here."

"No."

He moved her down to sit the bed.

"You're out of your mind," she resisted some.

With directing pressure he laid Lottie back next to Alecia.

Lottie sat up, "Let's stop this foolishness right now. Don't you know where we are? This is the President's bed."

"I know."

"Don't you realize what will happen if we're caught here? We'll all be ruined."

He shut off her words with his mouth and a hand that peeled her top down to touch her perfected breasts with various influential touches. She really wanted that, and he found their reconditioned quality so tensile and ideally sized that he was reminded of those brave and superstirring explorations above the waist with girls in high school.

"I want to. I really do," she admitted, "but not here. Please, darling. I'll never be able to here. Someplace, anyplace, but not here."

He took her hand to give it to his center, persuading. He told her the terms: "Either here or not at all."

She appreciated him, stroked and imagined for a while, and then sighed decisively. "Oh, well, what the hell," she said, letting her want dissolve her caution.

And there is where they did it.

They shoved the limp Alecia over for more room and Lottie remarked, "That's the trouble with today's youngsters. They don't take advantage of their opportunities."

They did it there, as luck would have it, with the element of chance oddly magnifying the stimulation. And from the moment she was open for total touch, offering and helping, Knight was sure of her completion. For Lottie, for the first time in years and years of time, was wet as a teen-ager.

* * *

Knight enjoyed it even more than he'd thought he would. And even more after, when he was remembering what he'd done. Lottie had just gone into her home for bed to sleep a satisfied sleep, and Knight was in the moving limousine alone with Alecia, who was not yet all awake. Alecia tried to hold her head up but it felt better dropped. She tried to keep her eyes open but they disobeyed her. The centrifugal force of every turn pitched her body, until Knight wedged her into a corner of the back seat and braced her with his arm.

She was completely useless. Knight thought that. He thought of the time he'd wasted on her. Maybe, he thought, if she'd gone all the way, if she'd felt and helped, he could have burned some of the hatred out of her. It would have been the best thing for her. But now here she was, escaping with her hate intact, perhaps increased. He heard her try talking. He asked her what.

"I feel sick," she repeated.

He asked her if she felt like throwing up, and her answer was a little giggle attached to some middle phrases of the national anthem sung through her sticking lips. Then she began to vomit what he considered to be vomit—her kind of patriotism that she was stuffed with. Even through torpidity it came squirting out.

"The Jews . . ." She mumbled her subject and managed to make her tongue work enough for accusations that were some he'd heard from her before and some new ones, including homosexuality, gold, opium, and the phony Commie Chinese, who were really doing only what the Jews told them to do. She was condemning them with white slavery when the limousine reached the street of her house.

Knight wouldn't have done it if she'd kept still, but her words brought the idea out of his imagination. He told the words to the driver, who steered to soon have them moving along a street of many neons. Knight ordered a stop, got out to inquire, and the next time they stopped they were there.

Alecia was finally sinking silent again. Knight pinched her upper arm for a test. She didn't seem to feel it, so he opened the car door and lifted her. He carried her inside to a small room where the walls were covered with red, blue, and green suggestions. The only person there was a big-nosed man with hairless skullskin reflecting. Knight deposited Alecia on a stool, and she immediately laid her head on her arm on the counter. Knight took out a pair of hundred-dollar bills before he said anything.

"For that you can get a special," the man informed, indicating a selection of the largest, most intricate.

"No. All we want is a little one about so," Knight told him, showing him approximately a half inch with index finger and thumb.

"Anything you say," agreed the man as he got ready.

"It's not for me. It's for the lady."

"What is she—drunk? I don't like to do drunks."

"No, she's just sleepy."

"Where's she want it?"

"I'll show you. Can I pull down the shades?"

"Sure."

Knight lowered yellowed venetian blinds and turned them shut. He also bolted the door.

"Draw me what you want," said the man, giving a pad and pencil.

Knight drew.

"That's nice," beamed the man.

"What's your name?" asked Knight, hoping.

"Abe Stein," the man replied. "What's that got to do with it?"

"Nothing, Abe, nothing," lied Knight. He lifted Alecia, who was really out, and doubled her face forward over the counter. He shoved at all the layers of petticoats until her ass was exposed. No underpants. Knight knew they were forgotten somewhere on the floor of that special bedroom and wondered what finding them would cause.

"Put it there," he told the man, who was stealing from the full twins of Alecia's bottom.

"Right or left?"

"Right. Emphatically right."

Abe Stein went to work. It required a most minimal expending of his special artistic ability, but he did it with flourish and flair, exactly as ordered.

Merely two miniature triangles in blue, overlapped, buzzed on, tattooed on the white right mount of Alecia's behind.

She wasn't able to say even one ouch while she got neatly needled with the Star of David.

The next morning Knight felt a big high, happy high. He'd done it a whole day ahead of deadline and he doubted that

Arnie or Rog or Eduardo could have done it better. He thought about them. Maybe they weren't making out at all.

Knight had slept late, taken no phone calls, and now he was at the hotel desk, checking out, signing his doubtless name instead of money for the bill. He was going out of the hotel when he saw her ahead of him. At first he wasn't sure it was her and then he was. She was dressed different but she was the same stunning one he'd softly collided with on the street in front of the jewelry store during his first day in Washington. The expensive high fashion one who was so choice. Knight hurried to reach her, but she was already in her waiting limousine, with the doorman slamming the shiny black door shut for her. When the doorman stepped aside, Knight saw her in there, all fluff and fine, her face creamy bright, flawlessly fragile. The window of her limousine, Knight saw, was open, and he went to it while he tried to think of some perfect thing to say. It didn't come to him, and in his hesitation she looked and pressed a little chrome switch to make glass climb the open space fast, enclosing her, separating.

Knight bent and stared through and knew from his inside feeling that, for him, she was singular, someone he'd sought, the found reason for all the hollow of his time. *Ne plus ultra.* He was eyes to eyes with her for a moment. He tried to talk with his look, but she turned profile and then was powered away.

The high Knight had felt was now erased. He tried to get it back and did manage to recover some. They'd already put his Gucci bag into his car's trunk and awaited him. There was the doorman holding open, expecting the famous-person tip.

Knight asked him, "Do you happen to know who that was, the lady who just left here?"

"Yes, sir," snapped the doorman and said her name that made Knight laugh at himself all the way back to New York City.

"That was Babs Bannon."

4

Rog needed the repair of sleep when he arrived home from Eduardo's. Actually he wasn't a good sleeper. His pattern was four to five deep hours to go on and a thirty-minute late afternoon nap for evening energy. He always wanted to sleep more, but his body took only the minimum it required for regeneration and then opened his eyes and mind all the way.

Rog was chronically aware that he didn't sleep as much as normal others. He was constantly looking mirrors, expecting to see sockets sunken and skin pale, but health always looked back at him.

It made him feel that somehow his substance was betraying him, pretending to look all right while it was being internally dissipated. To some extent that was true. The organic machinery of Rog was thirty-six years old but the texture of his skin and color of it and the distribution of it appeared a dozen years younger. Without trying, he was slim as a boy is slim. His facial structure also helped, with his features ideally balanced. His mouth and nose were delicate, like special perfect adjectives for the noun that was his pair of dark and lively eyes.

Those eyes that he now examined in the bathroom mirror illuminated by benevolent, slightly pink electric bulbs.

He thought he looked a little tired. He undressed there, taking time to fold his trousers and pair his shoes and stuff his shirt and undershorts into the dirty clothes hamper. He brushed his teeth electrically and splashed his face with water that he made sure was near the same temperature as him, not to stimulate. Then he went barefoot on the ancient expensive art of half a Persian rugmaker's lifetime, to his bed. On the velour-covered round table he was told the time by a three-hundred-year-old French crystal sphere clock that had fragile blue flowers enameled on its face so the warning turn of its black hands was blithely tempered.

Rog stretched under the finest sheets and then doubled up on his side, his hands near his face, perhaps protecting. He closed his eyes but a thought reopened them. He reached to the table for the slip of paper that had his assignment printed on it:

The ladies' toilet
of the main waiting room
in Grand Central Station

He put the slip of paper back on the table and got into sleeping position again. That place, he thought, had been his suggestion. It was ironic that he should get the place he'd proposed. Maybe there was a reason for it, his mind told him as it softly withdrew from thinking to sleep.

While he slept, Roger Elswyth Gifford's house was cared for by five women who knew he liked everything very clean and exactly placed. It wasn't a matter of simple order. For example, if a small bronze was an inch off its designated mark or the angle of a certain chair was not precise, it was considered an irregularity that might, just might, upset Mr. Roger. Although most of the sixteen rooms of the house were seldom used by him, and a few of them never, the women went over the same course every day, dusting, waxing, sweeping, quietly.

Rog chose his servants according to appearance, believing efficiency could be learned if demanded. So the five women who served him were worthy of visual appreciation. For Rog it was a valid arrangement. His home was full of beautiful things to feed the eyes or touch, and it would have been aesthetically destructive for homeliness to be in motion among them.

For that reason he never employed any male servants. He thought about it. He knew that in most species the male was the more beautiful and he wondered why the human animal was such an obvious exception. It was an odd evaluation, considering that he was, according to certain standards, a beautiful man. But he didn't appreciate himself in that respect. That is, he didn't think it significant to be masculine, and in no way did he try to magnify the fact. Actually, he preferred to ignore it and suffered some small emotional consequence whenever he allowed his mind to include himself in that awkward hirsute brute category he considered rather repugnant.

Of course, this attitude, which was reflected throughout his way of life, made his audience speculate. If he'd walked or gestured or talked mincingly, they'd have been sure he was a homosexual. But as it was, only his taste gave their judgment ammunition. Because Rog, despite the way he would have had it had he been asked before conception which sex he preferred to be, was unavoidably male.

He adored women as intensely as only a man who envies them can adore them. And in his living, except for Arnie and Knight and Eduardo with whom he shared a relative bond of worship, he permitted only the most absolutely necessary contact with men.

The thing his eyes were aimed at when they opened awake that afternoon at four was a good original nude by Klimt on the left wall. Rog got up for the bathroom and made the pale yellow ribbon that temporarily connected his center to all the sewers of the world. The flushing and then the washing and shaving sounds were signals his servants heard, so when he returned to the bedroom there was a silver tray holding hot coffee and fluffed eggs bordered by ribbons of crisp bacon. He'd had eggs that morning at Eduardo's and now his appetite wanted something solid as a steak, but he didn't demand it because there was too much hurry in him. He ate fast, then dressed fast. Everything he put on was entirely clean. He never wore anything twice, not even a tie, that hadn't been cleaned. What he put on now was a Cardin suit of subtle color and distinctive cut with its double-breasted longish jacket nipping his waist ever so slightly above trousers that were narrow straight down to where they flared some.

He buzzed the household intercom and was quickly answered. He said, "I want a car now."

"The black or the gray, sir?" The choice of Rolls Royces.

"The blue," he instructed, and in another part of the house one of the women who served him hurried to uniform herself in the twill that matched the blue Ferrari. Rog was always driven. He'd never had to learn to drive.

He was examining the skin below his eyes in a kind mirror when the phone rang, the positively private one. It was a call from Rome. It was Bibi. He was pleased to hear her lacy voice.

"I'm leaving for the airport now," she told him.

"Where are you off to?"

"There, of course. I hate Rome. I can't stay another second." It was the fifth or sixth time she'd hated Rome enough to fly from it. Rog knew why but asked her anyway.

"I'm sick," she said, sounding it.

"How do you feel?"

"Awful. My heart is broken."

"Has Berito been treating you badly?"

"Who?"

"Berito."

"Oh. No. I haven't seen him, except once, in over a month. It's Sebastian, the bastard."

"Who?"

"Sebastian. Didn't you get my letter?"

"No."

"Maybe Sebastian didn't mail it. I gave it to him to mail, but he probably thought there was money in it and opened it. Oh, Rog, I'm dying inside. Really, this time."

"Poor baby."

"My flight number's 362 Alitalia. I'm leaving everything here, just taking the bare essentials."

"Don't forget your jewelry."

"Funny you should mention that."

"Why?"

"All I've got left are the rings on my fingers."

"Poor baby," repeated Rog, knowing. "Did you consider going to the police?"

"I thought about it. But remember all the mess it caused that other time."

Rome has a voracious appetite for scandals. It is like watching gladiators in a colosseum that is the whole city.

"How are you?" she finally asked.

"Fine. The same."

"You sound different, sad a little."

"No, just preoccupied."

"Is someone there?" she asked and answered, "Of course,

you're with someone. I guess I'm just not thinking clearly. Is she good?"

"I'm alone right now."

"Well, don't be lonely. I'll be there in a few hours. Can I bring you something?"

"Only you," he said because it fit pretty.

"All right. *Arrivederci*, darling. No, to hell with the Italians. Good-bye, darling. I kiss you," she said and clicked off.

Darling and kisses. She was allowed darling and kisses over his positively private line because she was the make-believe mother. Rog's father had married Bibi for his last year and the nineteen-year-old Bibi had given the elder Gifford his final nice slippery slide. She'd been true and kind to him. The only bad thing she'd done inadvertently. The more Rog's father had touched the smooth and quick of Bibi's youth, the more his closer death was unacceptable to him. According to Bibi, who told it with serious sympathy and only to Rog, the old man had died with his hands on her. Rog thought it was more romantic than macabre.

Now ten years had passed and the twenty-nine-year-old Bibi, even more beautiful now, was the make-believe mother.

Rog wondered what she'd be wearing and how she'd have her hair, as he went down and out to the blue Ferrari and into the bucket seat of its blue leather next to his woman driver, who, in visored cap and high collar, was a disturbing mixture of military and feminine perfection.

The New York City landmark that is Grand Central Station was not strange to Rog. At least its exterior wasn't. But Rog hadn't been inside it for more than twenty years. The only reason for being there was a going or arriving train, and the only train that had been in his life since his year sixteen was the Roma-Parigi express just for fun with two underweight and over-libidinous models on their way to the Paris fall/winter collections about four years previous. So, inside, going down the ramp, was a curious experience for him. It was the beginning of the rush-for-home hour and he was in a crowd of hurry. He was the exceptional slow one, and non-identifiable humans flowed swiftly around him as if he were an obstruction. He felt that and he smelled the air of the place that was a particular odor caused by trains, a metallic black invisible float of stirred particles. Then he was poured off the ramp to the station level where the speed of everyone was various and he was collided. The surfaces there were different, hard slick for dirt to slide on, seeking edges and corners.

He went the most probable direction and was soon in the high and wide of the station proper where there was even more of the criss-cross confusion of movement. He saw a gargantuan rectangle of photographic color that was a brilliant boy and girl with American health on a sailboat with the wind and the sea stopped for them, fifty times larger than life. He heard the microphoned voice of the oracle of time and place that was not quite understandable. He looked for and found the title "WAITING ROOM" and went through one of many doors to be where thick indestructible benches were polished by millions of sittings.

And there it was. At one end of the room, announcing itself with a single segregating word:

WOMEN

Rog went to a newsstand and bought any paper. All the first row bench space was occupied, so he leaned an end of it and pretended to read while watching that opening. He appraised those women going in and coming out. He thought of them as prospects, judging, but that was difficult because there were so many. It was as if there were some form of entertainment in there that they had to see. Like Josie the Dogface Girl or Minnie the Moustached Lady or Big Bertha the Superfat Woman, he thought, and then realized his mind was describing, with some exaggeration, those he was seeing enter and exit. He stopped really looking at them, let them be vague shapes, instantly rejected, one after one. He waited for someone exceptional and, after about a half hour, during which only two out of perhaps a hundred were lean and stylish and pretty enough to be almost acceptable, he concluded that he'd probably have to endure repulsion unless he was extremely fortunate, and even then he'd have to compromise, for no beauties up to his standards were using the place.

He wondered what in there was like. He moved, hoping for a glimpse inside. He backed close to the near wall, trying for a sliver of view—trying that made him conspicuous. He gave up and turned to find the accusing eyes of a policeman on him. He smiled a weak, self-conscious smile at the officer, discarded the newspaper into a trash basket for something to do, and walked away and out, manufacturing incredible nonchalance.

From his first visit to the environs of his assignment, Roger acquired some beneficial realizations. He now knew it was doubtful that he'd find there anyone beautiful enough for him. He also knew it was too crowded there for success during the day hours. And most important, he was now convinced it was impossible, without attracting adverse attention, for a man, as a man, to enter that female sanctuary. Altogether, it seemed hopeless.

Rog thought about abandoning the idea. He reasoned it was absurd anyway. It couldn't be done. And even if he did somehow get into the place, even if he was in there with someone of adequate beauty, even if that someone cooperated ideally, it was still a ridiculous, grotesque thing to do. Ordinary logic, created by his intelligence but quickly converted by the nature of its various ingredients into the stimulation of challenge. Instead of a veto, his senses distilled the prohibitive elements of his assignment into excitement. He didn't hesitate to reason why. He merely accepted the fact that he wanted to do it and would, somehow, find ways to overcome the obstacles.

He had one of the problems mentally solved by the time he picked up Bibi at the airport at 2 A.M. Her flight was a half hour late due to air traffic and she complained about it.

"We were up there going around and around. I thought I'd flip. You know how I hate to fly."

"Try to calm yourself. You're safe now."

"Oh, I'm calm. I really am. You know me. Nothing bothers me except when it's bothering me."

"Did you sleep on the plane?"

"Hell, no. I hung on all the way."

"You must be tired then. It's nine in the morning Rome time."

"Really? I feel marvelous."

"You can sleep tomorrow."

"Oh, it's good to be here. So good to see you. Are you glad I'm here?"

"Of course," he told her with warmth because it was true.

They were in the ample plush of the black Rolls being

driven to the city. Rog thought Bibi looked even more beautiful than when he'd last seen her two years previous. He saw no effect of the distress she'd voiced on the phone. He looked for some signal of tension in her eyes, but they were dancing their usual alert brown dance and her mouth was not tight, not pretending smile. He noticed immediately that her blonde hair was done new, short with many wide fluffed curls. And her white sharkskin dress was contemporarily brief for her excellent legs, a good five inches above the knees and more when she was sitting as she was. She wasn't tan. She avoided sunlight always, believing it would bake something essential out of her skin, which was milk pale and baby-girl fine.

She took Roger's hand, held it just tight enough. "I'll stay at the Waldorf," she said.

"No. Absolutely no."

"Where then?" she asked, knowing.

He told her.

"I won't be lonely at the Waldorf," she said, meaning she would. "Are you sure you can put up with me?" She didn't give him a chance to say his nice answer because she saw the night skyline of the city. "Oh, I love New York," she said, song-like.

He appreciated her spirit. He also liked the smell of her, not entirely perfume. Fragile. He wondered how he smelled.

Whey they arrived home and her eight pieces of luggage were unbuckled and zipped open in her room, it was three o'clock. He tried to leave her to sleep but she found a small beige silk square, initialed, and she held it out with fingers as if it were contaminated.

"Sebastian's," she explained with a distasteful look that quickly softened. "Actually he wasn't a bad boy. Just Italian."

"What happened to Berito?"

"The same as with Sebastian," she answered. "You know what I think?"

"What?"

"They knew each other, Berito and Sebastian. Berito passed me on. I don't know that for a fact, but I suspect it."

"What were they like?"

"Pretty."

"Were they tall?"

"No. They just looked tall because they were so thin."

"How old were they?"

"I don't know. Twenty-two or -three perhaps. but they could have been eighteen. Maybe they were eighteen or nineteen, now that I think of it. I never asked. I wouldn't have gotten a true answer anyway."

"Did they really lie so much?"

"Oh, constantly, darling. But you can't blame them for that. It's natural for them, just like stealing. Actually, it was so obvious it was amusing. Nearly every day something would be missing—a compact or a cigarette case or a coat or something."

"What did they do with the things they stole?"

"Who knows? Probably sold them or gave them to some poor girl they really loved. You know what they are, don't you?"

Roger asked what with his eyes.

"They're sexual Robin Hoods. That's funny, isn't it. I just made it up."

"They lie, cheat, and steal. Why put up with them at all?"

She had the answer ready. "Because they're beautiful, darling. Because they're deliciously beautiful," she said and moved to drop the wayward handkerchief of Sebastian into the wastebasket.

She took a bunch of things into the bathroom and, after some minutes, came out changed into long cream silk bias-cut to repeat all the lovely inflections of her. She stood for his look a moment and then said, "I was buzzy inside, you know, feeling over electric, so I took something for sleep." She got into the big bed and pulled the sheet to her chin. She smiled a little closed-mouth smile at him. "Come kiss me good night before it works."

"Sleeping pills don't work so quickly."

"I took an up and out."

"What's that?"

"A suppository. Everyone takes them in Rome. They work faster. Hurry and kiss me."

He aimed at her cheek but she turned for her mouth. And when he drew back from her face her eyes were closed. She kept them closed. "Be sweet and turn out the light," she requested.

"Sleep well," he wished for her, doubting that she heard.

* * *

The next day was bright. Perhaps the day before had been also, but Rog hadn't noticed. He was up at ten to request an unusual outside breakfast. That caused some scurrying, but by the time he went down and out on the terrace a table was there, covered by pink linen under silver shining in the sun and an arrangement of miniature pink roses. On the way down he'd stopped at Bibi's door and opened enough to see she was asleep on her back with the sheet kicked off and her nightgown twisted up. So he had breakfast alone. Two broiled trout and biscuits that melted butter and a seedless orange sectioned and meticulously picked clean of pulp.

The terrace was pleasantly private, walled left and right and high enough above the East River. It was large for a place where land is precious. While Rog ate, he thought mostly of three things: Bibi, the flickery gold of the water disturbed by various small boats, and his assignment. During his second cup of coffee he focused completely on the last. He knew now what he must do to get in there. And he decided he'd do it that day. At least it would be a test run. It was going to be more difficult now with Bibi around, he thought. But his mind quickly turned that handicap into an opportunity. Actually, she could be useful. He'd have to lie to her, of course, but it wouldn't be a serious lie.

Having time, he went inside to the study to take care of some business that was papers he signed without reading and three long tubes of blueprints he didn't unroll to examine, merely pulled out a corner of each and initialed. He imagined the new theater for his ballet corps would be opening soon, and he assumed that the hotel he'd built on the island he'd bought in the Carribean was well-managed. As for the magazine he owned, he saw the cover of it looking more tasteful than most others on newsstands he passed. A thing that he thought he hadn't done that he thought he wanted to do was a boutique. There were many around the city, small going-for-broke side-street ones and large white and shiny Avenue ones, selling bright skimpy dresses and oversize plastic earrings and watches with big colored faces and wide neckties for girls and other such things. While he remembered wanting that sort of place, he telephoned for it.

He told the man he talked to exactly what he wanted and approximately where and all the man said was a yes and a sir. It was almost as simple as calling a prescription to the local pharmacy. Rog promised himself that he'd find out when his boutique was in business and go there someday, if he felt like it.

From then until one, Rog controlled his impatience by wandering the house. He opened doors to rediscover various organized rooms, looked at paintings that were hungry for eyes, especially the delicate dapple of a miraculous Monet. Also an Aubusson tapestry, perfect. He accepted the puffy invitation of a yellow silk damask cushion on a Louis XV chair that had been authentically rescued from the insensible anger of the Revolution. And he was touched to touch the ancient purity of a white marble girl who had somehow survived without wounds or amputation since before Christ.

Finally he was again on the terrace where he found Bibi in baby blue cotton beneath a wide brim, preventing sun. She greeted with cheek kisses left and right and he asked her how she'd slept.

"It's such a big bed," she told him. "It made me wake up a few times."

"Why?" He'd thought she'd like a big bed, as he did.

"It's so big I was lonely in it. All night I kept reaching with myself, you know, trying to touch, but there was only me."

He'd never had such a night but he understood.

She said, "I hate sleeping alone. That's been my trouble. At least a lot of it."

She looked thoughtful, vaguely sad, and he thought it made her more attractive.

He said, "Bibi darling, you're one of the world's two most beautiful women."

"Oh? Who's the other?"

"You choose her."

She laughed some. "That's a practiced line, isn't it? How many times before have you said those exact words? Now, come on. Be honest."

"Hundreds, probably," he admitted.

"You're worse than the Italians."

"I don't steal."

"Everyone steals," she said, wise.

"That's why everyone's in jail," he said.

"Trial by error."

"Sentenced by the great judge."

"No appeal."

"Absolutely. No appeal."

"Solitary confinement."

"But not you."

"Or you, darling Rog."

"A beautiful jailer with orchid eyes came with the key to unlock you."

"That was long ago."

"Not really."

"A long long time ago."

The mood was like a vessel that couldn't be steered to avoid sadness. But it was only a little melancholia that they skimmed over, past, when Bibi smiled and placed a flawless strawberry into the soft pink chamber of her mouth. She was sitting toward the river, sideways to the table. She lifted a leg and pointed her foot. "Do you like these shoes?"

They were blue to match. Rog thought they were pretty and said so.

"They're paper," she informed.

"Really?"

"They don't look it, do they?"

"No."

"They are."

"Then they won't last."

"They're disposable."

"They're pretty."

"They say that someday practically everything will be disposable. Just use once and throw away."

"I don't know if I'd like that."

"Very convenient."

"I suppose."

Some city sparrows were fluttering nervously in and out of the wall vines, hoping Rog and Bibi would abandon the table so they could hunt closer for crumbs. Bibi noticed them. "Do you feed the birds?" she asked.

"No."

"What kind are those?"

He told her. He told her they were ordinary.

"They aren't very pretty," she agreed. "And they all look alike." She was thinking of throwing an entire slice of toast that would be a feast for them but she changed her mind.

"What do you want to do today?" he asked.

"Anything."

He took some time pretending to invent a suggestion. "Want to help me do something?"

"Sure."

"It's a sort of joke I want to play on someone."

"Who?"

"Arnie Bruno. You know Arnie."

She'd never met the famous singer but, like most of the world, she knew him. "What's the joke?" she asked.

He told her. He used Arnie's known notorious appetite for women to build his lie. He told her he'd had a friendly verbal duel with Arnie over the quality of the females Arnie chose to bed. Arnie, of course, had defended his taste, claiming he selected only the best and boasting that he was an accomplished immediate appraiser.

Rog told her, "Just for the hell of it I want to prove even Arnie can be fooled."

"How?"

"By dressing someone up like a girl."

In Paris and Berlin she'd seen them. Female impersonators, pretty and good at it. "I'm sure we could hire some gay boy to do it," she said. "Do you know any?"

"No."

"We'll find one."

"He doesn't have to be a fag."

"Oh, yes. Only a fag could do it."

"Why?"

"He'd have to be swishy, real swishy."

"That's the trouble. I think a fag might overdo it."

She didn't agree.

"A fag would be too obvious," he said.

"Maybe."

"It can't be burlesque at all. It has to be underplayed. With poise and sophistication."

"Perhaps you're right."

She thought and he pretended to be thinking. He allowed enough time and then, with some mischief in his tone for protection, he said, "How about me?"

He expected her to laugh and she did.

"Could I get away with it?" he asked.

She leaned to him, took his chin with her fingers, tilted his face up for examination. She turned him profile and full face.

She smoothed each of his eyebrows, traced down his nose and around the outline of his lips with her touch. Then she sat back for a sip of coffee. Over the brim of pink flowers by Limoges her eyes remained on him, waiting. Into the cup for a delicate echo she said, "Without a doubt."

So Rog acquired an accomplice. He disliked having to lie to Bibi—not that he was normally opposed to convenient falsehoods, but because she was Bibi and they'd always been open honest with one another. Perhaps, he rationalized, he'd tell her all about it after. Then they'd laugh about it together, he was sure.

The more Bibi thought about it, the more willing she was to be a part of Rog's masquerade. She told him, "You'll have to shave very close."

"How about my legs? Won't I have to shave them too?"

"Unless you want to look lower European."

"I'll shave them."

"No. Use a depilatory. No need to have your skin full of nicks."

She's going to help a lot, thought Rog.

"I'll need all your sizes," she said, standing. "You measure while I go change. And be sure to measure everything."

"Everything?"

"Except that, darling," she tossed, twinkling as she went. "That's not necessary."

Rog found a tape measure and went up to privacy. He undressed and measured the exact inches of his chest, waist, and hips. He wrote them down along with his arm length and height and collar size that he already knew. He thought about shoes and was measuring from toe to heel when he heard Bibi's knock on the door. He put on a robe and let her in.

She examined the list of figures he'd made. "You forgot some," she told him. "You forgot shoulder to shoulder. That's important. And also shoulder to breast and shoulder to waist." She picked up the tape. "Turn around," she instructed. "I'll measure you." She did his shoulders and then had him turn about-face. She complained, "I can't tell where your breasts are."

He slipped his arms out of the robe that fell and he held it so half of him was bare. She measured from a shoulder to a tip of nipple. Then to his waist and she was finished. She started out but hesitated to ask, seriously, "B-cup or C-cup or what? How does Arnie like them?"

Rog saw himself with a pair of massive mounds on his front, protrusions out of proportion. He couldn't say.

"Probably a C-cup," she decided and went shopping.

Rog phoned for a rush drugstore delivery. He ordered several other things to camouflage his request for six tubes of the depilatory they recommended. It was brought to him within a half hour and he read the simple instructions on how to get rid of unwanted hair. He did it in the bathroom. He uncapped a tube, saw that it was a pale pink harmless-looking substance, smelled that it was clinically fragrant, squeezed some out and began coating his leg. The stuff went on easy as cream from five inches above his knees, which he designated as the upper boundary, all the way to his toes, that had some hair on them he didn't remember ever noticing before.

During the prescribed minutes he had to wait for the depilatory to work, he read the newest issue of *Connaissance* and noted that a good pair of unusually small Boulle commodes had sold for 18,000 francs and a bad porcelain figurine for nearly the same. Then it was time. He showered and watched the pink flow off his legs. He felt, and the smooth difference surprised him. He got out to dry and looked in the full-length mirror.

He felt again, rubbing down and especially up, testing for stubble. His skin was hairlessly slick both ways. He examined front and back and approved. The only imperfection was the contrasting circuit of growth on his upper legs, so he applied the cream there around his thighs and all the way up to the undersockets of his center.

Then his arms and the back of his hands.

Then the little bushes in his armpits.

He had to do it.

Soon every hair-growing area of his body, except for his head, eyebrows, and center, was covered with removing pink. And after he'd waited the waiting time and taken another shower and dried, he asked the mirror that told him he liked it.

He liked it very much.

It was nearly seven when Bibi returned.

"I got everything," she announced, signaling the help to

put down their carry of many boxes and bags. "It was fun. The most fun shopping spree I've ever been on."

After the help went, she asked him what he'd done. He had his robe on. He showed a leg.

She kneeled to see, close. She touched it with fingers, light. To him it felt like a kiss and he heard a brief appreciating sound from her. She remained on her knees and moved to be among the things she'd bought, to unwrap and show them. "Look, darling," she exclaimed, holding up some nylon stockings that unfurled like sheer snakes. "They're the new shiny kind that look wet on."

"Pretty."

"I got two dresses." She unboxed them. One was beige and the other black. They were much alike. "I got long sleeves to hide your biceps. You do have some muscles, you know."

"Smart."

She dismissed the dresses to display some shoes that were fashionably toed. "Good thing thick heels are in now," she said, holding one profile. "I can imagine you hobbling around on spiky ones. I hope these are wide enough for you. The length was no problem but I had to guess the width. It's almost impossible to buy shoes for someone."

She tossed a shoe to him for his hands to know how practically weightless and fine it was, so unlike even the best light man's shoe from Italy that he usually wore.

"These you have to try on," she said, taking out of a bag. "I didn't have to get them, really, but I thought we might as well go all the way."

They were bikini panties with a narrow frill of soft lace bordering each leg hole. Stretching them some, she said, "They're a match with the bra and garter belt. I got two sets, black and beige. But I suppose you won't try them."

He hesitated, only for effect. "Sure, why not?" And he took them from her. "Might as well try the shoes too while I'm at it."

"Here you go." She handed them up along with a pair of stockings for him to carry into the bathroom.

He had taken them off others so many times he had to know how to put them on him. First the panties. They fit snug as they were meant to, but there was no allowance for his center. What he had to do was tuck his soft self down and under. The brassiere was next. Although it was made well-padded, he found she'd bought a pair of extra pads that he inserted inside the cups to fill them. Then the garter belt. When he had its hooks in all its eyes, he slipped it down on his hips and slid it around so its hanging fasteners were in perfect control position, front and rear. That done, he sat to put on the stockings. He did it correctly, gathered the nylon from top to toe, to make a little ring that he pointed his foot into and pulled with stretch over his ankle and calf and knee and thighs. They were seamless. He smoothed them up with his palm, and, holding tension, fastened them to the elastic appendages of the garter belt. Left and right. Then he put on the shoes that fit exactly. The height of them under his heels felt peculiar and precarious. All the while he avoided the mirrors and didn't even look before going out for her to see him.

She was on the bed, her head propped up, eyes closed but aimed at him. She wasn't sleeping. She was waiting for his signal to open her eyes suddenly and see all at once, like a child expecting surprise. When she was sure, she opened and saw. She wanted to sit up, wanted to speak. But she couldn't. All her movement was inside and increasing. She had anticipated amusement, perhaps comedy, certainly not this serious interior reaction that simultaneously emptied and flooded her. For defense she tried to not look but her eyes disobeyed and she had to discipline her hands.

For a time that seemed long Rog stood there connected to her by exhibition. He'd expected to feel embarrassment but there was none of that in him. Nor did he feel particularly unnatural. The way Bibi was looking, combined with the messages his senses were transmitting, only one word passed repetitively across his mind.

Pretty.

"Well?" Rog asked for approval.

"You could fool me," said Bibi, carefully casual.

"The shoes may be a problem."

"Why?"

"I feel slanted forward."

"Walk for me."

He did, trying for balance that came off as an attempt for grace. It made Bibi feel invaded by more of that strange stir. Seeing him animated, seeing the black bra and panties and garter belt and liquid-like stockings in motion on the slim male body with its man face disturbingly incongruous, aroused some extremes she'd never known existed in her or yet understood. It was a synthesis of overpowering and surrendering, anger and appreciation.

"All you need is a little practice," she advised.

"How the hell do women walk in those really high heels? And why, anyway?"

"They do. Because it makes their legs look better."

"How do mine look?"

"You have nice legs."

"Not too muscular?"

"No."

"Shall I try on the dresses?"

"Not yet. I want a drink. You want one?"

"Okay."

"Tell you what. Let's have dinner up here tonight."

"If you want."

"And I'll help you with your makeup."

"Did you get everything I need?"

"Yes."

"How about my hair?"

"I bought a wig. Tonight we'll get you all dressed up for practice," she said, and then ordered drinks and dinner to be brought as soon as possible.

"I hope they knock before coming in," said Rog.

"Don't they usually?"

"Yes, but . . ."

"Relax."

He sat as a man does, knees apart. It made her laugh.

"Darling, not like that. Keep your legs together," she told him.

He put a leg over a knee. "How's this?"

"An exposé when you're in a short skirt."

"How short will mine be?"

"We'll see."

"What do you think of all this, really?"

She didn't answer true. She hesitated and told him, "It's entertaining. How do you feel so far?"

"Like a damn fool," he lied.

When the servants brought dinner, Rog rushed into the bathroom to be out of sight until Bibi gave the all-clear signal. When he came out Bibi had a martini at her lips and another offered to him. They drank and refilled and then began dinner. They were both hungry but didn't eat much, except dessert that was a creamy lime mousse of perfect consistency. Throughout the meal they tried to talk other subjects. It was difficult with Rog in a bra across from her.

"Really. How do you feel dressed—or should I say undressed—like that?" she asked.

"I don't know," he dodged, instead of lying again. She waited for a better reply that came out. "Actually, I think women have it nicer than men."

"Why?"

"The pretty things they can wear."

"Then you really don't mind?"

"Not really."

"Maybe you even find it a bit enjoyable."

"Perhaps."

She liked that for some reason. Because it meant yes.

"Most women feel men are the lucky ones," she said.

"I don't think so."

"I do sometimes."

"Men used to wear nice things, silks and laces."

"That's true."

"I wish I'd lived then. Don't you?"

"No. I like now."

"Really? Are you so happy?"

"Happy? That's something we invented, happiness. No one ever promised that living would be happy. Anyway, I like now. I mean right now, tonight."

"I'll take the past."

"Silks and laces?"

"That's part of it."

"But you've got silks and laces right now."

He thought about that. "So I have," he said, and they both laughed good laughs.

She said, "It's ridiculous, though, all this distinction between sexes. There's no logical reason why we have to look and act and be so opposite."

"Except for the way we're constructed."

"That shouldn't make such a difference."

"But it does."

"Did you know that from conception until the fetus is four months old its sex is undetermined?"

He didn't know that. And she didn't know if it was really true or not.

"That's nearly half the pregnant time," she went on, "so we're all about half mixed."

Her statement made him self-conscious. "Are you trying to excuse me? If you are I'm going to get out of these things fast."

"No. No. You misunderstood. I mean it. It's a theory I've often thought about but never expressed before."

He detoured the subject. "Want some cognac?"

"No. Let's put on your makeup."

"I think I've had enough for today," he told her.

"Oh, come on. Forget what I said."

He hadn't really reacted to it as strongly as she thought. But he felt like being persuaded. He shook a small no.

It irritated her. She was surprised that it did. Never had she generated such acute fury. She couldn't control it. "You'll do what I say," she snapped.

"To hell with you."

"What?" she exploded.

They were eyes to eyes. Hers over his. A need to submit dissolved all his defiance. "Whatever you want," he heard himself say.

That was that. She smiled her usual smile. "Let's go into the bathroom where the light's better," she suggested.

"Shall I turn on some music?"

"If you like."

It took nearly two hours for the makeup, including the false fingernails. His face had never received so much attention. To begin, she advised that he shave again and then she used her fingers to apply liquid foundation, spreading and blending it until his entire face and neck were one ideal tone. She hummed content with the music as she worked and she told him how to do the various things as she did them. All the way to the careful gluing on of the eyelashes and finally the outlining and filling in of his lips with a pale pink color and a coating of slick over that to have them look sensually wet.

Throughout the metamorphosis Rog sat before a mirror. It was his first view of himself dressed as he was. His immediate intellectual reaction demanded that he end this absurd escapade. But that initial impact quickly subsided to be replaced by a purely emotional force.

Look at me, look at me, he thought, accepting. His breath caught and his inside divided to allow a narrow passage for the direct run of his feelings from his eyes to his center, which began to receive. It was not an instant inflation. It seemed as slow as cell by cell until his center was hurting for space and he had to help it without being noticed by Bibi, who was preoccupied with brushing eyeshadow on him. When his center was completely full, he tried to command it to retract, but there was the fragrance of cosmetics, and the tickle of various prohibited brushes so delicate on his face skin, and Bibi's encouraging eyes. All he could do was hope she didn't see he was expanded. Another more courageous part of him said: so what if she does. Gradually, as he became more accustomed to the mirror and the many different touches he was receiving, the exterior evidence of his stimulation retreated. It went to be only inside, where it remained.

"Now for the wig," announced Bibi, hurrying to get and untie a circular box. Out of it she removed a faceless plastic head adorned with real hair duplicating the shade of his. "It was the first thing I bought," she said. "I had it set and then went back to get it." She took the wig off the plastic and transferred it to him, stretching it out and on. She adjusted it with gentle tugs, pinned it in place, and then fluffed it expertly. It was a short wig, about the same length as Bibi's and styled much the same.

When it was on, Bibi said what Rog was thinking. "You're beautiful. You really are." Then she helped him put on the black dress, that was a nice fit and a perfect length: inches above the knees.

Bibi backed away. "Walk for me," she told him.

He did a female parade. He was still not used to the shoes, but other than that all his imitations were convincing.

"Oh, sweet, you're marvelous!" exclaimed Bibi. "No one would ever guess you're not a woman."

"I rather feel like one."

"What kind of feeling is it?"

"I don't know exactly. Perhaps it's not at all like a woman feels."

"Anyway, you look beautiful."

Beautiful, he thought. Then he asked her, "What about my voice?"

"I thought about that. What you mustn't do is try to talk with a high pitch. You know, falsetto. That'll give you away sure as hell. Instead, just talk normally but a lot softer than usual, and with a lot of breath. Sort of like a half-whisper."

"Like this?" he tried.

"Even more."

"Do you mean like this, darling?"

"Yes, that's it exactly."

"How does it sound, this kind of voice?" he asked.

"Sexy. That's the impression you want to make, isn't it?"

"Naturally."

"Well," sighed Bibi, "we did it."

"Now what?"

"Take it all off, I suppose. Unless, of course, you want to go out and try for some whistles."

"No, thank you. Not tonight," he said but thought it a shame to destroy the illusion so quickly. "Maybe I should practice walking some more. And sitting."

"All right. You do that while I get ready for bed," she said and left him there.

At once he went to the mirror. He said hello to the female in it. He especially watched the lip movement. Then for a while he walked and sat from chair to chair. After enough, he undressed slowly, with a new gentleness toward his body and more respect for the things he took off. He removed the wig and put it in place on the plastic head. And after one last look, he peeled off the eyelashes and washed off the makeup. It was both a relief and a disappointment to be only him again. He put on a robe to go and see Bibi. She was already in bed.

"I hope you sleep better tonight," he told her, tender.

"I probably will. I took two up-and-outs."

She closed her eyes. "Good night kiss," she murmured.

He gave it.

He shut off her lights and went to his own bed. The sheets, he noticed, felt more indulgent than ever on his bare hairless skin.

The next night. Bibi helped him make up and get dressed again. To go out to fool Arnie, she thought.

"Can't I go along as witness?" she asked.

"No."

"Why not?"

"Arnie might go for you instead of me."

"I doubt that. The way you look."

"I don't need any competition," he told her.

"All right. But you've got to remember everything, every detail, so you can tell me about it. Promise?"

He promised and asked her for a final inspection.

She assured him. "You look ravishing, darling. But don't forget to use your sexy voice."

He swung his purse and went out. To Sutton Place where a taxi was his first test. He tried for female poise during the ride to Grand Central and felt a small victory when the driver said, "Thank you, lady," for his tip.

Minutes later Rog was in the waiting room with his destination in sight. He hesitated a moment, pretending he was looking for someone, while he accumulated courage. He noticed a different policeman was on duty there. Rog walked toward the word WOMEN, wondering if there was anything detectable about him. There was pounding in him and his legs felt floaty, all the way.

But as soon as he was in there, all symptons were replaced by curiosity. Actually, except for the absence of vertical urinals, the place appeared to be no different from any public toilet he'd ever been in. It was hard white and hard lighted. Its smell was mostly that strong camouflage of disinfectant, nearly successful. One wall was lined with wash basins with a long common mirror above them. The opposite wall was a regiment of enclosed toilet booths, each with a knob that required payment to open. Except two on the end that were dangerously free.

Rog's imagination had expected the place to be crowded. Perhaps it was an after-illusion from the constant in-and-out traffic he'd witnessed two days previous. But now there was no one. He was alone, a solitary trespasser staring at a sanitary napkin vending machine. At least he thought he was alone until he heard the sudden sucking flush of one of the toilets.

The one who came out was a Fat Fifty in a synthetic suit. She had a cotton mesh shopping bag crammed out of shape and a *Daily News* sticking up out of it. She went across to a wash basin, turned on the cold water, and faked putting a hand under it. She wasn't a good pretender because she forgot to fake drying with a paper towel. Instead she stuck a hand inside her top and adjusted the placements of her breasts. Under her hanging chins, she had a pair of glasses attached to a cheap chain so she wouldn't lose them.

Rog just stood there, as if he were an invisible observer. Until it came to him that he'd better move. He went by Fat Fifty, who was examining her lower gums close up in the mirror and didn't notice him, the chic and pretty lady in black.

There was nowhere for Rog to go except into one of the toilet booths. One of his hands went automatically to where a trouser pocket had always been, but he corrected fast to unsnap his purse and find the needed dime. He placed the coin in the slot and turned the handle but forgot to pull and it snapped itself locked again. Rog, like so many valiant others before him, had innocently lost his first encounter with the pay-before-you-go toilet. He jerked at the handle, believing it should open, but the little sign on it said "Vacant."

His nervous battle attracted some attention from Fat Fifty, who, like a veteran victim of society's various weapons, told him, "You've got to be careful, honey. Those things will steal you blind."

Rog smiled for the sympathy and produced another dime that he didn't put into the hungry slot until he'd read the instructions and knew his mistake. The door opened for him to enter and when it clicked its metallic shut he wondered if he'd have to pay to get out.

There was nothing to do in there but sit. His dressed rear fit on the slick seat and down some into the oval chasm. He placed his good black faille purse on the tiled floor between his feet. He waited for something. That was when he first noticed the graffiti—all the writing on the walls around him. Some of it was almost not readable because of attempts to scrub it clean off. Some was scratched on for sure preservation. Some was obviously new. The phrase he first noticed was done in lipstick, red and large, obviously by someone extremely disappointed with modern medicine. It said:

THE PILL IS A FRAUD

From that his eyes found others, such as this generous instruction:

FLUSH TWICE, NEW JERSEY NEEDS WATER

Next to a clever contagious greeting:

MERRY SYPHILIS AND A CLAPPY NEW YEAR

Some of the inscriptions he saw were answered by a second person. For example:

DO YOU KNOW MARY HUNT?

Answer:

NO, BUT I'M CLOSE TO HER BROTHER MIKE

It's a regular communication center, Rog thought. He then caught on a more graphic one: a badly-drawn penis somewhat larger than life. Under it the artist had written her candid desire:

I WANT ONE THIS BIG

Exactly beneath that someone else had drawn the same physical item three times larger along with an uncomplimentary comment:

YOU NEED ONE THIS BIG

Another in the same category was a boast:

MY TITS ARE BEAUTIFUL

Addition:

SO ARE THE EARS ON A COCKER SPANIEL

One that made Rog laugh inside was:

JOE THE CONDUCTOR IS A GREAT LAY
SIGNED: JOE THE CONDUCTOR

Rog had nothing to do but read the other wall, that, among numerous scribbles, offered this fragment of sadness:

I WISH I WAS WHAT I WAS
BEFORE I WISHED I WAS WHAT I AM NOW

And running diagonally up the end of that was one of probable truth:

MY MOTHER MADE ME A LESBIAN

Which inspired someone else to add:

IF I SENT HER SOME WOOL WOULD
SHE MAKE ME ONE TOO?

What were they like, Rog wondered, the women who sat and made these inscriptions? Were there just as many writings in all the other toilet booths? If so, that meant hundreds to thousands of scribbling participants. He pictured one of them with pants down and pencil out, privately performing minor public mischief. Probably they were mostly nose-high women with inhibitions. But maybe not.

Music entered.

It was a transistor radio tuned to some thumping screaming sounds. The voices that came with it, Rog decided, belonged to three in their early teens.

"Christ. Look what he did to my chin."

"Put some makeup on it."

"I'm going to be all broken out."

"Why didn't you make him shave?"

"He's growing a beard, that's why."

"My mother will flip. She'll know for sure."

"I think he's a groove."

"I don't want to go home yet."

"This is the last train."

"I don't give a shit."

" Me either. What a drag."

"Let's go."

"Suppose we miss the train."

"We could call and say we missed it."

"I ain't even supposed to be in the city. I'll really get hell."

"You'll get hell anyway."

"We could miss it and call."

"What do you think his friend looks like?"

"Groovy from what he said."

"Let's just miss it."

"Then we can make it back down to the Village with him."

"Wouldn't you dig that? I would."

"Sure, but what about school tomorrow?"

"Screw school."

"I've got to pee. You got a dime?"

"Use that one, you don't have to pay. That one's free."

"Give me a dime, for Christ's sake. I'll pay you back."

One of them borrowed and bought her way into the booth next to Rog's. He could see her feet. She had on bright red plastic shoes and pink stockings. In a few seconds he heard a thin stream hitting water. He wondered if she had pubic hair. He saw her feet move and turn and then there was the expected flush that continued after she went out.

"Hey, why didn't you hold the door? I could have gone without paying."

"Yeah, you're dumb."

"You didn't say you had to go. You should have told me."

"I don't have to go bad but I could have."

"We're going to miss the train."

"Who cares?"

"How does it look now?"

"You can still see it."

"It looks like a rash."

"I'm not going to kiss him anymore, the bastard."

"Want to bet?"

Giggles, while the radio announcer sold a cold soft drink hard.

"Go call."

"No, you."

"Call and say your watch was wrong."

"That's a groovy idea."

"Tell your mother to call mine."

"Why do I have to call?"

"I ain't got any bread."

"Yeah. You've got the bread. You call."

"Think she'll believe me?"

"What the hell else can she do?"

"I'll say that we'll take the first train in the morning."

"Tell her we're just going to hang around the station."

"Let's split."

"What's your hurry? I can't call until after the train's gone."

"Yeah, don't be so dumb."

"Let me borrow your lip gloss, will you?"

"Why should I?"

"Let's get out of here."

"You know what I'd like to do, don't you?"

"What?"

"Get lost."

"What do you mean?"

"Get lost down in the Village. Kids are doing it all the time. I read about it in the papers."

"That would really shake them up."

"They'd find us."

"Not for a while."

"Maybe we could stay at his place."

"With him and his friend."

"They'd let us."

"That would be a gas."

The music went with them. Rog had created faces to match their voices, and after images of them remained for him to advise. Go home, children, he said to their improbable virginities and forgot them. He wished he'd bought a magazine. There was nothing to do but sit and wait.

In minutes he heard the walking in of someone, the cadent clack of female shoes. It occurred to him that he could know a lot about anyone from seeing merely their feet. So he hunched down to look out below the door. He saw a pair of brown kid shoes, not inexpensive, and ankles that were slim enough. He got lower and saw that the legs weren't bad. But that was all he could see, unless he actually got down on the floor.

He did. Got down and saw the back of her, and although it was a difficult angle for precise judgment, one that exaggerated her behind, he thought she had a nice enough figure. He couldn't see her face, not even the reflection of it in the mirror, because she was directly in front of his booth. He decided to go out.

He went to a wash basin two away from her. She was teasing her hair with a sharp pointed comb, punishing it with short backward strokes and arranging it with pats.

She could be the one, thought Rog when he saw her face. Although not up to his usual standards, she was pretty in a brittle way. She was handicapped by too much makeup and too much forehead; however, her mouth was all right and so was her nose, with a slight mistake that made it vaguely noble. She had active brown eyes that caught the stare of Rog, who smiled a fast excusing smile and worked the hot and cold water handles to be doing anything. He almost washed his hands but suddenly feared that his false fingernails might come off, so he pretended to search his purse. When he again looked in the mirror, he saw her eyes were aimed at him and sending a deliberate message. He tried to translate.

"You wouldn't happen to have a cigarette, would you?" she asked.

"No," he answered, almost forgetting to use the softer, breathier voice. "I don't smoke."

"Neither do I," she said meaningfully, and waited. When he didn't say anything, she asked, "Are you taking a train?"

"No. Are you?"

"No."

She stepped back and lifted her dress to stretch her stockings smooth and refasten their tops. She lifted higher than necessary, showing.

"Did you just get into town?" she asked.

"No."

"That's a lovely dress you have on."

"Thank you," smiled Rog.

"I wish I could wear my skirts that short, but my legs aren't pretty enough."

"Sure they are."

"You think my legs are pretty?"

"You have nice legs."

"Glad you noticed," she said and turned from the mirror to lean the sink with her behind. "Why did you notice?"

"I had to."

"I thought so," she said. The way she was leaning, the mound of her center showed where it was. Although she was standing still, the impression was that she was moving small offering moves.

Rog felt that, along with the judgment that it was all happening too fast. How long had they been there together? Five minutes? Surely not ten. And, he estimated, as things were going, in five more *she'd* probably be inviting him to enjoy the privacy of her in a booth. And that would be that. For some reason, he resented its being that easy. Some part of him wanted to prolong the circumstances. So he was relieved when he suddenly realized a perverse obstacle. He'd been seeing the situation from a male point of view, forgetting completely that he looked female and she thought he was. Woman to woman were the terms of this encounter. Stupid bastard, he cursed himself, happier.

"I'm Marylou," she said, asking for a name in exchange.

He'd overlooked a name. He said the first that came.

"I'm Bibi."

It was then that the tall Bony Cleaner came in. She had a scarred official bucket with a squeezing mechanism attached to its edge and she was dragging a mop, leaving a swath of damp on the surface after her. There was some resemblance between the mop's gray twisted bunching strands and Bony Cleaner's hair. Instead of shoes, her feet were in a pair of men's rain rubbers. She had on a gray uniform, too long. Her face was like an oversized pale machine with mouth and eyes turned off. She walked past them to the end of the room where she began mopping.

The presence of Bony Cleaner turned Marylou. She shifted her attention to her lips, putting some slick red on them and tightening her mouth inward to press it smooth. While she swiveled the lipstick back into its tube and capped it, her eyes went aside briefly to Rog's. She sent him an obvious mixture of cruel and tender permission.

Rog didn't allow his reflection to return the smile.

She took a tissue from her purse and blotted her lips. She handed the tissue to Rog. She turned and walked out with her best-looking walk.

Rog examined the tissue. There was the red imprint of Marylou's open lips. And exactly between them was her phone number. Clever, he thought, and, as he dropped the tissue into the wastebasket, he felt motion near his feet. He had to move quickly to avoid the swabbing mop of Bony Cleaner, who hadn't warned.

In then came the Fat Talker who was a station sleeper. She washed her face and hands without soap before using a free toilet. All the while, she delivered sounds to some audience that Rog was sure didn't include him. She spoke as if her tongue were swollen, a continuous soliloquy of slurred words and short phrases connected to mumbles and agreeing angry grunts, incomprehensible. She was one of those who lived in the station. Her existence depended on knowing one valid psychological fragment. She knew that most travelers were happy, to arrive or be going, and in that mood they were generally generous. So almost any entrance/exit of Grand Central was a good location for handouts. Weekends and holidays were her best times. She was always especially glad to discover it was a holiday. But now was only another ordinary night and she was a victim of its empty. Now she was more noticed by police and oppressed. Now she would have to wait for a long-distance train, going or coming, to create enough travelers for enough coins for admission into the public asylum of the station's movie theater. Under no circumstances would she go outside where she hadn't been in five years.

She repulsed Rog. He thought of her as a woman, provided with female equipment, and it depressed him. However, she was also the cause of his thoughts about beggars and choosers that made him decide on his next move, that made him pay his way back into the toilet booth he calculated was the one he'd occupied before. Actually, it was another, but it didn't matter, for there was some of what he now believed might be useful. Telephone numbers. In lipstick, one said:

FOR THE HEAD OF THE CLASS CALL 211-8310

Another advertised:

FRENCH TEACHER 610-2615

He didn't have a pen or pencil so he had to memorize, choosing the more neutral notice that was:

IN CASE OF EMERGENCY DAY OR NIGHT
CALL 211-4929

He hurried out with that number in mind, repeating it to remember, all the way to a pay telephone in the waiting room. He slotted the required coin, dialed, and after three buzzes was answered by a voice that sounded sleepy.

"I'm Bibi," he said. "I saw your message."

"Where?"

"In Grand Central."

"Oh, Well, hello, Bibi."

"Did I wake you up?"

"Hell, no," she said. "Tell me about yourself, Bibi."

"What do you want to know?"

"Start with your age."

"I'm twenty-six."

"Blonde or brunette?"

"Brunette."

"Why did you call?"

"I saw your message, I told you."

"And you just felt like it, huh?"

"Sure, why not?"

"Where are you now?"

"Grand Central."

"Why don't you come over here?"

"All right."

"You got money for a cab?"

"Of course."

"I was going out but I'll wait for you, so don't hang me up."

"What's the address?"

She told him a West Side address and Rog was there in fifteen minutes. He knew it was only a chance with her but perhaps he could develop it into something that would eventually end up where he wanted it. Of course, that depended on if he wanted her. If she was pretty enough he'd persuade her. Facing her address, he hoped she wasn't constructed as ugly as the building she lived in. If she was, he'd retreat fast, back to Grand Central for another number.

Actually, Rog was intrigued with the gamble, and during the climb up and around to the third floor, he speculated on the looks of the stranger he was about to meet. She would be attractive, if not pretty, he hoped. She would have long hair, probably blonde or light brown. She would be thin but not skinny thin, with good legs and fingernails cared for. She would have a quick soft smile and generally otherwise she would also be soft. She would be lonely. Loneliness was the reason she wrote on the wall, he thought. She would be self-conscious about that and he wouldn't mention it again. She would probably be the frilly sort. She'd said she was ready to go out, so she'd have on her best dress, maybe blue, probably short.

He reached her door. He knocked and it was opened.

She was tall. She had on a blue denim shirt and black trousers held up by a wide belt with a huge metal buckle. Her complexion was sallow with no makeup. Her hair wasn't combed. It was an in-between shade of light brown cut short by a cheap barber. She appraised Rog from curls to toes with slow-motion eyes.

"Come in, Bibi," she said, not opening her mouth much.

Rog knew what she was, immediately. He knew this was no-man's-land and it would be wiser to turn and run. His excuse for not running was his shoes. He could hardly walk in them. His hesitation was noticed.

"In or out," said Blue Shirt, hard.

Rog stepped in, Blue Shirt closed the door and went to sit. She drank some from a bottle of beer. It was as if Rog weren't standing there.

The place was one large room with a high yellowed ceiling and a bare scarred floor. All the furniture was two black canvas chairs, a round Victorian table, and a phonograph. The phonograph was next to a mattress covered in orange denim. There was someone on the orange. Another one. She was dressed in a white shirt with sleeves rolled up to her biceps. She had on dark belled trousers and the same kind of belt with a big buckle. Her hair was black and kinky short. Rog guessed from her skin that she was Puerto Rican. When Rog looked she nodded one cool nod.

"Where you from Bibi?" asked Blue Shirt with eyes down.

"Los Angeles," lied Rog.

"What part of L.A.?"

"Actually Santa Monica."

"You don't look like the beach type. I've been there. I lived in Venice for almost a year."

"You smoke?" asked the one in the white shirt

"No."

"Come over here," ordered Blue Shirt.

Rog went and, when he was close enough, Blue Shirt grabbed his purse. She opened it upside down, so all its contents dropped on the floor. A lipstick, sixty-four dollars and some change.

"She travels light," commented White Shirt.

Blue Shirt examined the purse closely, feeling it inside. "Nothing," she said and asked White Shirt, "What do you think?"

"I think she's straight."

"I'm not sure," said Blue Shirt.

"What's the problem?" asked Rog.

"You could be fuzz."

Rog knew the term. "I'm not."

"She's not," said White Shirt.

Rog asked Blue Shirt, "What makes you think I am?"

"The way you look. Why would anyone who looks like you get a number off a shithouse wall?"

"I'm impetuous," Rog explained.

"Maybe she's just horny," said White Shirt.

"Could be," said Blue Shirt, giving in.

Rog knew they were high on grass. He'd smelled it right away.

Blue Shirt combed her hair with her fingers. She drank more beer from the bottle and then used her eyes on him. "You didn't expect two of us, did you?"

"No," answered Rog.

"How does that grab you? Two of us?"

Rog didn't answer but he smiled.

"Bibi," said Blue Shirt. "That your real name?"

"No."

"What's your real name?"

Rog shrugged.

"Okay. So it's just Bibi. That's good enough. I'm Jackie and that's Jo."

"Hi, Bibi," greeted Jo.

"You like music?" asked Jackie.

"Sure," Rog told her.

"We've got lots of sounds. What kind do you like?"

"Doesn't matter," said Rog.

"Why don't you go put on something you like?" suggested Jackie.

Rog went to the phonograph to read record covers. Jo rolled

across the mattress and kneeled next to him. "Want to smell something nice?" she asked.

"What?"

"Take a big breath," Jo instructed, putting her hand up to his nose.

Rog took a small cautious breath.

"Didn't you smell it?" asked Jo.

"No."

"Try again," said Jackie.

Rog did as he was told. He inhaled a long breath with his nose. Something went pop inside Jo's hand and Rog got it deep. Instantly he went hot all over. His fingers and toes felt like burning candles. His chest and stomach was a warm oven and his center was a torch. The room was liquid and laughter ran out of his throat. It lasted only a few minutes but Rog didn't know how long. Gradually he came down and cooled. When he did, he was horizontal on the mattress and there was Jo's face and Jackie was next to her next to him.

"How about that?" asked Jackie. "Wasn't that a nice little trip?"

"You can have more when the time comes."

"You'll dig it. Believe me, Bibi baby."

"Bibi baby," repeated Jo.

They all laughed and said it. Bibi baby. Jo got up and turned off all the lights so the red bulb she switched on had its effect. It was a private flattering hell.

Rog knew it was almost time for discovery. He didn't know what was going to happen when they found out.

Jackie came down on his mouth with hers. She kissed with tender authority. He'd never been kissed with such tender authority. Her tongue conquered his with alternate light play and rigid plunge. The feeling went separate ways through him and converged in his center that had to expand. He couldn't control it. He felt a hand that he thought was Jo's going up his leg. It reached him and clutched hard to make sure. Then it recoiled.

Jo shouted. "Hey! It's a man in drag. No shit. It's a man in drag."

That snapped Jackie's kiss off. Rog didn't move while she felt him.

"Achh," was the sound from Jackie's throat, as if her mouth had some horrible substance. She spat and tried to clear it out but it was done. She went on spitting. "The son of a bitch!"

"No-good bastard."

"Let's cut his joint off!"

"Get a knife. We'll cut his joint off."

They meant it. Jackie sprawled all her weight across his shoulders and arms, pinning him. Jo had gone for the knife.

Rog's center was still up. It seemed to be getting harder with the danger. He struggled under Jackie. He heaved and tried to roll. His hand found her head and grabbed her hair. That pain raised her enough for him to get free.

He stood. His heels dug into the give of the mattress and he couldn't move. Jackie backed away out of range of the red light. Jo was somewhere in the dark with her. He heard the sibilation of their whispers and then some short metallic noises connected to a pair of fast frictional sounds.

The lights went on.

There was Jackie and Jo between him and the only way out. They'd taken off their belts and now held them like wide whips with the heavy buckles dangling.

"Come and get it, Bibi baby," said Jackie.

No laughs this time.

"We're going to beat your balls off," promised Jo.

Jackie was still spitting out the kiss.

"Listen. It's not the way you think," Rog told them.

"You asked for it," said Jackie.

Rog slid out of his shoes. That let him move off the mattress. He rushed through them and had the doorknob in his hand when the first hit of leather stung him and the buckle cut in with its flash of punishment. The second hit followed. He jerked the door open and was hit again around the thighs, the buckle snapping painfully close to the prime target. He gained the hall and they ran after him, whipping with their weighted weapons. When he reached the top of the stairs, he tried to double up for protection. Jo kept hitting. Jackie put her foot on his back and shoved. He reached for anything to stop his fall but his body bumped and bruised all the way down to the next landing.

Through the cloud of his pain he knew he saw them up there, standing, legs apart, hating down. He had to use the banister to rise.

"So long, Bibi baby."

"Come again."

They began laughs. He stumbled around and down and out. He filled himself with air for revival. The street finally focused and stopped seesawing. He knew he was lucky to have escaped with his life. He knew he was without shoes. He knew he'd have to walk the entire width of Manhattan because all of his money was in his purse, left with them.

What he didn't know was why his center was still at maximum and remained that way for six long crosstown blocks.

It was three-thirty in the morning when he arrived home. Bibi was on his bed asleep in her clothes. Obviously she'd been waiting. He was careful not to wake her. He went to her room where he removed the injured black dress and the stockings that were ruined with up and down runs from where they were torn around his scraped raw knees. He took off the wig and everything and drew a deep hot bath. He hurt in many places and expected to be bleeding but wasn't. He got into the tub, under the hot of the water, hoping it would help. It did. After a fifteen-minute soak he dried tenderly and got into bed. He was tired. But his mind was electric. The sheets had the fragrance of Bibi on them and he filled with it, using its delicate abstract power to pleasantly turn himself off.

He slept seven hours. He dreamed some during the lighter last phase of his sleep. It was an enjoyable dream that transplanted him into another previous age of sensual nobility surrounded by all the tactile rewards of precious pretty things. He was pouring a rare silvery wine down the flawless silken shoulders of someone who was laughing a priceless string of perfect pearl laughter when he opened his eyes.

There was Bibi.

"Good morning," she said as if her words were a fragile gift wrapped in her smile.

As usual he was entirely awake.

"I was dreaming," he told her.

"In color?"

"I don't think so."

"I always dream in color. What were you dreaming about?"

"I can't remember except it was nice."

"I remember all my dreams. I really do. It's like going to the movies." She was on her side on the edge of the big bed with her head elbowed up right at him. "What happened last night?" she asked, making a line on the sheet with a fingernail. "Did you see Arnie?"

"No. I didn't run into him."

"You must have run into somebody or something," she said.

He sat up. He was achy but he tried not to show it. He saw that the dress, the wig, the stockings, and all the underthings weren't where he'd dropped them. Most likely she'd seen their condition.

"I had quite a night," he said.

"Tell me."

"They tried to rape me," he invented.

"Who?"

"Two of them."

"Where?"

"In an alley. Next to an apartment house. I don't know exactly where."

"Tell me."

"They grabbed me and pulled me into this dark place."

"What did they look like?"

"They were both huge. I didn't see their faces."

"Did you yell?"

"I couldn't. Suppose the police had come."

"That's right, you couldn't. So what happened?"

"One of them held me while the other one tried to rape me."

"Be more specific. Please?"

"He took his thing out and pulled up my skirt."

"I'll bet he was surprised."

"Furious."

"The joke was on them."

"They didn't think it was funny."

"What did they do then?"

"They tried to beat me up."

"Poor baby."

"But I kicked like hell and got away. They chased me in back of the building. I didn't know where I was. I hid behind some trash cans and eventually they went away. I lost my shoes and purse. Probably they got the purse."

"The one who was holding you must have squeezed very hard."

"Why do you say that?"

"He bruised you with his belt buckle." Her fingers tenderly touched the skin under his left breast where there was a distinct blue outline of a buckle and a red welt. She got up and hurried into the bathroom to get some lotion and cotton. She nursed.

"It must really hurt," she sympathized.

"I fell and scraped my knees," he said and showed her, keeping his center concealed by a bunch of the sheet.

While she lotioned his knees left and right, she noticed another swollen buckle imprint on his right thigh, high up. She didn't say anything about it with her voice but her face did. She treated that place and then told him, "Roll over."

He turned face down and she applied the lotion with care to several areas of his back and shoulders. Buckle bruises. Welts. She didn't comment, but when she was done she began to hum.

"What about Arnie?" she asked. "Are you going to try again?"

"I don't think so."

"I should have told you."

"What?"

"It's dangerous to be beautiful."

"Have you ever been raped?"

"No."

"But it could happen, couldn't it?"

"Not unless I wanted it to."

"Some girls get raped, don't they?"

"Very few," she said.

"Well, I got a taste of it."

"You certainly did," she said thoughtfully. "You really did."

He asked her, "What are you going to do today?"

"I'm going shopping."

"Not for me again."

"No. For me."

"What are you going to buy?"

"Just some things."

By the time he'd done his bathroom ritual and had something to eat, it was afternoon. Bibi had already left in the limousine to do her shopping. He dressed in a soft shirt and some summer slacks and put his bare feet into a pair of supple white antelope loafers.

It was a wet day, but he had the exterior double doors of his bedroom open. He could see down the river that was a slate-colored surface unbroken by ships. And he could see down the city to the upper limits of the United Nations building. He wondered what serious people were conducting what serious business in that hard tall rectangular monument. Was a small war being prevented today? It was a lovely day for it. The rain was a friendly rain, fine and friendly as lace. He went out on the narrow balcony and received the spray of some while he looked and thought how this nice little rain had prettied the city, increasing the depth of all its colors, slicking it kindly. Much more attractive than its usual dry tight high panic.

He went in and touched the top of his hair that was misted. He didn't disturb it. He went downstairs to the study and the desk that had accumulated just as many papers in only a day. He read the top one without interest. It was something about authorizing the trade of one called Plaxton for three other names. Just skimming as he was, it sounded like slavery but when he really read it he discovered they were football players and he remembered that he owned a team that played in the biggest league. He signed the paper and all the others under it in the proper places checked in red.

During the painful walk across the city the night before and since he'd awakened with the hangover of aches, he'd decided to give up the Grand Central project. It had forced him to lie to Bibi. Because he was who he was and had what he had, there was no reason ever to lie. But, he thought, as long as he'd already been circumstantially pressured into saying lies to Bibi, dear Bibi, surely it was a lesser offense to construct an ideal untrue story for the ears of Eduardo and Arnie and Knight. Now he could do it with knowledge, for he had been in the place and there had been an adventure because of it. All he had to do was add and subtract a few details.

That was his decision. He stuck with it until Bibi returned and they were sharing the pleasure of an early dinner. They took their coffee and cognac to the upper rear sitting room. The long windows of that place were all as open as possible. The rain had stopped. With crystal and cups in their hands, they sat facing the industrious neons that boasted brand names on the other side of the river.

She asked, ''What are you going to do?''

''About what?''

''About Arnie.''

''Just forget the whole thing. It was a stupid idea anyway.''

''I understand,'' she said, true.

She sipped and he twirled his cognac.

She asked, ''How are your bruises?''

''Better now. I can hardly feel them.''

She sighed and crossed her legs to make a foot bounce.

''Do you wish you were back in Rome?'' he asked.

''A little maybe.''

''But not enough to go, I hope.''

''No, not enough to go. At least not yet.''

''Do you think you'll go back?''

''Probably.''

''I don't see why. Rome has always treated you badly.''

''Maybe I deserve it.''

''No, you don't.''

''Maybe I think I do.''

''You can stay here, you know. I like sharing with you.''

''I know.'' She got up and walked the room some. He watched all her moves and felt as if he were doing them.

She sat again and suggested, ''Why don't you give it one more try?''

''You mean the trick on Arnie?''

''Yes.''

''It won't work.''

''It might.''

''I doubt it.''

''Are you afraid?''

He shrugged because he was and wasn't.

''Yes,'' he admitted.

''How about giving it one more try?''

''No. Anyway, Arnie's too smart. He won't be fooled.''

''You fooled those rapers,'' she inserted.

He thought about it: Jackie and Jo. She let him think, sensing his submission. ''I sure did,'' he said, turning a smile on.

''Come on.'' She stood and held her hand out for him to take for a lead. ''We've never seen you in the beige outfit.''

Rog had never in his life done anything he didn't want to do.

The makeup and everything went on faster this time. Within an hour he was in the beige, ready to leave.

"I should go with you," she said.

"No. Alone is better."

"You're beautiful. Don't forget. You're beautiful and it's dangerous," she warned.

"I won't."

"How do those shoes fit? They're the same size as the black ones."

"They feel fine."

"Walk for me."

He did. She watched, an intimate collaborator, sensitively aware of the illusion. He felt her appreciation and purposely prolonged his parade for her.

"I approve," she finally said.

"What about these fingernails?"

"They look real."

"Will they come off if I wash my hands?"

"Of course not," she said inside her lacy laugh.

"I guess I've got a lot to learn."

Grand Central was the same week-night slow. Rog went across the waiting room with more confidence this time, all the way into his destination. Although the place wasn't empty, it might as well have been. There were only two heavy travelers washing off the dirt of a long trip. They both had their tops off, revealing a lot of blotchy skin, thin shoulders, neck stumps, and wide blemished backs. Neither was wearing an adequate brassiere. Only about two-thirds of their breast flesh was contained. The rest was squeezed out and swollen around into ugly rolls of flab. When Rog entered, they were soaping their armpits, the lather making sucking vacuum sounds.

Rog immediately paid his way into a toilet booth. He tried not to listen to the pair of heavy travelers who were talking about the imperfections of various first-named people. Rog tried to turn them off, but their voices got through to inflate his impatience. Again he'd forgotten to bring anything to read. He took his interest to phone numbers on the walls. Very classified advertisements, he thought, remembering the previous night.

That was when he got the idea. He left the booth and

hurried out. He asked someone and was directed to the nearest open drugstore. He went there to buy ten tubes of the reddest red lipstick and got two dollars changed into dimes. Then he went back to do it.

By that time the two heavy travelers were brushing their teeth, spitting loud frothy spits into defenseless wash basins. Rog disregarded them. He began with the last pay booth.

He twisted the tip of a lipstick out and printed, obviously bold and bright, his positively private phone number. He did it on the back of the door at sitting position eye level where it couldn't be ignored. He paid his way into booth after booth and did the same. He broke five lipsticks, his hands were greasy red, and he still had three left to do. He was about to slot a dime into the next line when a crisp voice stopped him.

"What the hell are you doing?" she asked, hard. She was in a brown belted dress and comfortable order-woman shoes. She had neat gray hair and a solid face.

"None of your business," Rog told her. She took a leather folder out of her purse and flipped it open. She was police.

"I'm sorry," said Rog. "I didn't know who you were. I thought you were one of those, you know, the kind who bother people in places like this."

She didn't seem impressed. "I've been watching you. What are you doing?"

"Looking for something."

"What?"

"I dropped the tip off my lipstick tube. It rolled somewhere."

"That how you get your hands all smeared?"

"Yes," was all he could say. He saw himself being handcuffed and led to where they took women. He saw them discovering him. It would make the papers.

"Give me your purse," she ordered.

He obeyed. Fortunately, there was only one lipstick left in it. He'd thrown all the depleted and broken ones into toilet bowls and flushed them away. She inspected the purse, even more methodically than Jackie had the other one. Rog remembered that moment.

The policewoman handed it back. "I don't believe you," she said, "but get the hell out of here."

"Can I wash my hands?"

She nodded permission.

Rog wet and soaped his hands into a pink lather. For clean he had to wash them three times with her as a silent official audience.

"All you'll find in here is trouble," she warned.

He felt like saying: Listen, lady cop, let me tell you about a piece of double trouble I already found here. But instead he dried with a paper towel and didn't even thank her before he left, fast, feeling her eyes on his back.

For no conscious reason he didn't take a taxi. He walked east on 45th and up First Avenue, especially appraising the dark depths of dangerous alleys. He turned several male heads and one man in a sports car slowed and went around the block to pass again but wasn't brave enough to say anything.

When Rog reached home he found Bibi watching television in her room. She asked him why he was back so early. "Arnie's out of town," he told her.

"Oh," was her single-syllable reaction.

"I'm not having much luck."

"You will, darling," she said without taking her eyes off the color screen.

"I guess I'll change."

"Why don't you just kick your shoes off and curl up in that chair? There's a good old movie coming in a few minutes."

He took her suggestion. They watched the late late show together, laughing at ridiculous bad parts and criticizing the commercials and going down in stocking feet to get some fresh cookies and cold milk before the end. Like girl friends.

Two more nights.

If Rog was going to fulfill his assignment truthfully, he had only two more nights to do it. None of the experiences he'd had so far in and around *that place* were encouraging. When he analyzed the situation he concluded that he was a victim of unalterable circumstances. He was a man. But in order to enter *that place* he had to look like a woman. For success, he would eventually have to reveal himself as a man; however, what they wanted him to be was a woman. It was a paradox.

Now his chances were reduced to the improbability of a phone call. That someone would undoubtedly be expecting a woman. He would have to pretend to be a woman to get in there. Then, if that someone was willing to share intimately one of those booths, out would come his unexpected manhood.

He imagined the scream.

"He tried to attack me."

"She was all for it until she found out I was a man."

"He shoved me into the booth and tried to molest me."

"That's a lie. I didn't have to shove her. She went in voluntarily."

"I did not. I was minding my own business."

Official question: "Why were you dressed in woman's clothing?"

"I'd been to a masquerade party."

Official question: "What were you doing in the ladies' toilet?"

"I couldn't go in the men's toilet dressed like that, could I?"

"You're a man."

"You'd have arrested me if I'd gone in the men's toilet, wouldn't you?"

Official answer: "Yes."

"Well, I had to urinate. Where was I supposed to go, behind some luggage trunk?"

"He tore my clothes off."

"She took them off."

Official order: "Call the psychiatrist."

His being a man was the obstacle.

All afternoon he thought about it, staying in his room near his positively private phone in case it rang. He decided if someone did call, he'd explain what he was and simply, persuasively make the proposition. That was the best, least dangerous way.

Then it came to him that that wasn't necessary. According to the rules, all he had to do was please his partner in that particular place. How he pleased her was his choice. So, if she allowed herself merely to receive, if she didn't explore him, he could to it that way all the way, as a woman. If it was going to be, that was how. He didn't mind. But it depended on her, however she was, her sexual personality. She'd have to be a total taker.

He knew many who were.

"That was beautiful, just beautiful, darling."

"How do you feel?"

"Marvelous. Sleepy."

"Why don't you nap awhile?"

"But what about you? You don't mind?"

"No."

"I don't think I can move. You really don't mind?"

"No."

"I'll owe you one."

The debts mounted up and were seldom collected.

By nighttime he knew that hundreds of women had sat and seen the lipstick proclamation that was his positively private number. But no one called. All he could do was continue to wait. Bibi had been out shopping since early afternoon. He wished she were with him. She was always a perfect distraction. He was sure that she'd soon be bored enough with New York to fly away somewhere. She was lucky, he thought, for no reason except that she had all the advantages of being Bibi. If, through some miraculous influence, he was granted the fantasy of becoming someone else, his choice would be to be her. He'd thought that numerous times. He thought it now.

He also remembered a poem by someone that was a favorite because it expressed a relative emotion:

In another age
I would be
No more than a ribbon flying
On the hair of a beauty crying
Joy and running
The edge of a sea.
In another age
I would be
No more than a simple stone,
Alone on her fragile hand.
In another age,
Another land,
I would be
A smile,
For that short while
Only, on her lips exploding
From life's sad cage,
I would be
In another age.

The positively private phone rang.

He couldn't hear her very well, but he thought she had a nice voice. He used his soft breathy one.

"Why did you call?" he asked, knowing.

"It was written in lipstick."

"Tell me about yourself. What do you look like?"

"I'm pretty."

"You think so?"

"I know so."

"Well, at least you don't lack conceit."

"You'll see."

"When?"

"Whenever you want."

"Are you always so cooperative?"

"Only when I feel like it."

"Where are you now?"

"In a phone booth."

"Where?"

"Grand Central."

"What do you want to do?"

"You tell me."

"I'll meet you in an hour."

"All right."

"Make it an hour and a half."

"Whatever you say."

"At nine-thirty."

"Where?"

He told her.

"Why in there?" she asked.

"Why not?"

"Can't I meet you near the newsstand or someplace like that?"

"No."

"How will I know you?" she asked.

"I'll be wearing beige."

"Beige what?"

"Dress."

"Lots of people wear beige. You'll have to do better than that."

"You'll know me."

"How?"

"I'll be in the third booth from the end. That's the first pay one."

"You really know your toilets." She said, smart. "Third from the end?"

"Yes."

"What shall I do—knock?"

"Knock."

"You'll be there?"

"I'll be there."

She sounded like a good one, Rog thought, and with recharged spirit began putting on the beige.

It took him more than an hour to be ready to go. It was the first time he'd applied his makeup unassisted. He tried to imitate exactly the way Bibi had done it. He used all the correct little brushes for their special effects, but he had trouble with his eyes. No matter how carefully he shadowed and lined them, he couldn't get them to look identical. Either the left came out wider than the right or the right higher than the left, so he had to erase and start over several times before he finally got them perfectly matched. Hurrying, he also had difficulty with the false eyelashes. He got some of the adhesive on his fingers and the lashes stuck to them instead of his lids. They were like hairy incorrigible insects, but eventually he managed to glue them on.

He was fifteen minutes late arriving at Grand Central. He rushed to the waiting room and across it, but warned himself and stopped at the entrance of WOMEN to take a cautious look in. No woman cop. He saw six women in there, ranging from slightly to extremely unattractive. He remembered she'd promised she was pretty, and his imagination had magnified that adjective with hope. Now he thought she was probably one of those who needed to believe her own fraud, safely blind to every mirror.

Against his judgment he went in. He slotted the required dime to get into the appointed booth, third from the end. He had to wait only a few moments for her knock. He was sure she'd be one of those he'd seen and he was repulsed enough to almost not open the door. He knew she'd probably be the most unlovely one.

But he was wrong.

She was in a gray double-breasted trouser suit of finest English flannel, a shirt the color of an ideal blue sky with stylish long collar points, a wide black-on-black silk tie, and a pocket kerchief exposed to match. She had on lace-up shoes of black brilliant authentic alligator and short black kid gloves that accentuated the double diamonds of her cuff links. Her jacket was cut smartly long and subtly nipped, and her trousers were straight full. She was in every detail, right down to hand-turned bone buttons, expensive and tasteful.

Her face.

The blonde hair above it was a round of perfectly planned soft curls like fine spun springs.

Her face.

The skin of it was pleasingly pale, like precious porcelain and flawless as that, but surely soft, soft.

Her face.

Eyes artfully darkened around to make targets of her pupils that were set hard and brown as wet sea pebbles. A mouth faintly slicked, upper lip and lower lip exactly full, but not smiling, not even parted, together forming a serious transmission.

Her face.

It made him start to stand to speak, but her gloved hand splashed his left cheek with sting.

It was Bibi.

"Quiet," she whispered, commanding.

Eyes to eyes, his questioning.

She reached and took his head like a helpless bowl with both her gloved hands, the cool leather an exaggerated shock. She was a tower that fell on him with her lips. It was a long kiss, long to recoup from time all the kisses that had never been total kisses and all the kisses untaken. Before it ended there were words in his mouth, so when her lips released but remained loose and light against his, he said them into her.

"I love you."

He knew it was the first true time he'd said it because it made all other times so obviously false.

She received, tasted, let his words reach her entire system and then returned them.

"I love you."

They were sounds like seeds poured down the funnel of his throat to flower instantly.

"I worship you," he said.

"You must," she told him, knowing and requiring.

From the first moments of the first kiss there had been a rush to his center. Now she found him with her animal-skinned hands. Her fingers chewed and blessed alternately.

"Let's go home," he said wanting.

She disconnected and stepped back, and he thought she agreed. But then she unbuttoned her jacket, keeping the aim of her eyes on him. Her fingers went to the metal tab of the zipper of her trousers. She pulled and he heard the metallic teeth forced to part the front of her all the way down and half way under between. Not enough. But these were not ordinary trousers. These were her special accommodating design that allowed her to reach around and under to continue unzipping the back. Then she was split open and capable.

He didn't move. She did. She moved so the black of her silk tie was in his eyes that he shut black and used as a background for the overture his expectancy performed. She lowered until they touched exactly. No need for hands. She lowered more and much more and all to have them fit.

At once they were each answered.

At once they were seared, vised, each to hold and invade.

I am me. And you.

You are me, the penetrator, and the pierced, as I am.

Surrounded and enclosing.

I am the beauty and the beauty that is in me.

We are.

We are centrally melted.

We are both entered and admitting and now at last thankfully alloyed.

For them, motion was not necessary. Motion would have defined. They remained intensely still. And in their simple overlap, there was current and surge enough to surpass any previous experience. They stayed still all the way.

As for that place, they might as well have been in the private cradle of some luxurious balcony above the world. Or on the highest grassy head of some virgin hill with the sun bathing them purely. Or upon the slick and fragrant plush of some elegant ancient couch.

They were so immune and inseparable.

There was only one real problem. When Rog had opened the booth door to admit Bibi its device had accidentally jammed. They were locked in. Eventually, for discretion, they decided not to climb up and over. They called for attention and had to pass a coin underneath the door into an old hand.

Bony Cleaner rested her mop and slotted the toll for their freedom.

5

The private elevator about the size of a vertical sarcophagus lifted Eduardo to his third floor. Often he used the stairs for some exercise but now he was heavy in the legs from all-night nervous walking around the pool table.

He didn't know the correct time. He never wore a watch or wound energy into any of the clocks he owned for decoration. Not that he felt an aversion to such life-eating mechanisms, at least not consciously. It was just that knowing the minute wasn't necessary, according to his way of life, and the hour he could approximate through a sense he'd developed for that purpose.

As he got off on third he guessed it was after noon. Elaine Baine-Brice was due at one. He went into his bedroom, found her telephone number and dialed. The person who answered told him Miss Baine-Brice wasn't there. That meant she was on her way, and now it was impossible for him to prevent her visit with the excuse he'd invented.

Eduardo cursed her mildly, but reminded his anger that the compression he was feeling was self-inflicted. He had maneuvered Elaine Baine-Brice into this afternooner, inspired by the stir he'd felt then, at that party. But now was a different time, inconvenient. When Eduardo didn't want anyone around he really didn't want anyone around. Not even servants. He'd been through four housekeepers and three houseboys in the past several months. What always happened was: he'd want to be alone, they'd crowd him with their duties, he'd yell and swear, and they'd leave. The last one had departed just yesterday, crying but consoled by the extra two months salary Eduardo had gladly given her to get her the hell out of his life. He needed solitude when he needed solitude. Like now. But Elaine Baine-Brice was en route and there was no way of stopping her.

Eduardo made a resolution never again to commit even a fragment of his future—a vow he'd made and broken before many times, resulting more often than not in this sort of resentment. He thought perhaps what he'd do was not answer the door when Elaine Baine-Brice buzzed. He imagined her in her limousine, headed toward him, anticipation squeezing her, visions of various erotic possibilities accumulating. That's what his eyes and attention had promised her. So she wasn't really to blame. She was merely on her way to collect.

For no reason, he went from his bedroom up to the next floor, the highest one, his studio. Eduardo's house was like a rich cake with three layers of elegant living topped by one immense white room where he worked. He had replaced the original roof with framed frosted glass panes that could be opened electronically or covered if he wished by horizontal drapes that were also automatic. The floor was white Spanish tile, shining. At one end of the room was what served as a couch: a specially ordered mattress and box springs twice the size of king size. It was covered in basic yellow and had at least thirty puffy pillows on it, from small to giant. Near that was a sheer wall of hidden accommodations that mere touch revealed: refrigerator, hot and cold sink, amply bottled bar, food closet, biggest color television, truest hi-fi, and record storage. Altogether, the place was independent and immaculate. There were no paint spills on the floor or smudged cans and bottles around. All the tools of Eduardo's art were neatly cleaned and put out of sight when not in use.

Except the easel.

The easel was specifically constructed taller and heavier than necessary. It was made of two-by-fours lacquered slick white, about fourteen feet high and each of its three thick legs was inset with a noiseless roller for effortless mobility. The easel stood there in the filtered sunlight like an oversize camp replica of what it was supposed to be. It overpowered the canvas of normal proportions that was now on its ledge. The canvas had two converging wide swaths of cobalt blue on it, like a lopsided X anyone might quickly make with temper.

Eduardo caught on the blue X. He remembered he'd made

the first blue stroke with sincerity and how, twenty minutes later, apathy had speared through his concentration to make him erupt and cut across with the relinquishing second stroke. Now he thought about replacing that canvas with a fresh one. But he didn't. He retreated from the disturbance of it to the more comforting area where he made a gin on the rocks and sat on a corner of the yellow couch. The initial gulp of gin dissolved the old mucous flavor inside his mouth and made him want a cigarette. He put one to his lips and, going into a pocket for a match, also brought out the slip of paper with his assignment written on it. He unfolded the paper and dropped it on the floor between his feet. He lighted and looked down to read it:

Inside a cell
of a N.Y.C.
police station

He let the idea of it occupy him, as he swallowed more of the cold gin and felt his blood stream faster. The stimulation was from both the alcohol and the idea of doing someone in that unusual place. He'd never been in jail, even to visit, but he'd collected impressions of what jails were like from various visual aids such as television and movies and illustrated articles. He let his imagination run and it carried him to be barred from the world in what he thought was typical cold containment. At some point in past time his mind had connected imprisonment with martyrdom and that helped stimulate him more. In former centuries they always put artists in jail, he thought. Almost every effective one had been officially locked away for some time. Rembrandt came up as a perfect example. What had Rembrandt done? Nothing except be too poor to pay his debtors. History was redundant with such injustices. Eduardo was sure of that and felt a guilt because he'd never suffered so. But now was his chance. However, instead of joining the ranks of the great oppressed, he would, with one simple basic act, humiliate the oppressors once and for all. They deserved such ironic retribution as a good fucking.

The opportunity was obvious. It was there at his feet. He imagined Gauguin looking down at him and approving, amused. And all the others too.

The doorbell buzzed.

Eduardo knew it was Elaine Baine-Brice so he didn't ask, just shouted into the intercom for her to come to the top floor. He pressed the button that controlled the street entrance and in seconds he heard the elevator working.

For an effect he went to the center of the room and sat on the floor, his knees doubled up, his head bowed between them, his back to where she would enter. He heard the elevator open and her shoes on the tile for a few steps. He knew her eyes had found him, so, as planned, he didn't turn. She said a bright, slightly unsure hello, but he didn't respond. He continued his position. She walked a cautious walk around the right of him and paused, keeping distance. He knew this was unexpected, that she'd presumed a warm greeting awaited her and he had her off balance from the start.

She said his name with not much power.

He made her repeat it. Then he slowly, dramatically lifted his head to look her a look that said: Who are you? What are you doing here?

"Were you resting?" she answered, uncomfortable as an intruder.

"Of course not," he answered.

"What are you doing?"

"If you must know, I'm cooling off," he told her with obvious impatience.

"Oh."

He explained, "I'm letting my creative force descend to the common level. It's necessary."

"What happens if you don't?"

"I get sick."

"Really?"

"Oh, not sick as you know sick. It's a bisected feeling with my essentialness pitched high while my physical is on the ordinary lower plane. It's quite painful, like being overdosed with gravity." It was something he'd said many times before, but he made sure it didn't sound practiced.

"How do you feel now? You look all right."

"Only slightly sick but I'll get over it."

"I'm sorry. I caused it, didn't I?"

He stood up, sighing. "What time is it?"

"A little after one."

"Really?" He acted surprised. "I didn't realize. I thought it was early morning."

"You worked all night?"

He didn't answer, so she assumed yes. He asked her if she wanted a drink but not what kind. He went to get her gin over ice, easy and powerful. While he was doing that, she looked the place. She had anticipated a messy paint-flung atelier, crowded with canvases and temperament. She was examining the blue X on the easel when he returned. It looked simple enough to her, but she was sure it contained some extreme complexities.

"Is it finished?" she asked.

He parried the question. "Nothing ends," he said, wise. "Come sit down."

He led to the yellow couch. She sat with her knees together. He knew she was nervous. She was drinking the gin too fast.

"I have four of your works," she informed, thinking he'd ask which ones.

He wasn't impressed, said nothing.

"Three here in New York and one in Paris. The one in Paris is my favorite. I love it," she said.

He gave her his intense look.

She felt it and asked, "What's the matter?" Meaning, was something wrong with her, her appearance?

"I was appreciating you," he said, the usual explanation.

"Please don't. I was up too late last night. It probably shows."

"You didn't get enough sleep?"

"Not quite."

"There's a benefit to that."

"What do you mean?"

"Lack of sleep. At least not quite enough sleep makes the body more susceptible. To everything. You know the feeling?"

"Now that you mention it. Yes."

"Perhaps in such a stage the conscious is too tired to support habitual inhibitions. What do you think?"

"It's quite possible."

"What results is a sort of sensual lethargy. Have you ever felt that? From not enough sleep, I mean."

She didn't hesitate enough, he noticed. "I believe I have," she said.

"So all one has to do is permit, break down and through the meager tissue of any remaining restraint and let the senses receive."

"Sounds pleasant," she said.

"You must be uncomfortable sitting like that. Why don't you lean back on a pillow," he suggested, mixing concern with excuse.

The yellow couch was so spacious that in order to be propped by a pillow, she had to climb into its depths. She removed her shoes and did it.

"That feels better, doesn't it?"

"Yes," she said with some small settling moves. She handed her glass to him. He refilled it and brought it back to her. She expected him to share her position on the couch. He knew that, so he didn't. He just let her be there building herself, while he walked to the far end of the studio thinking about anything, for several minutes. Then, when he returned, she invited.

"Don't you want to relax with me?" she asked.

He took a moment to evaluate what he was about to get. She was a lot of clean blonde hair, a wealthy, pampered, pretty face, the twenty-five-year-old recently divorced darling of the daily and Sunday society pages getting her five-hundred-dollar dress wrinkled.

Through her want she saw him. He was not only a physically ideal specimen. There was also the artistic force she attributed to him, a superdimensional latency that was rare and sensitive, and she was about to reach it and be its beneficiary. He climbed across the couch for her. He wished it were jail.

After. After some sleep and some subtle approval from her in respect to his performance, she wanted to stay longer. But he used work as an excuse and while they dressed, promised the necessary encore soon. He went down to the street with her to make sure she got into her limo. He watched her out of sight, facing west where the sky was holding the going sun like a balloon with an orange light in it. He decided to walk the block that took him to the boundary of Central Park. Most others were leaving that green island and he went against the flow of them—mothers public mothering and fathers forced to carry. He went in and down to the large oval pond used by the children and the childish for sailing simple and complicated boats. He watched the testing of a dog by a man who threw a stick far out for the animal to plunge in and retrieve with much effort. The returned dog unclamped his jaws and dropped the stick at the man's feet, hoping for praise. But the man only picked up the stick and flung it again out to the water's middle, so the dog, already soaked and tired, had to paddle his paws furiously to it. Eduardo felt but decided it was insignificant cruelty and walked it off.

Up a hill and around the shoved-up shoulders of some rock. If it hadn't been for the high character of apartment buildings around the park he might have been lost. He stopped there. The sun was behind the west structures of the city but yet up and glowing the sky to tint everything more warm than bright. Below him was a wide shallow platter of grass speckled with dropped papers. Among them he saw the pink. It was a girl alone. She was on her back with her arms spread out, palms up. He watched her for some motion, but she remained still, the same for several minutes, and he thought perhaps there was something wrong with her. The idea that she might be unconscious, just left helpless in the green heart of this city of millions, was not so absurd. Live and let live is the code of the metropolis. But so is die and let die.

Eduardo went down the slight incline toward her, and when he was close enough he saw her eyes were shut. She was still in that same position, face up to the failing summer day sky. He went closer, alarmed. When he was less than a body length away he stopped and asked, "Are you all right?"

No response, no change.

He asked again louder and still got nothing from her. She looked unconscious limp. He kneeled and tried to see her breathing. He touched her wrist to find her pulse and she took it away from him.

"What do you want, creep?" she asked, her voice not quite as antagonistic as her words.

"I'm sorry. I thought you might be unconscious."

"Was I bugging you?"

"No."

"So like stop bugging me." She reshut her eyes.

That stepped Eduardo back, indignant. The ungrateful

bitch, he flared, and then controlled. He tried to nonchalant his anger and leave this nothing in the grass. However, her words had shrunk him. He sat down a few feet away to study her.

He saw the pink she was wearing was some woven cloth with two symmetrical designs of purple around the bodice. Definitely Indian. It ended above midthigh. She had on open raw leather sandals with tiny brass bells attached to the thongs. Her hair was stringy long, a natural color between brown and blonde. Horizontal and profile, as she was, it was difficult to appraise her face truly. She looked young. She looked pretty. But he wasn't sure. He was wondering how long she'd remain in her fixed pose, and why, when she rolled over on her side and elbowed her head up at him. She didn't say anything, just equalized his look with hers. He saw there was a painted green dot on her center forehead.

He smiled his best smile.

"It's a free park," he said to excuse his presence. He didn't expect an answer to that but got one.

"All the groovy things are free," she said.

She was extremely pretty, he saw. She had good bones. He guessed she was twenty.

"What were you doing? Really, you looked like you'd fainted or something." He said it with calculated soft concern.

She hesitated, obviously deciding to answer or not. "I was into my world thing," she told him.

"Solving world problems, I suppose."

"No. Feeling the world. Feeling it."

"You mean the grass, the earth underneath you?"

"More than that. The world goes around, man. It spins. Dig?"

He nodded his knowing and thought, what a simple child she is.

"It goes around thousands of miles an hour. Mind told me."

"Who told you?"

"Mind. One of my friends. He knows about everything. Just ask Mind and like he'll lay it on you."

"So you were trying to feel the world turning. Is that it?"

"Not trying, man, I *was* feeling it. Most people are too

hung up on other things so they can't feel it. They don't dig feeling anyway."

He felt she included him.

"You want to try it?" she asked.

"Sure."

She instructed him to lie next to her, on his back so as much of him as possible would be in contact with the world. She told him to close his eyes and concentrate on making his body absolutely motionless. "If you can make that, you might reach the sensitive range," she promised.

She did it with him. She held his hand lightly while they both were on their backs, trying to feel the ride the world was giving them. He really did try, tried to concentrate, but was distracted by his breathing. He told her.

"Oh. I forgot to tell you. You've got to take real short breaths," she said. "Little shallow breaths. Dig?"

He did that and concentrated on the turning idea of the world he was on. For a moment he lost contact with all the complications of reality and thought he felt space moving past him, a subtle sweet friction. Only for a moment. He tried to continue the feeling, but his imagination rebelled and went up above the park meadow to see himself and her, hand in hand, outlined on the park, and all the city and all the way up for a climbing view of the country and finally the world, a variegated sphere with their existence indistinguishable. He opened his eyes to come back and glanced carefully at her. She was dead-still as before and he was sure she was feeling the tender spin he'd just briefly experienced. He envied her but he didn't interrupt. He waited, pretending, aware of her hand's touch.

She opened her eyes. "Did you feel it?" she asked.

"Yes."

"Really? You're not sending me up?"

"No. I felt it for a while."

"The more you do it the more you feel it," she informed. She took her hand back. They both sat up. It was almost night. The greens around them were nearly out of color. But it was summer and warm.

"We should get out of the park," he said.

"Why?"

"It's dangerous here at night."

"You afraid?"

"No," he lied.

"Neither am I," she lied.

They stood and without more talk raced the unsafe dark to the nearest street. It was his neighborhood and he headed for his house. She went along without asking about destination. The tiny bells on her sandals accompanied her steps, more of a rhythmic tinkle than ringing. It attracted passers who criticized her short dress that was less than mini length, barely below the rounds of her bottom.

He asked, "Where do you live?"

"Around the Village."

He noticed she had no purse. He wondered where she carried her money and thought perhaps in her bra until he looked and with the help of a streetlight saw the little straight-out juts of her nipples that said she wasn't wearing and didn't need one.

"How do you get home? By subway?" he asked.

"Sometimes. Today I walked."

"Really? That's more than seventy blocks. At least seventy." He'd never walked that far in the city.

"When I'm high it's a groove, walking," she told him.

He knew what she meant. "But you're not high now," he said.

"I was this morning when I walked up. I'm on naturals now." She looked at him. "You're straight, aren't you?"

"Straight?"

"Like you never dig dope or anything."

"Smoke pot, you mean?"

"For example."

"Once in a while."

"You're probably a booze dropper."

"I drink," he admitted.

"It's a bad scene."

"Everybody drinks."

"I know a lot of people who don't."

They were in front of his house then, stopped. He told her it was where he lived.

She looked up. "Which is your pad?"

"All of it."

"You've got a big family?"

"No. I live alone."

"Must be a drag," she said.

"I'm an artist," he volunteered.

She looked at his house again. All the artists she knew only owned paints and had trouble doing that. She doubted that he was really an artist. She decided it was just a send-up, but she didn't care.

"I'm Eduardo Brant," he announced.

"I've heard of you."

"Ever seen any of my work?"

"Sure."

"What do you think?"

"It didn't grab me."

That made him angry some, a spontaneous reaction that he controlled. "What's your name?"

"Grateful."

"Grateful?"

"Just Grateful."

Maybe it was because she didn't admire his work or maybe it was because she could feel the ride of the world and he couldn't. Anyway, for him it was now a small contest with her. "I'd like to paint you," he said. He'd used that excuse many times but hadn't done a promised portrait since the very early days when it had been necessary. He thought she'd be eager to do it. But she didn't react.

"I'd pay you for sitting," he added.

"Like how much?"

He inflated the figure for some reason. "Five hundred dollars," he offered.

"That's a lot of bread," she said, mostly to herself.

"Do you want to?"

She thought and said no.

"Why not?"

She told him, "Because you've got to be some kind of freak. That's how I read you. Like probably all you want is for me to stand around bare-ass so you can look for five hundred dollars."

"What I had in mind was a portrait, from here up." He indicated the proposed innocence on his upper chest and above.

"Why?"

"You've got an unusual face," he said.

"Now I know you're sending me up."

"I swear I'm not."

"For all that bread?"

"In advance."

"Man, your head's all fucked up."

"I wish you'd consider it."

"I've got to split," she said.

"Look, you know where I live. You think about the portrait and if you decide you want to do it come see me tomorrow morning. Okay?"

She didn't say anything, started away.

He went with her a ways. "I'll get you a taxi."

"I can walk."

He got out ten dollars. "Take a cab," he told her.

The ten was out of his hand and in hers so quickly it was a moment before he felt any victory. He watched her going and thought he'd reached her. An old truth he'd often used for false starts came up: For success just find a need and fill it. It applied. He immediately canceled out all her resistance, all her frank abuse, with the judgment that she really preferred the convenience of a taxi instead of the long downtown walk. It was significant. It was enough proof that she wasn't as different as she tried to seem. The same. All the same.

He was tasting a mixture of triumph and disappointment when an available taxi passed her. She didn't stop it with a wave. She ignored another at the corner of Madison, where she turned.

Eduardo hurried to the corner to make sure. He watched the pink that was her diminishing, block after block. She was already too far away for him to hear the bells on her sandals that delicately announced her, all the way to somewhere in the Village. All the way, saving the ten for a better, prettier trip.

Eduardo had to think about more important things than a captious hippie girl called Grateful. He had to get started on his assignment, so he went home and into action with the first idea that came to him. He telephoned the police to ask the address of their station nearest him. It was only a few blocks away, although he'd never noticed it.

He found it was a short narrow building tight between larger, higher ones—a three-story old brownstone with its first floor front renovated by steel and glass. Its exterior lights were green for some reason. He'd expected some sort of proud lighted sign, perhaps even a brilliant flashing one, but there were only official square letters painted on the entrance to let anyone know.

It was just preliminary reconnaissance for Eduardo to get the feel of the place. He knew there were precinct police stations throughout the city, and he assumed that, in typical government fashion, they would all be similar. He created an excuse and went in.

In there was a large room with a gray streaky patterned floor of asbestos tile, walked and scrubbed to death. There were some invincible metal chairs and a standing cigarette disposer that was black and smelly because it was always emptied but never washed. The main thing was the metal desk and the dark uniform that swiveled behind it. Desk Cop had little dull eyes and a big shined badge, and Eduardo's entrance didn't make him pretend to be busy.

Eduardo introduced himself along with his address. Desk Cop knew the famous name and turned on some life, picking up a ball-point pen and ripping a doodled page off a pad for a clean start.

"What's your complaint?" asked Desk Cop.

"Nothing serious," Eduardo told him. "It's just that I was nearby and I thought I should tell you."

"Yes, sir. That's what we're here for," snapped Desk Cop.

Eduardo said, "For the past few days I've noticed some rather strange-looking characters in the area around my house."

That made Desk Cop begin writing.

Eduardo continued, "Not that they're causing any trouble, actually, but they do seem to be—well, you know, paying a lot of attention to my place."

"Is that so?" The little eyes of Desk Cop condensed more with suspicion.

"And I thought perhaps it would be a good idea if I alerted you to the fact."

"You're absolutely right, sir."

"Never can tell what people might do." Eduardo smiled.

Desk Cop tried to smile back. "I'll inform the patrols in that area. They'll keep an eye on things."

"I'd appreciate it," said Eduardo. He looked around, especially at the two closed doors behind Desk Cop. He thought one must be the way to jail. "I've never been in a police station before," he said, friendly.

"No?"

"I must say it's not what I expected."

"Why? What did you expect?"

"I had the impression there'd be cells and things like that."

"We've got 'em."

"I'm sure you do."

"Upstairs, second floor. That's where the lockup is."

"I suppose it's just a lot of bars and prisoners," said Eduardo with obvious curiosity.

"We're not holding anybody right now."

"Isn't that unusual?"

"The van came about an hour ago and took all prisoners down to Main. If you want to see a jail you ought to go down to Main. That's really a jail."

Eduardo was about to ask Desk Cop about taking a fast tour of the lockup but the others came in.

They were two behind three.

The two were Short Cop with a nose like a picked red ball, and Tall Cop, who was a cold square face. Both had holstered revolvers and belts full of polished bullets.

The three were all long-haired. You could tell one was a girl because her blouse had bumps. Other than that she was not much different from her two lean companions. All had on the same low-hung trousers and toe-bursted sneakers and similar tops—a slick purple, a reddest red, and a bluest blue. They were all strung with beads that looked like common rocks.

Eduardo stepped aside for them.

Desk Cop opened a drawer and took out some printed forms.

Tall Cop announced: "A five twenty-eight and a six eleven. Time of arrest, ten-o-five. Place of arrest, Central Park South opposite Plaza Hotel."

"Names," demanded Desk Cop without looking up.

The girl answered. "Apple, Desota, and Dud."

"They your real names?"

"Yes."

Desk Cop sighed his impatience. "Which is Apple?"

"Me," replied the girl. "I'm Apple. That's Desota and he's Dud."

"Those first names or last?" asked Desk Cop.

"Both," she told him, serious.

Eduardo noticed that the apprehended three were more relaxed than their captors. The girl's voice was soft and her eyes were sort of vague and heavy and comfortable. Her silent companions were the same. Eduardo thought it incongruous. They were being arrested for some reason, but they weren't tough or insolent, frightened or pleading. It was as if they had fallen into the hands of an enemy they felt sorry for.

Short Cop told the official story. According to him, the three were involved in a bad act against three good owners of certain horse-drawn carriages who were standing, with their vehicles and animals, across from the Plaza fountain, awaiting customers, usually tourists, whom they drive through the park. "They fed some sort of narcotic to the horses," he said, hitting his nose with a knuckle.

"We gave them sugar cubes," said Apple with a generous smile.

"Something was in the sugar," said Tall Cop. "Probably LSD. The horses wouldn't move."

"Like, man, we weren't trying to fix a race," said Dud.

Desk Cop told them, crisp, "The first charge against you is cruelty to animals."

"Why?"

"The horses dug it," said Desota.

"They told you, I suppose?" asked Desk Cop, sarcastic.

"No, but they were smiling," said Apple.

"Look, man, those steeds wanted to be turned on," Dud explained.

"Anyone could see they were uptight from pulling all those squares around," said Desota.

Desk Cop announced, "Second charge against you is disturbing the peace."

"What peace?" asked Apple innocently.

No one bothered to answer.

"All right, empty your pockets," ordered Desk Cop. They did as told, made three separate piles of things that altogether were:

$1.67
2 subway tokens
3 Hershey kisses soft inside their silver from body heat
a false fingernail

a miniature turtle shell with "Runner 1963" painted on it in pink nail enamel

a piece of orange chalk

a piece of green chalk

3 packages of Tip-Top roll-your-own cigarette paper

1 pair wire-framed eyeglasses with lenses cracked into a pattern on purpose

an acorn with its top still intact

a comb missing four teeth

and a square of waxed paper folded to contain some gray-green shreds of dried leaves

Desk Cop unfolded the square of waxed paper with superior satisfaction; he examined it and then asked Dud, its owner, "Now what could that possibly be?"

"Oregano," said Dud.

Desk Cop, Short Cop, and Tall Cop smiled ensemble.

"Oregano," verified Apple.

Desk Cop smelled the stuff. Wet a finger to pick some up for a taste. He was visibly disappointed when he had to say, "Oregano."

Dud explained, "It's for pizza. They never put enough on, so I carry my own."

"Goddam nuts," clenched Desk Cop as he finished the forms that booked them.

"Don't worry," soothed Tall Cop with venom, "they're carrying something. Some pills or grass or something. We'll find it."

But Apple, Desota, and Dud didn't look concerned.

"Okay. Let's have the beads," instructed Desk Cop.

"Why?" asked Apple.

"Take off the beads," Desk Cop told them, hard.

Desota and Dud took theirs off. Apple kept hers. The policemen waited for her to obey, but she stared ahead passively, as if she hadn't heard.

"Let's have your beads, Miss," said Desk Cop.

"No," she said, meaning it.

"We'll have to take them," he warned.

To defend she wrapped fingers around her string of colored rocks.

Short Cop reached for them with a grab and got hold. She flinched, protecting. He tried to loop them over her head. She twisted away and then it was a small struggle, with Tall Cop stepping in to help.

The string broke. The colored stones flew and rolled the tile floor.

Strands of Apple's hair were over her face. Her fingers brushed them aside. She was crying. Tears were down her cheeks and her eyes were swamped. "You broke my love," she accused, with hurt coming through the cracks in her voice. "I promised to never take it off and you broke it. They weren't just ordinary beads. You pig bastards. They were love. Don't you understand?"

Short Cop tried to take her arm. He missed as she dropped to her knees and began picking up her stones. She crawled around and collected until strong hands forced her to stand.

They took the three through the door.

One of her stones, a pink one, had landed between Eduardo's feet. He reached down and got it.

Desk Cop was shaking his head in disgust.

Eduardo just asked him, "Why didn't you let her keep her necklace?"

"Yeah. And sometime during the night probably she'd have hung herself with it."

Eduardo had the pink stone in his fist when he went from there, away from the keepers of peace.

At home, in his bedroom, Eduardo had a late light supper of cold white chicken and cold white Chablis, especially prepared and delivered by his favorite expensive restaurant. As he alternately chewed and refreshed his mouth, he couldn't prevent thoughts of Apple and Desota and Dud. He saw them in hard cells and wondered, when they were searched, if anything had been found. He wondered what they were feeling now. Were they still as warm passive as before? Perhaps they were already asleep on cell bunks, or maybe they were on the floor pressed against the bars to be as close to one another as possible. Probably they were hungry and wishing for the three Hershey kisses that had been confiscated. They were very young, he thought, and immediately realized somehow, that they were much older, by a more accurate measure, than those policemen.

Those policemen, Eduardo tried to believe, were only doing their job. There was no personal resentment, no special cruelty in their attitude toward these people. But that made him see all the possibilities for injustice:

"Patrolman Somename, tell us what you found."

"I found four amphetamine pills."

"Where did you find these amphetamine pills?"

"Hidden inside Desota's belt."

"State exhibit marked A. Did you find anything else?"

"Yes, sir."

"Tell us what else you found."

"Three marijuana cigarettes."

"And where did you find these marijuana cigarettes?"

"In the underclothing of Apple."

"State exhibit marked B. Now tell us, Patrolman Somename, what else did you find?"

"I found two capsules of lysergic acid."

"Where did you find these two capsules?"

"They were concealed by adhesive tape on the back of the neck under the hair of Dud."

"State exhibit marked C."

"Guilty or not guilty?"

"Not guilty. Not guilty. Not guilty."

"Do you have anything to say before sentence is passed?"

"Only—well, like it's not true. We weren't holding anything. We were clean."

Eduardo stopped in the middle of a chew of chicken and remembered how Tall Cop had been so sure of finding something on them. Tall Cop was a solid number-one absolutely doubtless American lawman. Desota and Apple and Dud were suspicious young long-haired blemishes to the pure face of the Stars and the Stripes, typical troublemakers, irresponsible. But weren't they also floaters on a cloud of higher heaven than earth, feelers of warm depths and infinite ascension, askers of all the free of the country which always promised?

Eduardo wondered where they would put them after guilt was pronounced. Was there a special place for their kind? Probably. He was sure it wouldn't be a place of acorns and sweet Hershey kisses or walk anywhere and far as you want.

Walk.

She'd walked, that honest rider of the world, that Grateful one. She had.

How much alike they were. Grateful and Apple, and, now that he thought of it, all the girls of that element. They were all transposable. They all had a special kind of tensile confidence in their movements and stands. It said they knew they were humans more emphatically than it tried to prove they were girls, and that somehow magnified their sex. And the message was the same whether they were covered with trousers or skirted just below the boundary of extreme exposure. They were different from the females usually encountered by Eduardo. Take off the clothes and regiment the breasts and triangle of crotches and they were still different. The girls of Eduardo's past and present and the future ones to enter all transmitted a primary weakness that was, in its traditional feminine way, protected by an intentionally pregnable wall. The game was catch-me-if-you-can with a parenthetical whisper reassuring success. Eduardo knew well how to play that game and had climbed wall after wall to reach the fair in their chambers of guilt. Each time it was only a temporary rescue.

But these hippie girls wore their crotches like medallions. They stirred the air with them. They met you eye to eye and center to center simultaneously. They seemed to bypass all the usual prerequisites, or was it only that their qualifications for admission were unique?

Of course, Eduardo wasn't just now discovering the hippies. He'd noticed them. His eyes had stolen from their legs and shown thighs. He'd seen them boy and girl, public walking, locked by what looked like love. But he'd never talked to one before Grateful. Not that he'd avoided them. He merely considered them an isolated minority, living opposite him. His acquired opinion was the general one. Hippies were selfish, unproductive, dirty, drug addicts, who were just one notch above or below the lost alcoholics of Skid Row. They went against the grain of America. They protested everything to get attention. They were not to be taken seriously. They were too young to know any better, but someone should teach them a lesson. Someone should cut their hair and make them clean up and send them back to wherever they came from.

Eduardo emptied his glass of Chablis into him and poured more, while he verified that he felt about hippies the same as most normal people. They had to be as dirty as they looked, as ignorant as they looked, irrational, alien, and impudent. And he included Grateful with her delusion of world-riding and Apple and Dud and Desota, who more likely than not were laden with concealed narcotics when properly arrested.

Eduardo decided he was giving them more thought than they deserved, a waste of emotional energy, so he shut them off. He took his Chablis and went across the room where there was a glass case he opened to let his eyes enjoy the romantic delicacy of numerous antique trifle boxes. Tiny expensive things he'd collected. All were finely worked, rare enough, decorated with various declarations, mostly pertaining to truth and love. He read his favorite that was scrolled in French:

If desire is the fruit of love,
Let us an orchard be.

He closed the case. He shut off the lights and opened the full windows. He took off his clothes and sat nude, listening to the variables of the city: the hurry of a siren, a fragment of shout, the wheeling hum of cars on streets. He wondered how Arnie and Knight and Rog were doing. He wondered if it had been as good as expected for Elaine Baine-Brice. She was a new one. She qualified. He could give it to her again in jail if there was some way to get into one together. He tried to think of some way other than getting arrested.

"Tell you what, baby, let's spend the night in jail together."

"Let's make your cells and my cells cellmates."

That's how absurd it was. Besides, Elaine Baine-Brice and jail were an impossible combination. He eliminated her and tried to remember if he had any other unlaid prospects. When he couldn't think of even one, he knew he'd have to pull someone new, and soon. He promised to do that tomorrow. He'd go along Madison into small galleries perhaps, or into the Whitney where he'd been successful several times with stimulated art lovers.

But connecting wasn't the problem, really. Getting in there was. Getting in there with someone for time enough to do the thing right. He hadn't expected it to be simple, but now he realized it was very, very complicated. So complicated that his imagination avoided the obstacles to have him already locked in and locked into her and maybe not on the cell bunk because it had noisy springs but on the floor with their excitement so intense they couldn't feel the cold and the hard underneath them. His knees would be hurt, he thought, but immediately prevented that and made a courteous point at the same time by volunteering for the bottom position.

Go, baby, go, he mentally encouraged, while she did.

That, my Grateful one, he thought, is what's known as really riding the world.

He got into bed, between the best kind of sheets. He was tired. He put a hand down to hold his soft center. His fingers were a diligent tender cup that assured him to sleep.

By nine the next morning he was trying to work. There was a fresh stretch of canvas on the easel, waiting to receive the paint that could transform it from blank to precious. Eduardo squeezed worms of color onto a new palette, selected a brush, and contemplated the vacant rectangle.

Today he felt the need to paint. Not the great absolute urge. He hadn't felt that in months, and for months prior to those months the big thing hadn't come to him often. But today he had a beginning in him. Just a meager opening, the smallest possible, microscopic. However, it was more than he'd felt in a long time and he was thankful for it. His eyes went for an undistracted swim in the white infinity confronting him, while he sent his concentration deep to help dilate the opening if it could.

Before, even in the beginning, whenever he faced a new canvas, every measure of his being was a wide, swift, nonstop passage for expression. The hand was the instrument with the brush, the eyes the guide, and the sensibilities crowded out of him, the next pushing the next, filling canvas after canvas with pure impetuous colors and forms that were truly care and pain, fruition and anxiety, vigor and sweet lassitude. Any emotional ingredient, no matter how abstract, he easily translated into substances that were extensions of himself, valuable.

Appreciation came early. Recognition came with it. They bought him, bid for him, hung him where eyes could come from an adjacent Monet or a Picasso to be on him. And it all happened without struggle, during his young life, so the rewards of fame and wealth were tasted full flavor. They titled him genius, and he believed it. He painted painting after painting, and they bought them away almost before they were dry, and even, in one instance, before he was finished. He let them go, believing in his perpetuity, the spring that was too deep and clear and fresh ever to empty.

What he hadn't anticipated was death, the premature death in life that is often inflicted on those who take time in double doses, those who gorge themselves with feeling and vomit and gorge and vomit, until the deadening. Only a fear at first but soon a deepening disease that one day becomes an unexpected block and then frequent inability and then total constriction.

Eduardo was a living example of such dead. Some, the most expert eyes, knew it. But most didn't.

Of course, since his death he'd continued to paint, hoping. And they still bought as eagerly as before, but he knew all they were buying now was his signature in the right-hand corner of anything. Ironically, the more he practiced this sort of fraud the tighter his death grew.

The luxury from the money from the work had killed him. And the most plentiful of all luxuries had been the principal weapon. Women. They came and took and wounded. They asked him to spend and spend until he felt nothing. They were not satisfied with simple sharing. Each of them wanted to digest his original force and used the mouths of their faces and their similar lower mouths for incessant attempts. No one ever succeeded. They all did. They devoured him by nibbles. They, piece by piece, corrupted the enchantment out of him.

He could have prevented it, had he not found it so pleasant. That was probably the most destructive part of it. He loved every minute of it. To Eduardo, a woman was the same as a canvas, a new surface, even more tractable, upon which he could stroke and dab and smear his feelings. They demanded technique and improvisation and, also like his paintings, they were let go when he decided he was finished. It went on and on and on, erotic repetition that continued to test him. Even after his living death, with them he could perform and maintain his sensual reputation. However, his mouth and finger and center, he realized, were collectively reduced to the same sort of mere residual significance as his signature in the lower right-hand corner.

But now he was yet young and he'd just recently read in an art journal that one of his paintings had been transferred from some owner to another for six figures.

"Oh, an early Brant," someone now remarked in the salon of a billionaire. "You must have paid a fortune for it."

Now he was the most fashionable painter alive.

Now, right now, he faced another new canvas, trying desperately to influence that pinpoint of feeling into opening. It was like reaching down through boiling ache hoping to retrieve something as unsubstantial as a particle of light. He stood fixed for many minutes, hand ready, prepared, and just as he was about to concede, the pinpoint dilated. It expanded into a swelling that overgrew his limits.

He quickly shoved bristles into orange that he gave to the canvas. It started with a simple round of orange and went on, went on fast with brush and knife and thumb, balancing delicately as required. This for love, that for hate, special allotments that finally gave a subtle advantage to the ideal of devotion. He knew what it was from the start of it. His unconscious was a spectator sitting atop his head like a seeing hat.

It was Apple and her broken beads, Apple crawling at the feet of hostility that had scattered her love all over the police station floor. It wasn't finished, but it was finished enough so he couldn't lose it. He stepped back, appraising, and knew it was good. As good as anything ever. It was there in the filtered sun, proof of his resurrection.

He felt like leaps.

He felt some song, any song.

He felt the want to run a ring around the room.

He went to reward himself with some gin over ice, and as he fixed it, he glanced several times at the canvas to make sure it was still there. It was. It was real and he was Eduardo Brant, the.

When Grateful didn't arrive that morning, Eduardo gave up on her. Despite his judgment that she was merely one of those hippie undesirables, he felt lightly disappointed that she'd decided against his proposition. Of course, that made him more glad to see her when she did arrive that afternoon around three.

She had on the same pink dress and belled sandals. The only change was no blue dot on her forehead and more eye makeup than yesterday. There was someone with her.

"This is Cherokee," announced Grateful. Cherokee was taller. She was wearing a tank shirt of blue and orange horizontal stripes and her skirt was more than short enough to exaggerate her long legs. So tall, and dressed as she was, she looked like a doll that had been stretched in a battle for possession. She had black hair, long black, and cheekbones high prominent, so her face was attractively concave left and right. Eduardo liked her looks.

"Cherokee?" he questioned her name. "Are you really?"

"A third," she told him. "And a third Sioux. The other third something or other."

Eduardo wondered how she calculated the thirds. "You brought her for protection, I suppose," he said to Grateful.

"No."

"I'd dig something to drink," said Cherokee.

"I'm having gin," said Eduardo.

"Got a Seven-up or a Fresca?"

Eduardo got them icy plain drinks. They took them and sat on the floor. Their skirts climbed for him to see white covered crotches. They didn't try to conceal any more than they were trying to show. He sat across from them. "About the portrait," he began.

Grateful interrupted. "Like, man, forget it."

"That's what you came for, isn't it?"

"We were around, just walking," said Grateful. "I know the portrait thing was a send-up."

"Maybe it was," he admitted.

"All we came for was to be someplace," Grateful told him.

Eduardo got up and when he returned with a large pad and a fist of charcoal pencils he saw Cherokee lighting the little end twist of a well-rolled marijuana cigarette. He understood then that they'd come to get in out of the public. Cherokee took two long noisy inhales and held while she passed to Grateful for her to do the same.

"You don't mind if I sketch you, do you?" he asked.

They shrugged permission. Grateful offered the marijuana at him.

"I'm on gin," he refused, but nicely. And while they passed back and forth until the cigarette was so short a stub it had to be burning their lips, Eduardo worked with the charcoal pencils, capturing various fragments of them: the lovely imperfect nose of Cherokee and one of her large dark eyes, quick impressions of both their physical attitudes sitting as they were, Grateful's mouth performing its slightly open kiss shapes around the thin shaft of marijuana. All the while there was no talk. He noticed that Cherokee had excellent long fingers and the nail of each was enameled red, white, and blue stripes. She must have spent hours doing it.

Grateful pointed with her chin. "That's dynamite," she said. She meant the new painting.

"I thought you didn't like my work."

"I dig that." She got up and went close to it and backed off to see it better.

Eduardo asked her what she saw.

She told him exactly.

He was surprised. An Elaine Baine-Brice would have probably said a sunset. Eduardo tore off the page of sketches he'd done to have a blank. He hadn't sketched in years, he realized, and was glad he was still good. Grateful looked at the sketches. She didn't say she liked them but he thought her eyes approved. She dropped them in front of Cherokee who asked, "Can I have them?"

He told her yes.

"I wish I could draw," said Cherokee.

"You probably do something else just as well," he said, kind.

"She makes pipes," informed Grateful, sitting again. "Real dynamite pipes."

"What kind of pipes?"

"For hash. She sells them to friends."

"I don't make any bread on them," said Cherokee.

"She only charges for the materials," said Grateful. "Everybody digs Cherokee's pipes."

"Why don't you charge more?" Eduardo asked.

"I don't do it for bread, man."

"How long does it take you to make such a pipe?"

Cherokee thought and told him, "Sometimes a week, sometimes a night. It depends."

"She does it for love," said Grateful. "When she really digs someone she shows it by making them a pipe."

Eduardo had never given a painting to anyone. Cherokee was looking at his sketches again. Eduardo felt like doing more and asked them if he could.

"Do us together," Cherokee suggested.

"If you want," he said.

Cherokee slid closer to Grateful who tucked herself into the arm of the taller girl and let her head fall against her shoulder. Eduardo began but had to stop when Cherokee broke the position. Without announcement Cherokee pulled her shirt up and off so the upper half of her was all bare. Then they went back to the pose.

They were lovely together and Eduardo sketched as quickly as possible to get it. He saw it as peaceful passion, fragile connection of two young creatures of feeling exempt from modern moral superimposition. He drew them like that, with Cherokee's breasts taut as they were, pointing a certain experienced purity.

Cherokee, lean and subtly primitive, surely strong enough to hold the light loving weight of Grateful, who had her eyes closed while Cherokee looked straight ahead with wide, rather arrogant innocence. He thought of Courbet and Klimt and knew he was trespassing their lands. When he was through he put the sketch on the floor for them to see but they didn't jump out of the pose. They came out of it slowly, almost unwillingly.

"Can I have this one?" asked Grateful. "I dig it a lot."

"No. I want to paint it," he said, true. It would be different from anything he'd ever done. He wanted to do it for himself.

Grateful didn't hide her disappointment, looked angry.

"I need it as a preliminary sketch. Then you can have it," he promised, to please her.

Inside her smile she got up and asked, "Don't you have any sounds?"

"You mean music?"

"Yeah. This place is like a tomb."

He got up and showed her where the hidden hi-fi was. He turned it on and pressed another part of the wall open to show her several hundred long-plays in their jackets. She read the titles, while he got a new drink of gin and returned to Cherokee, who was lying back now, bareback to the cool tiles, her nipples tiny brown towers on twin skin hills.

She aroused him but without trying. He wanted to say something to her; however, he couldn't think of anything perfect.

Music started at normal level. Grateful made it louder so it wasn't just a spear of sound but more of a whip that snapped its beat around them. Grateful danced with her head down so her hair fell to swish, her body mixed around moves with sharp breaks of punctuation by her crotch, while her arms conducted their own interpretation. She had her eyes shut. She wasn't dancing for him. Only for herself. She didn't stop until the music did. Then she sat down near Cherokee, who was still horizontal. She looked down at her. She touched with a finger across Cherokee's concave stomach, lightly over her navel as if she were trying either to erase or confirm it.

Eduardo wondered if they were physically involved all the way with one another. He thought so. He got up and lowered the music. He took some extra time doing it with his back to them, giving them a chance, hoping that when he turned around they might be more together. But when he turned, Cherokee was rolled over, pressing the clean tiles with her front, and Grateful was enjoying an ice cube from her glass, sucking it in her mouth and taking it out quickly as if it were too hot. Grateful's lips were reddened wet and her fingers were dripping.

"Are you lovers? You and Cherokee?" he asked.

"We love each other," Grateful told him.

"Do you make love?"

"We touch sometimes. Sometimes it's groovy to just touch." She looked over to Cherokee. "I guess we are sort of hung on each other."

"I think so," he commented, trying to communicate that he didn't condemn it.

"You think it's freaky," Grateful said, "but it's just when you get high, like you want to love, and if you're with somebody you dig you just have to."

"You're high now, aren't you?"

She read him. He wasn't cool enough not to read. She knew what he wanted was a scene. "Yeah," she said, "but you're not."

"What difference does that make?" Eduardo was encouraged by her last answer.

Grateful saw him as straight as he was. She decided to put him down. "Would you dig balling with us?"

"Very much."

"Then, like, shit, man, why don't you ask?"

"All right. How about it."

"It? What is it?"

"The three of us."

"Do what?"

"Make it together."

"You still haven't told me what *it* is. Like, shit, man."

He realized she was playing a game with him. It was sort of amusing. He pretended to be angry. "To hell with you."

"Hey, man, don't get up-tight."

"We were only sending you up a little."

"You probably send birds up all the time."

"Don't you?"

"Never," he lied, continuing his act, looking hard.

"Like right now. You're not really up-tight."

"How do you know?" he asked.

"We hope you're not, that's all."

"Why?"

"Because we were grooving with the drawings and everything and like we dig being here."

He had to smile.

It was what they were waiting for. The signal. They both began laughter. Cherokee rolled over and over and Grateful doubled up laughing. They laughed a lot and then it was reduced to sporadic giggles. Eduardo also had to laugh some, but not as much.

"Hey," shouted Cherokee. "I've just thought of a dynamite name for him."

"What?"

"Straight Man."

"Straight Man," repeated Grateful, approving.

Eduardo thought perhaps they were ridiculing him.

"I dig Straight Man," said Cherokee, meaning him, not the name. She seemed serious.

"Straight Man ought to turn on and relax," advised Grateful.

Eduardo liked them, more now. Now they were all past the physical and into what might be something closer. He liked the way they'd avoided him, playfully.

"Did you walk uptown today?" he asked.

"We took the subway."

"There was a guy on it with a telephone."

They laughed, remembering.

"He had this red phone, a real one, and, like, the wire was stuck down into his trousers."

"We watched him. He dialed and everything and then he

started shouting and swearing like he was really giving somebody a hard time.''

''I think he was talking to his joint.''

''It looked like it.''

''It was freaky.''

Eduardo imagined and said, ''I wonder what number he dialed?''

''Eight one eight two eight three,'' Cherokee invented, clever.

Grateful did an imitation with an invisible phone. ''Hello, is that you, joint? Well, I just want to tell you you're not as big as you think, see. And don't hand me any of this you've-been-up-all-night shit. I know exactly where you're at. What's that? Who's a jerk? You got balls talking to me like that, you little good-for-nothing. Next time you come when I call you. Understand? Don't you dare hang up on me. Okay, so short, I mean, so long.''

''And over in the park, how about the poodle?'' reminded Cherokee.

''Oh, Jesus, what a thing that was.''

Cherokee told it. ''There was this little square fat lady. She looked like she'd put her legs on upside down. She had this white poodle that was running around. And there was this guy sleeping on the grass, so the poodle runs up to him and sniffs and then raises its leg and pisses all over the guy's chest.''

''It was dynamite,'' verified Grateful.

Eduardo giggled with them.

''The guy said he was going to sue the lady.''

''He ought to sue the dog,'' inserted Eduardo.

''Yeah, he did it, not her.''

''Order in the court, order in the court,'' dramatized Cherokee. ''Little dog, did you piss on this man? Bark, Bark. That means yes, sir. Why did you do it? Bark, Bark. I didn't have my glasses on. Bark, Bark, Bark. I thought he was a hydrant. Bark, Bark. He smelled like a hydrant.''

More giggles. Then some warm silence, just enjoying camaraderie. Eduardo felt almost included. He asked Grateful where she was from and thought she'd say someplace strange like San Diego. He thought she probably came from the middle of many brothers and sisters of a poor family with a bad father and a careless mother from whom she was escaping.

But she told him Hartford, Connecticut, and Eduardo asked more to learn that her father was an insurance executive and that Grateful thought he was a groovy guy and she dug her mother too who had fixed a room up for her in their new house. They had two cars, a boat, and three cats.

"Don't they want you to come home?" he asked.

"They don't push it."

"What do you do for money?"

"I don't have any bread. After I got out of school I worked for an insurance company for a while. I was a secretary. It was a drag."

"How do you live now without any money?"

"All the groovy things are free," she said as before.

"Don't you have to pay rent?"

"There's always someplace to flake out. Lots of people have pads." She studied the palm of her hand as if it were saying something. "I thought about getting a job. A friend of mine named Glorie just started to work. Know what she does?"

He asked her what with his attention.

"Guys paint her. Not real artists. Just guys, like mostly squares. She works in this studio where they come to paint her. You know, like they make designs on her skin, all over."

Eduardo imagined the sensation of brushes on her various places and wondered if she felt it. "No finger painting allowed, I suppose?" he said.

"I guess they try."

"Have you ever been painted like that?"

"Sure, but not for bread."

"Tell me, if you suddenly had a lot of money what would you do with it?"

She thought and told him. "I'd get a real dynamite pad where everyone could turn on and be there. Either that or I'd buy a farm and put a big fence around it so nobody could bug us, and like we'd grow our own stuff and live there."

Eduardo realized he could make it come true for her with just his annual winnings from the weekly pool game.

There was more silence, a sort of dip in the mood, down. A period that was the end of something. Grateful broke it. Cherokee was lying next to her, just listening with her high. Grateful bent to her and placed her lips on the tip of the right breast of Cherokee, who merely accepted it. It wasn't a short peck kiss. It was several seconds of lips enclosing all the nipple.

Eduardo thought Grateful did it for his benefit. But he was wrong.

When Grateful raised her head from Cherokee, her expression said look what I can do, while her voice exclaimed, "I'm hungry. I'd sure dig munching some candy or something."

Cherokee sat up and put on her top.

Eduardo asked them to stay for dinner.

During the delivered dinner, that was steak and baked potatoes and thick-sliced sweet tomatoes, there was a phone call. Eduardo excused himself to take it in the study. It was Elaine Baine-Brice.

"What are you doing, darling?" she asked, bright.

"Having dinner with some friends." The "darling" he took as a measure of his success the day before.

"That's too bad. I'm at Warner's for cocktails and bored to death."

"That's too bad," he echoed. He realized how much more comfortable he was talking to Elaine than with his other two guests. Elaine was his league. Something he could handle, more predictable. Not as exciting, perhaps, but more predictable.

"What are you doing late, after dinner?" she asked.

"Work," he lied.

"Oh. Couldn't I come over and watch?"

"If you came over the only watching would be in a special mirror I have just for that."

"Let me," she pleaded.

"No. I need to work."

"You can work after."

"I never feel like work after."

"Then why don't you work for a while and I'll come over later."

She really wants that encore, thought Eduardo.

He got an anatomical picture of her wanting center, a closeup. "Will you be home?" he asked.

"Yes. Call me there. I'll go home and take a nap so I'll be nice and fresh."

What about me, thought Eduardo.

She said, "Don't worry about the time, call even if it's two or three in the morning. You have my perfectly personal permission."

"All right," he said, feeling like an all-night service station. As an afterthought he asked, "By the way, Elaine, have you ever been in jail?"

"Jail?" she reacted. "Christ, no. Why do you ask?"

"What do you think about jails?"

"They're nasty places," she said. "What is this, some joke you want me to bite on?"

"No. But now that you mention bite, next time a little less teeth, huh."

"Was I that bad? Really?"

"You could use some lessons," he advised, knowing it would get to her.

"I'll show you," she promised and said an *à bientôt* with a *mon amour* attached to it before she clicked off.

When he got back to his steak it was cold, but he ate some. Cherokee and Grateful had eaten their plates clean.

"Can we look around your pad?" asked Grateful.

"Sure, help yourself," he told them, and they left him there eating and wondering if they might steal anything. He decided they couldn't because the way they were dressed there was no place to hide anything on them. What he should have known was that they wouldn't have stolen anything even if they'd had on magicians' coats. After several cold mouthfuls he buttered a roll and ate it on the way to finding them downstairs in the first guest bedroom.

"Sure is a dynamite pad," approved Cherokee, trying the blue velour chaise longue.

"Dig this bathroom," cried Grateful from in there.

Cherokee didn't want to move, she was so sunk comfortable.

"I ate too much," she said. She tested the chaise cushion with her fingers. "What's this filled with?"

"Goose down," he told her.

Grateful asked, "You know where the softest goose feathers come from don't you?"

"England?" guessed Cherokee.

"No. I mean what part of the goose."

Eduardo knew. Cherokee wanted to.

"The ass feathers are the best," informed Grateful.

"Did Mind tell you that?" asked Eduardo, remembering what she'd said about the know-it-all named Mind.

"No. I'm an expert on gooses and asses." She arched brows to make them laugh.

"We ought to split," said Cherokee.

"Will you come back to see me?" asked Eduardo. Part of him wanted them to leave, the part that wanted to call Elaine Baine-Brice.

"Sure. We'll be back, won't we, Cherokee?"

"Straight Man, I guarantee it."

"How about tomorrow?" he asked.

"Not tomorrow," they both said, quick.

"Tomorrow's the draft thing," Grateful told him.

He asked what the draft thing was.

Cherokee explained, "It's a protest. Tomorrow is Stop the Draft Day. We've got to make it."

"How about the day after tomorrow?" Eduardo asked.

"Maybe Friday."

"Not until then?"

"We'll probably be in jail until Friday," Grateful said, serious.

She'd just said the magic word.

"Jail?" he asked.

"The fuzz are all up-tight about tomorrow's protest. They'll bust a lot of us."

"Where are you going to demonstrate?"

"At the induction center where the draftees have to report, down on Whitehall Street."

"Last demonstration I got busted," said Grateful, proud of it. "And, like, this one's going to be dynamite."

They were on their way to leave. Eduardo had to lie fast.

"I'm against the draft," he proclaimed.

"Lots of people are," said Cherokee.

"I hate it," said Eduardo, stronger.

They nodded and went down the stairs. Eduardo followed.

"Vietnam is wrong. The draft is wrong. Everything is wrong," he shouted. Actually, he'd never bothered with politics, never. Politics just happened and as long as his life continued the same he didn't care. But he had to act more vehement. "Stop the draft!" he yelled, desperate. "Stop the war!"

That made them blink at him. He was so loud and emphatic. It was his opportunity. He told them, "I'd like to paint a sign for the demonstration. How about it? How about DON'T GO, STAY AND PLAY OR how about BALL, DON'T BOMB?"

They dug that. "Why don't you paint them and meet us down there tomorrow?" Grateful suggested.

"What time?"

"We'll be there at dawn."

"That early?" He saw Elaine Baine-Brice fading from possibility. But this was more important. "Where shall I meet you?" he asked.

They shrugged. "We'll look for you," promised Cherokee. Eduardo got a better idea. "Why don't you stay here and we can go down there together in the morning?"

"You mean flake out here?"

"Sure, why not? You can sleep in the guest room," he assured, and persuaded. "The one with the pretty bath."

"Want to?" Grateful asked Cherokee.

"Might as well. Guide's pad's going to be crowded tonight, and Owsley's got all those heads in from Philadelphia. Like we'll be lucky to find a place."

"We could stay at Glorie's," said Grateful.

"Not anymore. I saw her yesterday. She got thrown out."

"I'd sure dig a bath," said Grateful.

"Me too," said Cherokee.

"I'll do the signs while you soak," said Eduardo.

"No," said Grateful.

"No," said Cherokee. "We want to make the signs too."

They helped him make the signs on stretched linen canvas. They got paint all over the studio tiles and their hands, red and blue. They took their baths with more than enough Dior bath oil, hot hot baths that made them weak. They were fast asleep fast.

Eduardo didn't call Elaine Baine-Brice. He thought about it but didn't for self-preservation. He took the phone off its cradle. He thought about what he should wear for the demonstration. He didn't want to look too straight, so he chose a pair of slacks and hung them in his shower for the steam to uncrease them, and when they were still damp, he bunched them up and threw them on the floor and kicked them around some. He picked out a shirt, cut its sleeves off and tore off a couple of buttons. For shoes he had some Italian canvas ones for sailing that he rubbed on the exterior of the building outside his bedroom window to give them some proper New York City dirt. Then he went to a mirror to muss his hair a different way, seeing if it could look longer.

It was dawn exactly when Eduardo, Grateful, and Cherokee arrived downtown. They had to walk three blocks with their signs because the taxi driver refused to take them closer. Eduardo saw why when they approached Whitehall Street, where the demonstrators were gathering.

Eduardo had expected perhaps a hundred there, not the thick, huge crowd they had to weave and push through. Actually, there were more than two thousand demonstrators. Also, five thousand police. Eduardo was a bit frightened by the unexpected scope of the thing, but for calm he told himself that it was a nonviolent protest and all the police were there only to make sure it was.

Most of the demonstrators, Eduardo noticed, were hippie types, long haired and young, as many birds as boys. Most were just milling around, greeting one another rather seriously. Some were in small groups, talking, not loud. Then, as if some signal had been given, the demonstrators moved into position. They massed on the sidewalk and sat down. The entire block was crowded with so many sitters that the sidewalk couldn't hold them, and hundreds overflowed onto the street, violating the boundary of wooden police barriers placed along the curb especially to prevent that.

Eduardo was just one of them. He made sure he didn't get separated from Grateful and Cherokee, who had joined a few of their friends. Eduardo was introduced but was so distracted he didn't hear names. He automatically offered his hand for a shake but all he got was a quick sliding of handskin across his, which he accepted as symbolic of something to them. His position was right on the curb with a wooden barrier at head level. Sitting there, he had a choice. He could either stay behind and see nothing but a close-up of gray painted wood or he could hunch under to be beyond the official perimeter. He did the latter like so many others. In front of him were hundreds sitting the street, tight together. Two were leaning against his legs. They were a fat bird with dandruff and a pretty blonde attached to the boy next to her. Eduardo saw the blonde had a tattoo on her upper arm. He wondered if it was real. It looked permanent enough. It said: LOVE IS FREE in a heart held by two fat-bellied cherubs. She also wore a hat stuck with a button that said: TO GO TOGETHER IS BLESSED, TO COME TOGETHER IS DIVINE. That made Eduardo look more at her, wondering if her verbal display was based on experience or hope.

Grateful elbowed him. "Hold your sign up," she told him. He held it high and imagined the police reading it. The police were everywhere. There was a thick string of them across the street with shining badges and baby blue helmets. Each carried a nightstick. There were also numerous mounted police on chestnut horses with NYPD in golden yellow on the corners of their saddle blankets. They backed and snorted and reined up and down the street. The police were also above in a pair of official helicopters that spun and hovered over the area, radios connected to the ground forces.

Everyone seemed to be waiting for something.

What they were waiting for soon arrived. It was a group of young men carrying satchels and small suitcases. The young men were walking double file, flanked left and right by a solid line of policemen. Eduardo thought they looked like prisoners, the way they were guarded. They were the draftees, coming to go. They were headed for the entrance of the building, but before they got there, the police barriers were disregarded and demonstrators blocked the way, a deep surge of them. The draftees looked embarrassed, having to stand there.

A chant started and grew. "Don't go. Don't go. Don't go," the demonstrators tried to discourage with encouragement.

A magnified voice blasted over the chant. A police lieutenant with a battery-powered bullhorn. "Move back from the entrance," he ordered. "Move out of the way. Move back. Move back."

The blocking demonstrators were parted by a spearhead of police who went into them with menacing looks and nightsticks ready. They forced a passage. The draftees entered the induction center. Eduardo realized they had to. There was no other direction for them to go. For them it was one way, all the way. Maybe they want to be drafted, Eduardo thought.

The chant ended. Eduardo told Grateful's ear, "They didn't stop the draft."

She didn't comment, because another chant began. This time it was, "Stop the draft. Stop the draft." Over and over and over. Eduardo had to contribute his voice. He felt loud. Grateful and Cherokee were screaming it. They looked over to Eduardo and nodded approval. The chant was like a flame under the police. Also opposite were some ordinary men, about forty or fifty of them, some with signs that said: BOMB THE COMMIES and FIGHT FOR RIGHT.

Most of these were longshoremen, who had themselves sat down on America many times, trying to get more per hour. Perhaps for expiation, now they were on the other side, fisting, flexing, taunting the sitters with threats that were dirty. Their hate was fed with those few demonstrators who had straggled from the main body and some who were arriving late. The longshoremen muscled and roughed them, punched them down, while the police stood by inactive, as if these were invisible battles. There were several unequal skirmishes, and one beaten demonstrator was thrown out into the street, with his face flowing blood. He tried to crawl across to his friends and some sitters got up to help him, but were immediately surrounded by police, who acted as if they were being attacked.

Those were the first arrests. Eduardo couldn't miss seeing it. It happened directly across from him. The unfairness of it gritted him, as it gritted all the others, but he covered it with his neutrality. What he then felt more than anything else was the desire to disengage himself from all this oversize drama.

He didn't care about the draft. As far as he was concerned, they could stop it or start it or shove it. It was not what he was there for. He had anticipated a harmless little demonstration that might possibly get him temporarily into jail with a bird. But this was full-scale opposition with hostility and defiance filling the air and expanding every moment. It had already drawn blood. He decided to hell with it. Maybe he looked like he'd chosen a side but he hadn't. Maybe he looked involved but he wasn't. He thought he'd just get up and leave. In order to do that he would have to wade the sitting pack in front of him. That was the fastest way out.

The chant of the demonstrators seemed more emphatic now, tribal. Just being there was adequately antagonistic, without irritating taunting violence with a chorus of opinion. Eduardo saw another stray demonstrator in the middle of shoves and hits by the longshoremen across the street, where the police didn't notice. It was a thin long-haired young man, who managed to escape, but not before he was beaten enough to be bleeding. Eduardo saw him run staggering to collapse among his own, who grumbled inside their chant. Some hippie shouted "Let's get the pig bastards."

That made Eduardo stand. He pushed his legs through the wedges of sitters until he was out of them. He heard some shouts behind him, "No, no, no," and he thought they were opposing his desertion, asking for loyalty. All Eduardo wanted to do was separate himself from them and hurry to some nice neutral street for a taxi to get him home. The police would help him, he thought. He started toward them.

Quick rear motion made him look left just in time to see the danger of high horses, trampling. He jumped aside but was brushed by flanks that spun him. He managed not to fall. News photographers focused on him and clicked. The motors of motion picture cameras were triggered to preserve the action. Eduardo was in a confusion of horses, a maze of heavy animals with perilous hooves clopping close. He dodged hurt. He saw an opening and got through it to be met by a half dozen policemen. He wanted to tell them he was neutral, but his voice didn't get out of his mouth before they grabbed and twisted him. He realized then that he was still carrying the sign and let it drop. He didn't resist but their roughing made him look struggling. His arm was forced behind him and turned with pressure that hurt. The pain made him react. He stumbled against the chests and shoulders of uniforms and flipped forward to break their hold.

It was then that he realized Grateful and Cherokee were mixed with the police around him. He saw dark blue arms clinching Cherokee, who was trying to kick shins. Grateful was also captured tight, held from behind, wiggling resistance. She lowered her head and clamped a sharp bite on the forearm of her captor, who had to release. Another tried frontal aggression on her and she took care of him with a bull's-eye kick in the groin that lifted him and bleached his face and doubled him. But the next who came at her used his nightstick for a short glancing hit that cut down the side of her head. She crumpled down.

Eduardo's intentions were lost in the violence of Grateful and Cherokee. Now it was not merely a matter of capturing him. Although he had his hands down and was only trying to retreat from the action, they included him in the fury. Nightsticks whizzed around his head. It was as if they were dueling to be the one to fell him. Wood hit wood and there was even a miss that followed through all the way to above the ear of a policeman, who dropped to the street. Outside the scuffle, it looked like Eduardo had done it. One nightstick whacked his shoulder. He buried his head in his arms for protection and the wood beat on his knuckles, splitting. He fell in defense and pretended unconscious. Down there he was in the lowland of round-tipped black city shoes, and through a forest of blue-trousered legs he saw Cherokee also down and being punished by the angry swing of an official foot. Eduardo hoped they didn't kick him. He knifed his legs up for protection. He was aware that his cheek was on the dirty street.

In moments they were lifting him. They carried and threw him like a sack into a van. Grateful and Cherokee were already in there, rubbing their wounds. Eduardo realized both his hands were bleeding and Grateful's hair was bright with blood. She touched it to bring down red fingers.

"The pigs," mumbled Grateful.

"The pig bastards," agreed Cherokee, holding her side.

"You all right?" Grateful asked him.

He nodded. "What happens now?"

"Jail," Cherokee told him.

Well, at least that's something, thought Eduardo, although he felt numb all over, incapable. "Just us?" he asked.

She didn't have to answer because the back door of the van was opened and other demonstrators were tossed in, one after one, until the compartment was overloaded.

On the bumping fume-breathing way to jail, Eduardo was between Grateful and Cherokee. He hung his head and tried to concentrate sense into his body. Cherokee's hand soothed the back of his neck. He received it for a while, hoping it might help, and it did, a little, at least to the extent that he could feel the existence of his center. When he looked up, Grateful put her lips to his ear. "You're dynamite," she told him and kissed him a soft promising cheek kiss. Eduardo looked across and two long-haired boys displayed their approval of him with a single cool nod.

"Straight Man, you've really got guts," said Cherokee to

him. She had her arm around him and his shoulder felt one of her breasts against him voluntarily.

More than five hundred demonstrators were arrested that morning. Only a few showed any active resistance. All the others merely defied the police order to disperse. They knew, of course, they would be arrested and they neither fought nor accommodated it. They just went limp where they were and forced the police to carry them to the vans. The police often got some revenge by allowing the deadweight bodies to sag and bump the street, bruising. But it was inadequate retaliation for the work forced upon them.

At the jail most of those arrested made a comedy of it. For the official record they gave such names as Mickey Mouse and Orphan Annie and Lyndon Bird. But they weren't boisterous. Actually, they were polite and submissive toward the interior police, who were more indulgent than their stick-wielding outside counterparts. The interior police joked and expressed serious and sometimes sympathetic comments regarding the reason for the demonstration and were generally not impatient. Evidently they had expected a mass arrest. They had prepared mimeographed forms along with a special system to care for the hundreds. The prisoners were divided into groups of twelve to fifteen. One officer was put in charge of each group and he acted more like a guide than a guard. To satisfy regulations more than anything else, the demonstrators were rather playfully searched for weapons and were allowed to keep all personal contents of pockets and purses.

Eduardo, to avoid publicity, self-consciously gave his name as Rembrandt. Unfortunately, in the random dividing into groups he was separated from Grateful and Cherokee. His plan, of course, included them. Either one or the other, or both were possible. So when they were led away he was disappointed and felt doubtful that he'd find anyone as willing.

The officer in charge noticed Eduardo's hands caked with blood. "Is that yours or ours?" he asked.

Eduardo said his blood was his and was immediately taken to a special room where a nice old nurse administered treatment. She washed his wounds, sprinkled them with a white infection-prevention powder, and bandaged them tight to make Eduardo look like a fighter minus boxing gloves. He thought the bandages might draw valuable attention and decided that sympathy or admiration were good emotions to start with. When the first aid was complete, he was taken to his cell. It was ready open. He went in and the bars of it were slid and locked shut.

He was alone. He hadn't expected to be alone. Alone spoiled everything. Maybe, he thought, they were giving him special treatment, honoring him with a private cell. He didn't want special treatment. He didn't want privacy. What the hell did they think he was there for? He went to the bars and looked the corridor. He got an angle view and saw other cells crowded. He decided to complain. He'd tell the guard some excuse, perhaps merely that he wanted to be with his friends. Maybe if he requested politely, they'd put him with Grateful and Cherokee, wherever they were.

Eduardo shouted. Loud four times. But no one came, so he gave up.

So close and yet so impossible, he thought. He examined his cell that was a built-in cot with a blanket and clean pillow. There was a washbasin in one corner and a barred high window in the exterior wall. He estimated the place was more than large enough for two. His being the only wasn't the way it should be.

He lay on the cot, in eyeshut, and reviewed what he'd done to get there. His hands hurt. It was absurd, his going to this extent and failing because of solitary. One thing for sure, he decided, he'd get out and forget about this ridiculous project. It was a foolish try for entertainment, a waste of time. He'd get out as soon as possible and call Elaine Baine-Brice or work some. He hoped he never saw another damn hippie again. However, that kiss on his cheek from Grateful had definitely communicated future pleasure and Cherokee's hands had said the same. Perhaps, he concluded, what he'd do was see and enjoy them one time as a sort of compensation for all this inconvenience. They owed it to him. He tried to think of something extra he could ask from them, for interest. Maybe a scene. Anyway, he'd do them once and then dismiss them forever. And from then on, he'd stay with his own element, like Elaine Baine-Brice. He knew Elaine wouldn't be angry from his not calling as promised. She might pretend some anger, but actually it would increase her want. That kind of indifference always did. Next time she'd be better, he was sure. She'd try to make it indelible.

What I want, darling, is to make it so good that you suffer.

Fill, you son of a bitch, so I can transform you into a beggar. When you want me, say please, and I'll burn you in the hot rejection game. Hunger, you bastard, for the food that is only me, so that I can starve the hell out of you. Here, have a morsel. Have some crust, have some crumbs, have some left-overs. Maybe later, maybe never, baby. Say please and I might let you. On your pleading knees.

He had the pampered center of Elaine Baine-Brice spread for mental penetration, when the cell door sounds brought him up fast.

They brought him eight for company. Five boys and three birds, who slouched in and immediately sat the floor. Eduardo looked them. One of the girls obviously belonged to one of the boys because she claimed her place tight with him. The other two birds were possibilities because they sat separate against the deepest wall. A blonde and a brunette, both long-haired. The blonde was tall and leaner and Eduardo decided he preferred her over the brunette who was slightly too round. Convenience also influenced his choice, as the blonde had on a short short skirt while the brunette was in slacks.

Eduardo also picked his spot, the deepest corner where the sink was, where he would be at least partially concealed by the cot. He got up and stepped over legs to be there. It was also within talking range of the blonde.

One of the boys replaced Eduardo on the cot, stretched out. That one asked, "Hey, man, aren't you the guy who gave the fuzz a hard time?"

Eduardo didn't know the question was for him until the asker finally looked over the edge at him. Eduardo decided to answer only with his eyes, playing it cool, imitating. He looked yes but said nothing.

"You sure got balls, man, walking right into them, like a whole goddam army."

"Is that the guy?"

"Yeah, it's him."

"I heard about him but I didn't see him do it."

"It was a bad scene." The one who said that was one of the protest organizers.

"You coming down on him after what he did?"

"What good did it do?"

"Better than sitting there dead-ass."

"The agreement was no violence."

"So that was his thing and he had to do it. You can't come down on him for that. Like, he got so up-tight he had to do it. Right, man?"

Eduardo gave him a cool nod. He was trying to look an extremely indifferent look. For it, he caught his eyes on nothing and froze them there, vacant. He really felt empty. He hadn't had any breakfast.

"Anyway, the demonstration didn't make it. It was a nothing scene."

"You're wrong. We had two thousand. It was big."

"It'll be all over the box tonight." Meaning television.

"So what the fuck good is that, man?"

"It helps define the problem. Makes people aware. Like a lot of people are up-tight about the war and the draft. Maybe next time we'll have four thousand."

"Yeah, I can see them now, rushing down from Scarsdale to sit among the dog turds."

"We shouldn't have gone limp. We should have marched."

"Yeah, right through the pigs and up Broadway."

"I tell you we accomplished a lot today."

"Sure, man, look at us."

"You knew you'd get busted, didn't you?"

"Don't give me that shit, man. I been busted in towns you never heard of. For just being there. So don't give me that shit."

"I still think we should have marched."

"What do you think?"

"I think, by comparison, this is a rather groovy jail."

All through it, Eduardo hoped the blonde would look at him, but she didn't. On the fringe of his fixed cool look he could see her profile. The more he saw her the prettier she seemed. She had an excellent nose and lips that were naturally pouted a little. She had her knees up some, so her skirt was folded down into her lap and showed her thighs almost to where they made the transitional curve and became her bottom. Eduardo thought the boys sitting the other wall had to have a crotch view of her and he hoped none of them got stirred. It was going to be difficult enough without competition.

By then they were all more settled in the cell. Someone took out a stub of pencil and a fold of paper to write a poem.

Someone began playing a harmonica, a bright rippling little song. Someone interrupted with a request.

"Play soul, man." And the harmonica changed its product to a slower, lamenting melody, almost musical crying.

The blonde took off her sandals and flexed her toes. Her legs were in the stretched rectangle of sunlight shaped by the window above her. The brunette was closer to the other far corner where it was darker. The electric light in the unreachable ceiling was low watt, ineffective.

The blonde was remembering a lake back in her other little girl time. A lake that was like a cool summer drink held in a mountain cup. She used to barefoot walk the road that curved with the lake's coves and get her underfeet black from the melt of tar. She used to pick roadside dark-eyed yellow flowers to take home but they always wilted and hung dead by the time she got there.

The brunette was wondering if she should. Caution wasn't enough to not risk it. And, anyway, there was the sink to wash it down for safety. So she pulled up one of her pants legs and from inside one of her socks brought out the rolled marijuana. Once she had it exposed she didn't care. She put it to her lips and from around it asked anyone for a match that she got and lighted to make the little reverse whistle of inhale. She passed to the blonde who took a deep share. The blonde passed to Eduardo who tried to pretend but got some. Eduardo passed to the boy on the cot and it went around like that until it came back to its origin as a mere stub with maybe one more lip-burning drag left in it. The brunette deserved it and took it, holding with fingernails. Then she got up and washed the tiny evidence down the pipes of the basin above Eduardo's head.

The harmonica player sucked and blew and ran from one song to another, all soul. Everyone else was quiet. From where he was, Eduardo could see only the head of the boy on the cot who had his eyes covered with arm. Eduardo thought about time. He reasoned that the police wouldn't leave them all in this one cell all night. They'd probably transfer them someplace. It might happen any moment. He wished Grateful or Cherokee was there. With the blonde he had to start from start. It wasn't even a pull. She was there because she had to be, so Eduardo had no measure to begin with.

He wondered whether he should smile first or say something. He decided smile was wrong and he was right about that. He was mentally suggesting and rejecting words to say to her when he felt her eyes on him. Not just a glance from her, but a steady regard that he took advantage of. He lowered his head into his bandaged hands for a while, took his hands away for a moment to reveal his eyes squinted shut and made his mouth as sad as possible and then again buried into the bandages. He wasn't surprised when he felt her bare toes touch one of his legs. He didn't respond. Next it was her hand on his arm and she was there, kneeling near him, a lot of her contacting because of the limited space.

Softly she asked, "Do your hands hurt much?"

He shook his head no.

"Did they beat you bad?"

He shrugged to transmit modest bravery. He noticed she had a foreign accent that gave her an interesting dimension. Without asking, she sat and he moved some for her but even then she had to be wedged against him. She touched his bandages, tender. "I saw what you did," she said. "You didn't have a chance, but you did it."

Eduardo got her eyes with his. He made his say lonely.

She asked, "You're not from the Village, are you? I've never seen you around."

"No," he told her with as much drama as he could put into one word.

"You don't know anybody here, do you?" she said with hope.

He told her no again, the same way.

"You're all alone."

He shifted his shoulders a little for his answer and she understood. Immediately she released herself. He felt her let go more, moving into the vacancy he'd indicated was there.

"My name is Flight," she said.

"Billy," he told her for his name. A true lie. His middle name was William. He thought Billy sounded young sweet in a dangerous way.

"Where are you from, Billy?"

"Everywhere."

"Ever been in Sweden?"

"Stockholm," he told her, true.

"That's where I'm from," she smiled. "Did you dig it there?"

"No," he lied. Actually he'd balled his center sore that week in Stockholm.

"I don't either. I dig New York."

They were cramped together. He lifted his arm for her to get inside it. He hit his elbow on the sink pipe, his funny bone; it sent sharp shock down to his fingertips and up to his neck. But he couldn't show it. He swore inside.

"I dig you," she said just like that. The top of her head, her hair, was against his cheek. After a moment she tilted her head up and all he had to do was turn his head to be lips to lips with her.

It was a nice new first kiss. The shape of her mouth was nice, slightly wider than average, and her tongue was a plump slippery pillow, alternately consenting and asserting. She kept her lips in touch with his between the open kiss that he could take whenever he wanted. The harmonica helped. Eduardo hoped it continued.

Her eyes were kept closed. She wasn't in a cell with eight others. She was in touch. That was where everything was for her, all concentrated down from wide-awake to the special point of intense want. Not want later. Not want when it's more convenient. Not want some other place that might not be, ever. Now want. Here want. Taking the time and location of it as part of it. "You're beautiful," she said to the inside of his mouth, so the words might go deeper down into him, reaching.

Even with all his experience, Eduardo didn't realize she was so willing. Minutes before, she'd been a separate stranger. Her kisses didn't convey any barriers, but he knew kisses were a long way from really connecting. Maybe not someplace alone, but here maybe she was offering so much because that much was impossible to deliver. He thought perhaps she was using the place and the presence of the others for protection. And even if she wasn't, it was so spontaneous he couldn't help but be apprehensive. But then, he remembered some words by Grateful about doing what she felt when she felt it and that encouraged him. He decided on a fast test. He shifted to be on his side with his head in a better position for it. He aimed his mouth at where her right nipple might be. He let his lips just touch the fabric of her blouse. He gave several long warm concentrated exhales to the area and then pressed his open mouth to find he was right on target. There was no bra underneath and her blouse was silky thin so her nipple was easily determined.

With a minimum of interruption her hand undid her blouse and his lips felt the fabric slide away to have him have direct skin. But it wasn't enough for him to know she wanted that. For more test he took her hand with one of his bandaged ones and led it down to find him. Her fingers kept still and he kept his hand over hers there for confidence for a moment. When he was more than half sure she wouldn't withdraw he removed his hand and hers began. She had an intuitive touch, with nice pressures and use of fingernail tips. As she played so seriously he became more conscious of where he was and what he was about to do. By that time they both had relinquished most of their lean on the wall, had gradually slid down so only their upper shoulders and head were against it. Eduardo looked up at the cell ceiling and it was a gray old sky. He looked up and back and saw the undercrust of the wash basin and the cracked painted pipes of it. He looked for and saw the brunette who was in the opposite corner curled into a tight independent form, her attention away, perhaps sleeping. There was still the playing of the harmonica, the same soul.

Flight found his zipper and worked it to have him out. As she touched the first direct touch, she again said, "You're beautiful," and kissed. Her tongue asked and suggested what he would have her do. He knew he could be selfish.

Eduardo wanted to use his hands but the way they were bandaged they were useless. It was as if he had on mittens with holes in their ends. His fingers were wrapped together, only the very tips of them free. He did the best he could. With her skirt high as it was, her center was within easy reach. Lean as she was, she had sockets left and right of her most upper inside thighs and they helped his fingertips get around and under the elastic of her nylon bikini. He stretched his way in and got to her. She was unfolded and his fingertips ran the short personal length of her center several times with expert tender and then gave more attention to increasing her excitement exactly.

If ever in all his loving days he needed to be good it was now. He had to take her all the way up to the coming edge and he was handicapped by the bandages. But he built her with patience, with strategic variety, tactile art, more care and time, until she was above the ordinary high warmth, her mind and center swarmed with a single simple correspondence.

They were on their sides, bodies facing. She lifted. She interrupted her contribution to use that hand for taking her bikini down to below the knees. Then she used her feet to help them off one leg all the way. Eduardo thought she might need more building but she moved into range, raised her top leg and guided. She did it. She found herself with him and took him in part way.

It was then that Eduardo was alarmed to stop.

He was being tapped on the shoulder and not by her.

It was the boy on the cot. His chin was over the edge above them. Perhaps he'd been watching all the while. His expression was intimate, wise.

Eduardo thought all the building he'd done was now destroyed, sunk into self-consciousness. Although Flight wasn't covering, wasn't reacting, Eduardo didn't want to continue under such close inspection. He was cursing inside, ready to stop, hating the intrusion and the intruder, when it was dropped on him.

It came from the boy on the cot, who immediately rolled over, nonchalant, took all his attention away. It changed Eduardo's opinion entirely.

Eduardo was thankful for the blanket. He spread it over them. It allowed. He moved between. He went in and felt the clutch of her. His careful preparation was partially the reason, but mostly it was her ability to feel deserving of feeling, without blame, that allowed her to start coming on his second stroke.

Posterotic courtesy. Eduardo let her be snuggled for a floating while. It had been especially good for him, so he kissed her an altruistic forehead kiss and she murmured, "You're beautiful," to his neck where her lips were. He remained like that almost long enough for her before he separated to replace and enclose himself. He sat up. She stayed horizontal, her arm over her face. He stood up and if he'd looked down at her he would have seen her pull the blanket over her head to prevent the world a while longer.

He went to one of the boys, the one who'd been writing. From him Eduardo borrowed a scrap of paper and dull pencil. Eduardo used them to write:

I am Eduardo Brant, the painter.
I have been arrested by error. I
demand immediate release. Call
my lawyer, Mr. Phillip Case.

He added a phone number. Then he returned the pencil, folded the note, and waited at the bars for a guard who finally came and took the message from Eduardo's extended, waving hand.

In less than an hour they were releasing him. For remembering, Eduardo looked a fast look back into the cell of his success. In the deep corner beyond the cot he saw some of the blanket and one of Flight's bare feet. The boy on the cot sent him a small gesture. The harmonica player was chin on chest, asleep now. No one really said good-bye except Eduardo, who said that word to the place more than its occupants. Then he turned to be led out, all the way out, after acting some indignant rage and receiving many official apologies.

In the big black car on the way uptown, his lawyer was legally concerned with Eduardo's hands. He suggested a possible lawsuit.

"What for?" asked Eduardo absently.

His lawyer mentioned several counts a suit could be based on. "Yours aren't just ordinary hands," he declared. "Who knows, these injuries might affect your work, perhaps temporarily, perhaps forever. Who knows?"

That would be a way out, thought Eduardo. "My hands will be all right," he said.

"You shouldn't take it so lightly," his lawyer advised. "Have your doctor look at them. Have X-rays. Even if there's nothing seriously wrong we could sue. Look at it this way. If not being able to use your hands prevents your painting just one painting it's enough for us to sue."

My hands aren't the problem, Eduardo almost said, but revised to tell him, "My hands are fine. Forget about them."

"I think you're wrong."

Eduardo flared. "Look, goddam it. Stop all this shit about lawsuits. It was just a mistake."

His lawyer wanted to inquire about Eduardo's appearance. He could understand how the police mistook Eduardo for one of those hippies, the way he was dressed. But he kept quiet.

Eduardo looked the avenue they were riding north on: a fruit and vegetable stand with regimented oranges outstanding, a stainless steel hot dog cart, some unpainted furniture on the sidewalk, pink nylon panty hose on inverted plastic legs in a store window display, red stoplight. People crossing. He saw especially then a long-haired young man with short-skirted young birds connected to each side of him. They were the difference in the crowd. All others seemed to be treading furiously anonymous, but to Eduardo, the three together seemed conspicuous, unhurried, exempt. He wondered if they were high. He thought he heard harmonica music, felt the drop of that blanket on his legs, had the uncomplicated response of Flight around him.

"I want you to do something for me," he told his lawyer.

"Sure. What?"

"After you take me home I want you to go back to that jail and get them out."

"Get who out?"

"The demonstrators they arrested this morning."

"All of them?"

"All of them."

"Why? What did they ever do for you?"

"Nothing. I just want to do it."

"I don't know if it's possible."

"Pay their fines. Talk to whomever you have to. Get them out today."

"I can try."

"Do it, Phil." That was an order from a very paying client. It was the most Eduardo could do.

Home where he belonged, Eduardo took off his make-believe hippie clothes and threw them away. He bathed away the street and jail dirt and got his bandages soaked, so he unwound them and saw his hands were more bruised and swollen than cut. However, while he was shaving they began to bleed. The red of them ran up to his wrists and arms, so he called his doctor who rushed over to treat with efficient sympathy. While his doctor rebandaged his fingers individually, Eduardo explained an unbelievable accident that wasn't questioned. His doctor also advised X-rays and left.

Not until he had a glass of cold gin and was relaxed on his

bed did Eduardo enjoy the credit of his accomplishment. He'd done it. In less than three days out of the allotted seven, he'd done it. He was sure that Knight or Rog or even Arnie couldn't have pulled it off so fast and well. He wondered how they were doing. Maybe failing, he hoped. Maybe they'd have to lie when they all got together again. At least he wouldn't. He even had evidence of his story with his hurt hands.

He closed his eyes and remembered the entire episode from the time he'd first seen Grateful in the grass of the park, riding the world. He remembered every detail, every impression and word spoken. It was like a rehearsal. He got some help from the television during the six o'clock news that he never usually watched.

It came right after the latest reports from Vietnam that showed some young men with guns living in shallow holes among dead trees that had all their leaves and tops exploded and burned off them. And then:

> "This morning more than two thousand demonstrators gathered around Whitehall Induction Center to protest the draft."

Eduardo saw his sign but it was too fast for him to see himself.

> "The police were prepared for any violence. More than five thousand of New York's men in blue were on duty in the area . . ."

Low angle shot. Eduardo saw some police who looked strong and tall as the skyline buildings behind them.

> ". . . to maintain law and order. Generally the protest was peaceful. Many of the demonstrators, it seems, had other, more important things on their minds."

Insert close shot. Eduardo saw a pair of hippies, boy and girl, kissing a long public kiss while sitting.

> "But there were some instances when the police had their hands full."

Full shot. Eduardo saw himself. Surrounded by the pushing prance of mounted policemen. He saw panic distorting his face. He saw other policemen rush to help. He saw Grateful and Cherokee struggling. He saw the wielding of nightsticks and one policeman fall, hit. He saw flashes of himself bent and trying to protect his head with his hands and then down on his knees and finally curled up on the street, defeated.

"There was the usual burning of draft cards . . ."

Several views. Eduardo saw hippies lighting the small cardboard rectangles with serious pleasure.

". . . and many arrests."

Traveling shot. Eduardo saw voluntarily limp forms being hauled and tossed into police vans.

"However, the draftees, destined to strengthen our effort in Vietnam, successfully entered the induction center to take their oaths."

Overhead angle. Eduardo saw one in the line of draftees look up at the camera and wave a good-bye for identification before he was lost.

And that was that. Eduardo wondered how recognizable he'd been on the screen. He looked like him. He wondered if anyone such as Elaine Baine-Brice would know it was him. He could always deny it. Using the excuse of possible recognition, he turned on the television news again at eleven o'clock and saw it all repeated. And before he went to sleep he thought about the demonstrators and how they were now out free, instead of in jail, because he'd really wanted to help them, he told himself.

Anyway, no more hippies. The score was even.

He was up early. He had a large rich breakfast and then went above to the studio to work. The unfinished good canvas he'd done was on the easel but he replaced it with a fresh one, and when he had the paints squeezed out and brushes and oil and turp ready, he concentrated, expecting as a result of his last effort to be wide open. But he wasn't. He was tighter than ever, entirely closed, not even that hopeful pinpoint of inspiration in him. For an hour he tried but finally capitulated. He tried to analyze it. He looked at the last great work and couldn't understand why he'd had it then but had nothing now. Was it just a bad day? Maybe tomorrow? Maybe tomorrow. No use forcing it. He'd learned that from all the previous tight time. Maybe it *was* his hands. They didn't feel right. They were sore stiff. He tried to rationalize but knew better.

He wandered his house for no reason and he was downstairs when the doorbell sounded. He saw it was Grateful and Cherokee and after some brief indecision he let them in.

But it was not only Grateful and Cherokee. It was also a half dozen others he'd never seen before. They slouched in, a mixture of young men and birds, while Grateful and Cherokee gave him simultaneous hugs and cheek kisses left and right. The part of him that needed distraction was glad they were there. The other lesser part didn't want it but had to allow. Grateful and Cherokee led the way upstairs with authority, all the way up to the studio. There the group disintegrated to various areas of the large room, some to the floor, some to the expanse of the yellow couch, some to the hi-fi. They'd brought their own music that Grateful loaded on the turntable to make their kind of sounds fill the space around them.

"Straight Man," Grateful called him fondly and hugged again and remained attached. He wasn't formally introduced to the others. Grateful merely gave him their names. There was Guide and Mind and Fitz and Hope and Lita and Chip. And one especially physical girl called Glorie, whom Eduardo first saw from the back, the perfect round of her bottom that seemed to be unconsciously winking with soft tension. Glorie turned, her ample breasts pointing at the disturbance they caused. Eduardo decided he was thoroughly glad he had visitors.

They'd come to show their appreciation. But none of them actually verbalized thanks. They reasoned that he knew why they were there and that was enough. Eduardo did know. He could feel their gratitude and it was pleasant being the target of it. They also admired the courage he'd displayed the day before at the demonstration. Their spontaneous acceptance of him communicated that. Only Grateful and Cherokee mentioned it, however. And all they said was, "You were dynamite yesterday, Straight Man, like dynamite."

Eduardo thought they were there for the day and perhaps some of them would stay on for some of the night. He hoped he had a chance at Glorie. He noticed she didn't seem to be claimed by anyone. Maybe, he thought, they'd all eventually leave except her. He decided to try to arrange that. He watched them dance. They danced apart, tribal, doing all the moves that were obviously sexual in a simian manner. Eduardo was amused and laughed to himself that they looked like aroused spastics.

They turned on. Rolled marijuana into tight white sticks lighted and passed to one another, many times, almost constantly.

Eduardo talked some with Guide, who was the oldest of them. They called Guide by another name sometimes. They called him "the head head," but Eduardo didn't know why, although he thought it was some form of respect. Guide didn't dance, nor did he move from where he'd first placed himself on the yellow couch. It was as if he were content to observe the others, watching over them, the play of his children. What Eduardo and Guide talked about mostly was the war in Vietnam and the draft. Eduardo didn't contribute much but Guide went on about it, emphatic. Behind Guide's vehement opinions regarding the draft was his guilt unexpressed. He was from a money family. They'd sent him to Princeton. And while mentally or financially deficient young men had been drafted because they didn't have a college to protect them, Guide had been automatically deferred. Now, in retrospect, he felt the unfairness of the partiality. Now he was trying to make up for it, but, no matter how loud he shouted or how much he humiliated himself, it wouldn't balance out.

Eduardo also talked to the one called Mind. He was short and thick and his features hung enough to convey lack of intellect. Eduardo tested him. Eduardo asked him if he knew the earliest paintings ever discovered.

"The earliest," answered Mind without hesitation, "are ascribed to the Aurignacian Third period of around twenty-five thousand B.C. They're in La Ferrassie, black and red pigments used to portray animals, probably deer."

Eduardo knew Mind was correct. He asked about the Mona Lisa.

"Painted by da Vinci around 1503, believed to be a portrait of Lisa Gherardini of Florence," said Mind. "The painting was bought by Francis I, king of Florence, who installed it in his bathroom. He paid four thousand gold florins for it. The painting was stolen, you know."

"Really?"

"Yes. From the Louvre in August, 1911—on the twenty-first, to be exact. A guy named Vincenzo Peruggia copped it."

That was news to Eduardo. He decided to try another subject. "Know anything about boxing?" he asked.

Mind shrugged modest.

"Know who held the heavyweight championship for the longest time?"

Mind thought a few seconds and came out with the name. "Joe Louis. He was champion for eleven years, eight months, and nine days, from the twenty-second of June, 1937, to the first of March, 1949. His last name wasn't really Louis—it was Barrow. Joe Louis Barrow."

Eduardo couldn't help but be impressed. He tried a final quickie. "How many people died in the Black Plague epidemic?"

"Seventy-five million in the four years between 1347 and 1351," replied Mind with ease.

Anything, everything that Mind's eye contacted was instantly stored in his brain, just like everyone else, except Mind could get it out whenever he wanted. He could, for example, recite verbatim entire pages of Einstein's Theory of Relativity. However, he didn't understand a word of it.

"What time is it?" asked Eduardo.

"Shit, man, I don't know," said Mind and went to dance some in the vicinity of Glorie.

Eduardo was wrong about these hippies staying all day and part of the night. They stayed two days and two nights and they increased in numbers. What had been eight gradually multiplied to three times that number. They were everywhere Eduardo looked, exploring his house and possessions, using toilets without shutting doors, curled in pairs in chairs, stretched out for sleep on his soft rugs, drinking his milk straight from cartons, depleting his food and soft drinks, ordering more from Gristede's via phone, calling long distance as far as Calcutta, balling in his beds two by two or more, taking baths.

The music never stopped.

There was always someone dancing.

They were constantly turned on.

They painted the body of Glorie, who sat completely bare in the filtered sunlight of the second afternoon while they covered her with bright designs, spirals and circles and dots and lettering, all over. They demanded that Eduardo do her back and he painted a series of green arching strokes left and right symetrically from the crack of her bottom all the way up to her shoulders, using the little nubs of her spine for exact spacing. It took several hours for them to complete her, and then they were finished, Glorie was very cramped from sitting, so she danced and Eduardo saw her writhing and snapping like a decorated savage, stimulating.

There was another girl, a pretty one, who had her hair fuzzed up and stuck with at least a dozen sticks of incense, lighted. She left a trail of Oriental fragrance everywhere she moved. Eduardo asked her if she wasn't afraid of setting herself on fire.

She smiled. "I take them out and put in new sticks when they get too short."

"But how can you tell when they're short?"

"When I smell hair burning," she explained. "Shit, man, anyone can tell the difference between burning hair and incense."

With their special brand of insanity, Eduardo thought, they'd come to stay. He wanted them to leave, but he was helpless. He got the idea of calling the police but didn't want to do it enough to do it. They might stay forever, he feared, and his nerves were already electric from their antics. He saw one young man in a pair of slacks and a crisp shirt that Eduardo was sure were his from his dressing room compartment, but he didn't complain because his impatience was beyond that point. He was in the middle of a mad storm, a storm of mad. Who the hell did they think they were, he kept asking himself. How could they assume? What made them think they could take over his place, use his things, superimpose their mass derangement on him? They had merely used the excuse of paying homage to him for the opportunity to free-load. That's what they were, he decided, free-loading freaks. He had to think of some way to get them out.

They thought of it for him on the third morning.

Guide suggested that they all go to the country and turn on out there where they could also feel some naturals. Of course, they insisted that Eduardo go along, and he didn't refuse, fearing they might change their plans if he did.

"How do you get to the country?" asked Eduardo.

"Bus and walk, man," was the answer.

Eduardo hadn't been on a bus in fifteen years. He detested buses for all the slow, smelly, ordinary reasons. But he went.

They sang on the way, oblivious to all the other passengers, who complained futilely. They sang folk and soul accompanied by guitar and harmonica, while Eduardo watched the ugly upper city become the backs of suburban houses, become long stretches of trees and rock walls. For nearly two hours. Where they got out seemed to be nowhere, just a crossing of a narrow asphalt road that they walked to a dirt road they climbed. They seemed to know where they were going and finally Eduardo saw their destination.

It was an old huge house, on a New England hill with a lot of open fields and woods around it. It was overgrown, apparently abandoned. All of its windows were smashed out and its front porch was broken through. Inside it was dust and shatters of glass. Eduardo estimated it had about twenty rooms.

"What's this place?" he asked Grateful, who was attached to him.

"Just a place we come to."

"Doesn't anyone own it?"

"I suppose."

Eduardo noticed signs that warned: NO TRESPASSING—old weathered yellow signs.

"Wish I owned it," wished Grateful.

"What would you do with it? It's a mess."

"Oh, we could fix it up. We could paint it and work on it. I told you I'd dig having a place in the country that I could build a high fence around. Remember? A place, like where we could all just be without any bother?"

Eduardo remembered.

"Well, this is the place," she told him.

They sat in the high grass on the slope in front of the rundown house. Some turned on with LSD but Eduardo didn't know it. They sat and didn't talk much. Some stretched out and looked up at the sky as if they were reading it. Some walked down to the brook. Someone found some wild flowers and shared with everyone.

Eduardo wandered alone around the back of the house where the woods were nearest. He entered the woods, zigzagged his way among old and young trees, maples and oaks. Lower branches switched his thighs. Under his feet was a carpet of last year's leaves and sometimes there was a fallen trunk to step over. He stopped and looked back and couldn't see the house. He sat down and sunlight dappled him. Everything there was new and old. Extreme. New with hope. Old with elemental punishment. The innocent brave naturally mixed with the habitually compromised, the deformed. The moss giving up the north of a rock. Two trees matured too near one another, so their branches fought. Acorns rotting at his feet. A small piece of granite he turned over to expose a horde of little things running for their lives. Because of the catastrophe he'd caused, it would never be the same for them. He gently replaced the granite and hoped they got over the shock.

Was he really there? He didn't feel there. Where he was, really, was somewhere between Elaine Baine-Brice's voracious center and the work he couldn't do. He wasn't in a New England grove where blue jays flapped screeches at one another on the tip of the high branch he looked up at. Those irregular fragments of sky weren't there. Not for him, anyway. He was a leftover form of something that had once lived. Only the rot hadn't begun. Or perhaps it had. He felt very down as he walked back to the deserted house and around to be with them again.

By that time some of them were overdecorated with flowers: almost all had wreaths of blossoms on their heads. They were holding hands in a circle, sitting cross-legged, like Indians or children or both. Two of them broke connection and made space for him, inviting. He sat imitating them. His right hand was held, and his left.

When they returned to the city it was almost night. Eduardo hoped they'd leave him at the bus station. He actually tried to walk away, but they merely joined him in his direction. He felt like running. And when he was at his door, he wanted to rush in first to bolt them out. But they followed him in and again they were all over his house. Again there was the thumping of their music. Eduardo began to feel that he was being punished with them, that some supreme force had inflicted them on him.

They were dancing again.

They were turning on again.

They were on all the beds and all the floors again.

The telephone rang.

It was the precinct police station. Eduardo listened and immediately calculated that he could use what they told him. The police had kept a special watch on his house. As a result, they'd picked up four suspicious characters, who, Eduardo knew, according to the description the police gave him, were only hippies who'd gotten the word and were trying to join their confederates.

Eduardo hung up the phone and shouted a demand for everyone's attention. He told them that the police were holding four of their friends. He told them they had to get them out.

"It'll take some bread," said Guide.

"Like we don't have that kind of bread," said someone else.

They all looked lost.

Then it was Eduardo once more to the rescue.

He went to the studio storage area. He brought out the blue X canvas. He got a brush and some black and signed his famous name in the right-hand corner. He gave it to Grateful. "Take this to the gallery on the corner of Madison," he instructed.

"And then do what with it?" she asked, examining the simple meaningless X.

"They'll buy it," he told her. "They'll pay you more then enough to get your friends out."

"You've got to be jiving," said Cherokee.

"Hurry before the gallery closes," urged Eduardo.

They streamed down and out. All of them. Eduardo immediately double-locked the street door and the inside foyer door and blew a big breath of relief.

Grateful dubiously took the canvas to the gallery. The

owner examined it, and her and her friends, and Eduardo's signature closely. She was astonished that he gave her $1200 for it. She would have taken $10. He should have given her at least $5000, based on the current market.

Eduardo went up and shut off the twanging hi-fi. The quick quiet was a shock. He went room to room and decided they really hadn't destroyed anything. Actually, the place wasn't as messy as he'd thought. Perhaps it was their personal dishevelment that had created the impression of disorder.

He was exhausted but he took a bath and changed the sheets on his bed they'd used. He opened the tall double doors in his room for air to eliminate the heavy mixed odor of marijuana and incense. When he was about to click off the wall light switch near the little case that contained his trifle box collection, he noticed that one box was gone. Only the one that was his favorite. The one that said, "If desire is the fruit of love, let us an orchard be." They'd stolen it. The dirty bastards had stolen it. Not only were they filthy free-loading freak dope addicts. They were also thieves. He made the room dark and got into bed. Anger stabbed through the thick of his tired. He heard them on the street below. They were trying the door, pushing the bell, knocking. A voice he thought was Grateful's called his name that the night carried loud. Three, four times. Then they went away and Eduardo went to sleep for a normal tomorrow.

He slept shallow and stayed in bed longer than usual, lay there listening to the outside sound of the city, an accumulated buzz punctuated by impatient horns. His body reminded him that he hadn't done anyone since Flight in jail. Four days. He'd appreciated Glorie and all her exposures but he hadn't pursued. Grateful and Cherokee had been available but he hadn't tried. It was ironic. All the young balling there'd been around him, while the most he'd taken was teasing observations and a few fast handfuls. Now he thought he'd try to work this morning and have Elaine Baine-Brice over to have in the afternoon. He didn't really know why he hadn't done Glorie or Grateful or Cherokee. He was sure he could have. He decided it was better that he hadn't. Four days. It would be extra good with Elaine.

He dressed and went down to the kitchen for breakfast. He filled a bowl with dry cereal, sprinkled on some sugar and then found there was no milk, only four empty wax cartons in the refrigerator. He wondered how long it would take before his living was completely unaffected by them. Post hippie. What he had for breakfast was only an orange, slightly wrinkled and overripe.

From the kitchen he went out to the hall for the elevator. He glanced to the foyer. On the floor there was some mail that had been delivered through the slot. He went for it and among several letters was a small package wrapped in pink paper tied with blue ribbon. There were no stamps on it nor address. He took it up to the studio with him, wondering.

When he unwrapped he found the package contained the missing trifle box. He examined and saw it wasn't damaged. There was also a note, written in eyebrow pencil on a piece of brown bag paper:

It was so beautiful
I just wanted to have it,
to hold it for a while.

No other explanation or excuse. Eduardo read the note several times and imagined the writer. Obviously a girl.

Skeptical, he placed a fresh canvas on the easel and prepared a palette with squeezes of paint and flexed the bristles of a brush. For several intense moments he sought within him for the opening. It wasn't there. He broke concentration. His eyes wandered to the returned trifle box and from that to a twined ring of flowers left by one of them on the floor. Delicate lavender blossoms now limp with wilt. But they took him back to just yesterday, when he had sat in high grass in a living, loving circle and linked tenderly right and left.

His attention went back to the blank canvas. He tried again for the opening. He went deep to probe for it and it wasn't there. It wasn't.

It never would be again, for as his try for it began to retreat, to surface, there was suddenly a different dilation in him. It was wide. A new channel from a fresh generating source, a new passage rushing with emotion.

He could not paint fast enough.

He used every brush, every finger, every palette knife, and even applied directly from the mouths of tubes.

He did one, two, three, four canvases.

The demonstrators and their victorious futility.

Flight in the freedom of herself in a cell.

Grateful riding the wonder of the world.

The country green field circle of love currenting.

It was late afternoon when the time and place of then and there came focusing back to him. He wanted to paint more but he stopped to appraise the canvases he'd done.

They were different from anything ever.

They were a giant step ahead to now.

He didn't care if anyone else liked them or not.

He knew now he could be open forever.

He decided he wouldn't paint anymore that day. He would go downtown and find them. He would really hug Grateful and kiss her his feelings. He would touch Cherokee and send his message. He would even dance like an ape in heat with all of them.

He cleaned his arms and hands with turpentine. There were smears on his clothes and many on the floor, he noticed. He didn't care.

He thought with a leaping fear that perhaps he'd lost them. That they were gone forever. Perhaps his rejection had scattered them out of reach. And even if he did find them would they forgive him? He had no excuse. Now he was beyond the inanity of excuses. Besides, they were so wise about such things.

He walked with his thoughts to the front window. He looked down.

There was the green and black of a police car at the curb, and, across the street, sitting, leaning, slouching, were Grateful and Guide and Cherokee and Mind and Flight and Fitz and Glorie and Chip and Lita and Hope and thirty or more others who had been there for hours.

Stretched above them, attached to poles held up, was a big banner of paper with nine beautiful red letters on it, and, of course, some flowers.

WE LOVE YOU

6

The girl had to get up at seven every weekday to get dressed and get some coffee and get to the bus uptown and walk four blocks to get there by the starting time of nine-fifteen so she could be behind the typewriter to get the check the first and fifteenth of every month. But she stayed in bed until eleven that day because it was a Saturday day. Not that she'd been out late the previous night and needed the rest. It was just that the horizontal position, along with eyeshut self-cuddle, made it easy for her to be anything else she wanted to pretend to be. She wasn't fat as she was. She didn't have eyes too close together and a nose too long for her mouth that was too small. Her hair wasn't brittle and dead from trying to color more life into her life with it, and her breasts weren't small and droopy. She wasn't in a fifth floor rear anything room with three pairs of shoes on the closet floor below four half-size dresses. Most important, she wasn't alone. At least in the limitless better land of dark behind her closed eyes she wasn't. She was letting her generous FM radio put Arnie Bruno in her. His only desire was her, so it wasn't her own hands that were down there on her, knowing exactly where and how.

The woman scraped the breakfast dishes over the bag in the flip-top garbage pail to rinse them before she put them into the built-in dishwasher. Husband and both children were gone with their morning meals in them and she had on rubber gloves to keep her hands young. The built-in fan over the built-in electric stove was still whirring needlessly. She clicked it off and transferred butter and jam into the built-in refrigerator and went back to rinsing dishes. The number thirty-four that was her years was printed in erasable chalk on the built-in slate background of her mind. She was always partially wiping away the four to replace it with an inevitable five. She sponged toast crumbs off the white counter, little things, while the FM radio on the sill of the window over the sink tried to sell her a cigarette she didn't hear. She looked absently out the window to her exterior territory. Then there was an arrangement of strings and brass for a voice that entered her and lifted the heavy of the house from around her so love could get in. Different from the regulation weekly relief in the cloud of Mother's Day perfume. Different from the sheets she'd washed mother-clean in the built-in washer, automatically. Somewhere Arnie Bruno took her. Soft animal in the sunshine. Having to moan. The sacrificial stretch marks on her thighs and stomach not there where he touched.

The two girls on the beach. The straps of their tops unhooked so their backs would get all tan. Baking like muffins, desperately still, breasts flattened under them. Exposed skin oiled to fry. Broiling their teen-age vanities for the reward of attention from boys. Boys in their warm minds. Boys with hair-trigger centers. Boys they were supposed to match according to the law of age for age. But time ripening unequally. And there was the portable radio sending the ingredient to accompany the inside lower squeeze of both the girls. Their imaginations, projecting boys, slid a quick change to Arnie Bruno. The man got into them simultaneously. His voice, the perfect size and shape and experience, filled them as they flexed their bikini-covered bottoms, so their bikini-covered unsatisfied centers pushed some, secretly.

At that time Arnie was scratching his pubic hair. Winner had just given him a rubdown and he felt loose and good. He was just standing there in the air-conditioned air of his fiftieth floor looking the vertical profile of Manhattan. Toward the river was a new high building going up. No steel or glass skin on it yet and no expensive guts. Only its tomato-colored skeleton being worked on. Arnie saw workers on it. He noticed the highest, a figure in blue who stepped little dangerous steps nonchalantly out on an extended girder, all the way out to the end of it. He saw the man stop and look up, as if asking the sky if he should take the final fatal step, and then, suddenly, the worker opened his fly. He took out his center and urinated, made a thin arcing stream that glistened in the

Saturday summer sun and broke into drops as it fell onto the city. He shook and replaced himself and walked back to work.

Arnie had to smile because he was laughing inside. Aloud he said, "You know it, baby. Piss on them all."

"Huh?" asked Winner, bringing beer.

"I just saw a guy take a leak off a girder over there."

"Must be a nut."

"He just hung his joint out and let them have it," Arnie admired.

"So?"

"He probably does it all the time."

"Here. Drink your beer. When you got to piss I'll open the window for you."

"Heads up," smiled Arnie and drank some of Munich's best from its bottle.

"You had two calls last night, one this morning," Winner told him. "The one this morning was a repeat."

"Nothing on the good line."

"No."

Only three people had the good line number. Arnie's ex-wife, his son and daughter.

"Get the number on the regular line changed again," he ordered without asking who called.

Winner told him, "The one yesterday, the blonde from the recording studio, she called late. She must have got the number off the phone."

"Don't scam me."

Winner went innocent. "What do you mean?"

"You had her here all night."

"Then it wasn't her."

Winner started the vacuum cleaner. To also sweep away thoughts. Letting him get away with it, Arnie went to the bedside table.

From under a Tiffany money clip holding some hundreds, he picked up the piece of paper with his assignment on it:

Aboard a regularly scheduled
transcontinental flight

He'd been thinking some about it. The way he had it figured he didn't think it was going to be difficult. They had flights going all night, and usually the night flights weren't crowded.

He wouldn't go first class because going tourist gave him better odds. Besides, in tourist they had three seats next to each other, so he'd get all three for plenty of room. He didn't know if the dividing arm rests were removable, but he hoped.

There was only one problem.

Arnie Bruno was afraid of flying.

Not the usual grit-your-teeth-and-try-not-to-think-about-it kind of fright. Arnie's fear was animal terror. Even when he was on the ground and a jet passed overhead he felt an inside lurch that had to be dissolved by the happy realization that he wasn't up there.

"Did you call for the tickets?" he shouted to Winner, who clicked off the sweeper with a foot and asked what with his head.

"The tickets."

"Yeah. They already delivered them."

"Why the hell didn't you tell me? Did they send the seating plan like I wanted?"

"Everything's out on the hall table," Winner told him and kicked the sweeper on again.

Arnie went out to the hall and got them. He ripped open the envelope and there were the three. He opened one and saw his famous name and tried to translate some of the special abbreviations used by airline ticket clerks. Departure time was 1 A.M. from Kennedy. Return open. Just having the tickets in his hand made Arnie go speeding over a hundred in the seventy-two-per heart zone.

And when he studied the seating plan that was an overhead cutaway drawing of the plane, his armpits got wet enough to run a trickle down. He'd read someplace that the safest, strongest place of any plane was where the wing joined the fuselage, so he decided on seats in that area. He also made sure the numbers were right, that they didn't have a four in them. He didn't like fours because he didn't think fours liked him. He remembered, for instance, a four in Vegas that came up on the top of a lot of passes and refused to repeat during a long roll that ended with a seven, losing the most ever. When he was a child he'd been sick and hurt most of his year four, and his fourth-grade classroom was where they'd come to tell him his father was dead. Of course, the reasonable part of Arnie said it was ridiculous. Four was just a number between three and five. But when he started counting all the times four had been bad for him, he was sure it wasn't all coincidence.

Now he thought, with a take-off time of one, he'd be high up there at four. Jesus Christ, he said inside, as if blaming Him.

He went in and told Winner, "I want to go to Nickie's."

"He ain't open yet. It's only one."

"Call and see if anybody's there."

"He opens at three."

"Call anyway."

"By the time you get dressed and ready it'll be three."

That sharpened the edge Arnie already had. "Look, bellhead," he shouted, "you do what I tell you." Arnie usually accepted Winner's insubordination. It was part of their closeness, for Arnie a relief from sycophancy. So he was immediately sorry for his temper, especially for calling Winner a bellhead, which was a direct hit on Winner's having absorbed too many punches.

Winner kept his head down and went to the phone. Before he could touch it, it rang, so he picked up and asked who. Without covering the mouthpiece he told Arnie, "It's Connie."

"Which one's that?"

"I think it's the one you pulled coming out of the flower shop."

Arnie tried to remember.

Winner tried to help. "The one who had her picture bare-ass in that magazine."

Arnie remembered.

"Want to talk to her?" asked Winner.

"No."

"He says he can't talk now," Winner informed.

Arnie decided on the distraction. Connie was the one who'd dug fingernails into her own breasts. "Tell her to meet us at Nickie's."

"Meet us at Nickie's," relayed Winner and didn't wait for her yes or no because he knew she'd be there.

She was there when they got there at half-past three. The owner, Nickie, hugged Arnie a ritual hug and held arm all the way to the table where Connie's 38C-cups dominated. Connie was an unnatural blonde, of average height and weight; however, her front abundance made the rest of her look thin. Arnie sat next to her on the wall side of the table, thigh against thigh. He slid his arm over and around and his hand got the edge of her right breast that wasn't in a bra. She hadn't forgotten he didn't like bras. He aimed a cheek kiss at her but she turned so he got some of her mouth. There was the taste of her drink on her lips. A stinger. The waiter brought Kentucky whiskey for him and Winner.

"You didn't call me like you promised," she complained, careful.

"I thought about it. Didn't I, Winner?"

Winner nodded automatic.

What's he, a goddam mind reader, Connie wanted to ask but only smiled instead, so Arnie would notice when she quickly changed her expression to worried. She wanted Arnie to ask about it, but he didn't.

Arnie said his thoughts: "I'm flying to the Coast tonight."

Maybe talking about it would keep it from building.

"When you coming back?" she asked.

"Soon as possible. Tomorrow or the next day."

"I need to talk to you," she said.

"So talk."

"Alone."

"We are alone, baby."

She looked at Winner, who blinked blank at her. She lighted a cigarette and tortured the matchbook cover some. "I need your help," she said.

"You need money," Arnie told her.

She was surprised he knew. She nodded at him, hoping her eyes said hope.

"How much?"

"Eight hundred," she said, adding on an extra two hundred at the last moment.

"What for?"

"Something personal."

"You're knocked up."

That was exactly what she was going to tell him in different words. Her silence told him he was right.

"It wasn't me, baby," Arnie told her. "I know it wasn't." He really did because that only time with her had been one of his pretend times.

"I didn't say it was," she told him.

"Eight hundred? Christ, everything's going up."

Her eyes were starting to flood and her mouth was tightening. She was slouched now and that was bad for her front, made it hang. "I tried to borrow it from my friends," she said, thick and futile.

Arnie went into his jacket pocket for his money clip. She didn't see him do it. She didn't see him pass it under the table to Winner. "Winner will give it to you," he told her.

She didn't believe Winner had money.

"I'll loan it to you," said Winner.

"I doubt if I can ever pay you back," she said, poor.

"You can give me a little at a time," Winner assured. Without looking down he counted eight of Arnie's hundreds that he folded and passed across to her. When they were in her hand and going into her purse she checked the double zeros in their green corners. She didn't say thanks. She said, "I'm empty," and Winner signaled another drink for her. When she got it she took a victorious sip. Because the eight hundred was the finishing touch that put her over the goal with plenty to spare. From nothing three days previous to more than enough now, just from doing the same number to different audiences. Now she could pay cash for that blue convertible Triumph 4A she wanted to drive home to Ohio with the young actor who was in and out of her life. Now she had extra dollars to buy New York City presents for her jealous married sisters and her mother.

She looked across at Winner and wondered how long it would take her to get even with him.

Arnie got up and went to the bar, no longer in debt to himself for calling Winner a bellhead. Nickie was behind the bar now. He put a fresh drink in front of Arnie. "You going to close this summer?" Arnie asked him. There were no other customers there. Nickie's was a typical narrow place with no front window so it was the same inside no matter what time it was outside.

Nickie asked, "You staying in town?"

"In and out."

"You stay. I stay," said Nickie. He knew when Arnie was in town he could count on plugs in all the columns. They all knew his place was Arnie's place. Arnie had been faithful to it for over two years. People came to eat and drink there because Arnie might at the same time.

Arnie knew it. "I'll be around," he promised. He looked at his watch that told him precisely four.

The front door opened. She came in on a splash of temporary sunlight and stood there near the entrance, afraid to move until her eyes regulated to the dim. She couldn't see anything for a few moments. Arnie had to see her.

She was thin but not very tall, sort of gangly in a miniature way. She'd put in some sunning hours to make her skin an ideal color, and that was helped some by the contrast of her white silk jersey dress, short and swishy loose. Her eyes, he saw, were blue, bright as children's marbles, and her hair was blond-light, chopped shaggy like a boy's on purpose, no fluff or curl, but straight and mussed some. Her face wasn't made up much. She was plain pretty in an unusual candid way. The impression was that she was more girl than woman, more little girl than big girl. Arnie thought maybe she was sixteen, possibly seventeen. Nickie, who was also looking, thought he didn't want to risk his liquor license by serving this underage one.

"Do you have a telephone?" she asked, her voice slightly flavored with drama. Nickie indicated where the telephone was behind a door next to the coat-check room. She walked the few steps to it and went in.

"You ought to be out on your boat today," Nickie told Arnie. "Nice day today."

"I'm going to sell the boat."

"How much you want? Maybe I buy it."

"Two hundred thou." Arnie was sure Nickie couldn't come up with that much. Arnie had paid three.

"I take a look," said Nickie, serious.

Then the phone door opened and she came out with all her attention on the inside of her purse. She had white gloves bunched in one hand and the open purse in the other. Arnie looked at her and was removing his look when it happened. Her face shocked. Her eyes went big while her mouth made a silent oval. She grabbed at her hips and then her thighs.

Arnie thought perhaps she was suffering some sort of physical fit, contorting. But then he saw the problem.

They were white silk. They were already exposed below her hemline and sliding farther down. She caught them for a moment with her knees but they got away and gravity dropped them around her tan ankles. She didn't look up for looks. She just stepped out of the white double ring of lacy silk that was her panties and bent to get them. She bunched them into her purse that she snapped shut.

Arnie felt the urge to applaud.

She walked a head-high walk to the bar as if it hadn't happened. She sat on a stool far enough from Arnie, put her purse on the polished surface, and ordered a gin and tonic, specifying a particular good gin.

Nickie, polite, asked her for identification to show she was old enough.

"I'm twenty-two," she told him.

"I've got to see proof," said Nickie, nice. "A driver's license or something."

"I don't have anything."

"Can't serve you without proof. Sorry."

Arnie advised, "Have a plain ginger ale. It's better for you anyway."

She looked Arnie a mind-your-own-business look while Nickie poured her a ginger ale. As soon as he put it in front of her, she took two thirsty swallows. She didn't comment on the omitted alcohol. Arnie noticed some of her panties, a little lace, sticking out of her shut purse. He wanted to tell her but decided not to. He brought his eyes to the icy amber of his drink that had no relationship to the jet roaring in his mind with its danger. You don't have to go, his fear told him and told him while he knew he would. He felt like an object being poured down a funnel of time into a container of probable death. Over the engines he heard a voice say, "I thought you were skinnier."

He smiled his public smile. "My tailor gives me ten pounds." Words he'd said before. He would have let that end it, but because he was nervous he said, "I thought you had more freckles."

She had them across her nose and some on each cheek.

"Would more be better?" she asked, sparkling.

"Two or three maybe."

She opened her purse and her panties sprung out some. She dug in under them and brought out a little flat plastic box that she got a tiny brush out of. She wet the brush tip with her tongue and dabbed it on the cake of color in the box. "Where should I put them?" she asked, ready.

Arnie went closer to play her game. "You're a fake," he said.

"Not completely," she defended.

"You paint freckles," he accused.

"I've got ten real ones."

"Ten's not enough?"

"You're the one who wanted more."

"I'll settle for ten."

"All right." She spun off the bar stool and went into the ladies' room. She was back in a minute, presenting her face up to him for inspection like a schoolgirl.

"What did you do?"

"I washed off the fakes. These are all guaranteed real."

He counted. "I get eleven," he told her. "You said ten."

"Maybe they breed."

She laughed at herself. He noticed that her nose changed when she laughed, cuter.

"You're not really twenty-two, are you?"

She nodded yes and he believed her. She didn't have the kind of eyes that could lie. "You look younger," he said.

"So do you," she flipped.

"What's that mean?"

"I thought you'd look . . . well, you know."

"Look how?"

She hesitated and let the words out. "Spent," she said.

"Why should I?"

She shrugged innocent and drank some. He waited for her answer. She changed direction. "If you weren't here, where would you be?" she asked.

"Someplace like here."

"That's sad."

That hurt a little. He retaliated. "You're here, aren't you?"

"Not really. I needed to use the phone."

Arnie looked over to the table and saw that Winner had taken his place closer to Connie and was on the way. Arnie thought from Connie to this little one at the bar, comparing. This little one was in a different league. He didn't know if she was worth any time or not. She was about as sexy as a boy scout, although the bit with the dropped panties, the way she'd carried it off, was in her favor. "You like boats?" he asked her.

"You've got a boat," she said.

"How do you know?"

"You asked."

Little smart ass, thought Arnie.

"I love boats," she volunteered. "Where's yours?"

He told her.

"Let's go see it!" she shouted young and took it for granted that was what he wanted to do because she was already on the way out. Arnie finished his drink too fast, waved stay to Winner, and followed her.

Outside, he looked for a taxi.

"Let's walk," she suggested and started before he could disagree.

It was twenty blocks. After the first two or three he couldn't help catching the fun of her. It was contagious the way she looked at everything as if she were discovering. She was the only girl he'd known who said hello to lamp posts and felt sorry for beat-up garbage pails. He'd never known any other twenty-two-year-old girls who literally skipped across streets across the grain of taxis and their drivers at whom she stuck her tongue out. "Don't be self-conscious," she told Arnie when people stared. "They only think you're somebody who looks like you."

They walked east as far as they could and then downtown. They adopted a very mangy street dog for five blocks and bought him a two-pound sirloin steak that he ran away with, afraid he'd have to share it if he didn't. At a fruit stand she stole a pear that was too hard green to eat. At an Italian grocery that Arnie couldn't pass, they got some Genoa salami slices and a round of sesame seed bread and some peppers that burned her mouth so much she swore and cried for water that he got for her from a fat lady fanning herself in the window of a ground-floor oven apartment. They tore at the bread with their mouths and Arnie folded the salami slices small enough for hers. When more people stared at him and walked backwards for a longer look at his fame, she told them, "You think he's Arnie Bruno, don't you? Well, actually he's Barnie Runo. Honest." She crossed her heart and added for good measure, "He can't sing a note. He's just a player piano player."

Many times she ran ahead and waited for him. One time he thought he'd lost her and felt small panic until she came jumping at him out of a cheap clothing store with a pair of working-man's wide suspenders. "For holding up pants," she laughed, and he remembered she didn't have any on. Altogether, it was the longest walk in fifteen years and it was also the kookiest. When they were approaching the river landing where his boat was, she started to run ahead again, but he caught her hand, snapping her back to him. "What's your name?" he asked.

"Jen," she said and spelled it for him.

"What's your last name?" he wanted to know.

"Last names don't count." She funnied her face and broke away.

"I'll bet you're Irish," he yelled at her, and that made her stop and turn and put her hands on her hips.

"My mother, God bless her soul, told me to watch out for hot-blooded sorts from Italy," she said with exaggerated brogue.

Arnie didn't know exactly where his boat was. He hadn't been on it in over a year and it wasn't where it had been then. He told her its name and they looked separately. Jen found it and waved victory. She was aboard by the time he got there. Lots of it was covered with protecting canvas and the door to the inside cabin was locked. He didn't have the key with him and Jen was disappointed for a moment. She took her shoes off and tried to sit the varnished wood of the stern but it was too hot on her bare bottom, made her leap up and run for shade. "Damn near fried my precious asset," she complained, and told him, "Take off your coat. I don't care how skinny you are."

"You're no heavyweight yourself," he said as he got out of his jacket.

She tried to slide his necktie down and nearly choked him doing it. He undid it and unbuttoned his collar. She unbuttoned another button and some of his dark chest hair was exposed.

"Ape," she called him, squinching her nose to let him know she wasn't serious.

And there they were, sitting on the outboard side where they could see other boats, including some big commercial ones coming and going.

"You know what I'd do if this was my boat?" Jen said.

"What?"

"Sell it."

"Why?"

"I get awful seasick."

"You said you loved boats."

"I do. People can love things that aren't good for them, can't they?"

He didn't have to answer, it was so true. He looked at her profile. The jersey dress told him she was definitely no more than a 32A-cup, and it occurred to him that she was through growing. She didn't have an inch of glamour that he could see, although she had nice-enough skin and a nice-enough nose and her hair was sort of funny-nice. Looking, Arnie decided he liked being with her but she wasn't for bed. She didn't promise enough comfort.

Wanting to know, he asked what she did for a living. Her answer surprised.

"I'm a sex expert," she said, serious.

"You work for someone like Kinsey?"

"No, for a magazine." She named the magazine that was one with a high circulation among women. "Every month we have new recipes, new fashions, and one old love story," she explained.

"You write the love story or make up the recipes?"

"Neither, stupid. I do feature articles. For instance, last month I did one on extra-extra-marital relations. You know, cheating on who you're cheating with."

"How do you know about that?"

"Well, I got a lot of percentage figures from research and translated them my way."

"What can you learn from percentage figures?"

"Things like how many do and how many don't according to education, age, income, and all that crap. It was interesting."

"Was it?"

"Not really. All my article did was give those who do something to ease their guilts and those who don't a reason to wish they did or something to feel superior about for not doing it."

He tried to decipher that. "Somehow I'd never take you for an expert on sex," he said, looking.

"Well, I am," she defended.

And she was. Her first article, when she was nineteen, was a precocious sensation entitled "Is Your Sex Drive Automatic?" The magazine had announced it on a day-glo ribbon across its cover that issue and sold nearly a hundred thousand extra copies. After that, she'd done "Take it Slow and Enjoy the Big O," and that earned her a contract from the editor-in-chief. Since then she'd written "Low-Fidelity Husbands (How to Turn them On)" and "Try an Afro-Aphrodisiac" and "Improve your Sexual Vocabulary (Don't Just Lie There, Say Something)," just to mention a few. She'd been invited to speak to various women's groups who loved her, and she'd appeared on several television discussion shows as an authority.

"I probably know more about it than you do," she told Arnie.

He doubted that and told her so.

"Are you really such a lover?" she challenged.

That was a warning signal for Arnie. Magazines were always wanting to do articles on that side of him. Although such publicity helped more than it damaged, he disliked being tricked into an interview and he suspected that was her motive. "No comment," he said, cold.

Jen felt his change and the reason for it. "I was asking unofficially," she assured and asked again. "Well, are you?"

"They don't come any better," he replied, clever.

"Do women really enjoy you?"

"You know it, baby."

"No, I don't."

"What do you want, some testimonials?"

"They wouldn't be valid."

"Why not?"

"A lot of them would say they liked it because they were supposed to like it and if they didn't really like it they blamed themselves and wouldn't admit it. Know what I mean?"

"They all like it," he said, sure.

"Did you know that half the time most women pretend enjoyment?"

That made Arnie wonder if whenever he was pretending they were also pretending. He didn't want to believe that. Both pretending would be a bad joke. "I don't think you're much of a sex expert," he said.

"Oh?" she arched. "Well, according to research averages, what you get is make-believe passion at least 50 percent of the time."

That was one out of every two fooling him. He refused to believe it. He couldn't remember even one he hadn't made good.

Jen went on. "A little moan at the right moment, a few appropriate sounds, a well-timed scream perhaps, some scratching and biting along with typical gyrations to simulate abandon. Any woman can do it any time and make it believable."

"The birds I know don't have to," he said.

"They're different, huh?"

"They want it, they do it, they like it," he said, trying to repair the damage of doubt as fast as she could inflict it.

She unexpectedly reversed to help him. "Then you really must be everything they say you are."

"What do you think?"

She got him eyes to eyes. She put her hand to her chin, studying. She smiled her best smile and told him, softly, "I believe it."

He liked her more for it. "How do you feel about spaghetti?" he asked.

"I think it's stringy, messy, and delicious."

Arnie cooked the sauce, Jen made the salad. They both burned their tongues tasting and their fingers testing spaghetti strands. Winner observed, thinking about Connie and seeing her late late after he got back from the airport.

The meal was good. They had it out on the terrace where the going sun made everything orangy soft. Jen ate the most.

"Where's she putting it all?" asked Winner as Jen finished her second heaping helping.

"Thatsa besta pasta I ever tasta," she said. "Where you learna cooka lika that?"

"Where you learna talka lika that?"

A jet went over for Arnie to watch, expecting it to explode every moment, but it went safe until it was a speck and out of sight. "What time's my plane leave?" he asked, knowing.

"One," Winner told him, clearing dishes and taking them inside.

"You going away?" asked Jen.

"To the Coast."

"I don't like it out there," she said, down. His trip was

news that changed her inside and she tried not to show it outside. "I don't like it."

"It's not that bad."

"Everything out there looks too temporary, including the people."

"I would have thought you'd like the Coast."

"Why should I?"

"Being a sex expert and all that."

She said, "You know what they do, don't you?"

He thought he knew but asked what to hear her.

"They annihilate sex."

"Yeah, piece by piece."

"They do. They all hate it so much they have to destroy it. That's the reason for all their orgies and things."

"It's just kicks," said Arnie. "Maybe they're just doing what everyone else would like to do."

She didn't believe that. "With them sex is always a performance. No, I take that back. It's a rehearsal meant to be serious but played like a comedy. Those orgies, for example, are just everyone on-stage at the same time yelling for physical attention, yelling look at me, look at mine, look what I'm doing, isn't this exciting? Isn't it lovely that we're all so bored together?"

"What do you consider an orgy? More than two?"

She thought and, for intrigue, answered, "More than three."

"How about in your fantasies?"

"What about them?"

"Never more than three?"

She stood suddenly, made her paper napkin into a ball that he thought she might throw at him. She tossed it over her shoulder and it went over the railing. "I'm the second best gin player in the world," she announced to all New York City below.

"Who's the best?"

"Whoever beats me, and you can't."

"It's a deal," he said and they went in to find a deck of cards.

She didn't beat him, she murdered him. Her game was unorthodox. She picked up a lot of discards for speculation, confusing. She outboxed him all the way and blitzed him several times. For a penny a point. She played fast and confident and kept score like she had a built-in adding machine. Actually, Arnie was good at gin. Losing, he blamed the distraction half of her but mostly the impending jet.

Her. Arnie felt she was unusual, so much so that he didn't classify her as a woman woman. He put her in neutral because, with her, his mind didn't have to be pointing toward the eventual bed. She just wasn't bed material, according to his anatomical standards. This skinny little girl who laughed a lot and had eyes that were always dancing around bright blue, who talked quick and unpredictable, didn't affect him that way. He felt it was a nice change, no challenge, no demands, no spending but time. He also found refreshment in her because he thought she was uncomplicated, not a tangle of depressions and hang-ups. It was a relieving contrast to his own layer over layer over layer of time after time hurt and indelible scars.

For most of the gin game Winner watched her play, at first there to help her if she needed help, and then just to enjoy her skill against Arnie. Winner liked her. When they'd been in the kitchen fixing dinner she'd held up her fists at him, inviting him to spar some. She'd danced some fancy footwork around him and flicked out her left pretty good, brushing her nose with her right thumb, fighter style. Winner had invited her to hit him in the stomach with her best punch and without hesitation she'd shot out a sharp right that surprised him. Winner liked her. She was fun to have around, different.

They played gin until eleven. Then she made coffee that Arnie laced with Kentucky for flying courage. As the safe time until departure time was eaten away, Arnie got edgier. He tried not to show it but he couldn't just sit and his talk diminished. Jen asked if she could ride to the airport with him and he wanted her to.

On the way she saw a poster announcing a middleweight fight that made her talk about going to see it. It was Monroe versus Atkins for a shot at the title.

"Atkins will take him," Arnie forecast.

"He's a bleeder. Monroe will cut him up inside six rounds," she contradicted to make Winner smile.

Arnie contended, "Atkins is a good puncher."

"Nothing in his left hand. All he's got is a right."

"He beat Jenkins with it," Arnie told her.

"Right hand lead. Lucky punch," she said.

"Bet?"

"Twenty on Monroe."

"Bet."

"The line gives seven to five on Atkins."

"Okay. You've got seven to five."

The radio was on. It sent them Arnie's current big song and she didn't talk while it was on. With her ears getting it, she looked over at him and put the song beside the man. It was about disillusion, a love of a lover out of reach with touches remembered to hurt, lonely. It was him, she thought, and thought perhaps he really was the oracle of love for everyone that his voice had made him. There was a pain around him in reality, as there was around his sung words. She wondered how he'd come to that and she wanted to ask but couldn't think of the question that might ask enough for answer.

During his song Arnie recalled the session when he'd taped it. The orchestra had been mostly guys who'd backed him before, so first there'd been some personal joking to take the edge off. He'd come to the song cold, so he'd had them run through it twice while he followed with the words inside his mouth, and then he was ready with the tension of knowing they all expected him to be as good as he was supposed to be. He hadn't made it look easy because it wasn't and there was no need to fool. On the first take, as usual, the words weren't just words, they were individual feelings contributing to the total feeling, meant to be swollen into strong soft complaint or shaped down to thin exposed hurt. The first take had been good enough but not good enough for him and, after some terse suggestions from him, they tried again. And that was the second take, the one now coming from the car radio. The orchestra had applauded, he remembered, appreciating him and his performance. He also remembered now the other session that night after that session. With a girl tall and black-haired, who'd called the big night club that missed her showing almost everything in little feathers and a sewn sequin crotch that night, because she had the phony flu. She'd had her purse stolen and needed rent money along with a long horizontal display of various talents. Arnie wondered if she were on-stage walking her flat, child-rejecting stomach around on the beat, being hard on anonymous customers at that moment when he was looking out at the giant red neon that said a bad local beer at him.

Arnie's hand was on the seat between them. Just there. Jen put hers there also, atop, not large enough to cover, but he was surprised to feel it. All the rest of him seemed so numb.

At the airport Winner waited while Jen saw him off. At the passenger check-in counter the almost pretty clerk recognized immediately and tried for blasé.

"Are you traveling alone, Mr. Bruno?" she asked.

Only a nod from Arnie. He no longer felt human, more machine.

"But you have three tickets," the clerk said.

"Three," verified Arnie.

"One is sufficient."

"Three," Arnie insisted. "Seats together."

"It won't be a crowded flight," the clerk informed, and questioned with her eyes a moment before processing the three. "Your luggage, Mr. Bruno?" Arnie didn't have any. He didn't need any because his place in Beverly Hills had everything there.

While he was checking in, Jen hurried to a magazine counter and returned to walk the long walk to the boarding gate. From the passage window Arnie saw out to the gigantic silver shape of his fear with men in white coveralls around it. At first sight he stopped in his mind and walked away instead of toward, but his legs continued on to the sign that was his way to go.

"I bought you this to read." Jen gave him a magazine that he rolled into a tube. She faced up to him.

You're so lucky, he thought, you don't have to get on that thing out there and drop dead. Then it registered through his fear that she expected a good-bye kiss. For him it was quite possible, nearly a fatalistic certainty, that it was good-bye kisses, forever. So he brought her to him with his arms. Not for a neutral quick dry kiss. For a long connection, desperate.

"Here," she said, when they finally broke. "Promise not to read it until after you take off." She put a slip of paper in his breast pocket, tucking it behind the silk handkerchief already there. He tried to smile. She smiled enough for them both. "You kissed the legs out of me," she said. "Hurry back, Barney Runo. Please?"

It sounded to him as if he said yes before he went inside

and farther in to be really inside, past the welcomes of the two pretty stewardesses to where the seats were three by three. He found his and made sure there was no number four. He sat the seat near the window, put his head back and shut his eyes. But his ears were wide open, and it was as if his sense of sight had been transferred to them when all the sharp and muffled mechanical sounds began. They were on total volume for him, making the needle jump. Then there was the sibilant power of the engines increasing. He opened his eyes and looked the window and outside was moving slowly, away. A stewardess came by to smile and instruct him to fasten his seat belt. He strapped himself in tighter than necessary and thought her spirit was foolish. No going back now, he thought, unless he jumped up and went to the control cabin and shouted for them to stop and return him. He wouldn't let them know his fear, of course. He was ashamed of it, so he started to invent excuses important enough. "I'm on the wrong plane," he thought he could lie. Or: "I'm not feeling well, I need to see a doctor," which was half-true.

By that time they were down the runway and turning and stopping for a moment.

Get off now, all of Arnie told himself.

The engines grew and grew and grew and vibrated him and everything around him. For seconds the ship was a giant power, held back, but then it was released to spring forward. Arnie in eyeshut felt the sudden thrust, and the speed he knew was still touching ground because there were some jars and bumps on it. Long, long fast, faster roll, until the wheels had to be off the concrete that was now Arnie's earth and he was an object inside the rising float, unnatural. All through the slanting shoot up to altitude he was closed eyes, trying but failing to think of anything other than falling to death. The plane leveled. Arnie opened eyes. Although the seat-belt sign was off he kept his tight around him. He looked the window and saw dark nothing below, and that was bad and good. Perhaps some ground lights would have been reassuring, but they would have also been the frightful gauge of how far up he was. All he could see out there were the flaming exhausts of two engines and the reflection of a red light on the wing tip, revolving blink blink.

It came to him that he was soaked with the perspiration of his tension. His shirt was sticking to his skin and his eyes were stinging and his scalp felt as if each hair were electric. But, at least, feeling meant feeling was returning through the emulsion of his anxiety. He had to think of thousands of feet of possible fall beneath him. The plane, that had looked too large and heavy to lift into the air, now seemed flimsy and incapable. He was sure that they, those who were at the controls, didn't know enough to be absolutely safe. He imagined the plane's captain surrounded by dials and other indicators and wondered how much guess there was in that man, and how much apprehension really, as the ship shot through the high dark.

Arnie had to turn off such thoughts. He tried, forced their volume down, but they continued to needle with warning like a long-playing record, stuck. He unsnapped his seat belt and told his imagination that instead of there he was in an ordinary chair some ordinary place on earth. He remembered the slip of paper from Jen and took it from his breast pocket.

> Think of all the thousands of planes that fly every day and never crash. Besides, the wicked always live to be very, very old.

In her writing. Arnie read it three times. Had his fear been so apparent? He wondered and decided no. It was just that this girl Jen was perceptive. She probably had some sort of witch's mind. How else could she have beaten him so badly at gin? She probably knew what cards he had all the time. And even if she wasn't a witch, he thought, because he really didn't believe in such things, there was definitely something abnormal about her.

He put the note back into his pocket to read again when he needed to. That slip of paper reminded him of another—his assignment, the reason for all this risk. A look at his watch told him they'd been flying over an hour. He had plenty of time if there was anyone among the other passengers. He got up to see, to search for a pretty girl alone. He walked the aisle forward and back and saw there were no more than a dozen passengers, mostly men. The only female alone was a chunk of pigeon-breasted woman in a gray suit who was reading the *Wall Street Journal* through nose-pinching glasses. Arnie noticed her hair was like an oversize steel scouring pad. Nevertheless, she was the only prospect, repelling, adjusted to her change of life that probably hadn't even been a change. Arnie passed.

He walked the aisle all the way back and into one of the three toilets. He didn't feel the need to urinate but when his center was out and aimed it performed its secondary function. Arnie pressed the flush button and watched his liquid get swirled away. He thought of it dropping somewhere on America. Like the worker on the girder, the pisser. He reiterated the philosophy. To wash, he took off his jacket and undid his collar and sleeves. The water that jounced in the miniature stainless steel sink was reviving and he felt better when he went out.

That was when the answer came to him in the form of the stewardesses. It had been so obvious he hadn't thought of it. There were two of them in the cubicle that was the plane's galley. One was an angular brunette and the other a rounder blonde who also looked younger.

"Hey, conductor, how about a drink?" Arnie asked for a start.

They both smiled.

"Scotch, vodka, or gin?" the brunette asked.

"Got any orange juice?"

"Sure," the blonde answered and got out a container.

"Plain orange juice?" asked the brunette.

"Plain with vodka," said Arnie. He noticed they had their names in plastic on them. Miss Bryan and Miss Whitney. The blonde was Whitney. She mixed and handed Arnie his drink. "Here you are, Mr. Bruno," she said, sort of sing-y.

"Do I have to drink alone?" asked Arnie.

"We're on duty," said the brunette inside a cool company smile.

Before that Arnie had wondered which. Now it was definitely the blonde, who was squatting to a compartment when a single chime sounded and the brunette moved around her to answer it, a passenger's need. The blonde came up with a tray of sandwiches wrapped sterile. "Want a nibble?" she offered.

"No, thanks. Want a sip?" Arnie offered back.

"Regulations. I shouldn't."

"I won't squeal."

She took a gulp that was a lot more than a sip.

"Make me another," requested Arnie.

She did, with more emphasis on the vodka this time. Arnie drank some of the first drink and gave it to her. "Finish it," he told her. She hesitated and nodded no.

Arnie warned, "Hurry, here comes Miss Rulebook." That made her drink the rest of the drink so fast some of it dribbled her chin. She was innocent by the time Miss Bryan got there to pour two coffees and carry them to someone. As she went sideways past Arnie in the narrow aisle, Bryan gave him a look that ordered him to his seat. Arnie ignored it.

"You like night flying?" Arnie asked Whitney.

"Yes. Working nights I can go to the beach days."

She had a good blonde's tan. She also had a nice pair inside her crisp white blouse, Arnie noticed. She was about as all-American as an airline could get.

"When do you sleep?" he asked.

"I get enough."

She probably does, thought Arnie.

She told him, "We take turns napping on flights like this when there's only a few passengers."

"Give me another drink."

"Two's the limit. You've already had two."

"Afraid of Bryan?"

"She's senior."

"She's an airborne cop."

"Not really."

"But you're a lawbreaker. I can tell. That's why I like you more."

She poured him another juice and vodka.

"When it's time for your nap, come sit with me," he said and whispered confederately, "I'll save you one of these."

He went back to his seat with a drink in each hand. The plane was dark except for very dim lights over the aisle and the individual beam that old gray pigeon was reading with. He had to wait only a few minutes for Whitney to be beside him. He tried to hand her the promised full glass.

"You hold it. I'll drink it," she told him.

She lighted a cigarette. He put the glass to her lips and poured more vodka into her. He made sure their talk was about her for a while. She was twenty. She was from St. Louis, originally. She shared an apartment in Hermosa Beach with two other stewardesses. Her only brother had just left for the Vietnam fight. She signaled with her lips for a vodka encore from Arnie who tipped the glass so high she had to get a lot but she didn't complain. She liked surfing and was good at it. She really didn't want to be a stewardess but she didn't want to be anything else either. She had a dog named Pete, a West Highland terrier that a passenger had sent her. Her first name she thought was awful. It was Roberta. Her friends called her Whit. Whit was feeling the vodka. "I saw you in person once before," she told him.

"Where?"

"Vegas."

"At a crap table?"

"No. Singing. You were marvelous."

"When was that?"

"Last year."

Last year is so old, thought Arnie. It reminded him that he didn't have much time. He gave her the last of the drink and put the glass in the elasticized pocket on the back of the empty seat in front of him. He was going to put his hand on hers but she beat him to it, found his and held.

"Your hands are cold," she said. She stood and got a blanket from the above rack. When she was spreading it, he asked her about the arm rest that separated him. She knew how to remove it and did. Then she was under the blanket, a third of her against him. He put his arm up and around and she moved closer into the cave of it. He let her just be like that for a few minutes, using it for the foundation he felt she needed before he started really building her. Actually, in that time she was prefabricating a kiss with her hope. Because this was Arnie Bruno. So when he moved his head she moved hers to it. He kissed his best kiss. He had to teach her mouth some. She learned spontaneously. During the second kiss her tongue told him her breasts were waiting.

She had a brassiere on. His fingers had to squeeze in and gather until he finally found a nipple that was full from anticipating. But he couldn't define her breasts, harnessed as they were. He thought perhaps she would rebel when he maneuvered in a try to find where her bra was fastened. He felt for the place but the band across her back was smooth and that puzzled him. She had to help. She reached with both her hands into the V front of her blouse and her bra uncupped left and right. Then he could play them, both. His touch told him her breasts didn't really need the bra.

This was Arnie Bruno. Whit was feeling his feel. Arnie measured how much by the way she was breathing into his mouth. He gave her left and right more than enough tease and slight hurt and perfect other attentions before he sent his hand down for the more serious occupation.

This was Arnie Bruno. She didn't clamp her legs. She parted more to allow and his hand went up to nearly reach but down to increase her crave for it to be up again. Arnie wasn't lost in the loverland. He was on the perimeter of it, feeding her, the target. He expected her to be wet with want when his fingers stretched in between her skin and the elastic of her panties, and she was, puffed and streaming, and her most special place was distended maximum to receive. He pressured that place perfectly, rolling its little long rise and flicking its exposure with experience.

Whit had to move some, grabbing animal moves.

She wanted it.

She'd never been lost so high so fast.

She didn't care. This was Arnie Bruno.

She wanted it in.

Arnie plunged a finger.

At the same time there was someone else.

"Whit," called Miss Bryan, not loud.

"She's asleep," said Arnie.

Miss Bryan disregarded his excuse. She called the name again to make Whit separate and Arnie's hand retreat.

"Captain Eliot is looking for you," said Miss Bryan. She waited for Whit to get up. She took Whit away.

Cunt. Arnie cursed Bryan a couple of times. His watch told him they had a little more than an hour to go. He looked the window and the same black was out there being burned by the engines that were more glowing now. He wondered what mechanical device prevented such heat from reaching the fuel tanks and exploding them.

Headline:

BRUNO DIES IN AIR CRASH

He saw thousands of mourning females, and some less inhibited ones, overcome by grief, unable to restrain from rubbing themselves on the corners of his coffin, closed because he'd been scorched beyond recognition.

He dissolved dark death by clicking on the light above. Less than an hour to landing. He gave up on Whit and making it on this flight. For distraction he started on the magazine Jen had brought for him. He read anything, including an article by her that was boldly titled:

BORED SUBURBAN HOUSEWIVES TAKE UP THE OLDEST PROFESSION

Why are thousands of American women out selling when they say they're out shopping?

It was after three, Coast time, when he got to his Beverly Hills apartment. He stripped, dropping his clothes anywhere. He was exhausted, his body let down as if it had been through hours of battle. He got into bed and felt, by contrast to what he had felt, a safe content that took him to sleep for seven hours. When he awoke, some of him had a tension hangover; especially around the shoulders he was stiff and sore. He wished Winner were there to rub it away and he thought about calling for a massage but he took a sauna instead and the heat loosened him. He dressed fresh and called the office.

"When did you get in?" asked the voice Arnie paid.

"Last night. I need a car right away."

"We weren't expecting you."

Arnie asked, "Is Eunice here or in Palm Springs?"

"She's here, I think. Do you want me to call and make sure?"

"No, I'll call. What I want you to do is cast somebody for me."

"Who?"

"How the hell do I know who?"

"What type?"

"You know."

"There are lots of new ones around."

"So show me some."

"When do you want to see them?"

"Tomorrow. I'll be in Palm Springs."

"Anything else?"

"What else is there?"

"You could sign some things while you're here, save sending them to you."

"Send them."

After that he realized how hungry he was. He went to the kitchen that wasn't ready for his arrival. Nothing fresh. He found a can of cling peaches and opened it. He ate some fast right out of the can, just to stop being so hungry. He thought maybe Eunice would fix him some bacon and eggs.

He didn't bother with calling her. He knew he should but decided on surprise, so in fifteen minutes the car had him up Coldwater Canyon and into the drive of the house. He didn't like having to ring the doorbell and avoided it by going around and down the long side of the house. There were tall hedges and a gate that he opened to go in to the rear terrace, large with grass and inset with the marble swimming pool he'd designed himself. Also, in the far corner was the putting green he'd had put in with special grass flown from Scotland. Everything the same. But there was no one. He walked to the pool's edge and looked down into the water where a yellow plastic toy boat was sunk. On the pool's surface, where the overflow drain was, an inflated plastic tube floated, bright. Yesterday's play that he'd missed, he thought and sat in one of the cushioned chairs facing the rear of the house.

He looked windows for life but saw none. He felt as outside as he was, a kind of expiating pain that didn't discontinue even when he told himself everything was better as it was. The house. The house had been extremes for him, penitentiary and empire. The ambivalence had split him from the crotch up, slowly, and he still felt it, being there. A part of him made him fiction that he'd never left. But the other part of him that had been a prisoner stuck him with the points of reality that were all the ins and outs and various breasts and crotches he'd done in the time that was now a one-way span of years. The problem was, for him, both sides were really counterfeit.

Now there was a face in a second-floor bedroom that discovered him and he had to get ready for her. He decided to stay where he was, sitting, because he wanted to look relaxed and happy enough.

Eunice came out the terrace door and down the few steps without hurry all the way to him. She had a full-length cotton robe, straight, with a front zip. It was oversize blue flowers and leaves on a white background. On her feet were little strapless heels of cracked gold, and her head was wrapped in an orange chiffon scarf so no hair showed. She had a red drink in her right hand and a bracelet heavy with gold charms on a wrist. "No one said you were here," she told him.

He got up and put his hand out to her and they touched fingers meaninglessly. "I let myself in," he explained. They sat opposite. The sun made them both squint. "How are things?" he asked.

"Fine."

"Where are the kids?"

"We didn't know you were coming. They're not here."

"They're in school?"

"No. It's summer vacation." She thought that was like him, not knowing that. "They left for Acapulco the day before yesterday. They're sailing down with the Bruces."

"That'll be fun for them," he said, down. He thought he might as well leave.

"Want one?" she asked with her drink.

"What is it?"

"Bloody Mary. The way you used to fix them."

"No, thanks." He remembered she'd never liked Bloody Marys. He watched her gulp. "The place looks the same," he said, just to say something.

"I'm having a fountain and fish pond put in. They begin it next week."

"Where?"

She indicated the far corner where his putting green was. He didn't care, he told himself.

She asked, "What brings you out? An emergency?"

"Just a little problem."

"Sorry the kids aren't here."

He looked Eunice. She didn't have any eyebrows. She'd plucked them all because her natural ones were too low and made her look glowering. Now, without makeup, no eyebrows. She wasn't pretty anyway. She never had been. He wondered if she was letting her body go. He couldn't tell, the loose way she was dressed, but the last time he'd seen her in a bathing suit and noticed. "You still go to the shrinker?" he asked.

"Don't use that term, please."

"Dr. what's-his-name?"

"Richards."

"You still use him?"

"Of course. I'm down to three a week now."

She'd gone five a week for seven years. Maybe three a week was improvement, or possibly less hope.

"I may try LSD," she said. "We're undecided on it but I'd like to. What do you think?"

"Why not?"

"I'm afraid I'll flip out. It happens, you know. Some people flip under LSD and never get back."

He could see her flipping. He knew her scream. He always thought she was the ugliest animal in the world when she was angry. He really didn't think LSD or Dr. Richards or a dozen a week would help her. The trouble was the way she was born, with a hole between her legs, a nothing hole, a vacancy that didn't want to be filled but needed to be. He wondered what she did now for sex. He knew she needed once a month. But probably she just clenched and concentrated herself numb until the urge passed. Or maybe she had someone. He couldn't imagine that.

"Like some lunch?" she invited.

"No, I had a big breakfast."

"The kids loved your last television special."

The kids. Georgio, the oldest, wanted to be a doctor and there was nothing to stop him. Arnie didn't know how a twelve-year-old boy could really decide doctor but Georgio was serious and read medical journals instead of comic books.

"Dad, your eyes are bloodshot."

"What's your diagnosis?"

"I need to give you an examination."

"All right, examine."

"Is your stomach upset?"

"No."

"You need glasses."

"What kind?"

"Dark glasses. I'll get them for you."

"Okay, doc."

"Also I noticed something else bad."

"What?"

"You've got wax in your ears."

Maria, the girl, was different, more like Arnie at ten. She didn't like school and could spend hours just wondering. She entertained. Maria knew all the words to his songs and would duet any time. Arnie remembered once driving along the coast highway with her only six and singing with him. Despite the resistance of Eunice, Arnie knew Ria would come to him someday wanting to do what she wanted to do. That's what Arnie called her, Ria. No one but him.

"I hate geography."

"Why, Ria? What did geography ever do to you?"

"Stupid maps."

"Don't you want to know where you're at?"

"I know."

"All right, where are you?"

"With you."

"Learned any new songs lately?"

"Three."

Ria had a good transistor radio Arnie had bought her, that she kept under her pillow at night and listened with the ear attachment so Eunice wouldn't know.

Now Eunice sighed the old sigh and asked, "When you going back?"

"Tomorrow night."

"Still afraid of flying?"

"Not so much."

"That's a change," she said as if there'd never been many.

"I'm going down to the Springs for the night."

"Too hot down there. But you like it hot, don't you?"

Eyes to eyes. "Yeah, I like it hot."

Eunice had come to the conclusion that she really didn't know him as well as she knew him. Sometimes she'd tried to keep up but just when she thought she was with him something always happened to make her realize how ahead he was. There'd never been the period of separate bedrooms for them. When the time for that came he left. There had been one brief reconciliation, a week in Las Vegas when she'd unplugged. She'd forced herself to be by his side urging the dice at the crap tables, and she'd laughed and gone without her usual long sleeps, and once when he was shaving she'd come up behind him to reach around and make him hard. And she'd gone down there, acting as if she wanted to, right there in the bathroom. For four days she'd acted against her normal currents before giving up to stay in the suite alone and sleep most of the time away and admit that she really hated him because she couldn't love him. Of course, she blamed him for it. It was his fault because it looked as if it were, the way he'd gone right from her into some tighter-bodied dancer from the show line that week.

Now there he was, sitting the sun with his fame. Every chance now Eunice tried to destroy the lover legend of him. After all, she'd had him for years and should know. But no one believed her. They preferred to believe in him, illuminating the truth that he was too much for her. She often thought there must have been a time in all that time when she'd been equal to him and she tried to feel when. She was sure it had been some time before fame. Perhaps when she'd waited on a stairway while he auditioned and they'd shared one beer afterward. Or was it when he'd bought her that first mink without asking the price and sneaked in that morning while she was still asleep to throw it over her and waited until she awakened to discover it, feeling loved? Perhaps there'd been more than one time when she was up to him. But then, perhaps there'd never been even once. He'd always been faster.

As he was now, saying, "I have to go."

"I'm sorry the kids weren't here."

"Tell them I was."

"Of course."

"Tell them to call more often, will you?"

"I can't make them."

"You can remind them."

The rest of the Bloody Mary went down into her.

"Good-bye, Eunice."

It is martyrdom to be in Palm Springs midsummer.

The mountain that hovers the town is like a high bleached spiny beast too blistered to move, threatless. All the land puffs and reflects a gassy insanity, contrary to the slow motion of humans in the heat. The only outside chance is a swimming pool, although even that purified private liquid is not really as cool as its invitation, another sun trick.

Arnie was in his, bare. He swam mostly underwater, an exercise to improve his singing breath. For about twenty minutes, and then he got out to let the baking air dry him. But it didn't. The swimming water on his skin was quickly evaporated but immediately replaced by perspiration from every pore. It was punishment and he retreated from it to inside air conditioning. He showered, wrapped in a blanket-size towel and, with a Kentucky whiskey, sank into one of the deep white couches in the living room. The quiet irritated him. He got up and clicked on the hi-fi that was kept loaded with two-hour tapes of him. That was better. He tried to relax again but had too much impatience. He went for a telephone, and the long white cord of it followed him like a trained snake as he walked the room and dialed. He got the office. He told them, "I'm going back to New York tonight."

"We set up the casting for tomorrow."

"How many?"

"Six."

"All good ones?"

"Of course."

"Have them here by seven."

"It's almost four now."

"Fly them down."

"All right, they'll be there."

Before hanging up, Arnie thought of another prerequisite.

"Make sure none of them are sick," he said.

"Sick?"

"You know what I mean."

"How'll I determine that?"

"Ask them."

After that he called New York to get Winner. He called the good number. It rang more than enough and he was about to disconnect when Winner answered.

"I was in the tub," Winner excused.

"Soaking?"

"Yeah."

"Don't forget to change the sheets."

Winner knew Arnie knew. "Don't worry."

"How much have you got it down to?" asked Arnie.

"What do you mean?"

"With Connie. Starting at eight hundred, how much per piece?"

"Maybe a hundred."

"Try for fifty."

"When you coming back?"

"I'll leave here around midnight."

"That'll put you in about seven in the morning."

"Be at the airport."

"I thought you were going to stay out there a couple of days."

"I'm bringing someone with me."

"She going to stay here?"

"No. Get a hotel."

"Okay. Hey, we saw that guy today."

"What guy?"

"The one who pisses off the girder."

"Did he wave it at you?"

"He waved it at the world."

"See you in the morning."

While he dressed, Arnie thought about Eduardo and Rog and Knight. He liked the possibility of them not making out, of him being the only successful one. So far, he'd made only one mistake. He shouldn't have counted on the mere chance of there being anyone to do on the plane, although even under those long-shot circumstances he'd almost scored, would have if that other stewardess hadn't interfered. The way he had it figured now, he couldn't miss. He'd bring his own. That's what he should have done originally; however, he'd have had to make the return flight anyway, so nothing was lost. He was sure he now had a sure thing.

And even more sure when the girls arrived at seven for casting. One first fast survey told him he could pick blind and come up with a cooperator. Three shades of brunette, two shades of blonde, and a red. Their hair colors were the only individual thing about them. They all had the same very helping makeup and the same partly parted smiles, promisingly hungry. They all had fronts that pointed proud of size and good legs shown by short skirts that were also tight enough to contain their bottoms with flattering tension.

Arnie started it with a business handshake for each and let them say their names. He offered a drink and told them to relax. Some sat to make their skirts ride up. Some walked around to look but really to be looked at. Arnie said something clever and they all laughed easy eager laughs.

"I'm sure you've all had experience," he said.

That got a unified yes.

"Do any of you dance?"

They all danced.

"Okay, so far it's a six-way draw. Hell, I'd take the six of you if I could."

"Why don't you?" asked one of the brunettes.

Arnie gave it a thought. He saw himself boarding the plane with these six. He imagined them up there with him. The only way to go, he thought. He saw himself landing in New York with them. Twelve sensational tits wouldn't hurt the image any. He'd give them to Winner for a coming coming-home present, after he'd had firsts, of course.

"Put on your bathing suits," he told them.

They all looked quizzically at him and one another.

"Didn't they tell you to bring bikinis?"

They all said no.

"They didn't?" Arnie acted anger at *they.* He went for the phone, picked it up, and then put it back, disgusted. "I told them bikinis."

Arnie knew one of them would see the advantage. It was one of the blondes. She got up from the couch and asked with her expression and went where Arnie indicated, out of the room. It had the effect he wanted on all the others. They let some of their nerves show; those smoking dragged harder. In less than a minute the blonde was back. She hesitated in the doorway to frame her pose in panties and bra. She had it and she showed she had it. She turned for an all-around view. She kept her shoes on to better her legs.

"Very nice," approved Arnie, and the blonde, encouraged, walked toward him to pivot within reach. That made one of the brunettes get into competition. She didn't bother with going to the next room. She took her dress up and off right there and came around the couch so she'd have the benefit of his unobstructed appreciation. In minutes the room was decorated with removed dresses and choice, nearly nude bodies fighting variously for attention.

Arnie remained impartial. He flattered and gave equal interest to each. He acted confused, transmitting the impression that they'd have to make up his mind for him. "You all look good," he told them.

The redhead took the next step. She reached around back and unhooked and her bra dropped while her breasts didn't. Then she got the elastic top of her panties with her thumbs and showed that she was either a true redhead or a perfectionist. Then for all it was a serious race to get bare. They all kept their shoes on.

Arnie continued blase.

The redhead complained with pout, "It's not fair."

"What?" asked Arnie.

"You're the only one dressed."

They all playfully demanded the equality that would be him with nothing on.

He was tempted. "Let's keep this on a business basis," he said, faking formalism. "I want you to line up," he told them. "Over there."

They did as he said, avoided contact with one another while they got into formation, all using the standard stance of one knee bent out and overlapping, weight on rear foot for suggestive side curve, shoulders back to maximize fronts, and one hand on hip. Arnie let his eyes enjoy them ensemble for some time and then he went in for closer inspection. Actually, he'd been so erotically amused that he hadn't yet made a choice. They were all choice. To eliminate he had to look for minor flaws. He walked the row of them, front and around.

One, he observed, had slightly inverted nipples that, of course, could be aroused out but he used it as an excuse to exclude her. Another had a small spoiling appendectomy scar. Another had just a hint of stretched tissue on her back upper thighs. One of the blondes needed a bleaching retouch because her hair roots were showing the same darker color as her pubic triangle, and a brunette had too many moles.

Arnie asked the redhead, "What was your name again?"

Her name, she said, was Laurie.

She had ideal redhead skin, newborn texture, a tight drumhead stomach dotted with a fortunate navel, pale pink baby-finger nipples, taut, and a waist that made a nice roller coaster dip for the good of her hips.

"Okay, the rest of you can go," he said.

They broke the line and kept their smiles for the chance of next time, while they put on their clothes quickly to leave. They sang their individual good-byes to him.

The victorious Laurie stayed bare. She walked to the wall of glass and showed him the dimpled punctuations above the twins of her rear while she appreciated the swimming pool. "I'd love a swim," she said. She slid the glass door open and went out. She sat on the pool's edge and splashed the water gently with her feet.

Arnie wondered if he should get her ready here, build her some before the plane, just for insurance. He decided he didn't need to. He went out to her.

The day was going. It was cooler out but still too hot.

Laurie tossed her hair from her face. She was on the shallow end of the pool and she lowered herself into the water so half of her was submerged. She looked up at him and asked, "What kind of part is it?"

He was thinking about the plane. "What?"

"The part you chose me for. What kind of part is it?"

"The best part," he assured.

She began swimming. Arnie watched her cut the water, her ass white rounds following the streaming red of her hair. She rolled over to float some and her breasts were wet identical islands and her crotch mound glistened its hairs like a patch of delicate water weeds.

For Laurie to pack some things for the trip East, they stopped at her apartment that was close enough to Schwab's just south of Sunset. The building she lived in looked more like a nightclub with its color lights, plastic facade, and cheap molded fountain. Arnie waited in the car. His flying tension was increasing every minute, and he wished with his fear that it was some future time when there was teletransportation instead of this terrible risk of valuable life. He tried for calm with the fact that he was returning home and vowed, if he arrived there safely, never for any reason to put himself again at the mercy of another jet monster.

Laurie rushed out with a single suitcase and plenty of excitement. She'd changed to a summer suit that Arnie didn't think would be a problem. He was glad she hadn't decided on slacks.

And in less than an hour and a half they were in the belly of the plane, belted in, moving toward take-off. Arnie watched blue lights marking the runway, ominous blue. By that time he was inflated numb, unaware of the lovely Laurie beside him, not wanting to believe he was where he was. He put his head back and closed his eyes and was again a victim shot up into the air, depending on the unknown quality of some mechanic, who really wanted to be a singer, and the fallible judgment of some pilot who might possibly be emotionally or alcoholically distracted.

They finally leveled off at 30,000 feet. The same soaking perspiration for Arnie. He opened his eyes to look at Laurie. "Warm in here," he commented, making the corners of his mouth smile.

"I'm cold," she said.

"How many films have you done?" he asked just for talk.

"Seven. But only one good bit," she said and asked if he'd seen a certain movie. He told her no. "It was an Arabian Nights thing," she explained and said she'd played a harem slave girl with a lot of close-ups. "I got quite a few calls from that but nothing developed." She added, "Until now."

Arnie was looking at her but not really seeing her yet because of the jet.

"I never thought I'd be here with you," she said.

"Why not?" shrugged Arnie.

"It's a big break. I guess I've got it coming, though."

Arnie was phasing back to near-normal tension now, his large anxiety settling under, but just under, remaining mercurial.

Laurie asked, "Why did you choose me? The others were so pretty."

"Red's my favorite color."

"That the only reason?"

"You look talented. I've got an eye for it."

"I'm really cold," she said, hunching.

He stood and got a blanket from above. While he was unfolding it, she asked, "Could you get the stewardess to bring me some water?"

He rang and requested and the water was brought.

He looked out to see the afterflames of the engines. He thought he'd get started on her in a few minutes. He'd give her a long building, take her up to such a degree that when he finally put it to her she wouldn't be able not to come immediately. He turned to begin.

She had some things on her tongue.

Blue capsules, two of them.

She brought the glass of water to her lips and swallowed.

She saw his concern. "Just sodium amytal," she explained. "Sleeping pills. I always sleep when I fly. It's nice to go to sleep and wake up when you're there. Want a couple?''

''Hell, no,'' he told her, sharp. He wanted to tell her to go stick her fingers down her throat and vomit the damn things up before they started working.

''I'll be asleep in a few minutes,'' she said. ''If I snuggle against you, please excuse.'' She scrunched down and got into a comfortable sleeping position.

''Good night,'' she said and closed her eyes but opened them again to smile contentedly. ''Thanks for everything,'' she said. ''You're a nice guy.''

Arnie cursed inside, every curse he knew, but mostly the word ''fuck'' vehemently.

In minutes Laurie was sleeping limp.

Arnie wished he'd chosen the brunette with the moles. All he could do now was sit tight and listen to the hissing power that was six hundred miles per hour and hope the damn machine he was captured in didn't fall to death. All the way home.

Winner was waiting for them when they came down the passenger ramp at Kennedy International. Arnie's initial impression was that the big man appeared blanched and tired, but when Arnie looked again and caught Winner stealing up and down Laurie he saw Winner's color had returned.

They rode into the city. Winner drove first to the hotel he'd arranged for Laurie. She was still a little remote from the sleeping pills. ''I'll see you later,'' Arnie told her. He put five hundred into her hand. ''Do some shopping.''

''When do we start rehearsals?'' she asked.

He almost told her the show was over but decided to save her. Perhaps he really would find something for her. Although the little trick she'd done with the sleeping pills wasn't in her favor. ''I'll call you,'' he promised. ''In a few days.''

''In a few days?''

''I've got a tough schedule,'' he excused and left her and her one piece of luggage to the doorman.

''Wild-looking bird,'' said Winner about Laurie on the way to the apartment. ''She really a redhead?''

''Yeah,'' was all that Arnie wanted to say.

''She's got nice milky-ways.''

''Not only that.''

"She got talent?"
"She's a sleeper."
"A real comer, eh?"
"A sleeper."

Arnie's body was thankful to be home. He took his suit and tie and shoes off and lay on the couch in his shirt, while Winner fixed some breakfast. Arnie felt as if he'd been tortured. He had a back-of-the-neck headache and his ears still had pressure in them from the altitude drop. He worked his jaw some, trying to pop his ears, but failed.

He'd also failed at his assignment, he thought, but didn't really care. Nothing, not even that, could get him up in the air again, he assured his nerves. It was dumb anyway, this doing-it-on-a-plane thing. What the hell difference did it make where he did it? That question made him feel it would have been different-good up there. But now he'd never know. To hell with it. No more planes, son of a bitch, no more planes.

After bacon and two scrambled, Winner gave him a rub and Arnie fell asleep for five hours. When he got up he opened the drapes to watch the construction workers on the girders. He hoped the pisser would go into his act, but after fifteen minutes Arnie gave up on him.

Winner answered the phone and said, "It's Jen."

"Who?"

"The one who beat you at gin."

Arnie took the call. "How'd you know I was back?" he asked, still partially convinced she possessed some extrasensory powers.

"I just felt you might be," Jen told him. "How was the trip?"

That was a chance to unload some of his suffering but he let it go by. "Fine," he lied and then told her a truth: "I read your article in the magazine."

"What did you think of it?"

"I got a few laughs."

"It wasn't funny."

"You made it all up."

"I didn't. It was based on facts, every word."

"Anyway, why shouldn't a housewife hustle around some if she wants to?"

"You don't understand. What makes it so exceptional is

the lie they live. And the idea that most of them do it for kicks, not the money. Of course, they take the money because that's part of the kicks."

"I read that."

"How do you feel?"

"Okay. Why?"

"Well, I was just sitting here contemplating three pieces of cardboard that say Monroe versus Atkins, ringside. Interested?"

"When is it?"

"Tonight."

He felt like it. "Who's the third ticket for, Winner?"

"Unless you want to bring along one of your 38C-cuppers."

"You're enough to handle."

"Me? I'm just a slip of a girl, sir."

"Speaking about slips, how are your pants holding up?"

No answer from her about that. He thought maybe she was irritated by his mentioning it. He asked.

"No," she laughed, "I just wanted you to ask if I was."

"Smart ass."

"The bishop also said that to the showgirl."

Before good-byes, Arnie got her address to pick her up at eight. They decided to get there early to see some of the preliminary bouts.

Jen had on silk jersey again but this time bright blue. She was the same blonde cap of mussed hair and batch of freckles. She gave Winner a hug for seeing him again and Arnie got a fast cheek kiss.

During the prelims she picked two out of three and the third was a draw she thought an unfair decision and said so loud enough to be heard by one of the judges. She ate two hot dogs with plenty of mustard and had a pair of orange drinks. She didn't yell during the fighting. She urged her favorite with mumbles and slight jerks of her left and right shoulders that was punching of her own, restrained. She amused Arnie. He'd taken girls to fights before but usually they were either bored or screamed for punishment; never were they so sympathetically involved.

"You really like fights, don't you?" he asked.

"When they're fair."

"Where did you learn to like fights?"

"At home."

"How's that?"

"My mother and father were fighters."

"They didn't like each other?"

"They loved each other," she explained. "Some married people do nothing but sulk and repress. My mother and father always square off and let each other have it. Whenever I go to see them I can always count on at least one good battle."

"They actually slug one another?"

"With words. My mother's a screamer. My father shouts. She's a good jabber and he's more of a counterpuncher."

"What do you do, referee?"

"Hell, no. They don't need a ref. They hit below the belt sometimes but that's not dirty. And whenever they clinch nobody can break them apart anyway. It's very romantic, really."

He thought perhaps she was inventing. He remembered she was Irish.

Then it was almost time for the main event. Anticipation was in the air as thick as the smoke. This was the one they'd all come to see, and when the boxers made their entrances to climb up through the ropes and be in the lights, the crowd glorified them.

Atkins was a mean pale chunk with a pile of scar tissue on his brows and a ridge of previous tortures across his flat nose. He looked as if he'd been purposely constructed, or at least reconstructed, for his profession. All his flesh, his hard leg stumps, bull neck, back and chest full of built muscle, seemed to be ready to work as a living weapon, lethal.

His opponent, Monroe, was different. Monroe was taller, rather spindly, a Negro more National Geographic than Hollywood jungle movie. The sinews of his legs showed and so did his rib cage. He had a lean long neck and a small head. There were glistens of perspiration on his tight hair from warming up in the dressing room. Monroe's arms hung relaxed, and they looked out of proportion, too long for the rest of him.

Appraising the two fighters, Arnie felt even more that Atkins' respectable right would do its expected work. "Who do you like?" he asked Winner.

"Monroe," Winner told him.

Jen smiled.

"Shit. They don't belong in the same ring. Look at them," said Arnie.

The fighters were in the ring's center with the referee saying the official litany that was the instructions already known. When you compared the brute of Atkins to the flimsier Monroe, it did look like a mismatch.

"I'll take Monroe for twenty at seven to five," Winner told Arnie, who quickly snapped, "Bet."

And when it was two minutes and five seconds of the first round it seemed to be a good bet for Arnie. It was then that Atkins' right hooked around and caught Monroe on the temple. The thin Negro went down like broken sticks. The crowd cheered and moaned accordingly.

Jen said, "He'll get up."

Monroe did and escaped further pummel from Atkins by staying in close and hanging on almost all the remaining time until the bell. When he went to his corner for repairs, Monroe's walk was as if he had a pair of fractured ankles.

"Told you," said Arnie, nodding with knowledge. "Atkins will finish him next round."

But deep sniffs of ammonia stimulant cleared Monroe.

He came dancing out for the second round as if he'd never been hit. He stayed out of Atkins' range and managed not to get cornered, while flicking stings over and around Atkins' guard, again and again.

"That's my baby," encouraged Jen.

By the end of the third, Monroe had opened a cut over Atkins' left eye and during the fourth the knifing of his long left had sliced the skin across Atkins' nose. Atkins fought with more fury, wilder, while Monroe evaded and damaged as if the leather around his fists were edged with razors. Early in the fifth the ridgy right brow of Atkins was jabbed open and blood streamed. Monroe went to work on Atkins' eye and soon his left glove looked as if it had been dipped in a bucket of ketchup. Atkins' face was a red ball trying to breathe and see. He was missing badly now, not able to gauge his enemy, who danced and bobbed behind the film of blood that Atkins couldn't blink away. They tried to patch Atkins for the sixth but the collodion only held for a couple of punches and within a minute Atkins was helpless. Monroe slashed across two consecutive rights and Atkins was actually facing to fight in the wrong direction when the referee felt enough mercy to stop it. More moaned than cheered in the crowd that began leaving.

In the car on the way to Nickie's, Jen stated with authority, "They should have stopped it in the fifth."

"You said Monroe inside six," Winner reminded how exactly she'd forecasted.

"Shut up," snapped Arnie, who was normally a poor loser and recently had been unlucky various ways. He thought what he might do is have a steak and call Laurie the redhead, to see her after he'd taken Jen home. He needed it.

At Nickie's the usual stares hit Arnie from all directions. Arnie instructed Winner to sit at the bar for punishment. Arnie was self-conscious of Jen because she wasn't the speedy-looking sort of specimen he was usually seen with. She didn't have the promising buttocks and pointing breasts to create the envy, so Arnie was glad when they were sitting and less of her could be appraised. The redhead Laurie would have strutted and flipped them, he thought, but here he was with this bony little creature smiling her inextinguishable smile and ready to order everything on the menu. Arnie had received the usual important reception from Nickie who disapproved of Jen because he had much at stake in the ardent reputation of his most famous customer. Jen was definitely damage to the image.

"We should have gone someplace else," said Jen, not knowing she was expressing Arnie's exact thoughts.

"Why? This is my place."

"You own a piece of the business?"

"No."

"You ought to."

"What makes you say that?"

She answered by holding the oversize menu up between her face and his. She pretended to read: "Appetizer Arnie Bruno, Entree Arnie Bruno, Dessert Arnie Bruno."

The truth made him angry some. "We can leave," he said.

"No. I'm hungry. Besides, you think you really like it here."

"You think I don't?"

He was nodding around at people he didn't know, generous. She told him, "It's not a supper, it's a benefit. For two different proceeds, Nickie's cash register and your ego."

"I like the food here."

"So let's eat."

They ordered. He didn't think she could eat as much as she asked for but didn't care. While they waited for the food, she told him about an article she was writing on latent lesbianism. She was in the middle of a sentence regarding the amazing statistical frequency of homosexuality among overweight women when someone interrupted.

He was looking down at them. He was a few inches over six feet, a young man with an old face full of alcoholic resentment. "That the best you can do, lover boy?" he slurred, indicating Jen with his chin. Arnie expected Winner to be there immediately to handle this one, who was already getting his sleeve politely tugged by Nickie, trying to coax him away. All the room's eyes were aimed, and talking stopped for everyone to hear the man continue his belligerence. "You wouldn't know what to do with a good piece," he said.

Jen felt Arnie stiffen. She looked for Winner. "Ignore him," she advised.

The man said, "You know what I think? I think you've got more publicity than balls."

"Blow, creep," snapped Arnie.

The man telegraphed his punch. Arnie saw it coming and it never touched him. It pounded harmlessly on the leather back cushion and the weight of the man went against the table, off balance. Arnie had a fist made but never got to deliver it, because Jen had slouched down and reached with her feet.

It was a beautiful trip.

The man went stumbling with spin, crashing off a table and grabbing the dessert cart on the way down to cover him with cream cake and brandied peaches. He tried to get up but Winner's foot was on his forehead. Nickie was screaming Italian when Arnie and Jen left with hurry. The car was in front. They got in and waited for Winner who finally came out wiping whipped cream from the back of a hand with a napkin.

"Where the hell were you?" Arnie asked him.

"I was making a phone call when it happened. Who floored him?"

"She did."

"No shit?"

They all laughed. They drove up Park, laughing. Arnie and Jen laughed in a hug and Winner could hardly steer, he had to laugh so much. When they could talk again, Jen said, "I'm hungry."

"Take us someplace." Arnie told Winner to have him turn off Park and over to Third and up some blocks. He stopped at a little place that looked empty.

"Good hamburgers," recommended Winner and they all went in to have rare ones with raw onions and draft beer.

"I guess that happens to you a lot," said Jen about the trouble at Nickie's.

Arnie shrugged.

Winner said, "Only a couple of times a week."

"Oh, well," sighed Jen and exaggerated admiration, "I guess that's what you get when you're the fastest gun in the East."

"I'm very slow, baby. Good and slow," said Arnie.

"Yeah. Bang, bang," she teased.

The owner of the place slotted some house money into the jukebox to play three Arnie Bruno songs as a tribute. Again Jen put the singing of the man around the flesh of him. It was the same current big song they'd heard on the way to the airport, and again she felt his musical hurt was a reality. It was a voice with more than performed lonely. It was pure lonely. She heard it and went through his famous face to his private deep where she was surrounded by the pain of his disconnection. She felt sorry for him. She wanted to help. "Take me home," she said, changing.

"Don't you feel well?"

"You sick?" concerned Winner.

"No. I just want to go," she said and led the way fast out to the car.

The quick change in her made a difference in Arnie. Since the Garden he'd been the quiet sullen one, but now she sat as far from him as possible, withdrawn, looking the New York night streets, and he had to go out to her.

"Did I say something wrong?"

"No," she replied, staying the same.

He thought maybe she was having a delayed reaction from the fight at Nickie's but the way she'd been at ringside canceled that. He didn't know what was wrong. There was no reason for her mood. When they reached her apartment she got out immediately and said good night without looking. They watched her go in, her blue dress swishing with her sharp walk. She shoved the lobby door as if she hated it and was out of sight.

"Nice kid," said Winner.

"What happened to her?"

"I don't know. You must have said something."

"I didn't."

"Maybe you should have."

Arnie didn't care. "Let's go."

"Where?"

"Call the redhead."

"I got a late one with Connie. That okay with you?" Winner asked permission.

"Go."

Jen tried to get her mind off it. First she took a bath and tried to scrub it away. It helped some but not enough, and when she was drying she got herself in the bathroom mirror and it all came back full force. She stood there and contemplated her reflection as if it were another person, with hipbones studding like that and breasts not large enough for their mature nipples. That body in the glass had hardly any woman curve to it from underarm all the side down to her thighs. No nice in of waist because there was no nice out of hips. She stood with legs apart and thought of it, "Freak," she said and retreated from it.

She always felt it was incongruous for her body to have so much want. Her mind was more than rich enough to deserve full soft curves and full-size breasts. Often she tried to convince herself that her body was literally retarded, incapable. But her center always heated and contradicted that excuse, so she had to go on envying the proud-bodied women she saw, overcompensating with her mind. That was how she became occupied with writing oblique erotica. A sex expert.

But now, as she turned off the light, hoping to turn off her thoughts, it wasn't her body that she was devaluating. She was ashamed of herself generally. She'd chosen Arnie for a target because of his lover reputation. She'd planned it all, a simple-enough plot, starting with the premeditated dropping of her panties. She remembered how she'd used her cuticle scissors to snip the elastic of them while she was in the phone booth at Nickie's. Just for initial shock. It had worked, had helped get her into his attention, into his life.

From that point on, she'd expected a development, either quick or eventual, that would take her body under the publicized skill of his. Her reason was candid enough. She'd never done it. Never had it done, and she thought she might as well start with the best. All the sexual research she'd accumulated, along with the nourishment of her own contemplation, had brought her to that scheme. She'd even gone so far as to prepare her mental attitude for an absolutely brave acceptance of his insertion. If there was pain, instead of a painful cry, she was determined she'd moan. She wouldn't tell him virgin. Not only because she was ashamed that she still was, but also because she didn't want to restrict him with carefulness. She wanted full force feeling the very first time, including all the variety and techniques his experience promised. She'd even practiced her part. On the very bed she was now on, she'd exercised, making diverse pleasure circles with her center and hungry interior muscle grabs.

She knew how, theoretically. She'd even gone to the extent of training her hands to touch how and where they should. And her mouth as well. She'd been prepared for the experience. All ready to deceive and use him. What she hadn't counted on was anything beyond the physical, either her own emotions or any consideration of his.

Now in her bed in the dark, her mind and body had an argument.

"I want it," her body said.

"I know," her mind tried to soothe.

"I want it absolutely the best in the world the first time. No fumbling, no mistakes. First-class the very first time."

"I agree."

"Then why the hell did you run out on the plan?"

"I felt his hurt."

"So what? It was there before you. You're not to blame."

"He's got so many scars from being used."

"It's his own fault," her body contended.

"He's a victim."

"You're depriving me."

"Keep still. You'll get yours somewhere."

"Sure. But not like from him. You know, he probably is as good as he's supposed to be."

"Stop it. I said no and I mean no."

"You're afraid."

"Not really. Not physically."

"I want it."

"Forget it."

"I can't."

"You can."

"I won't," her body protested.

"You will. You're nothing but a skinny, flat-chested, inexperienced undesirable."

"All the more reason not to feel sorry for anyone else. Especially him."

"I promise. You'll get it soon."

"From him?"

"Maybe."

"Call him right now. Lie about tonight. Get on with the plan."

"No."

"Why not?"

"I've had a change of heart."

"Don't give me that. You mean love, don't you?"

"Yes, love."

"How can you love him? You hardly know him."

"I saw into him."

"I want him."

"So do I."

"You don't stand a chance. I'm impatient. I'm already overloaded with want. You know that."

"We could change our plan."

"Will it include me?"

"Of course."

"Will I get it good? From him?"

"Better."

"I want it, him, it, now."

"Control yourself."

"Get him for me."

"I'll try. But it won't be easy. If you were round-soft like you should be, full, hot-looking with ideal breasts and a pretty, twinkling ass, it would help."

"I'm sorry. You'll just have to make do," her body said.

Jen turned the light on. She looked down at her toes. She got up and turned on the hi-fi for some of his records that she stacked to the limit on the automatic changer. Then she turned off the light again and went horizontal. She rolled over on her stomach to try to stifle the voice of her center that was crying more for attention by the singing of him. She had the hi-fi volume loud and his voice covered her. She let it. She listened to every word and after a while she sent her concentration against the stream of his sounds to speculate on the love of Arnie Bruno.

By then Arnie was home, He'd tried to call Laurie but the hotel switchboard told him the line was busy. Three times. He walked the apartment, turned on the television to not watch an old movie. He had Winner fix him a drink. He wondered some about Eduardo and Knight and Rog. His own failure made him think they'd probably all succeeded by now. It didn't matter, he told himself. He wasn't going to give it another try in a plane. He thought he'd lie to them Friday night. It wasn't much of a lie anyway. He'd use the stewardess story and just stretch it a half hour. After all, another half hour or maybe less and he'd have had her. He took the phone to his lap and dialed the hotel again. This time the switchboard rang Laurie's room. After four rings someone answered, but it wasn't her.

Arnie asked for her.

"Who's calling?" the voice asked, definitely male.

"A benefactor," snapped Arnie.

Laurie got on and said hello with a question mark.

"What are you doing?" asked Arnie.

"Nothing. Just talking with an old friend."

"Send the old friend home and come over."

"It's one-thirty."

"What's the difference?"

"I'm tired."

"From what?"

"I walked all over today. I'm not used to walking. You know how we drive everywhere in Hollywood."

"Get a cab and come over."

"I can't."

"Why not?"

"My friend is here."

"Get rid of him."

"I'll see you tomorrow, please?"

"Forget it."

"Don't be angry."

"I told you I'd call."

"I know you did, but . . ."

"Are you coming over or not?"

There were some noises that Arnie heard, along with some protesting whispers by Laurie, simultaneous with what sounded like a brief minor struggle. Then it was her friend on the phone who said, "Look, I suggest you go play with yourself."

"Fuck you, fink."

"If you want somebody to come over, it'll be me and I'll break your goddam head in."

"Come on over, you bastard, I'll get on you faster than stink gets on shit." Arnie slammed the phone down. His stomach was flipping, his heart at high-speed anger.

Winner had heard it all. "Want me to go get her?" he asked.

"No."

"Then can I leave? I got Connie."

"No."

"What you want to do? Just sit here all night? Why don't you call somebody else?"

"Who we got?"

"How about the receptionist from the recording studio? She was a good one."

"You had her."

"So? She was good."

"I don't want to follow your act."

Winner held back a remark regarding that. He suggested, "The blonde at the Copa. You told me to remind you about her. She gets off about two."

Not all of Arnie felt like having her, but he nodded for Winner to dial. After a brief conversation Winner hung up. "She got married," he said.

"Was she there?"

"Yeah."

"Well, why didn't you ask her to come over?"

"I told you. She got married."

"Means nothing."

"She only got married last week."

"So she needs a honeymoon."

"We got lots of numbers. How about a rematch?" Winner named a few first names from before. But Arnie rejected them all. He couldn't think of anyone he'd had that he wanted enough again.

Winner said, "There must be somebody."

Somebody. Some body.

To put some time into. To take from with pleasure of giving ganglions their greedy due and blood its rush, disturbed. To smother a skin and cover all its possible inches with discovery by effective fingers, arousing from their lair the little animals of sensation, packing them for ferocity. Pressing pore to pore and asking every opening for entrance. Feeding on the surfaces of somebody. Devouring reaction in fragments of cultivated convulsions and particles of pyramidal spasms. Playing with cellular specialties.

Response is the fill of loneliness, temporary but adequate. It is proof of living, at least.

Horizontal crucifixion.

Delicious gnawing of the glands to extract heaves and humps. Turning the tissue into tactile proof that there really is no disconnection, that separate birth and death does not brace a hopeless cavity. Plunge to disprove it. Lick the overwhelming vacancy. Shove down the throat of breathing the long tongue of reality so time must gag and give up its tasteless digestion for all to be sweetness and reassuring physical fragrances, melting on the tongue like communion wafers.

We are connected by feeling alone.

From a singular beginning the protest against solitary confinement, futile, but demanding attempt with hands that hope to heat, and lips, to such a degree that centers glow and fuse forever. But never forever.

"Did you like it?"

"Very much."

"You came good?"

"Oh, God, yes. You did me in."

"How many times?"

"I don't know. I lost count. You give marvelous head."

Not many variations on the desperate theme. And aloneness, that was never really dissolved, that hovered all the while, claims its place to ache its habitual ache, slides its exact duplicate transpicuous shape into focus with the flesh that tried to burn and plunge and probe and grab and give it away. Again and again and again. Always, all ways the constant aching parallel, now predictable.

Piston into the flesh sleeves of similar engines but realize the transient coupling.

Heat passes through time without consequence.

Sperm pours down the numbered face of the clock.

Although all the nerves are ignited cleverly together:

"Now, darling. Now."

"Come with me. Come with me."

"Oh, God, I'm coming."

"Come with me. With me."

I am with you, isolated with you. Arnie Bruno is alone with you, feeling the echo of his separate punishment in the hollow of your manipulated rapture.

Abandoned.

Winner filled Arnie's empty glass. "I'm late for Connie," he said.

"She'll wait."

"To hell with her. I don't need her," sacrificed Winner, knowing Arnie's disposition from previous times.

Arnie appreciated the loyalty but it wasn't really what he needed. "No. Go on. Bang thc hell out of her."

"I've got an idea," Winner brightened. "The little one. Jen. Why don't we call her?"

"What for?"

"She could be better than she looks."

"I doubt it."

"She's got a motor. You've got to say that for her."

"I wonder what pissed her off."

"Just a mood. She's over it by now."

Arnie considered it a compromise. But the more he thought about it the more intrigued he was with doing this different little skinny girl who advertised herself as an authority on sex. However, simultaneously, another part of him measured her against those his want usually chose and almost convinced him it would be a waste of sensual effort. Ambivalence. He eliminated it by deciding to give her a break. She'd be grateful for it. They all were but she'd be more. His generosity appealed to him.

"Call her," he told Winner.

Winner didn't have her number. He tried information and learned she was unlisted. He told Arnie.

"Okay. Forget her."

"I can go pick her up," Winner volunteered.

"Too much trouble."

"I'll go get her," said Winner and went.

While Winner was gone Arnie took a fast shower and shave. He put a long tape of himself on the hi-fi, so it was ready. There were clean sheets on the bed. He wondered if he should use the mirror. He pressed a button and some of the ceiling directly over the bed slid away to let the glass it revealed reflect the surface of the expecting bed. He decided on a 20-watt pink light bulb and arranged so all other illumination could be switched off with a single snap. The usual anticipation of doing someone new was highing him. He remembered what Jen had said about only half the girls truly enjoying it. He was inspired to demonstrate how he contradicted her statistics. When he was through with her, she wouldn't be able to move. Sex expert. He thought it likely that she'd experimented a lot, but nothing compared to what she was about to get. As far as real pleasure was concerned, she was still a virgin. For the first time she was going to get it good. The best.

He heard the front door and waited for Winner to come in with her. But Winner was alone, with a pained expression.

Arnie asked, "Where is she?"

Winner didn't want to say.

"Did you see her?"

"Yeah."

"Where the hell is she?"

"She didn't want to."

"What do you mean, she didn't want to."

"I told her straight."

"What did she say?"

"She said, 'I'd sew it up first.' "

"You're shitting me." Arnie went out and looked the hall, hoping she'd be there to laugh at this play. But she wasn't.

Winner explained more. "I told her you wanted her. She told me what I just told you she told me, word for word."

"The ungrateful little bitch," cursed Arnie. He had some anger but mostly disappointment. He began dressing. He told Winner, "Take me over to her place. You can leave me there."

* * *

The front door of Jen's apartment house was open but it was a large building and there were about fifty names on the black plastic plates in the lobby, each with a signaling buzzer. There was also a metal plate with perforations that was a speaker.

Arnie was glad he knew her last name. He found it. Apartment 14C. He pressed a long buzz until her filtered voice asked, "Who is it?"

He told her.

"Go away," was all she said.

He shoved her button in again and again but she didn't answer. So he pressed a lot of others, playing the odds. Various voices came from the speaker. He mumbled some nonsense syllables into it that sounded like he'd forgotten his key. Immediately the door buzzed permission for his entrance. He went up to 14 and found C. He knocked three firm knocks. He heard her say, "The door's open, Arnie."

He went in to find her in a fat-armed chair near the window. She had on a pink innocent nightgown. She was all in the chair, her feet and legs curled up under her. Arnie didn't sit.

"Why didn't you accept my invitation?" he asked.

"Because it wasn't an invitation."

"What was it then?"

"A command performance."

"I thought we could play some gin."

"That's not how Winner put it."

"So what's wrong with that?"

She didn't answer. Arnie moved to the hi-fi. He examined empty album covers. All him. She got up for some reason. As she walked past him he blocked her. She didn't try to get around. He put his arms around her. He kissed her his best kiss. She just received it with her arms at her sides, her mouth inactive. Her passivity made him break short.

"What's the matter with you?"

She wasn't angry. She wasn't anything. Just blank.

"Nothing," she said.

"Don't you want me?"

"No," she lied.

"I want you."

No reaction. He released her.

"It's almost three," she said.

"Time to be in bed."

"Yes. Why don't you leave?" She didn't say it acidly, merely a suggestion. He stepped out of her way and she went into the kitchen for a drink of water she didn't really want. She listened, hoping not to hear his departure. She had to risk it. When she came out he was the same.

"Reconsider," he told her.

"I haven't even considered it."

"Why not?"

"It's not worth considering."

"You'd like it. I promise."

"Let's not talk about it."

He went to her and held her again. He tried another kiss. She had to think of cruel things and neutral things. She kept her eyes open and concentrated on the wall behind him. Blank.

He gave up. "I guess I don't affect you."

"I guess not."

He turned and started to go. She hoped he'd say something else. With his hand on the doorknob he said, sarcastically, "Sex expert."

She had to smile. "Are you sleepy?" she asked.

"No."

"I'm not either. Want to go for a walk?"

"You know what I'd rather do."

"Forget it."

"Okay. A walk."

She went into the bedroom and closed the door to put on bell-bottomed tan twill slacks and a pale yellow tank top of silk jersey. She thought about putting on a bra with falsies for courage but decided to just let her normal nipples punctuate. The slick of the fabric would rub them to attention.

When they were on the city streets she did another quick change. She let her laugh out. Her walk was practically a dance, floaty and diverse. She wanted to go to Times Square. He didn't think they should and she knew his fame was bothering him.

"Don't worry," she assured. "I'll tell them you're not you. Better yet, don't act like you. Laugh more."

Times Square at 3 A.M. on a weekday isn't quite the same as Times Square at midnight on a weekday. Some of the stores are closed, half the people are gone, and a few of the lights are out. But it is not unconscious. While most of the city turns off and slumps in the black to replenish for survival in tomorrow, Times Square is a perpetual pit of glow, attracting those who are too alone to sleep, those with night causes, those who need to be actively reassured that life is synonymous with motion and sight. Most nourish one another and receive nourishment at a safe separating distance. The exceptions are lovers locked by arms and minds, representing hope. Their presence is respected with envy.

Arnie and Jen went around there hand in hand, looking lighted windows of closed stores, going into some that were open.

Arnie was on a campaign. He took Jen's advice and forgot about his fame. He laughed at things, at her. He communicated his desire for her with frequent physical messages—a hand around her waist brushed up for a fast exploration of her right breast. The young size of it and its erected tip he found pleasing. He held her lower, around to touch one of her hipbones and past it to the concave section where her legs and torso made their transition. From that he imagined the sensational tight of her center. He embraced the back of her against his front and liked the fit. His lips gave a fast traveling kiss to her neck, just above where it joined her shoulder and up its smooth to her ear that he also paid some extra teasing. He cupped the shape of her head with a tender stroke. And he kissed her short laughing cheek and mouth kisses, depending on the position of her face, spontaneous.

Jen received. She wisely didn't translate his attention into more than surface language. She allowed his touches but suppressed response, merely continued on her merry mood, being with him.

They had a newspaper headline printed for them that shouted in 4″ high letters.

SEX EXPERT VS. SEX EXPERT

They spent coins and good time in a flashing arcade for amusement with various machines, including an electric eye rifle that had to be aimed at a moving bear. She could have gotten a better score but let him win by ten. There they also tested their love capacity on a device that lighted his squeeze as warm and hers torrid. They also stamped their names on aluminum good-luck disks and exchanged them for keeps.

They paid their way into an all-night thrill movie that had an overstated title with the word "orgy" in it. They giggled at the serious parts of unbelievable girls who were, not to violate the law, acting for the sunny health of nudity in a camp where volleyball was a convenient sport that made their huge breasts bounce.

After that they had an orange drink standing up. And went on.

They were stopped by a ten-year-old boy selling plastic orchids for the sympathy of two dollars each. The boy ached his face and hunched and uttered something inaudible as he tried to shove the overpriced flower into Arnie's hand. The boy did his best deaf, dumb, and maimed imitation and Arnie was reaching for money when Jen pulled him away. The boy straightened immediately and found his voice. "Fucking cheapskate!" he yelled.

They went into an all-night record store and saw on its high wall a giant, faded picture of Arnie ten years younger, smiling for the world. Jen told him he hadn't changed much. Outside again they saw a dyed-hair fag doing his cutest look-at-me walk that no one else noticed. They saw two sailors cruising for girls or anyone. They saw a pair of fat-assed hookers flanking a bald man on the way to taking him. They saw the selling of magazines covered with overgrown breasts and paperback books showing waist-cinched, mean girls dressed tight-black and accessorized with whips and sky-scraper heels. Next to the art of pouting muscular blond boys kissing. Next to an ideal girl in a wisp of dress curled at the feet and begging up to her shorter-haired female duplicate in trousers, shirt, and tie. It was all a matter of taste.

They saw a wild man striding and talking loud anger to himself about Jesus and war and the President and commies.

They walked east to the next avenue where Arnie's wave got them a taxi. He didn't ask Jen. He gave his address to the driver. Jen didn't say anything.

He kissed her a long kiss on the way and his hands went under her sweater. Jen didn't say anything.

In the elevator going up fifty floors he pressed against her for her to feel his excitement. Jen didn't say anything. And when they were up there inside his place he repeated the close holding to combine it with an open darting kiss.

Jen's body was crying. Her center was flooded. The cool blue of her intentions was dissolving in the red of want. She was on the edge of yield and he was pushing. He was grinding. One of his hands wedged between their lower press to take his fingers down there where she wanted them. They began, sure now.

She gritted and reinforced. She separated to be more than a reach away. "No," she said, surprised that she could say it because her breath felt molten. He moved toward her for more persuasion. She stepped back the same distance and said another "No."

"Why not, baby?"

"The name's Jen," she said for some reprieve.

"Jen," he conceded. "Why not?"

"I just don't want you."

"That's ridiculous."

Her body agreed but she said, "I just don't, that's all."

"Sure you do."

She made a sympathetic face and nodded no.

"What's wrong with me?" he asked.

She knew she was gaining. "Nothing. I like you. But I don't want you sexually."

"Not at all?"

"Oh, I could go through the motions but it wouldn't mean anything."

He had confidence. "Let's try," he suggested.

She walked to the window and looked the dawn that was happening to the city. The first sun was hitting just the top of the highest buildings. A half-moon was still in the sky but losing.

"You must be frigid."

She laughed. "Like hell. I love sex."

"But you don't want me. Is that it?"

"That's it."

"Why?"

"Why should I? Just because you're Arnie Bruno?"

"You're a cock teaser."

"Not really."

"Then why'd you let me touch you?"

"I had to find out."

"What?"

"If I wanted you or not. I don't."

"Sure you do. I could make you want it."

"It would only be vaginal masturbation."

"You don't like me at all."

"Yes, I do, Arnie. Even though you are a sorry creature."

"Me? I've got the world by the balls."

"That's the general impression. But you're a fake."

It hit a nerve, exposed. He captured her with his arms. He expected her to struggle but she stayed passive.

"Maybe you're the kind who wants to be raped," he said.

"Maybe."

"I could accommodate you."

"Do you want me that much?"

"Sure."

"Why?" she asked, calm.

He didn't know why. He really did want her that much. It flashed to him that he hadn't wanted her at all before, but now he held her and pulled her sweater up to get one of her small breasts. He had to have the nipple. He bent her roughly but his mouth was tender with it.

She was melting. She felt like falling, heaping-helpless.

"Do you like that?" she asked, flat.

He didn't stop to answer.

"It's doing nothing for me," she said, sighing for boredom.

That stopped him. He released her. He walked to the couch and across the room, threw her a look and then back to the couch to sit. "You're frigid," he accused.

"Don't be silly. If there's one thing I'm not it's frigid."

"Then why?"

"You really want to know?"

He nodded yes. She thought he looked very vulnerable.

"You're a machine," she told him.

"A machine?"

"An orgasm machine."

He laughed a short laugh, nervous.

She went on. "The stupid thing about it is you think this machine that you are is capable of making love."

"Go on, expert," he flipped.

"But all it ever produced is hate."

"I don't hate anyone," he defended.

"You don't love anyone."

"Love is a four-letter word. Spelled different."

"Don't you wish it weren't?"

He didn't answer. What she'd said was finding a place in him. He looked her eyes to eyes for reassurance. She was steady. He lowered his eyes and was a child she wanted to go to for arms around.

"Suppose we'd done it," she said. "What would it have meant to you?" He couldn't answer.

She answered for him. "Nothing. It'd be just one more stab at your trying to feel more than alone."

"You're full of shit."

"Am I?"

He lowered his head again, clamped his hands in his lap. He thought a moment before he said, "No."

"Don't you think anyone could really care for you?"

"No."

"I do."

"You think someone could?"

"I mean I do. Me. I do," she admitted.

"You feel sorry for me."

"More than sorry."

"What do you mean by care?"

"You know."

"Tell me."

"All right. What you've been doing is spending your time as if it were counterfeit. Actually, time is the currency of love."

She stopped to see if his reception was on. It seemed to be.

She went on. "When you care for someone you want to be with them as much as possible. You want to *spend* your time with them, or more precisely, you want to spend your time on them."

"Yeah, *on* them," he quipped.

She continued as if he hadn't spoken. "When people care the only thing of real value they can give one another is time. And in that time they give themselves."

He was serious now, receiving.

"Lovers say, 'I want to be with you. I want to go with you.' Lovers ask, 'Please be with me. Will you go with me?'

And even when they're apart they spend their apart time on one another."

"You said you cared for me," he reminded.

She parried. "In a way the act of lovemaking isn't half so much proof as the given time in which it happens."

"You said you cared for me," he repeated.

"I do."

"Does that mean you want to be with me?"

She had to say yes.

"Then why don't you take off your clothes and be with me?" he grinned.

She walked over to him, looked down.

"That's my baby," he said. "We'll spend some beautiful time together." He was reaching for her slacks button when she did it.

She almost did it with her fist. At the last moment she opened her hand so it was only a slap. But it had all her temper in it and hurt.

"Know what you are? You're an ignorant, one-way hopeless bastard," she said and left him, fast.

With the sting of her still on his face, Arnie mustered his egotism and thought he was glad she was gone. He needed her like he needed a disease. He took off his shoes. He went to the kitchen and made a cup of instant coffee. Motion made him realize he felt heavy and he had a strange abstract sense that every move he made allowed the air to refill the space he vacated. His imagination could hear invisibility rushing to occupy the train of him, replacing him with nothing, testifying that no part of him, not even the merest mark, remained to prove he'd been there.

With his cup of steaming black burning the knuckle of his right forefinger, he returned to the couch and tried to resume his position. He blamed her for this bizarre feeling. It was the infection of her, left over, that would be cured almost immediately by other thoughts. He sipped the coffee that was too hot but the anesthesia of his emotions prevented burn. He didn't care. He didn't care if he never saw her again. He switched his mind to other pictures of relief: bodies opposite from her, pleasure-built figures female full, exaggerated.

That was what he needed, he thought. It had been nearly a week since he'd had. A long time for him. That was his problem, not her. For distraction, he planned the extra large breasts and cushioning crotch he'd find somewhere to put into his day. However, it was only a slight shift of focus from that future form to a parade of past used skin and parts and faces. He was surprised they were all so distinct. They were supposed to be forgotten. He'd had them, they were already consumed and wasted. There was no need for reunion. But he couldn't stop them from reminding him that they were what they were: grown from helpless infancy into usable proportions like a crop of phenomenal fruits to be munched to their cores again and again, but always replenished to their original substance.

That was how it had to be, he thought, including Eunice. Commitment didn't change that. Commitment was worse with its sharing of toilet and paring of nails, brushing of teeth and chewing of dinners, laundry and lipstick and monthly soil.

Winner came in. Arnie didn't know he was there until he spoke. "Did you see Jen?" asked Winner.

"Yeah."

"She still pissed off?"

"Yeah."

"Did you find out why?"

"She told me."

"Connie sends her regards," said Winner, taking off his jacket.

"How was she?" asked Arnie, trying.

"You know Connie."

Sure, thought Arnie, I know Connie and all the Connies. Life is a mushy fucked-up ball of Connies. Arnie said, "I've got to connect today."

"It's a nice day."

"Got any suggestions?"

"We could go shopping. Saks, Lord and Taylor, Bergdorf, like we used to. We always scored. Remember the doctor's wife? The one who wanted her clothes ripped off?"

Arnie got a flash of her. "Okay. We'll go shopping."

"I'll make some breakfast," said Winner and went to do it.

Arnie got up and moved a chair to the window. He sat there. He didn't eat the fixed breakfast. On the steel frame of the building being constructed he saw workers and the actual stars of welding. He wished the man who pissed on the world would do his act. Arnie waited, ready. But the pisser didn't appear. Arnie sat like a toad, feeling heavy, silent, blobby. In that time he reheard some of the words Jen had said to him, her tender and angry ones alternating. As he looked over the city, he received some reassuring mental applause to drown her voice that came in octaves, delivering her prescription for heal.

Eventually the applauding diminished to be only that one loud slap her fury had dispensed, and then there was only her single word "care" to be examined, depreciated, and valued. From that he was taken to look through the prism that he thought was her past. He saw other hands and lips on her thin body, and jealousy invaded him, especially when he improvised her willingly spread for the hard pierce of someone. He was sure it had happened, and while he hated it, he was astonished that he hated it.

Why the hell should he care?

He looked with increased hope for the man who could walk nonchalantly out on the high beam to piss on everyone below. But he wasn't there for Arnie. Arnie needed him but he wasn't there. Arnie had to talk to Jen. He resisted, using Winner for diversion. "Let's go shopping," he said. "Let's go."

"Any time you're ready."

"Right now."

"Don't you want to shave and put something else on? You need a shave."

Arnie felt his jaw that was rough with enough growth to make him go to his electric razor. By the time his face was buzzed smooth and cooled by lotion, he and himself in the bathroom mirror had come to a decision. "Let's go," he said to Winner.

"Aren't you going to change?"

He didn't answer. "I want to stop by Jen's."

"What for?"

He didn't reply to that either because he didn't yet know the true answer.

But he knew when he got to her place, when he went up and knocked her door and she didn't open. He listened against the panel of it but heard nothing. He hoped she was in there sleeping. He knocked more and tried the knob that told him locked and he had to knock more until his give-up told him she was gone. At once hope, that he hadn't realized was in him, poured out, and he was empty.

She was lost. It meant something to him that she was lost. He tried to refill himself with the confidence that she was only temporarily gone but his anxiety told him different. He leaned the corridor wall to wait some. He walked the corridor to consume time. He went down to the lobby of the place and sat there for her. All the while he fought against believing she was forever lost. He kept watch on the street door with his imagination seeing the fragile blithe form of her entering any moment. He planned on what he'd say to her. He'd gradually reveal his feelings, he thought. He'd guide their conversation cautiously to a point. He'd lead her to repeating what she'd said about time being the currency of love and also another declaration of her care for him. But this time he'd respond in a different enough way to let her know. That was one plan. Another one was more impetuous and true. He'd just blurt it out.

There was someone coming in. It was only Winner.

"Did you see Jen?"

"No."

"What are you waiting for?"

"Nothing," lied Arnie.

"Let's go shopping."

"I'm tired."

"Let's go home. You look tired."

"Let's wait another ten or fifteen minutes."

Home, Arnie got bare and again took up his vigil for the pisser. For some curious reason his mind had created a race between seeing the pisser and Jen, seeing one or the other first. Impatience inflated him. "Call and see if she's home," he ordered Winner.

"Her number's unlisted."

"Give the operator a spiel. Tell her you're a doctor or a detective or something. Use your goddam imagination."

Winner dialed. After a lot of arguing he got the number and tried it. "No answer," he reported.

Arnie tried it himself every fifteen minutes all afternoon until he was saturated with futility. He felt very young and very old. He fell asleep with the phone in his nude lap. When he awoke it was after nine. At once he dialed her again, but still no answer. He had a double Kentucky to freshen his mouth and dissolve the dead feeling. He thought about how many dead people there were who just didn't know enough to lie down and stay down. He yelled for Winner. Arnie told him, "I'm going to the Coast. Get some reservations. Three seats like before."

At midnight Arnie was where he'd promised his fear he'd never be again, belted tight in the belly of a jet. Although terror was again sweating him and every muscle was contracted by danger, there was a resigned sort of despair sharing him.

The engines increased from a whine into a sibilant scream and the jet rolled the runway for the velocity it needed to finally make its diagonal try, carrying Arnie and a few other night travelers up to the unnatural height of five, nearly six miles.

For Arnie, survival now was valued more and less. There was now a hollow in him, a measure of desolation defined. At the same time, and equally intense, he felt something new stirring him. It was a giddy feeling, a fresh sort of pride, an unexpected sensation of well-being to a degree he hadn't experienced since his kiss-stealing youth. He knew it was precious. He tried to enlarge it, and in that attempt its source became explicit. It was so simple. Now he knew he was capable of feeling. He'd lost Jen but in losing he'd reacquired a dimension that had for so long been submerged beneath the layer upon layer of erotic error, covered by all that false plunge and mounting, mounting, mounting. He didn't expect ever to see Jen again. Surely, that instant, he was flying from her. Besides, he really didn't know how much he cared for her. He'd not had the chance to face her and measure it. All he had to go on was what he'd felt as a result of her. He was thankful for it, even though he didn't trust it completely yet. He'd have to get used to it. At least it had happened. She had broken through the hurt barrier.

To relieve tension, Arnie got up and walked the dim aisle of the plane. He got a drink from a mechanically smiling stewardess and brought it back to his seat, along with a plastic-protected magazine.

He was turning pages and sipping when he glanced and

had to look again to the window seat opposite his. A very pretty bird.

He stole some from her for a while. She was puffs of dark hair curls and a perfect nose and eyes that turned toward him. She recognized and her mouth smiled. He knew she was a model. He returned his attention to the magazine and flipped a few pages until, coincidentally, there was her face in print, a full-color photograph for a cosmetic company's newest shade of lipstick. He held the page up to show her to her. He didn't have to try for her attention. Her eyes hadn't left him since his first look. Arnie pointed at the reproduction of her and the real her. He nodded approval with an appreciating face. She considered it an invitation. She clicked off her overhead light beam and came over to sit with him. She was tall and rather lean. She had on a very short skirt and a sheer blouse.

"I saw you when you got on," she said. "I thought you were someone who looked like you." That reminded him of Jen.

"Shouldn't you be up in first class?" she asked.

"Too lonely up there," he told her. "Want a drink?"

She didn't. She told him her name that was Paula.

"No last name?"

"Sure but last names don't mean much in modeling. Everyone just calls me Paula."

"There must be more than one model named Paula."

"Not that I know of."

"Suppose there was?"

"She'd change her name."

"Why?"

"The face that belongs to the name Paula belongs to me."

"Do you like being a model?"

"It's sort of super. But sometimes it's a drag. Like now where we're going is Yuma because there's sand dunes near there. Somebody got the idea to shoot fur coats on the desert, just to be different. They're always trying to be different. Shit, I'll bet it's a hundred and ten there, and I'm supposed to look like I feel super while I roast in chinchilla. It's dumb, really. Once I had to do bathing suits in an icehouse. But it's better than being a secretary or something. I make more for a day's booking than most secretaries make in a month." She went on to tell him the name of the famous photographer who was going to punish her on this hot job. "He's flaked out but I can 't sleep on a plane."

"Me either."

"You want to read?"

"No."

"Would you mind killing that light? It's glary. I've got sensitive eyes."

He clicked the beam off.

She asked, "Those things they say about you, are they true?"

"Probably."

"They say you have a pink-tinted mirror over your bed. You don't really, do you?"

"Why not?"

"Isn't that rather vain?"

"Depends on how you look at it."

That made her laugh.

He told her, "You should like mirrors."

She took it as a compliment. "I know a model who says she went out with you a few times. A blonde named Erica. German."

Arnie remembered but "out" and "a few times" were exaggerations. It had been in and one weekend, every minute bare.

"Erica's a blabber," criticized Paula.

"What did she tell you?"

"Not just me. Everyone."

"So?"

"You come highly recommended," smiled Paula, arching.

They talked for nearly an hour. About places and him, but mostly about her good life that included a time when she'd witnessed a sexual exhibition in Paris. She told him, "It was in this super house, a mansion really, right on Avenue Kleber. All red velour and Louis furniture. I thought I'd be embarrassed but I wasn't."

"Did it affect you?"

"You mean did I dig it?"

"Did you?"

"It got to me," she admitted, "but not a lot. Actually, I thought it was too contrived. It was like they had a script and were changing positions on cue. What I really dig is spontaneity."

"How's that?"

"It's why I don't think I'll ever get married. Most married people get all hung up on routine. Like every Tuesday they take baths and do it early and every Saturday they get bombed and do it late. It's ridiculous. I'm too impetuous for that."

He didn't have to ask her to elucidate. She went on, exposing, "I dig letting life surprise me. Unexpected things, things that just happen are a lot more exciting. Don't you think?"

Her face was turned to him. For his answer he gave her a light kiss, merely a soft meeting of lips. She consented to that mild extent for a few moments until her mouth became impatient. Then there was nothing cautious about her tongue. It communicated for the rest of her. Arnie felt as if he were observing himself kissing her. His assignment came to mind. Evidently he wasn't going to have to lie about it after all. There was nothing to stop him from having this splendid, impulsive model animal.

After the first kiss, after she'd kissed a pattern of extra kisses around his lips, she stood abruptly. "I'll be right back," she said. She got her purse from her seat and went to the rear of the plane into one of the washrooms.

In the ten private minutes she was in there she lighted and inflated herself six times with deep helping drags of marijuana. She wanted to elevate further the stimulation from this chance meeting with Arnie Bruno, *the* Arnie Bruno.

Although she was already high, she was determined to make it exceptionally gratifying, so she turned her brain and all nerve ends up to their most receptive frequency. After the sixth long-held inhale was let out, she carefully squeezed the spark off the cigarette, put the remainder of it inside the little purse in her purse, and sprayed the air with expensive perfume from a tiny atomizer. Then, for future convenience, she removed her bikini underpants and went out to be with him.

The moment she sat she was more relaxed against him. They immediately kissed again, and Arnie detected the particular odor of marijuana on her breath and knew the purpose of her brief interruption. It supplied him with positive permission.

Continuing the kiss, he began inside her blouse to get her breasts that were not dimensionally large but proportionately perfect with pleasing pliant tension. He played for their benefit left and right and adored her nipples with all his tricks, subtle and precisely severe. He determined the increased temperature of her breaths, more shallow now. He got a blanket from above.

Her legs were bare. She welcomed his hand down there by parting, and his touch was surprised to find no barrier of fabric all the way up. Her lower hair was silky thick and the mound of her center was nice for him to cup with pressure for a short while, until he split her with one finger and commenced delicately where her sensations concentrated.

She had to move, tightening preliminary spasms. She had to make little animal noises.

Animal trainer, Arnie thought of himself and continued the perfect friction.

She had to whisper into him, "Fuck me, Arnie, please fuck me."

He couldn't.

She expected him to undo himself and maneuver between her for the long hard slide in. But he didn't. She reached for him and found him not ready. She squeezed some without result. She unbuttoned and unzippered and took the soft bunch of him out. She kissed his mouth to convey the pleasure she received from doing it, hoping that would help. She tried her entire hand and then fingers alone and then only fingernails for sensual scratch. She tried tender and tease and finally resorted to hurt, that she knew was sometimes the needed influence.

Arnie didn't respond. Actually he seemed to be shrinking.

"What's the matter?" she asked.

"I don't know," he answered, true. Panic. It had never happened to him before. His center had always obeyed, but now, for some reason, it was rebelling. His mind rushed to diagnose the reason and dispel it. He thought perhaps it was because he was so tired, but he'd been more exhausted previous times. He thought maybe it was this girl, Paula, but she was more desirable than many had been.

Her want wouldn't let her give up. She was floating, erotic, hungry determined. Her fingers kept trying. However, the more she touched him the more he despised the doughy proof of his inadequacy. He tried with all his mind to concentrate on her tactile efforts. It feels good, he imagined, hoping to make his brain make his center believe it, but his center wouldn't cooperate and neither would his mind that voluntarily altered the phrase into it should feel good.

Paula withdrew her hand and moved into position for a different attempt. Then the soft dark curls on her head were in his lap and he felt her mouth include him, warm and pleasant. He was sure that would do it, that would certainly overwhelm the block and cause the blood to cooperate with a hard rush. For the first few moments it seemed possible. Some of the sensation demanded acknowledgment. It encouraged him to think he'd soon be swollen with it, normally capable. But it was merely the initial comfort of warmth and wet that soon reduced itself to faint futile chewing. He lifted her head away and placed it against his chest.

"I'm sorry," he told her.

Now he thought he knew the reason. He blamed the airplane. He accused his flying anxiety. That was the problem. He was so tense with thick fear that feeling couldn't get through. It was a state of shock causing temporary paralysis. That was it.

Again he told Paula he was sorry.

She turned her face up and kissed him. He thought it was a condoning kiss. He was embarrassed and needed understanding. When their lips parted, she told him, "I'm turned on, baby. Jesus, I'm turned on. I've got to have it."

"I can't."

"Do me, then."

He knew what she meant.

"Please," she begged. "Feel how hot I am." She led his hand down to her. "Don't leave me hung up like this."

Just a little head, that's all she was asking for. That was the most he could do. He'd always said he gave the best. He was about to move her into the position for it when he realized. The reason, the real reason for his impotence came suddenly clear. It stopped him with its truth. He should have known.

"I can't," he said again and pushed Paula away.

She sulked silent for a few minutes, cooling. "You're a fucking fraud," she said hard and left him to go to another seat somewhere in the plane.

Arnie looked out at the flaming engines. Once more he felt very young and very old. He didn't think he'd ever again be as he'd been. Maybe in time, but he doubted that even time would restore him. He touched his center to make sure it was there. It felt puny and powerless. He zipped up and buttoned. He looked at his watch. Four o'clock. Less than an hour to landing. Four, hard-luck four. Time, he thought, for this giant silver bird to explode its guts out. He kept his attention on the minute hand until it passed straight-up four without calamity. He felt sorry for Paula. At least now she had something extraordinary to talk about. Arnie Bruno couldn't get it up. Who would believe her? He felt sorry for himself. He tried to wallow in feeling sorry. But the core of him, a limited space that fluctuated between his lower belly and throat, contained a piece of laughter like a blown glowing coal.

Hell, he chastised, this was nothing to laugh about.

This was serious.

The reason was Jen.

His office had a car waiting for him at the airport, long important car with a white telephone in the back. Arnie told the driver where, and as soon as they were on the way he called long distance, trying to connect with her.

No answer.

And the same nothing when he tried again a half hour later.

He stretched out for a while to uncramp and then doubled up on his side across the plush of the seat. He'd never felt so tired, coated-thick depression. He was driven for almost five hours over the black ribbon of road, through dry lonely land that reminded him of him. And finally down the last long desert steep.

He hadn't been in his hotel suite more than a minute before he was phoning long distance again for her. No answer. He called Winner.

There was Las Vegas.

Vegas will help, he thought.

"You sound down," Winner told him.

"I feel fine," lied Arnie.

"Want me to come out there?"

"Yeah, why don't you." Arnie didn't want to be alone with this bad thing. Not that he was going to tell Winner. "There's lots of new gash all over this place," he said, trying to sound regular.

Winner always enjoyed more fringe benefits in Vegas. "I'll

take the first plane I can get,'' he promised. ''You sure you're okay?''

''Couldn't be better. I've got two here with me right now,'' Arnie pretended. ''Hey, baby, come here and say hello to Winner. Come on,'' he urged and hesitated for effect. ''They're taking a shower together,'' he told Winner.

''They dancers?''

''Legs all the way up to the ass.''

''Blondes or brunettes?''

''Blondes with brunette where it counts.''

''I'll be there.''

''By the way,'' Arnie had to inquire, ''you heard from Jen?''

''No. Want me to call her?''

''I was just wondering.''

''I'll call her.''

''You don't have to.''

''Whatever you say.''

''See you.''

It was midafternoon. Arnie shaved and changed clothes and went down to the pool. There was plenty of exposure—bronze skin in minimum bikinis, well-oiled rows of them on plastic cushions. A glistening sunlight display of night-performing flesh, typically horizontal. Arnie walked around. They recognized. Some sent him smiles. Many were girls from the hotel's well-stocked show, a customary source of late entertainment for Arnie. Although these were new girls, they'd learned the legend of him from their rhinestone-crotched predecessors.

Arnie chose an advantageous chair, shaded by a bright pink umbrella. He ordered a Kentucky and observed. He stirred the ice in his glass. He stirred the girls. Instead of staying still for the sun, now, one by one or by pairs, they aroused to pose up or walk their most provocative walks for Arnie's eyes. Their similar show-bodies communicated similar probable pleasures, some shout, some whisper.

Arnie was there to hear them, to especially test his reception. He sipped Kentucky and hoped for susceptibility. But his point of view wasn't normal. Instead of helping to create want, it saw only the unmysterious human function of these female bodies, common anatomy of practical tissues, actually rather grotesque when observed from that objective standard. Nothing to get excited about.

He abandoned half his drink and escaped to his suite. He again attempted long distance. Again no answer. He ordered a massage and the hands of a muscular Swede punished his back and legs and arms until they had to submit to relaxation. Arnie thought then he could sleep and he did, but it wasn't good sleep. It was several hours of eyeshut with half his brain and body aware that the other half of his brain and body was unconscious. When he got up he felt thick and slow-motion, more tired than he'd felt before. He ordered some Kentucky and a steak and while he had the phone he had to try long distance again. He slammed the instrument back into place, futile.

The Kentucky helped. He drank it fast. He ate the steak without tasting it and ordered more Kentucky that he gulped while he shaved again. He took a long shower and by that time it was night enough for him to put some faith in the distractions he knew Vegas offered. He dressed for action and was about to go out when Winner arrived. Arnie was relieved to see him.

"Did you check in?"

"No," replied Winner, "the guy at the desk said they were full."

Arnie called with angry demand to get the next nearest room for Winner. "Want to wash up?" he asked.

"Yeah."

"Do it here if you want."

"I left my stuff downstairs at the desk. What number's my room?"

"Ten-o-two, right next door."

"Where are the girls you had?"

"They're doing the show. But we'll see them later."

Winner looked the room. The bed was mussed but not like there'd been three in it, or even two. And there was no typical evidence anywhere around. "See you in a minute," said Winner, going.

When Winner and Arnie went down to the hotel's casino, it was half past midnight, still too early for Arnie, and he had to pay the penalty of recognition from the crowd of slot-machine pullers and the islands of players around the crap and twenty-one and roulette tables. Arnie wanted to shoot craps but didn't want an audience, so he put on a public smile and went across the bright of the large room to the adjacent darker lounge. They sat and a waiter brought Kentucky without asking. On a small stage there was a blonde singer of semifame fighting for attention with her loudest number. Through the flatter of the spotlight on her she saw Arnie and immediately improved her smile, gestures, and voice.

Arnie asked Winner, "How's everything back in New York?"

"The same."

"No phone calls or anything?"

"Nothing important."

"You still making it with Connie?"

"No."

"What did you do last night?"

"The one from the Copa."

"The one who just got married?"

"Yeah."

"I told you. How was it?"

"She says her old man's a fag."

"That's her story."

Arnie pretended attention at the blonde singer who was now especially doing one of Arnie's current songs, badly. He tried to nonchalant it. "Did you call Jen?" he asked Winner without looking.

"Who?"

"Jen."

"Oh, yeah, I called her."

"What did she say?"

"She said to say hello."

"Is that all?"

"She said you can call her if you want."

"Why the hell should I call her?"

"I don't know."

"Did she sound okay? I mean, she wasn't pissed off or anything, was she?"

"No."

"She really wants me to call?"

"She said you could if you wanted."

"When?"

"When I talked to her."

"I mean when did she want me to call?"

"When you feel like it."

"No special time?"

"She mentioned nine o'clock."

"This time or that time?"

"Probably that time."

"Morning or night?"

"Probably morning."

"Nine o'clock. She's out until nine?"

"Guess so."

"That's six here."

"What time's the last show over?" asked Winner.

"What's that got to do with it?"

"The girls. Remember?"

Arnie left Winner sitting there. He was gone less than ten minutes. When he returned he brought three tall ones from the show, two blondes and a brunette. They all sat and got drinks to sip while they maneuvered who was for who. Winner obviously liked one of the blondes, so Arnie let her know. She was disappointed and took her glass to her lips to hide it. The other two allied with glances and shifted slightly toward Arnie who looked his watch. Almost five hours to go until six. He turned to the casino. The crowd wasn't so many. "I'm going to play," he announced, getting up. His blonde and brunette got up with him. He took out a fold of money and counted off some. "Here's the five I owe you," he said. Winner took the five hundreds, nodding.

They opened and lighted a closed table especially for Arnie. From one end of it he demanded ten thousand in chips that he scribbled his famous name for. He asked that the limit be removed. The prettiest waitress had the privilege of bringing him a Kentucky he hadn't requested. A few other players came to the table but stayed on the opposite end to not crowd him and there were numerous spectators, reverent. Flanked by the most beautiful blonde and brunette in the place, Arnie chose a pair of red dice from the dozen the stickman shoved at him. He put a thousand on the line and two hundred on each number. He didn't shake the dice or blow on them or talk to them. That wasn't his style. He merely flipped the dotted cubes backhand, a blasé gesture.

Someone shouted for him, "Yo-leven!"

Arnie brought the Kentucky to his lips and turned to smile

at the blonde, who couldn't camouflage her excitement. He wasn't even watching the dice as they bounced and rolled their unpredictable roll to stop with a six and a five on top.

"Eleven. Pay the line," said the stickman, automatic.

By four o'clock Arnie was seventy-eight thousand ahead. His tie was down and collar unbuttoned. The blonde and the brunette had deposited enough hundred-dollar chips in their cleavages to excuse themselves so they could cash in for large bills that they secreted in an even more intimate location on themselves before returning to flank him with their divine fronts ready for refill. They brushed Arnie's arms with them to remind him.

All the while, Arnie kept aware of the time that seemed unusually slow. When his watch approached four straight-up he interrupted his play and didn't resume until that bad-luck time was passed.

By five minutes to six Arnie was a hundred and twelve thousand ahead. Now there were only two other players at the other end of the table. The blonde and the brunette had achy legs and sleepiness but were getting rich too fast to complain or leave. Arnie, knowing the time exactly, called for a break in the game and left his chips there to go for a phone. On the way he noticed dawn outside. He dialed the hotel operator. He asked for Jen's New York number that he knew so well by now. He heard it ringing. It sounded different but he attributed that to the hour.

After the third ring he got Jen's voice saying a distant hello.

"It's me, Arnie," he said.

"I know," she said.

"How are you?"

"Sleepy."

"Did I wake you?"

"No."

"I've been trying to reach you."

"Why?"

"I have to tell you something."

"What?"

"I've been trying to call you all day."

"Must be important."

"Yeah. But now I don't know if I can tell you or not."

"Is it a secret?"

"No."

"Then go ahead."

"I don't think I can."

"Try."

"I love you."

She clicked off as soon as he said it.

Arnie put the phone back into place slow motion. He felt emptier than ever. Her hanging up after those true words was like a puncture that had allowed everything to run out of him. He was out of everything. He took a couple of deep breaths trying to get something back into him. Piss on them all, he thought and returned to the dice.

He made the largest bet of the night. A hundred thousand on the pass line.

The blonde and brunette blinked their false eyelashes to believe their tired eyes. They rubbed their breasts more on his upper arms.

Arnie tossed the dice.

"Four," pronounced the stickman. "The point is four."

Hard-ass four, thought Arnie. He remembered that afternoon at Nickie's. It had been exactly four o'clock when she'd entered his life. He should have known then.

He threw the dice again, expecting the seven that would make him more of a loser. The number that came up was an inconsequential eight. The stickman retrieved the dice and pushed them to Arnie's waiting fingers.

Arnie was about to throw again when he froze.

There she was. There. She'd cut between him and the brunette, who was indignant.

Jen.

"I just talked to you long distance," he told her, not believing.

Jen smiled her best. "Not real long distance, just room ten-o-two," she explained, as she gave a sharp elbow to the brunette who was trying to regain her position.

Arnie realized. "Winner," he said. "That beautiful bastard Winner." He'd never been so happy. The total hollow he'd felt a few minutes before was now packed with happiness.

"I got here about a half hour ago," Jen said.

"Pretty sure of yourself, weren't you?"

"Not really. I figured it was worth a chance. After all, what's a plane ride?"

"The point is four," said the stickman, polite but impatient.

"Go ahead and play," Jen told Arnie. She moved in front of him between him and the table.

"I'll be through in a second," said Arnie.

"Is that your point, four?"

"Yeah. But I can't make it. Not four."

"Nonsense." She smiled back and up at him.

"Hell, I don't care. It's only money."

"You want to throw a four?"

"Roll them for me." He offered her the dice.

"No." She folded his hand around the cubes.

"The point is four," the stickman reminded nasally.

"Press it," Jen told Arnie.

In the jargon of gambling, to press means to place an additional bet and, in that confident way, influence the dice to produce the desired number. But to Arnie and Jen it also meant something more. In front of him as she was she merely had to move back some to be in nice touch with him, while he pressured forward to meet the contact, tight.

Arnie bet fifty thousand more.

"Now," Jen suggested, "the hard way."

To any crap shooter, making a number the hard way is to make it with an identical pair, such as, in this case, a pair of deuces. The house gives odds. But to Arnie and Jen, the hard way also referred to Arnie's center as Jen made subtle frictions with her rear lower half against him. At once it grew him up full and potent. In all his adult life it had never happened so quickly.

He bet ten thousand on the hard way.

"Now you can make it, darling," Jen assured.

Arnie lobbed the dice.

He didn't watch them. His attention was on the nice little neglected skin place behind Jen's left ear. He got some of the fringes of her funny haircut with his kiss there.

The dice hit the green felt of the opposite end, rebounded, and, without wasted tumble or spinning suspense, they snapped to a stop next to each other, actually touching.

Two by two.

7

The time of one week was through.

The night for reunion had arrived.

Eduardo awaited Arnie, Rog, and Knight. Usually on game nights he had everything ready for them in advance. By this time the traditional green of the table was usually uncovered and lighted and brushed flawless with the balls racked into the proper beginning triangle. But all he'd done this night was make sure the ice bucket contained and the various favorite alcohols were enough. He sat and expected them, sure they would soon be there bringing reports of adventures in their mouths. Eduardo didn't feel like playing. He'd have rather been two floors above, where other, newer friends were, higher.

He waited. And when it was an hour past the scheduled gathering hour, Eduardo was about to give in to his hope that they wouldn't come. But then the door chime told him someone.

It was Knight.

The beautiful man of motion pictures helped himself to a drink. He made no comment about the dark pool table. "I thought the others would already be here," said Knight as he sat the edge of a chair and rotated his glass to mix and make its contents colder.

"They're late."

Both men looked their watches.

Knight said, "I can't play tonight."

"Why not?"

"Got to be in Rome in the morning."

"For work?"

Knight nodded.

They allowed silence until it became too obvious.

"Wonder where the others are?"

"Haven't heard from them," said Eduardo.

"They'll be here."

Knight sat back but in a moment returned to the edge again. Edgy, he looked down into his drink.

Eduardo said what he was thinking. "I'm going to sell this house."

"Thought you liked it?"

"I did."

"Find something better?"

"Yes."

"I've been thinking of getting a bigger place."

"This would be a good house for you."

Knight agreed it would.

"I've decided to get out of the city," Eduardo told him.

"Why?"

"Like there are too many bad vibes here," said Eduardo, not realizing how different he sounded.

Knight was too distracted to notice. "Where you going?" he asked just to continue talk.

"I found a place in the country." Eduardo stopped himself from revealing the rest of the true dream that was: So we can all be together to do what we want where no one will bug us.

The phone rang. Eduardo answered while Knight listened with half his mind to Eduardo's half of the conversation. When he hung up, Eduardo said, "That was Arnie."

"Is he coming?"

"He's in Vegas."

"Then he won't be here," said Knight, relieved.

"He said he was getting married."

"Arnie?"

"That's what he said."

"Probably a joke."

"He seemed serious."

"What else did he say? Did he say who he was marrying?"

"No. But he sounded good. He said he wanted us to know."

"I suppose it's possible," said Knight, comparing.

They thought about Arnie and themselves in some silence.

"Wonder where Rog is?"

At that moment a Western Union messenger was en route with words from Rog:

TRANSACTION FULFILLED BUT UNABLE TO PLAY TONIGHT DUE TO FAMILY DEMANDS.

"I can't wait any longer." Knight got up. He hadn't finished his drink. "I have to catch that plane."

"Let me know about the house, if you want it or not."

"Okay."

Eduardo went down to the door with him. Knight hesitated before going out. "Did Arnie say anything about how he made out? Whether he did or not?"

"I should have asked him."

"Knowing Arnie, he probably did."

"No doubt."

"How about you?"

"Yeah," answered Eduardo, plain.

Knight expected to be asked in return, so he volunteered, nodding. "It was kicks," he said.

"Looks like none of us have to retreat," said Eduardo, primarily referring to the two months' monastic solitude they'd wagered. Two whole months without birds.

"Not now," said Knight.

"I don't think I could have taken it, anyway," Eduardo admitted.

"No birds would have been hell," said Knight.

"I would have lied if I hadn't made it."

"Me too."

And that was all there was to it.

After good-bye, Eduardo hurried up to the studio where he wanted to be, inside the loud music with them. Some were dancing. Others were wherever they felt like being. Eduardo went to the large yellow couch. The only acknowledgement of his entrance was the taking of his hand by the hand of Grateful, the girl who could ride the world.

In that same time in time, Knight had walked to the corner of Madison for a taxi that took him up and around the block to be headed downtown. He was on his way. He'd had her phone number and phoned and phoned until she'd finally accepted his apology and promised to see him. They wanted him in Rome, but he didn't really have to be there for another week. He had a whole week and perhaps, he thought, that would be time enough. Anyway, in an hour he'd be on a shuttle-flight to Washington and Babs Bannon. And maybe, if he called again and asked nice, she'd meet him when he landed. He was on his way.

As the taxi that carried Knight went down Park, it had to pass a certain expensive address. At that number, twenty-five floors up, above the ordinary world, was a large terrace apartment. Inside there on a deep down couch was a woman relaxed on her side. She had on a long cream silk Geoffrey Beene gown trimmed with matching maribou. The delicate feathers seemed to be in perpetual motion for its wearer, Elaine Baine-Brice.

Elaine's lips had a fresh cigarette between them. She was snapping a costly gold table lighter that was sparkless. She was saying, "I've got twenty fucking lighters in this house and none of them work."

Someone offered a little solid-gold Dunhill for her to flick into flame on the first try. She tossed it back to its owner, while exhaling.

Besides Elaine, there were three other women in the luxurious room. Altogether, four of the beautiful. Now they were having their fifth martinis. Before the third they'd depleted talk about other things, and since the third their words had been on *the* subject.

"Oh, come on, he's definitely a fag!"

"Don't you believe it. I know. That's only his bit. He admits he's a fag and then says you're the first woman ever to get him a hard on."

The actress with the face of sensitive contours and body full of fame. Now on the floor, careless about her Courreges ensemble.

"He put on one of those things and I make him take it off."

"What did it look like?"

"It had big soft bumps and things all over it."

"Darling, you don't know what you missed."

"Have you ever been done with one?"

"There are all different kinds."

"Some feel better than others."

The heiress of countless wealth and incredible loveliness. Unfair God, how unfair. Now with her Vivier shoes off and her legs over the arm of a soft chair.

"In the dark I thought it was regular vaseline. I found out damn soon it was the carbolated kind."

"Get closer to the fire or wheel out more hose."

"I know he looks good, but forget him."

"I heard he gives fabulous head."

"Sounds like firsthand information to me."

"Not hand, darling. Head."

"He used to be a whore, literally."

"He still is, in a way."

"Well, at least she got her money's worth out of him."

"Know why a man won't marry a mermaid?"

"Why?"

"Not enough woman to ball and too much fish to eat."

Laughs. Together laughs. League of laughs.

"How's your new young one?"

"Isn't he beautiful?"

"Yeah. But how is he?"

"Learning."

"If you ever want to send him to finishing school, I'll open one for him."

"Let me know when he's perfected his French."

"Darling, that was his first lesson."

The musical comedy star with the world's most talked-about legs. Now, as always, in her color: pale yellow. A short very short skirt to her advantage and her blouse unbuttoned more than enough to boast better breasts.

"He's a switch-hitter."

"I was with Alexis the night I met him. You know Alexis, the hairdresser. We ended up fighting over him and Alexis won."

"He's hung-up on doing it with two girls."

"He pulled that on me once. I went home with him and he had a little blonde dancer waiting there."

"What did you do?"

"I walked out, naturally."

"Really?"

"The next day."

"He's vile. He really is."

"You know what he said to me? The first thing?"

"What?"

"He said, 'I'd love to go down on you and get lockjaw and let you drag me to death.' "

"I was in Beverly Hills on Bedford in the middle of the afternoon when this marvelous-looking young stud stopped me and came right out and asked for it."

"So?"

"Actually he didn't ask. He told me what he wanted."

"And everyone went to the seashore."

"That's right. Malibu. How'd you guess?"

"His whole damn bedroom is electronic with a control panel next to the bed. It's wild. Push a button and a movie screen comes down. He has a projector built in the wall over the bed. Push another button and the show begins. In color."

"Why do they call them blue films?"

"I don't know. They're not sad."

"I've seen some pretty sad ones."

"I'll give you his number."

"Don't you ever get enough?"

"Do you?"

"Never, darling. Never."

Average seven male inches used every time. At least three times a week. That's 21 inches a week each. Multiplied, that's 1092 inches each a year and over ten years 10,920 inches or 910 feet. For the four beautiful women, altogether a total of 3640 feet of male center. A modest estimate is 300 in-and-out strokes per session makes the super total of erotic distance come to 1,092,000 feet, or approximately 200 miles.

They went on. The same mutual subject. Their talk eventually came to the point when Elaine Baine-Brice told about the teen daughter of her former personal secretary.

"She told her mother she wasn't feeling well," said Elaine. "So her mother took her to the doctor, who found nothing wrong with her except she was pregnant. The girl insisted she couldn't be, claiming she hadn't done anything to get herself that way. They ran a second test that showed positive. The girl still said it couldn't be. She explained that she'd only done it once. Of course, the doctor informed her that once was often enough. As it came out, it seems she'd done it with someone while standing in the waiting line at Radio City

Music Hall. Somewhere she'd gotten the idea that it was impossible to get pregnant standing up."

"Imagine doing it in a pubic place like that."

"He must have just lifted her mini and slipped it to her."

"I don't believe it."

"It's the truth, darling."

"It could happen."

"I don't think it's so incredible. It probably happens in lots of strange places like that."

"How about St. Patrick's Cathedral?"

"By candlelight."

"The locker room of the Green Bay Packers?"

"At half time."

"A pass up the middle."

"A quick opener."

"An end-around play."

They all laughed, but that got them started on it. They began suggesting places, not impossible ones but places that would be a challenge, requiring ingenuity.

And in less than an hour, to relieve their beautiful boredom, they were seriously drawing separate slips from a Bergdorf hat box.